I0758031

Copyright © 2003-2023; 2025 by Cassandra Featherstone
Hardcover: 978-1-960935-33-5
Paperback: 978-1-960935-42-7

All rights reserved.

No part of this book may be reproduced in any form or by any electronic or mechanical means, including information storage and retrieval systems, without written permission from the author, except for the use of brief quotations in a book review. Any unauthorized copies will be pursued through DMCA, legal channels, and reporting to all appropriate companies and law enforcements agency, both foreign and domestic.

Contact the author for permissions or rights inquiries at www.cassandrafeatherstone.com

The characters and events portrayed in this book are fictitious. Any similarity to persons, places, brands, or locations—real or fictional—are coincidental and not intended by the authors.

No part of this book my used to train generative AI/LLMs/or any future technologies without express written permission from the author.

AMAZON Version ONLY

Ebook/Print Cover: CAROL MARQUES DESIGNS
Editing, Proofing, backgrounds, & Formatting: Dirty Sexy Words/ Storm shield Editing/Little Tailfeather Publishing
Cassandra's logos: Pretty in Ink Creations/Artlogo
Goosebusters Alpha team: Kat Silver, Becky Ross, Erica Taryn
Duckhunters Proofing Team: Jackie H, Jaemi Serrano
Sensitivity Readers: Brit Mason, Gail Jericho
Translation Consultant: Mo Jacobs
Legal Services: Joshua Farley, esq.
Agent: Laura Pink at SBR Media
Images/Fonts: Depositphotos, Shutterstock, Canva, & Photoshop

No GenAI was used within this book. All errors and greatness are by an ADHD muppet.

Little Tailfeather Publishing

Signature Page

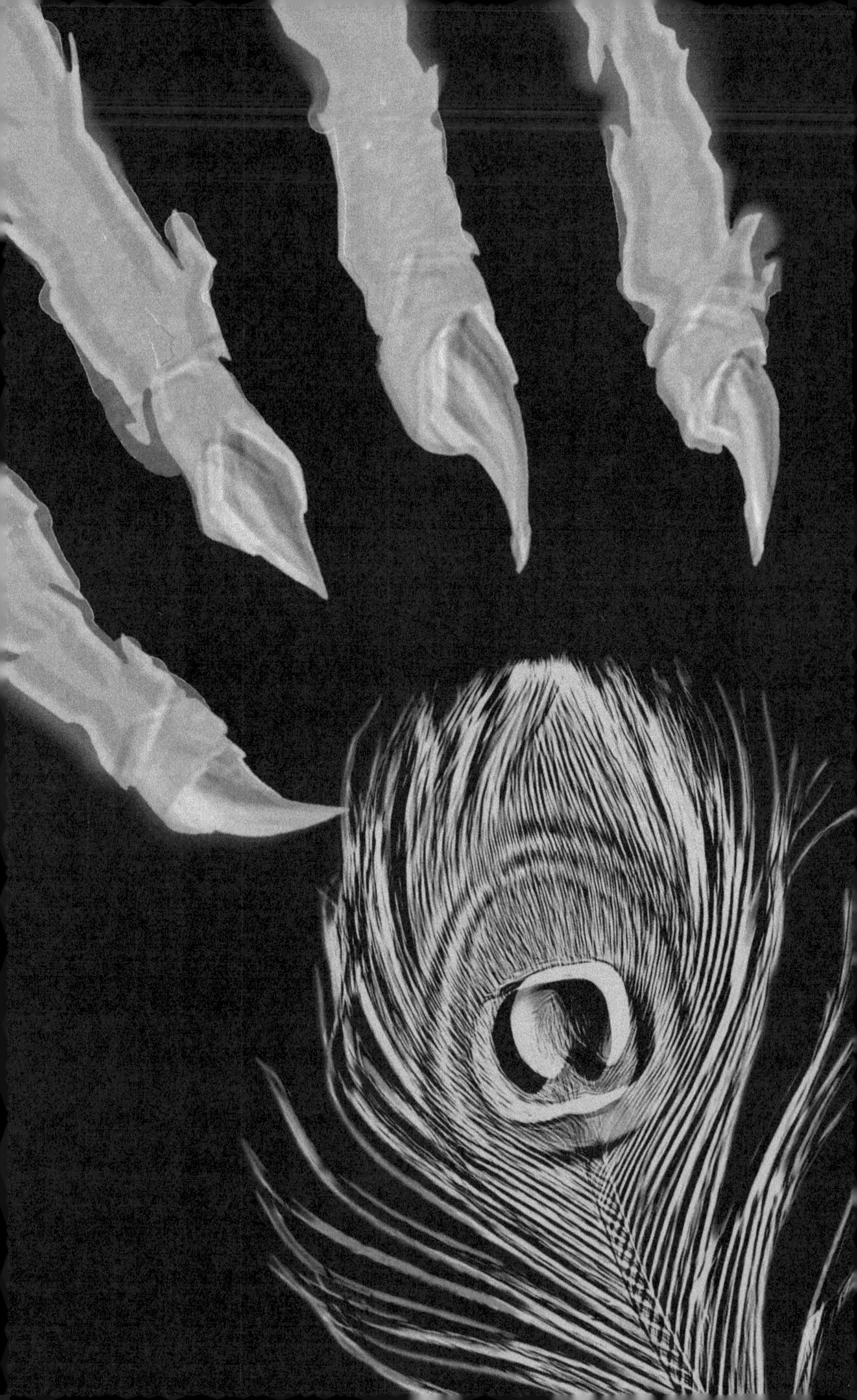

PEACOCK ME LIKE A HURRICANE

INTERNATIONAL BEST SELLING AUTHOR
CASSANDRA FEATHERSTONE

Stalk Cassandra Featherstone in the Dark Corners of the Web

JOIN MY FACEBOOK GROUP AND FOLLOW ME EVERYWHERE!

WANT MORE?

SIGN UP FOR MY BI-WEEKLY MANIFESTO FOR A FREE SERIES SAMPLER:

Join my Ream as a FREE follower or exclusive subscriber to get access to cover reveals, WIPs, Serial Stories, and personal chats from me!

CASSANDRA FEATHERSTONE

Content Information

This is a *paranormal whychoose romance with poly elements*—our FMC, Delilah, **will** make choices, but it will be to protect her peace and her family. She will make more choices throughout the series, so don't worry that you've been 'RH baited.' It's coming, I promise.

There are many situations included that are intended for <u>mature audiences (18+).</u>

In these books, there may be instances/references (be they small or lengthy) that could trigger some individuals such as:

- liberal use of appropriate consent
- Mention off-page of dubious consent situations
- group scenes
- MMF, MM, MFM, MF, MFMMM, FF, FFM, FFMM, relationships and more throughout series
- emotional abuse by mates
- physical abuse (off-page) by mates
- alphahole/possessive MMCs
- cinnamon roll MMCs

- multiple POVs— including ones beyond the MCs
- unhinged MMC
- unhealthy coping mechanisms
- selfish, narcissistic mates
- boundaries being crossed
- BDSM
- raw sex
- traumatic childhood
- alcohol use and abuse
- threats of bodily harm
- death
- body modifications
- fancy genitalia
- mating bites/marks
- androids and building androids
- bullying (in person and on social media)
- PTSD
- blood
- emotional abuse from outside poly group
- body dysmorphia
- adult language
- pop culture references
- literary references
- emotional manipulation
- power play
- adorable nicknames
- physical intimidation
- rough sex
- markings/tattoos
- family dysfunction
- Community of various poly families
- animal companion
- brief mentions of non-body positive dieting culture
- very liberal re-imagining of history

- morally gray secret organization that monitors mercenaries/dimension
- official corruption
- name calling
- occasional misogyny
- exhibitionism
- hand necklaces
- adult bullying
- magical kinks
- impact play
- elitism
- bribery
- corpses
- drama
- physical threats to FMC and others
- species-ism
- pregnancy (in future books, no loss)

No sexual practices in this book should be taken as safe or appropriate for real life application.

Content information is important and I don't ever want to harm a reader with inaccurate information.

A Note To My Loving Family Members and Friends...

THANK YOU FOR SUPPORTING ME BY BUYING MY WORK.

YOU KNOW I THINK YOU SHOULD WALK AWAY FROM THIS, PUTTING IT ON YOUR BOOKSHELF LIKE A PAPER TROPHY RATHER THAN READ IT.

I HAVEN'T BEEN VERY SUCCESSFUL WITH SOME OF YOU IN THAT REGARD.

SINCE MY MOM KEEPS TELLING PEOPLE I WRITE PORN THAT SHE DOESN'T KNOW IF IT MAKES ANY MONEY... I GUESS I'M JUST GOING TO HAVE TO LIVE WITH IT.

THIS IS BOOK TWO OF A SERIES THAT IS DEFINITELY GETTING WILDER AS WE GO. IF YOU READ VAMPIRE SLAYING FANFIC IN THE 90S, YOU PROBABLY DON'T KNOW WHAT WAS ME AND ARE NOT READY FOR WHERE THIS WILL GO.

CAVEAT: IF YOU CHOOSE TO KEEP READING, KNOW THAT AT NO TIME WILL I EXPLAIN TERMS, POSITIONS, THEMES, TROPES, OR ANY OTHER PART OF THIS NOVEL AT FAMILY EVENTS, IN GROUP CHATS, OR ON SOCIAL MEDIA.

DON'T ASK.

Peacock Me Like A Hurricane
Playlist

The De
The
Firehous
The Cabal Qvarter
The Port

The
Homestead
Company HQ

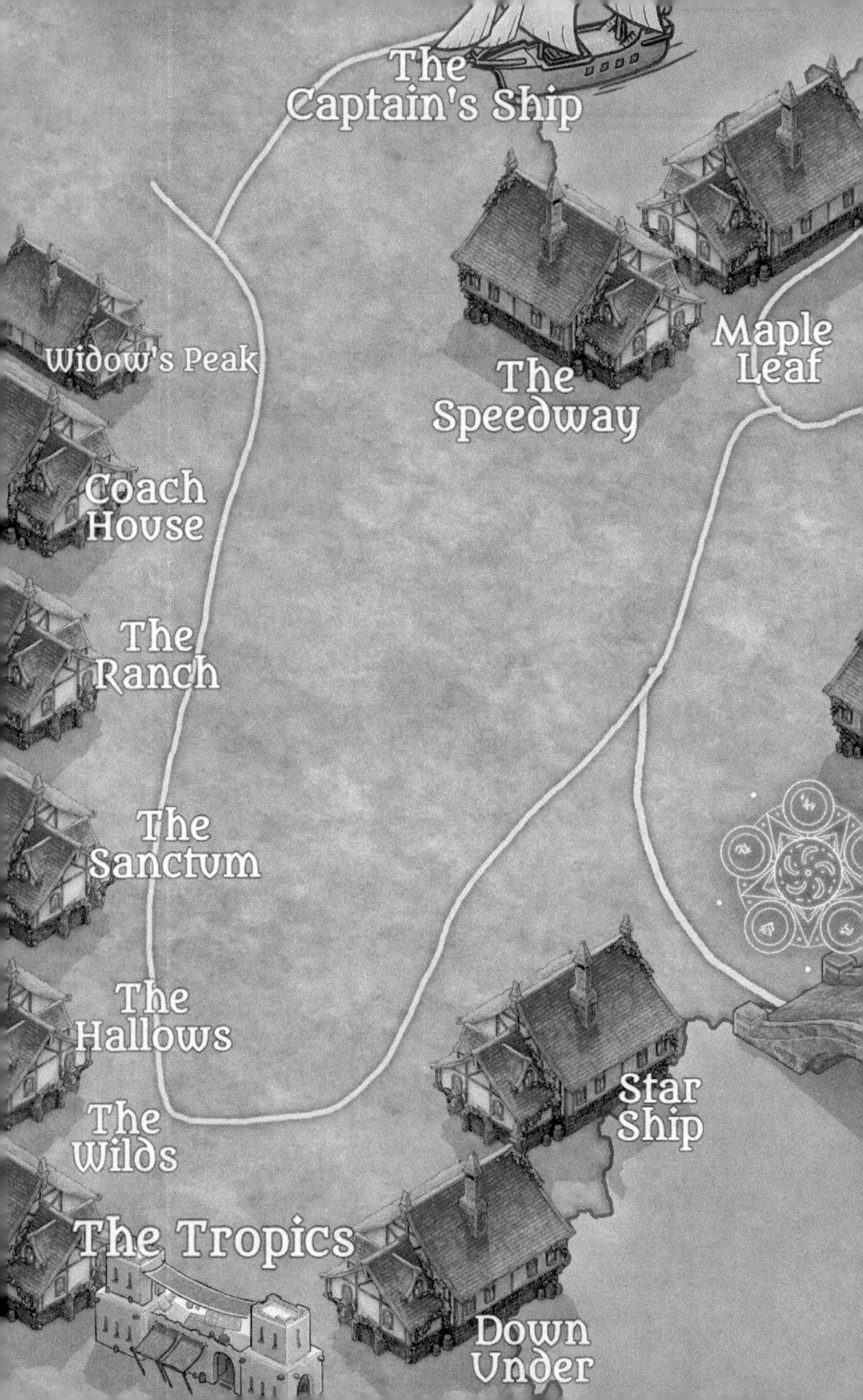

The Captain's Ship
Widow's Peak
Coach House
The Ranch
The Sanctum
The Hallows
The Wilds
The Tropics
The Speedway
Maple Leaf
Star Ship
Down Under

The Portal
The Maison
The Frat
Jagvars
The Resistance Quarter

Dedication

To the dreamers who are hoping, wishing, and waiting for their passion to become their job
For the writers, artists, and creators who think it won't ever be possible

You can do this—never give up.

for everyone who told me I wasn't good enough to make it on my own

Grab your cape and get superfucked, kiddos.

How starved you must have been that my heart became a meal for your ego.

— ANONYMOUS

Wait!

A FINAL REMINDER BEFORE YOU READ…

My series typically have prequels, gap novellas/novels, and bonus material that are integral to your having a satisfying reading experience.

If you have not read the other pieces in this series, you may feel as though you have missed critical details, developments, plot points, and other information. This will cause the book to appear to have continuity gaps that it does not have.

If you have not read the bonus material for this series, it is available online here, in audio versions (if applicable), and in print special editions (if applicable).

I highly recommend consulting the bonus page prior to reading this new title so you're up to speed on all the things going on in this world.

Happy reading!

Prologue

As with all good romances, this starts with a man and a woman—or rather, two men and a woman...

Centuries ago, humans believed in things beyond their comprehension more readily. Supernaturals and their non-magical counterparts co-existed by using fairy tales, myths, and folklore to create a world where they interacted on specific terms that protected everyone. But as all species do, both sides of the coin evolved and dissension within their ranks and with one another caused internal wars, famine, and other tragedies.

The supernaturals evolved more quickly than humans, so the ancient bloodlines gathered together to form a governing body for all the non-human species. For a long time, this group made sure to curate history in a way that did not dishonor the gods or destiny, but kept humans from interfering in their business.

The stories of conflict, triumph, and regret from human history were often supernatural, but the truth was concealed. Eventually, humans turned their efforts towards science rather than spiritualism and the tales of things that go bump in the night became legend. This allowed the Society to focus solely on their own and as time went on, they expanded across the globe.

Our love story begins with an ancient woman who drew the attention of two supes in the Society. A warlock and a vampire, brothers in spirit if not blood, ascended to their council seats to become the last survivors of their names. Their families were decimated in various conflicts over the years and these two men grew resentful of the Society's leniency towards humans and lower tier supes alike. They were both in love with the ancient woman, though, and for a time after they mated with her, it settled their need for vengeance.

But evolution never ends and once humans advanced far enough to threaten supernaturals again, their thirst for revenge flared again. When they couldn't convince the Society council to conquer the non-magical beings, the brothers left their positions to work as undercover agents within a growing organization of humans dedicated to fomenting crime and strife. The warlock climbed the ranks of leadership over many decades and the vampire dove into the scientific program; together, they conspired to control the human population through their own weapons and technology.

When their true aims were discovered by the Society and their mate, they got exiled. By then, the warlock was in full control of the global criminal organization that operated under many names in many countries. He and his brother pleaded with their mate to join them, and when she refused to alter the course of Fate, he performed a forbidden ritual to unmate them from her.

The consequences of his reckless, selfish decision echoed through the world like wildfire. Wars broke out, treaties soured, crops died, and disease raged across the lands. Society members around the world confiscated all the tomes containing information on revoking a mate bond to prevent another ripple of magic that powerful from being released.

Unfortunately, the anguish of being cut off from their magically intended partner affected the vampire and the warlock as well. Their organization was thriving in the chaos the revocation caused, but they could barely stand to be in the same room as one another. The time came when they argued so often that it threatened their mission and they split the organization in half.

Each took the half they preferred—the warlock keeping the criminal wing and the vampire taking the technological sector. They vowed to share resources when required, but their empires would remain separated for good.

As technology continued to advance, The Company branched out into mercenary pursuits and the vampire blended magic and science so well that he created a pocket dimension to hide his labs, agents, and their secrets within. He named it The Rift in honor of the divide between him and his brother and once it was fully operational, he retreated into a world far away from the humans he despised.

That seclusion kept him from knowing his brother and their former lover were briefly reunited during the sparkling days of disco. Despite the cadre of new mates the Fates provided the ancient one, she relented one last time and from that tragic mistake, a child was born.

In order to protect her from her heritage, the child was left at one of the hybrid enclaves created by the Society and eventually adopted. She lived an inauspicious life as a 'lost one' until one day, the small amount of magic she could access sparked and she ran from her life, including the Guardian watching from the shadows.

Only the Fates could have conspired for this child to find her way to the portal to The Rift and settle there without knowing what she'd discover on the other side.

Delilah Lenore O'Hara was *never* meant to set foot in The Rift, but once she did, it started a cascade of events that cannot be prevented.

This time, the story begins with a a woman who has lots of men, but one who is changing her entire world.

The story kicks off with me freezing my tail off in a park, waiting for Taurus, the infuriatingly smug enigma who just might hold the answers I've been chasing for years.

Two years as the leader of the Resistance, and I've grown used to shouldering the impossible—holding the group together, fighting The Cabal's grip on The Rift, and now keeping my Beast under control.

But my personal quest? That's the one thing I haven't cracked.

My transformation into a half-human, half-cat hybrid still feels like a cosmic joke, and Taurus might be the only one with the punchline.

When he finally shows up, radiating his signature blend of arrogance and power, I don't bother hiding my irritation. Leading a rebellion against an all-powerful organization has left me with zero patience for games. I'm here for answers about my mutation, and while Taurus is as evasive as ever, I rattle him by demonstrating my accelerated healing ability.

It's a small win, but in this game, I take what I can get. He's not ready to give me the whole truth, but I leave with enough to keep digging.

The Beast within me has been my constant companion through all of this. It's not just a side effect of my transformation—it's a force I have to wrestle with every day.

As the leader of the Resistance, I've mastered the art of staying calm under pressure, but The Beast is always there, lurking, waiting for a moment of weakness to take over. It's exhausting, but giving in isn't an option. The Resistance depends on me to keep it together.

Taurus becomes a reluctant ally in my search for answers, though "reluctant" doesn't quite capture the vibe. He's frustratingly cryptic, but he knows more than he lets on, and his personal stakes—protecting his mate Talia—give me leverage. Talia's near-death experience last year left Taurus desperate, and my healing abilities offer him a glimmer of hope. I promise to help if she's ever in danger again, and in return, I piece together the larger picture.

The "Creation" that made the clones is tied to The Rift, a pocket dimension where The Company conducts its experiments (not that the inhabitants know that's what they're doing).

I've always known The Rift is a playground for The Company's twisted ambitions. Clones, pulled from alternate timelines and reshaped, populate this world, each a fragment of their original selves. Taurus and his fellow clones aren't just connected by DNA—they're variations of the same person, split across realities.

It's a mind-bending truth that only deepens the mystery of my existence, because I'm not one of them. I'm something else entirely.

The Resistance formed to fight back against The Cabal's control, and for two years, I've kept it afloat through sheer determination.

Trust is a scarce commodity in this world, and alliances shift as easily as sand in a storm. My circle is as chaotic as the world we're fighting in. Rhea and Sari, two of my closest allies, develop similar mutant powers to mine that threaten to spiral out of control.

I take Rhea on a hunting expedition with Taurus, hoping to teach her discipline, but it only highlights the fractures in our group. Power dynamics, jealousy, and manipulation swirl around us, and keeping everyone on the same page feels like herding cats—pun very much intended.

Taurus complicates everything. I've built my leadership on clarity and focus, but he shakes me in ways I don't like to admit. He's arrogant, infuriating, and maddeningly magnetic. Our bond grows stronger, but it's a constant source of friction. He challenges me in ways no one else does, forcing me to confront the parts of myself I'd rather ignore. It's a strange, volatile connection that feels equal parts strength and vulnerability.

My search for a solution to The Beast takes a turn when I finally face the truth: The Company's tech will not help me. If they had the answers, they would know I'm a walking threat to everything in this little reality and come for me. That realization hits hard, but it pushes me to explore a different path—one rooted in the old ways, in gods, goddesses, and magic.

It's a long shot, but if science can't fix me, maybe something divine can.

The ritual becomes my last-ditch effort to rid myself of The Beast. It's meant to be a renewal ceremony, a calling down of power from the gods and goddesses of The Rift.

As the leader, I'm supposed to guide it with calm authority, but inside, I'm anything but calm. I've kept my desperation hidden from the others, but this ritual is personal. I don't just want to renew energy or please some deity—I want to excise the part of me that feels like it's eating me alive.

The ceremony is chaos, as expected.

The Rift itself feels alive, its energy volatile and unpredictable, as though it's mocking our attempt to control it. I pour everything I have into the ritual, invoking every god and goddess I can think of, begging them to take The Beast from me. The power of a goddess surges through me, overwhelming and raw, and for a moment, I think it's working.

The Beast seems to calm at the beginning of the ritual, and I feel a glimmer of hope.

But the gods, it seems, have a sense of humor.

Instead of banishing The Beast, the ritual leaves me more connected to it than ever. It's not gone—it's integrated. The primal force I've fought for so long is now a part of my magic, my identity, my power. The realization is both freeing and terrifying.

I can't escape what I've become, but maybe I don't need to.

The aftermath of the ritual is sobering. The Resistance still faces the constant threat of my two-faced allies, and my leadership is more critical than ever. The cracks in our group deepen, and I'm forced to make tough decisions that weigh heavily on me. My bond with Taurus grows stronger, though it remains complicated and messy. He sees me—both the leader and the Beast—and somehow; he doesn't flinch.

It's infuriating and comforting in equal measure.

By the end, I stand on the precipice of something new. I'm no longer running from The Beast or what it means to me.

I'm Delilah—leader, fighter, and survivor.

The path ahead is uncertain, but for the first time, I feel ready to walk it on my own terms, claws and all.

The Cat Pretends Nothing Happened

DELILAH

It's been a week since they opened that stupid bar, and though we had a serious discussion with Belle and Sari, I don't think it did a damn bit of good. Every day I hear about shit going on there that concerns me, but I don't get involved. They've already developed a persecuted narrative and I don't want to feed into it. But I know it will be the source of major conflicts and breaches of boundaries soon—it's inevitable with those two in charge.

Unfortunately, I can't do a fucking thing about it without looking like a tyrant.

The worst part is having to contact people I want nothing to do with about this damn ritual. If I didn't need it, if that dream woman hadn't been adamant about me having more powers... I would have just abandoned the whole idea. But if that odd chat with the hooded specter was more of a premonition, I should *not* skip our biggest spring holiday. I just have to survive doing this shit with a bunch of witchy tourists and asshole mates that I'd rather punch in the teeth.

Piece of cake, right?

"I think I'm going to pick Kali," Sari says as she chews on a licorice twist. She bobs her brows, making a slashing motion like she has a sword and I groan inwardly.

Of course, she is. That's a fitting choice for someone bent on avenging every imagined slight in the worst possible ways.

"She's a dangerous choice," Lily says, trying to tactfully relay to Sari that inviting a Hindu goddess of vengeance might not be prudent. " might choose Athena."

I wouldn't bat a lash at that choice. Lily is highly intelligent, introverted, and values logic over all else. Athena is perfect for her, and it's not a dangerous one if this damn ceremony has any reality attached to it.

"I-I believe... I'm g-g-going with Artemis," Calista murmurs. Being that she's all about nature and thinks she's calling a wolf in Veruca, that also fits. Artemis has a strong sense of justice and fairness, too, so I'm less worried she'll use that against me in Sari's name.

Calista has been thrust into a bigger role in this adventure because Rhea's not at the meeting. No one is comfortable enough with her to have an intimate experience with her. I don't know if anyone has spoken to her directly, but the meeting has focused on kicking her out and deciding which goddesses to call. It's funny because Sari is totally cool with giving Rhea the boot for her betrayal and didn't for a second consider bowing out herself.

Fucking hypocrite.

"Hel," Amanda says bluntly, her tone daring anyone to challenge her decision. Sari claps and I have to grit my teeth not to growl in irritation. All Sari's besties are choosing very aggressive avatars, and it makes my ass clench.

I'm concerned about her part in my ritual as it is. Given the shenanigans Amanda has been up to with her 'quest' that she's been blogging about, this worries me even more. I bet she's been encouraged to emulate the patented Sari 'disaster strikes' method of working through personal problems. Her current posts suggest that she's right on the edge of suicidal tendencies, despite the fact that she looks fine right now. So, of course she's decided to call the Norse goddess of Death.

Jesus. H. Motherfucking. Christ. Sometimes, I want to strangle everyone I know and dance on their graves.

"Who are you calling, Deli?" Sari asks, grabbing the wine bottle to pour another glass. "I can't imagine what will happen when you take your turn. Your goddess can't call fifty clones at once. You'll have to survive with only one dick this time around."

I whip my head around to look at her as a silence falls over the room. The edge in her voice tells me what she's accusing me of. She might as well have called me a tramp, and she's not kidding. "That's not my purview. The goddess calls her true mate and we respond, Sari. Given the crowd in this room, I don't think the choices are clear for anyone."

Everyone looks at one another, and I sit back, grinning in satisfaction. I know that I've squashed her completely for that thoughtless, tacky comment. She won't notice, but it's important to keep others from seeing someone step on you in your home. It's especially important when that someone is your mate, your friend, and your family.

Letting her get away with that would have made me look weak.

"Are you hens done with your planning?" Philomena glides in, looking suave and comfortable in some designer jumpsuit with her trademark martini in hand. The glint in her eyes tells me she overheard and is stepping in before it gets ugly. "If so, Leo has the grill going. All the blonde dimwits are out by the pool waiting for you ladies."

I chuckle. "I think we're done for today, DP. Thanks for letting us know."

"I guess we know who *won't* be making an appearance that night, though," Sari snarks.

Philomena narrows her eyes, waiting for my mate to continue her wine-fueled tirade. "I think people know what is and is not appropriate behavior, even for that mumbo jumbo stuff. I'm not sure if I can say the same about other public behavior, but at least the unwelcome won't crash your hippie party."

Ouch. She made it about Rhea *and* Sari. Sari's aim was more dangerous, letting me know that she's certain Taurus won't be around. I don't think he will, but she needs to tread more carefully. She's going to be deeply sorry if she keeps poking that bear with a short stick.

I don't leash him, and I certainly don't have control of Talia.

"Guys, let's take our drinks out by the pool," Lily says, playing peacemaker as usual. "All the boys are waiting and it's a pretty day."

Amanda rolls her eyes and Calista smiles shyly. I stand, ignoring Sari's dark countenance as I stretch my cramped limbs. I toss back the rest of my drink, looking at them expectantly. "I guess we could do that. I don't know if I'm ready for a bathing suit," Amanda says, chewing on her lip.

Sari snorts. "Hell, woman, this is Deli's house. We strictly forbid swimwear."

Philomena glares again. "With family. There is more mixed company than is acceptable for that. We have plenty of spares in the guest cabana. Sari, yours should be in your room. See if any of the extras float your boat, ladies."

"I'm going to go get mine," I say, starting towards the stairs. Everyone looks at me for a moment, stunned, and I shrug. "She's right. There's more non-family than I'm comfortable with."

I give DP a grateful smile, trying to keep my spine straight and head held high as I go up the steps. I will not cave to Sari's abuse—not in public. Besides, I can't swim naked with my plumage showing yet anyways. I'll have to wear a rash guard and bikini bottoms to hide it.

We're still semi-under wraps and today is *not* the day to tempt Sari's ire.

I wish I wasn't here.

That's sad.

The Cat Hides From Life

DELILAH

The afternoon sun had given way to a starry night as we lay on the plush couch, tangled in each other's embrace. I could feel his warm breath on the top of my head as he mumbled something indistinct into my hair.

"Deli," he whispers again, and I can't help but giggle. Despite feeling lightheaded from the blood loss, his voice still sends shivers down my spine.

"Mmm, love?" I look up at him through half-closed eyes, trying not to succumb to the dizziness.

"Nothing, love. I just wanted to say it." His fingers trace lazy circles on my back as he speaks. "I'd ask how you're doing, but that giggle tells me it can't be too bad."

I can't help but giggle again, the sound almost girlish. "Definitely not bad," I said, covering my mouth with my hand.

"Sandwich, are you alright?" His concern is evident in his voice as he props himself up on one elbow to look at me.

"It's just the alcohol," I reassure him with another small laugh. "I'm a bit giddy. It'll pass."

"We shouldn't have done it again so soon," he murmurs regretfully. "The nitrogen and carbon dioxide in the blood...it's not good for you."

"I told you it was fine, worrywart." I lean up to kiss him lightly on the lips before sinking back into his arms.

"How is your hunger? Better?" His expression turns serious as he asks the question.

"Well, duh," I reply with a playful smile. "You always do this to me."

It's true; I hadn't fed in days and was struggling to keep everything under control until we were more settled. On top of that, I was also carrying Rafe's pain over his recent breakup with Rhea and Alistair, and keeping our relationship hidden from everyone we knew. Plus, we hadn't slept much in the past week due to our passionate encounters.

I'm running on fumes, but it's worth it.

"Cut me some slack, love," he murmurs, snuggling closer to me.

"My body heals rapidly," I say as he wraps his arms protectively around me. "I'm pretty sure my blood replenishes itself as well. The white cells at least; that's how I heal. It won't be a problem."

He relaxes into our embrace, making me feel safe and content. "Are you sleepy now, my foxy feline?"

"A little bit," I admit with a stifled yawn.

"You're exhausted." He traces a finger along my cheek before continuing. "Will you...um..." He hesitates, looking nervous. "Is it alright if we spend the night together? I haven't mated with anyone in a while and I don't know how you do it, but I've found that I just want to hold you."

I can't help but smile sleepily at his words. "Of course it's alright, love." I reach down and pull a large blanket off the end of the couch, covering us both with its soft warmth.

He pulls the blanket up to our shoulders and nuzzles into my neck. His tongue flicks out to lick at his mark on my skin before settling in to sleep. "Goodnight, love."

"Night, baby." Another yawn escapes my lips before I add, "Oh, and don't be surprised if Aradia shows up. She's used to sleeping with me."

His brow furrows in concern. "She won't come between us, will she? That wouldn't be good."

"No need to worry," I reassure him with a small laugh. "She'll just sleep at our feet."

"Uh, how much does she weigh exactly?" His tone is slightly hesitant now.

"Not that much, you big baby," I tease, running a hand through his hair. "She still jumps on my lap all the time, doesn't she?"

With a resigned sigh, he finally gives in. "I guess I'll have to get used to it." But I can tell he doesn't mind; he's already drifting off to sleep.

"Two bundles of purring warmth cuddled around you? You won't mind a bit," I say with a yawn, snuggling into him even more.

"I'll take your word for it, pet," he replies before closing his eyes. "But if I wake up tomorrow morning in an intestine, don't say I didn't warn you."

I can't help but laugh at his comment. "Don't worry, she's never eaten one of my clones before."

"Goodnight," he says with a tired smile.

"Goodnight," I reply, feeling myself drifting off to sleep as well.

"I love you, mate," he murmurs in my ear.

"I love you, too."

With that final exchange, we fall asleep in each other's arms, surrounded by warmth and love.

The Cat Gets Cornered

DELILAH

I awaken, turning to look for Taurus and only finding Aradia. She yawns, her large head butting up against me as she purrs. Stretching my legs, I sigh. His absence is probably work related, but disheartening.

"Well, love, it's time for us to go home and get cleaned up. Uncle Leo will feed you and we can find out what madness is going on today. Maybe you can check on Rafe, eh? He's been quiet since the traitors stopped coming around."

She dips her head as if she is nodding, then tugs her blanket off the couch.

"Let's go see what the crazies have for us."

I push the button on the phone and pop into my bedroom, watching as Aradia pads off to find her meal. Peeping around in my room, I frown. He's not here. Time to head downstairs.

"Hellooooo?" I call, heading down the stairs to find my family.

~In the studio, love. Good night? ~

I wrinkle my nose, hiding my worry for my mate in case anyone sees me. *~Okay, darling. It was an exceptionally good night. Come find me when you're done. ~*

He sends me an affirmative, but it's half-hearted and I feel his depression. Losing Alistair and being left with the terror twins is making him even more internal, more insular, and all I can do is support him. I tuck that thought away as I head for the fridge, needing caffeine and fuel to deal with whatever the hell is coming.

"Well, well. Look what the cat dragged in—literally."

I blink, turning my head at the voice. Why didn't Rafe warn me that he was here? Does he not know? Where is everyone else? Damnit, I was *not* ready for a fucking visitor this morning. "Hello, Constantine. What are you doing here?"

What I mean is 'what in the fuck are you doing at my house following me to my kitchen like a fucking stalker?', but I don't say it. Where the hell is everyone? Leo, Hex, and the gang are usually hanging out; they would have warned me that the lovesick droid I can't seem to shake is haunting my halls.

"I came to see you because I haven't gotten much of your time lately. It's making me sad, Twinkles."

This is my fault. I let him in when I was hurt by the stupid four way mating thing. It was a mistake, and I let it happen because I needed comfort. I slept with him for a while, but most people know that doesn't mean that it's serious for me. At a spectacularly low point—prior to Taurus' arrival—he managed to use the high point of sex to get me to say something I wasn't ready to say and didn't actually feel. It's never good to show weakness, and this passive aggressive courting that he's done is why.

Afterward, I couldn't bring myself to cut him loose. So I didn't make a big deal when he did the creepy 'sneak in my room' thing on my birthday. I continued to let him hang on like a puppy because I felt bad that I said something I can't take back. I do care about him, but I don't love him, and the guilt of leading him on— even if it was forced—eats me alive. So I can't kick him to curb, especially with the hurt I can feel radiating off of him. Amanda's stupid quest must be taking its toll on him as well.

Now I struggle with feeling guilty for leading him on and angry because I can't get rid of him.

"I've been out and about, working on my project and the ritual. Amanda's probably told you about that. Besides that, I'm just trying to keep everything on an even keel. You?"

"It's hard times, pet. My woman's lost her mind, everything's in a mess, and I'm adrift."

Crap. He's here for comfort and support. I definitely can't tell him to fuck off now. Damn my soft heart. "What can I do to help you, dear?"

"I'm feeling needy, cast off, and I wanted to spend some time with you, Twinkles."

I don't have an excuse, and I have no idea how to back myself out of this. I've been trying to get out of this for a couple weeks without hurting him and I haven't come up with anything yet, so I'm stuck. "Maybe we can go out for lunch?"

"I don't feel like being around people, pet. Can we stay here and watch a movie?"

Shit. That's not going to end well. I'll end up trapped and I'll do something that I don't want to do because he's hurting. Where in the *fuck* is everyone when I need them? If I use the bond to call Rafe, I have no idea what he'll do in his current state. He's never liked Constantine, and he doesn't even know about the coerced confession. It'll start a huge fucking fight if he tosses him out on his ass.

I sigh, realizing that no one is going to save me. I'm going to have to take one for the team, so that I can keep the peace. "Okay. Let me feed Aradia and I'll meet you in the living room. Pick something and I'll be in soon."

I swear to Christ, my inability to say 'no' because of guilt is going to get me in a *lot* of trouble someday.

I'm absolutely certain of it.

I finally managed to get rid of Constantine, after what felt like hours of his incessant moping and a supremely unsatisfying liaison. The thought makes me frown as I head for the shower, eager to rinse off the uneasy feeling that has been simmering beneath my skin since he left.

This is not how it's supposed to be, I tell myself, trying to shake off the lingering sense of discomfort that settled in my bones ever since I gave in to his pleading demands. It's not that I regret being with him - as a succubus, physical intimacy is as natural to me as breathing. No, what bothers me is the fact that for once, I didn't do it because I wanted to show him affection or comfort him; instead, I felt like I had no other choice.

That's where things start to go wrong with Constantine.

Then again, our relationship was never exactly smooth sailing. After he took me in during the worst of the Winter shit, I felt indebted to him and it's why I haven't been able to shake loose from his grasp. It's become a vicious cycle - he does something nice for me, and I feel like I owe him something in return. And so when he asked for intimacy tonight, I couldn't bring myself to say no, even though deep down I knew it wasn't what I truly wanted.

Sighing heavily, I step into the steamy shower and start scrubbing away at my skin, hoping to wash away the uncomfortable feeling along with the dirt and grime. But even as I cleanse myself, my mind is still twisting around this problem, trying to find a solution before it becomes an even bigger issue.

It's moments like these when I hate being so damn fairminded. My sense of fairness and obligation often leads me down paths that make me want to vomit afterwards. How do you fix something like that, I wonder, as I wrap a towel around myself and start drying off my wet hair.

Suddenly, I feel a tug deep inside me, letting me know that Taurus is back at our place. A smile stretches across my face for the first time in hours, pushing away the unease and discomfort that had been gnawing at me. Despite my desire to go to him immediately before he decides to just beam me up without permission, I know I need to check on things here first.

Using my magick, I close my eyes and reach out to sense the energy in the house. To my relief, it's quiet - the boys are downstairs playing pool in the game room and the girls are engrossed in a game of Hearts. Rafe is still holed up in his studio, probably working on some new piece of art. After the debacle at the Beltane meeting last week, Sari and her coven have been surprisingly subdued today, with the exception of a mysterious text about a visitor they received earlier. But for now, it seems like everyone is keeping to themselves.

In this moment, I feel free—free from Constantine's grasp and free to be myself without feeling obligated or indebted to anyone.

It's a rare and precious feeling for someone like me, who has always struggled with boundaries and fulfilling others' needs at the expense of my own. As I slip into my clothes and prepare to join Taurus at our home base, I can't help but wonder how long this freedom will last before someone else comes along needing something from me.

For now, I'll enjoy this brief respite before diving back into the endless cycle once again.

The Cat Retreats to the Birdhouse

DELILAH

Grabbing my phone, I hit the button and pop into our room. I smile when I see him. He's snoozing, sprawled on the couch with the stuffed panther tucked in the crook of his arm. His hand is resting on the bird on his bare tummy, and he looks deliciously comfortable.

My lips curl and I pounce on him, nipping his jaw. "Why, hello there, handsome. How are you?"

He opens his eyes, grinning slyly. "Not bad."

I arch a brow, crossing my arms over my chest as I sit on his hips. "That expression makes me suspicious."

"I always said you were a bright one."

"What mischief have you been up to?"

"I was seeing a lady about a twig."

"Oh, shit." I blink, something clicking inside. "*That's* why she's been quiet. *You* were her visitor." I try not to let the instant panic rippling through my chest make it hard to breathe. What did she tell him? Doesn't he know that any contact with her is asking to be drawn into her web of pain? She'll be after him like the coyote she is now.

Damn, damn, damn. I can't let him see me panic. He looks proud of himself, so he doesn't know about any of the bad stuff. She kept her fucking mouth shut for *once*.

"Moi?" he asks, trying to look innocent.

He must think that going to Sari to build a bridge will make me happy. That's a fair assumption, but only because I haven't told him the depth of our issues. I can't crush his insanely stupid surprise. "I'm very pleased," I manage, trying to smile despite the fear of her meddling welling in my chest.

His eyes glow with emotion. "That's why I did it."

Oh, Goddess. You jumped straight into hell and dragged the demon out, that's what you did. I hug him tightly, because I know what it cost him to do it. Dropping a kiss on his jaw, I murmur hoarsely, "Thank you."

"There's not much I wouldn't do for you, love of mine. I suppose she filled you in on what went down. What did she do, tackle you before you got here?"

I shake my head. "No, she didn't. She mentioned a visitor in passing when she texted to cancel our weekly dinner. You probably rocked her world view, and she needs time to deal with that. I'm sure I'll be told tomorrow all about the meeting of the two titans."

"I would have laid money that she wouldn't keep her yap shut. Huh," he muses.

"Only one person tackled me today—which is significantly less than usual when I get home." My face darkens briefly at the memory, but I pull it back, schooling myself before he catches it.

"You're a loved woman, heart of mine."

"Sari's... well, Sari. She'll fret and analyze and worry wort as if some major smack down will happen because you tried to offer an olive branch."

He rolls his eyes, huffing. "Speaking of paranoid loonies, Blondie tapped me today. She wanted to tell me that she's never hanging around the gnome again. I suppose she blames her for falling out with you and yours?"

"Probably, but it won't last. Rhea slipped her gears long ago. Sari didn't make it worse; she only went along for the jalopy ride."

"Let's leave the loonies to each other then, shall we?" He pulls me down on him, rubbing his cheek on my shoulder.

I kick up a purr, but something is niggling at me. I don't know what it is, but I'm worried. "Are you okay, baby?" He squeezes me tighter, nodding against my skin but not speaking. "I missed you."

Pulling back to look into my eyes, he softens that admission with a smile. "I missed you more than you will *ever* know." His hands flex on my hips and he whispers, "I almost told Sari that I'm in love with you."

I run my fingers along his jaw, my eyes dropping when I can't look at him. I swallow hard and ask, "Yeah?"

"Yeah. I wasn't intending to do it, but I…" His voice is soft as he finishes. "I'll always try for you."

Oh, sweet baby Jesus, I hope I didn't break him.

I don't want him to do things that violate his code for me. I have lots of people in my life that violate my lines hoping to make someone—including themselves—happy. Hell, I do it all the time and I *do not* recommend it. Most of the time, the reward is fleeting and you feel awful about yourself for much longer than it lasts.

"I appreciate your effort. I hope you realize, though, that she'll expect you and Talia out in the community more."

"That is not gonna happen." His brow furrows, and he shrugs. "Though, more than a few rules like that have changed lately, I suppose."

"I'll relay that you're not ready for that yet when she mentions it."

He grins. "Oh, sure. You're only saying that because you don't want anyone else to get their hands on me. Tsk, tsk, tsk, greedy minx."

I give him a huffy look. "I said that because you looked like you wanted to hurl at the idea."

"So you *don't* mind others getting their hands on me? Good to know," Taurus taunts, whistling low.

This time the look I give him is filthy, and I know it. "I didn't say that, either, did I?"

"Is it so hard for you to tell me that you don't want others getting their mitts on me, baby?"

I blink, my expression changing to one of incredulity. "Yes."

"Why?"

"My human brain and my animal brain don't agree on the subject. Even the concept of that emotion makes me struggle. It's not *fair* for me to feel that way. I can't ask you what I can't reciprocate. I get mad, frustrated, and confused, then I feel guilty. It's a big ass jumble of mismatched emotions that I don't know how to resolve."

"Sometimes I need to hear it, baby." His lips quirk and he jerks my chin up to look into his eyes. "I'm a relatively simple clone. I know two things: I love you and you love me. I know in my head that you would never stand in my way if you thought something would make me happy, but my heart needs to hear that you want me all to yourself. The demon wants to hear that you would seriously debate maiming someone that tried to make a move on me. Understand?"

To him, this is the simplest thing in the world.

He wants me to know that I can be selfish without thinking about the consequences or how it will affect our entire world if I am. I don't know how to tell him I've been down this road a little way before. The path it led us down—Rafe and I—did not pay off. In fact, it blew up in our faces. But he needs to hear this and I've never been one to deny those I love what they need, even if it costs me to do so.

So I shrug and give him a smirk. "I'm not saying for sure or anything, but I might consider putting a few holes in the stupid bint if she even looked at you sideways. Maybe. You know, if I was in that kind of mood."

The irony is that I'm not lying. My beast would happily put more than a few holes in anyone that came near him. I can't reconcile that with my belief system, but she is unconcerned with my philosophical dilemma. She lets me know that I won't have a choice in the matter. Given her vehemence, perhaps I don't.

"Thanks for that, love," he says, squeezing my hips. "Though, I'm fairly certain that you'd do more than CONSIDER putting a few holes in someone. Seeing some bint slither up to me, ready for a shag, would DEFINITELY put you in the mood, regardless of what else you felt." He winks, looking pleased with me. "Now that I've got the neurotic, chest thumping neediness out of the way, how was your day?"

"Nothing much to report. I dealt with one needy droid, one hungry tiger, one weird message in re: you, and one clone locked in his studio all day. No explosions." Constantine was a much bigger issue than I'm letting on, but I'm not getting into my neurosis. There's enough family bullshit on my plate as it is.

His eyes narrow and he studies me for a moment. "I think you LIKE me all unsure and neurotic. That's why you're downplaying your day. I'm onto you, hussy."

I shake my head, looking amused. "I'm only yanking your chain, baby."

Suddenly, his phone vibrates in his pocket and he jumps up. The movement dumps me off the couch, making me shriek. His eyes have almost rolled into the back of head and he curses. "Bugger!"

Rubbing my bum, I try to untangle my limbs as I look up at him from the floor. What in the actual fuck?

"Ahem. Tattoo," he clarifies as he looks at the screen. "Be right back." He walks over to the wall by the bathroom door and pushes a spot on the panel to reveal a doorway as he talks into the phone quietly.

I get up and plop on the couch to wait, studying the ceiling absently. Where in the hell does that door go? Do all of them open with a touch panel? How does he keep adding to this place in such a short time? What even IS this place? I'm so caught up in my thoughts that I miss him returning until he pounces on me like a cat.

"Quid pro quo, love!" he yells, laughing as I grumble. His hand groping everywhere as he pretends to right himself.

I burst out laughing, pinching his bum. "You ninny!"

"How dare you take liberties with my fair self! I'm a mated clone!"

I goose him again. "Uh-oh. I better beware."

"You know, I decided not to shag you today."

I sniff. "Maybe I wasn't going to shag you, ego man."

He chuckles darkly. "I won't then."

I grin as his hands roam over me, making his declaration a lie. "Definitely not."

We're both full of it.

The Cat and Bird Have No Restraint

DELILAH

His sapphire eyes gleam down at me as we curl together, sweaty and happy. "See, baby? It's all about restraint."

"We have serious willpower," I murmur, sliding my fingers down his spine lightly. That's about as far as I can move.

"Does our fantastic lack of willpower bother you? Do you wish I had more? We don't always have to shag. I'm not with you just for the sex."

I laugh throatily. "Yeah, I was hoping you'd make me moan *less* in pleasure. It's going on my Christmas list this year."

"Christmas is rather far away, love. Are you sure you want to suffer through the wild, crazy orgasms until then?" His grin is infectious, and I reach up to push a lock of hair off his forehead.

"I could make it a New Year's resolution, I suppose. Maybe for Valentine's Day…"

"My Minx, I'm starting to think that you don't actually *want* to give up the blood play and brain melting orgasms."

"You know, you might be right." I tap his nose playfully, smiling.

"Bloody right I am." He holds me close, turning us so we're snuggled in.

I nuzzle his shoulder before my eyes pop open. "You've made me a lech."

"*Me*? I made *you* a lech? How could I make *you*— Wait a tic... what's a lech?"

Lifting my index finger, I quote, "One, especially a male, who is excessively concerned with sexual pleasure."

His jaw drops open. The humor in my statement suddenly catches up with him and he starts to laugh. He wipes his eyes when they leak—positively hooting with mirth—as he tries to calm himself. Taurus kisses my shoulder, only to howl again when he looks at me. "Me?! I've made you a lech."

"Yup. It's all your fault. That's my story and I'm sticking to it." I nod, looking serious as I cross my arms over my chest.

He rests his forehead against mine, finally able to control the snorts. "I think we're both letches, and we corrupt each other. How about that for a compromise?"

"Agreed," I take his hand and shake it.

My phone pings from the table and I pick it up, frowning at the email. Tossing it back with a growl, I settle in. He takes in my sour expression with the arch of a brow. I'll have to explain or he'll wig out.

"Town biz. Lily and I have to read everything for rule viola-tions. Something's in the water today because there are a lot of posts and I've been ignoring them. Lily pinged me because this is a person she refuses to manage. We both have folks like that and we trade off. She wants me to make sure I read it because it's appar-ently fucking long, so it could be hiding all manner of bullshit."

He nods, understanding. "Is that why you look like you fucked a cactus?"

Covering my mouth as a giggle escapes, I shoot him a dirty look. "*No*. It's because if people don't quit writing bad romance crap that I have to read, I'm going to firebomb their house." He snickers and I glare harder. "Do you know *why*? Because of their tripe, I almost said *ridiculous* phrases to you to prove that the lechery is your fault. They all come from that shit!"

"Like what?" he asks, trying to look innocent.

Growling, I smack his chest. "Pulsating. Nuances. Gates of my womanhood... Ugh."

"Gates of your womanhood? Is that like some hotel card swipe thing? Where do you tuck that away then?"

I rub my face, irritated beyond belief as I throw my hands in the air to plead to the heavens. "I'm going to say this one more time to everyone in the universe. There is no key to my pants!"

His expression hardens and he lets go of my hips. "I'd really rather you not wax philosophic about what you've told others about getting into your knickers."

My arms drop and I frown as I look down at him. "It's some 'ha-ha funny' rumor people bring up every once in a while— like an urban legend. When you asked that, I thought you'd heard and decided to tease me about it."

"Telling me isn't quite the same as 'telling everyone in the universe' like you said on the first go round."

"The very idea is a French farce in the making, so I'm denying it yet again."

"Interesting."

"I don't think you imagining a chastity belt for Christmas is what I hoped you'd glean from that confession."

"Probably not, as one of those would probably spontaneously rust right off of you."

Ouch. Maybe I'm sensitive because Sari called me a tramp yesterday, but I think he just slammed my sex life. My lips curl into a sneer as the anger fills my veins. Everyone loves 'good time' Deli when she's with them, but when they feel threatened they get ugly.

The hurt makes me vindictive and I tilt my head, purposefully musing aloud. "I wonder who'd have *that* key."

He doesn't look at me, only swallows and looks out the window.

"Planning on hiding it?" I push again, needing to get my power back.

"Suddenly not really liking this conversation."

He started this when he slung a nasty at me. I swallow hard, my hands shaking as I push all my emotions into my feet so I can pretend it's all okay. I have a *lot* of experience doing this to make people feel better about hurting me, but I didn't think I'd have to do it with him. "We can talk about something else."

"It doesn't matter." He sits up quickly, shifting me off of him. I watch as he locates his pants, shirt and duster. After putting them on, he grabs his phone and pockets it. "I've got to get going."

I'm still smarting from the blow and now I'm worried as fuck. I can't let him see the weakness, though, because then he will have a weapon for later. So I nod. "I see."

Taurus still doesn't look at me, but he sits down next to me to put on his Ferragamos. I stand, feeling like more than my body is naked. I tug on my clothes quietly, finally dropping onto the other end of the couch. I'm raw and exposed and I'm not giving him access to wound me further.

"It's not you; it's me," he starts, looking over at the gap between us with a frown.

I wave my hand dismissively. "It's nothing." I'll be damned if I let another person that's supposed to love me make me feel like garbage this week. I can do that all on my own.

"Why, because it doesn't matter to you or because it shouldn't matter to me?" He holds up his hand and shakes his head. "Stop— don't answer that."

Joke's on you, asshole, because I wasn't going to answer shit. I stay silent, building the walls up inside of me again. This fucking bullshit is why I don't let anyone past them anymore. Everyone is a goddamned disappointment if you give them enough time.

He sighs. "I'm extra sensitive about some things because of

yesterday—it's the blood. It makes me more... Well, it does something to a clone. I'm close to saying something I'd regret. I'm not going to say it, but I want you to know that this is not your problem, nor is it your fault. You are who you are, and I am who I am."

My eyes darken and I force myself to grind out an answer even though it makes my stomach roil in protest. "You are my mate. That's all that matters."

If he's surprised at the arctic chill in my tone, he doesn't show it. He drops his head and exhales, as if he has to carefully select what he's going to say. "That's not true, is it? When I'm here, that's how it feels and I'm fine. But others intrude, the truth comes home with a kick and a slice."

The beast rumbles inside of me, Her need to protect flaring as my pulse speeds up. Anger, pain, and fear are making my survival instincts kick into gear. My skin feels hot and my veins throb, but I keep pushing the emotions down so that he won't have the satisfaction of knowing what his words are doing to me.

My voice is flat and emotionless as I reply, "If it makes you feel better, I haven't bled anyone since the feather."

"Oh, baby," he sighs and I shoot daggers at the side of his head as he looks at the floor. He doesn't get to call me that when he's ripping me to shreds. "Yes, that makes me feel better, but also so much worse. I know there will be a day when you won't be able to say that, and I'm not talking about Rafe."

I don't react. I don't even flinch when he gets up and walks over to run his fingers over my jaw.

"I'm raw. This is all new—the drinking and the claiming. It makes me a thousand times more possessive than normal. At least, I hope that's what it is."

"Yeah," I say, not moving a muscle as he stands there looking at me.

"You are still listening to me rip the heart out of my chest, right?"

My eyes flick up to him, the rage in them cloaked behind

nonchalance. I refuse to let him know that I'm trying to figure out what I'm going to do when he finishes breaking my heart after this. Because I know as surely as the sun will rise, I'll be getting a heartfelt kiss off when we next meet. "Yes. I'm processing."

"Maybe I should leave you to it. I've got to get out of here, anyway," he says, his voice sad.

I can't stop him. I can't be the one to reach out; it hurts too much. "Okay."

He closes the distance between us long enough to press a kiss to my forehead before turning around and walking towards the door. "I'll miss you," he mumbles.

Watching him go, I wait until he's gone before I murmur to myself, "I'll miss you, too."

Goddess above, I am so fucked.

The Cat and The Bird Mend Bridges

DELILAH

I sigh, not able to focus on my Book of Shadows and the notes I'm making for the Beltane ritual. I haven't been able to concentrate on anything all day.

Truthfully, I haven't been able to focus since the fight.

Taurus has been gone for almost a week. Why hasn't he called? Is he ever coming back? The uncertainty is killing me, and I don't know what to do.

I refused to talk about it when I got home that night and since then, I've flat out ditched everyone. I made it clear I wanted no one from outside of our family in our house. Hell, I didn't even take messages. I'm still pissed at Sari over the Zoo thing, Rhea's being shunned, and I have no patience for anyone else.

He's gone and I can't seem to function.

This week I've tried to distract myself by reading, working on Beltane, updating my blog, organizing my closet... All I've managed to accomplish so far is brooding. One by one, the boys come up to check in, offering food and drinks and treats, but nothing has appealed to me. I haven't been able to do anything but sit here, thinking about all of the losses I've suffered in the past six months.

I'm too emotional to even think about food, work, or sleep.

"Oi, woman." Rafe peeps his head in and I try to smile for him.

"I can't focus. Do you have days like that in your studio?"

He bobs his head, braid swinging at his waist as he does so. "I do, especially recently."

The same night that I was getting my heart pulverized by Taurus, Rafe was destroying his own. He told Rhea and Alistair to get help or get lost. The constant lies and affronts to her mates in the name of bedding Taurus caught up to her. He gave them the boot, told the members of our house, added locks to our doors, cleaned out their things and shipped them, and locked himself in his studio.

He did it for both of us, but he's taking the hit for it emotionally.

My primary is the only person I've spent any length of time with since Taurus left. Rafe begged to come up the next morning and I let him because I could feel the pain that was a twin to mine. My original mate sat here with me, explaining how he lost his temper and ended it when they showed up and tried to pretend nothing had happened.

I thought I'd be more upset about losing Alistair, but there were too many things that that clone allowed to happen despite it being hurtful. He may not have condoned Rhea's behavior towards her mates, but he enabled it. I was surprised to find that the pain of Taurus' betrayal hurt far worse.

We were ready to let them go, I think.

Studying my mate as he comes in and sits down in front of me, I notice that the loss has changed him. He's taming his wild locks, keeping them bound in the sleek braid. Instead of skintight jeans and fashionable shirts, he's donning track pants and cotton tanks. For days now, he's locked himself in his studio, cutting himself off from the world just as I am. When he comes out—like now—he's covered in paints, pastels, and charcoal. He's walled himself off to deal with his pain, but here he is, checking on mine.

Rafe truly is the best of all of us.

"Usually, I start doing things like slinging paint — messy, unstructured things—that make me feel like I'm letting my emotions free so I can think again," he says softly.

"I don't think that's going to help me."

Taking my hand, he kisses my knuckles. "If not, my love, then you need to do what no one ever does for us: seek him out and force a conversation. Clear the bloody air. Don't let the one thing that's been making you happy amongst all this mess slip away out of fear or stubbornness."

His smile is so heartbroken that my words catch in my throat before I can even speak. I can't help but wonder who that pain is for: Rhea or Alistair. I have a guess and if I'm right, I understand. It's hard to make a clean break with someone that didn't actually commit the atrocities.

A dull, nauseating ache throbs inside me, but I don't know if it's from their loss, Taurus, or the shambles my life is in. Rafe is probably right about what I should do, but I don't know if I can do it. "But..."

"No buts. You've been moping in this closet all week, but think about what you should have been doing. There are three member disputes that need negotiating—all of which are being raised because they sense weakness. That bloody bar opened and it's packed every day, despite the ongoing dispute with the owners and the council that still isn't resolved. Tamara is trying her hardest to throw a party for Shea's birthday month and having a hissy that no one wants to come because of the turmoil here. It's a *bloody mess* here and you have to fix this problem with the bird. Our town *needs* you to lead and you are in no condition to do it. Lily cannot hold the fort down forever while you mope. Find him."

I furrow my brows. "You're not happy."

"I don't have to be. I'm not the de facto mayor of our little burg, am I? People aren't testing my limits. They are testing you and they sure as shit are watching to see how you handle all of this."

Closing my eyes, I nod. "I know. Pushing limits and boundaries comes from fear, too. Sari must be whipping up the froth because she's pissed at Rhea and scared to death of the unknown that Taurus represents. It will only get worse if I can't be open about what's going on."

"Exactly. So, pop off and fix it, my night bloom. Figure it out together."

I lean in and drop a kiss on his jaw. "Only if you promise to stay out of the studio and be around the family. I don't like you stewing alone."

"If you insist." Rolling to his feet, he winks and heads out, leaving the door open for me.

Hell. I guess I need to go find out how badly I've fucked things up.

Taurus isn't here when I arrive, so I walk over to the bar. Fixing myself a drink, I toss it back and then pour another. It can't hurt to have a little liquid courage. Looking down at the mini-fridge, I open it. I'll be damned if it isn't filled with snacks I like. I swear to Christ, he thinks of everything, even when he isn't here. Swiping a container of freshly sliced fruit, I head over to the couch to wait.

Curling up, I try to focus on the right words and chants for Beltane. I brought my binder so that I could at least *attempt* to do something if he wasn't here. Since this needs to be finished, I sip my vodka again, munching on a piece of kiwi as I scribble. I shiver a little, and I frown. Pausing for a moment, I scoot over to grab the blanket draped on the back of the couch and a scent tickles my nose.

He's here.

I can feel him outside in the hallway. There's a sweet scent mixed in with his usual aroma of expensive cologne and leather—

fear. I don't turn around, but I murmur, "Are you going to stand out there all night with the door hanging open?"

When he finally speaks, his voice is low and gravelly. "People think they're in love because of how their loved ones make them feel. That's not love—it's selfishness because it's all about you."

A philosophical debate about love will not help us move past what happened last week.; I didn't come here to be lectured.

"While I was gone, I thought about what I feel for you. I love how you make me feel when we're together. That part might be selfish, but it's not the only reason I love you. It's not even the most important reason I love you. More than anything, I love you for who you are—your heart and your mind. I realized that your experiences are what have and will continue to shape who you are."

Nodding slowly, I stay silent and sit my chin on my knees. I wasn't the one who broke us—despite what my guilty conscience wants me to believe—so I need him to show me that he knows he was wrong.

"I'm a lesser person when the selfish bits pinch me. I'm less of a man."

Setting all my trappings aside, I turn my head to the doorway. I hold a hand out, gesturing for him to come in. He steps in the room and gets close enough to touch my fingertips. I grasp at his fingers, pulling him closer bit by bit. He grips my hand tightly and I can feel the emotions swirling inside him.

"I'm sorry."

I smile softly, squeezing his hand. He knows that he fucked up and he knows why. It's more than I get from any of my other mates, so I can accept it. "It's okay."

"No, it's not." He slowly rounds the couch and joins me, wrapping his arms around me. "I forgot something during my whacked out tantrum last week."

"What was that?" I ask curiously.

"My absolute *best* bloody moments are when I'm doing something that I think will make you happy. That has nothing to do with me at all. I'm complete when I'm with you, Deli." He gives me a rueful grin. "Movie sound bite as that may be, I'm head over ass in love with you."

Unable to think of anything except how wonderful it feels to be back in his arms, I give him a tender look. My voice is low when I respond. "I love you so very much, Taurus. I always want you to be honest with me, and you were. You went about it the wrong way, and you said hurtful things, but you apologized. So, we're okay now."

I should tell him that while he was gone, I struggled to function because he's my solace from the crazy. I should also tell him how much it hurt for him to say he could deal with my past, then fling it in my face. I should let him know that with him gone, it felt like a third of me was missing and I ached with the loss. I don't because I can't deal with that right now.

I just want to sink into his arms and feel right for the first time since he left.

"I can't promise that I'll never feel that selfishness again, but I'll be honest with you. I'll deal with it differently, so I don't hurt you."

Stroking my fingers through his hair, I murmur, "No one is perfect. We're all selfish sometimes." I've had people treat me much worse for no reason, and never once did they apologize or regret their actions. I can give him a pass for being an ass because he got possessive this time.

"Are you still mine, heart of mine?"

"Always, baby."

"Do you forgive me?" His expression is heartbreakingly unsure, and it makes my chest ache.

"I do." How could I not when he's clearly agonized over his transgression? I rest my forehead on his, soaking in the calm that is settling into my soul.

"I didn't mean to worry you, kitty. I should have texted while I was gone, but I needed to do this in person." He tilts his head to kiss my nose. "On a lighter note, I missed you like the air I breathe."

"I missed you too. So much."

"Want to sit on Daddy's lap, little girl?" He smirks playfully and I scoot over to curl up on his lap as requested. He reaches for my hand, linking our fingers. Bringing them to his mouth, he nips my index finger before dropping his fangs to pierce it. Sucking gently on the single drop of blood that swells, he growls softly.

I blink, the tingling from that tiny draw making the beast stir inside. Taurus ignites the primal in me like no other, and even a small bite gets her going.

He chuckles. "I love that I get to do that whenever I want." As if proving his words, he moves to my pinky and repeats the action, a small droplet of blood welling before he suckles tenderly.

Laughing softly, I ask, "What, snack on me?"

"Not exactly. I mean I get to be a part of you."

"You're a part of me all the time now, mate."

"I know, baby, but I've led such a poor, sheltered life that sipping from you randomly is a new experience." He makes a face like a poor little orphan and let me tell you, it works no better than the angelic one.

"Oh, poor you," I chuckle, swatting his shoulder. Giving him a crooked grin, I say, "Honestly? I love when you get excited about little stuff. Things that most take for granted, you cherish. It's endearing."

Looking embarrassed, he shrugs. "I'm naive, huh?"

"You enjoy everything and it makes me feel special." It took me a while to figure out why this reaction makes my heart squeeze. I haven't felt that way in a long time—everyone else just assumes access to me is part and parcel.

"Look at that. You get prickly when someone picks on me, even when it's me. That doesn't bode well for you in public, beautiful." He grins boyishly, looking pleased with himself, then frowns. "Wait. You *are* special."

"Oh, yeah?" I huff, pretending to look peeved.

"Are you going to get stompy now?" He struggles not to look hopeful, and it's a riot.

I cross my arms over my chest, my eyes narrowing.

"I love when you're irritated. You turn an adorable shade of red," he growls, his expression hungry,

"I do not!"

"I beg to differ, woman of mine." His fingers trace over my jaw as if to highlight it and I fume.

"You're only saying that to get me pissier so I'll stomp."

"Will it work?" he asks hopefully.

"No, it won't."

He looks crushed. "Well, hell."

"Oh, fine. If it'll make you happy." I stand up and stomp around the room huffily before coming to stand in front of him. "Better?"

A cheerful grin splits his face. He looks up at me, his heart in his eyes. "You're a kind woman, and I love you, my mate. "

"Because I stomped for you? Man, you're easy."

"Only in part. If I tell you the rest, you really will get stompy on me." His gaze falls on the table and he tilts his head when he sees the books and notebook. "Am I disturbing you? Were you working?"

"Not disturbing, no. I was planning the wretched Beltane thing that I told you about. It wasn't late when I got here, but it is getting late now, so I'm tired."

"Me too, baby. I've got a premature death scheduled early tomorrow. I was going to crash on the couch and let you work, but I'll go. After the other day, I—I wanted to be near you, even if you weren't here."

"You can still do that; I wouldn't mind."

"Do you want to sleep here? With me?" He gives me another unsure look and it makes my heart thump.

"That might be nice, actually." He looks pleased and squeezes me again. "Are we ready to clock out?"

Giving me a soft kiss, he nods. "Yes, love." He strips down to his silk boxers, then he wraps his arms around me. Stretching us out on the couch so we're curled close, he buries his face in my hair with a sigh.

I reach down, grab the blanket, and pull it onto us. "Night, my love."

"Night, heart of mine."

Yawning, I murmur, "I love you, baby."

"I love you too, beautiful. Mine."

With that, we both drift off to sleep.

The Stoat, The Witch, and The Cast Iron Bed

"Okay, lift!"

My primary frowns, studying the placement in relation to doors, windows, couch area, and other décor. "Hmm... To the left, I think. It's not centered."

"For the love of everything unholy woman, this thing weighs a metric ton. Decide before we all end up with hernias." Leo gives her a dirty look, wiping his brow.

I roll my eyes, knowing full well that droids cannot get hernias and individually, they could probably dead lift a F-150. They're all so damn dramatic, though, and like me, they love giving her shit.

"She's right, mate. It's definitely off-center."

Every droid in the room gives Hex a scowl of disapproval as we coordinate, lift, and move the wrought iron monstrosity again. It's not too heavy for us, but it *is* a pain in the ass and this is taking forever.

"Who let Mr. 'Flip This House' come? Between the two of them, we're going to be moving this sodding thing until we're all old and gray," I grumble.

"Again, with the dramatics. Clones do *not* get old and gray and droids certainly don't. Jeez, you're such whiny babies," my night bloom says with a sigh of irritation. "Come on. It's not like I can get a moving company here in this weird in-between place. Please?"

The whole group sighs and hefts again, swearing under our breath colorfully enough to make a trucker blush. It's performative at best, but I know it makes *me* feel better.

"I think it's good now." She smiles brightly. "Hex, where did you put the linens?"

"Linens? We needed to bring something besides this?" Hex arches his brow, looking at me to make sure he didn't miss something.

"Oh, hell. We didn't bring the damned linens! Back to the store we go," our girl says, not looking sorry in the slightest.

"Abso-bloody-lutely not." Leo stomps his foot. "I have to get my roast on and Hex has a half-painted bathroom. You can come back with them yourself, Juliet."

She pouts, hoping to sway him. "Aw, but Hex's so much better at this than me. If he didn't buy any, we have to go shopping."

Hex blinks, a grin creeping over his handsome face. "Oi. Sod the bathroom." We groan and he grins. "What? I love home stores. You gits feck off; I'm going with Nancy."

"You did that on purpose, Night Bloom. Now the guest bathroom will have to be completely redone because the shades will dry differently," I say.

Not that Hex will care; he'll happily strip it and paint again because he loves that shit.

"Who fucking cares? That's his problem," Leo grumbles, heading for the door. "You two have fun finding home and garden stuff for the secret lair. We're going back to the Maison so I can make sure dinner isn't ruined."

The cat grins at Hex, clapping her hands in excitement. "Where should we go first?"

"For this git? We gotta start at Neiman Marcus."

Once Leo and I decided to leave them to their décor journey, we were promptly sent back to the Maison. The quirky chef looks relieved as fuck, but honestly, I'm indifferent. Since I broke things off for us with Rhea and Alistair, I've been staying cloistered in my studio to avoid attention. The pain of losing Victor and now them is too much, especially with the other mates being so... unpredictable.

Aradia saunters up to me with Twist on her back and I scratch her ears. Seeing the little ferret doesn't make that spot where the jokester used to live ache anymore because we weren't nearly as close as the mates. This has been one hell of a year for my heart.

If I didn't have art, I'd definitely be in need of some heavy medication.

Leo jerks his chin and I nod at him before he scampers off to deal with his roast. It's no surprise when the tiger follows him: he spoils the shit out of her when she's not with our girl. I'm alone again, but I know what to do—I have things to work on.

It probably sounds as if I'm lamenting the cat's sudden absence while she's gallivanting with the bird. I'm not—at least, not how it might be perceived. I miss my mate when she's gone and I definitely wish I had her around more so I could use her as support. But I don't begrudge her happiness with that jackass, nor would I ask her to cool it until I'm in a better place mentally.

That's just not how our bond or our family work.

With a heavy sigh, I throw open the double doors of my studio. It's perfectly set-up for all the various mediums I experiment with, including a sitting area, a bathroom, and a closet so I can work without interruption. When I go on a 'project bender'. I can't be bothered to leave the room even for basic needs. Leo even has a specific knock to let me know he's bringing food or Hex has laundry because I won't open the door when I'm focused.

"Should I paint or sketch?" I murmur as I look around the room.

The walls and shelves are filled with the evidence of my pain. I haven't let my primary or anyone else in here since I started using this as my way of coping; it's way too obvious what state I'm in if you look at the various paintings and drawings hanging up. Every ounce of my heartache is shown in dark shades and rich colors, and I know they'd be able to sense it.

I'm a moody git and I don't want anyone's pity.

My eyes catch on one of the unfinished works on an easel and I know what I'm going to do. "Painting it is."

Turning on the music on the wall panel, I close my eyes as I begin the ritual of preparing to work. The music helps me get in the right headspace, then I set up my oils and brushes, and at last, I stand in front of the canvas to get the vibe from where I left off. Once everything clicks into place in my mind, I dip my brush in the paint. These won't hang in galleries or even on the walls in our house, but they are masterpieces of emotion just the same.

Everything I am is going into these artworks and hopefully, when they're done, I'll be healed.

The Cat Admits Something Big

DELILAH

Hex and I finished up my 'surprise' with relative ease. His eye for design is exquisite. We got a fluffy black down comforter and achingly soft Egyptian cotton sheets in blood red. There are piles of accent pillows in satin and lace, but I'm sure they'll never again see the light of day once I've shown this to Taurus. He doesn't seem like the accent pillow type. Once the bed is perfect, I curl up on the huge wrought iron bed amongst the mounds of pillows and fall right to sleep.

The hairs on the back of my neck prick up, waking me. I open my eyes, knowing what that means: he's here. Yawning, I stretch limb by limb, rolling onto my tummy with a smile. "Hello, my love."

Leaning against the doorjamb casually, he smiles. He must have been watching me sleep. "Hello, love. You look beautiful." It hits him suddenly because he gapes at me. "Wait. Bed. You." He looks around as if trying to make certain that he's in the right place.

Grinning, I tilt my head. "Nice to know your keen observation skills haven't failed you."

His jaw works, but he doesn't seem to get anything out. "You… you. It's a bed."

Nodding, I give him a satisfied expression. "With pillows and everything."

Taurus walks into the room cautiously. "I see that—you know, now." He winks and I wonder if he's trying to hide how he feels. "You bought us an exquisite, gigantic bed with all the frills."

"Yup." I wriggle my toes, spreading out on the softness happily.

Tilting his head, he sends a caress through our bond. "I thought you didn't do beds, love."

"Don't be silly—I'm not a heathen. I just have a hard time making it to them." I squirm, not wanting to explain how beds tie to fear of commitment.

I didn't used to be this way, but I am now and telling the tale will ruin the mood.

He takes another few steps and runs his hands over the wrought iron with a wide grin on his face. "I love it. Very manly—except for the dust ruffles."

"I'm a sucker for old fashioned stuff. Besides, the sheets are blood colored. I thought that'd be handy—no stains!"

"Look at all those places to tie you down and have my wicked way with you."

His eyes glow and I know he's being playful, but I feel my chest tighten. My breathing gets thready as the images flood my brain. It was fine with Alistair. He's gone now, but Taurus won't do what Wilde does. He won't take my power and make me small and afraid.

Shit. Shit. I can do this. It's okay. Just breathe, Deli, and it'll be okay.

I squirm, finally forcing husky words out of my dry mouth. "I knew you'd be all lecherous about it."

"You'd be disappointed down to your cute little toes if I didn't, so don't even try it, Minx."

"Maybe." I give him a sly smile as I work to push the panic away before he notices.

"You bought your lover—your *mate*—a bed. That sends a message." Eyes bright with love and passion, he stares as he slowly unbuttons his shirt. "Mind if I try out the mattress?"

Flopping onto my side, I let my hair spill over my shoulders like a pose from the cover of a romance novel. His growl tells me that I made a perfect 'come hither' picture and satisfaction rumbles through me. "Help yourself."

He tosses his burgundy silk over the foot rail and bunches his muscles, leaping onto the bed with delighted exuberance. Laughing happily, he pulls me towards him. "Oh no, minx. One cannot try out a bed properly without the person you intend to share it with as often as non-humanly possible."

I kiss him lightly, my heart filled with sappy emotions. He's taken this one little gesture and made it feel like I gave him the greatest gift he's ever received. Christ, it's nice to have someone who wants to share things with me that aren't to make themselves feel better or to look good in front of others. I purr softly as he holds me close.

Taurus groans low in his throat, enjoying the purr. Drawing back, he looks at me. "I like this setup."

"Oh, good. I hoped you would."

His smile is tender. His arms spread out over the expanse of the comforter as he relaxes. "This is wonderful. What made you think of this, love? Last I heard, you scoffed at the ultra-breakable beds and only wanted a sofa in here."

I wrinkle my nose, suddenly feeling exposed. "I might have been looking for the right time and place. I'm a softy about stuff like this."

Tilting his head as he leans over me, caressing his feather. He leans down and kisses me gently, stroking the feather eye with his thumb, then whispers, "I hate to tell you this, love of mine, but you're a softy about more than just 'stuff like this'. In all seriousness, you humble me. This is perfect and I'm honored to be the right time and place."

My eyelids flutter, a contented hum escaping into the kiss. I smooth my hands over his hair and down to rest on his shoulders. "Maybe I am soft, but you'd better not tell anyone."

He arches an eyebrow. "Who would I tell? You keep me locked away in this room, hoarding me all to yourself."

"I'm sure that disappoints you *so* much." I shrug, pretending to be nonchalant. This is the first time he's seriously talking about us going out in public as a couple and it terrifies me. "If you want to go strutting around together, I'm always game. I know how you love to spread your feathers."

"That's a conundrum. On one hand, I have a chance to sport you on my arm with a side order of proud and mighty; on the other, I have you all to myself for all manner of wicked naked fun on this new bed. What's a proud, ornery, love-struck, arrogant peacock to do?"

"You know, Mr. Polar Extremes, you could split the difference. I'm not going anywhere, and neither is the bed."

He eyes me oddly, a twinkle sparking in the sapphire depths. "My, my, kitty. If I didn't know better, I'd say you're interested in keeping me with you all the time." He leans back into the soft mattress, sighing in pleasure. "Split the difference, eh?"

Sighing dramatically, I roll my eyes. "Every time I'm accommodating, you get difficult. It must be a reverse corollary or something."

"I was being difficult?" He hides a grin behind a pillow sham. "How was I difficult?"

I huff in response.

"You mean saying you want me around all the time?"

"See how often I'm accommodating now." I cross my arms over my chest.

It's not very threatening, given that I'm flat on my back, but it's the principle that matters.

"Baby, you know the only thing that matters to me is being with you. I'm sorry I poked. I like it when you get possessive." Taurus rolls over and looks down at me seriously. "It occurs to me we've never been out on a date. I'd like the world to know I've mated with you, beautiful. That means a trip around town for mayhem and chaos." His smile is evil, and I can hear the wheels turning in his head.

"Ooh," I clap in excitement.

"Oh, sure. *Now* you want to dash out the front door with me in tow. Mention a date and the chits get all anticipatory."

"You are pushing my buttons, buster." I poke his chest playfully.

"You want a night out on the town. Hunting, stealing, chick flick, maybe a bit of a walk on the beach? Let me ponder a chaotic, glorious show."

"That sounds like a lot for a first date. Maybe we should pick a few?"

"What would you like to do, baby? Riot, random pyromania, girlie film...?"

"Surprise me. I like surprises."

His expression is evil. "Right then. Just ignore that buxom blonde that's going to hit on me while we're out then."

I arch my brow at him, the beast rumbling to life within a second.

"You mentioned preening, darling. I thought it would be an excellent opportunity for you to say, 'mine'. I know how much you like it."

"You are incorrigible," I huff.

"Though, you haven't said it of late. Maybe that buxom blonde will be more receptive."

My eyes narrow and I mutter, "She would be less buxom without her spine."

He laughs and rolls over to look down in my eyes, sapphire meeting sapphire. "Say it."

"Mine." I drop a single fang and lick it, my lips curling up.

My control is getting better now that she's not caged. I've been practicing things I've seen my boys do. The one fang thing is Victor's signature schtick and I was pleased as fuck to master a trick that none of the others can do.

I have twice as many as them, so that has to be slick as hell, right?

"Bloody right. Nice work on the control, minx—you've been practicing." His warm hand strokes along my skin as his eyes burn with pride. "I love you and I'm going to work hard to give you a decent time when we go out." His head lowers and his lips move over my collarbone, then quirk up in devilment when he draws away an inch. "You'll probably only have to kill three—maybe four—stunningly gorgeous chits with a yen to get me horizontal."

Making a face, I push him away. "I'm onto you, Mister. You *want* to see me slice people up over you."

"Well, yeah, but I'm an equal opportunity chest-thumper. I'll eviscerate a few flockers if you'd like." His eyes say that he'd not only do it, but enjoy it thoroughly.

Chuckling, I say, "No need. Unless you're eager to thump and bellow."

Leering, he sniffs. "Whatever gave you the idea that I was... how did you put it? Eager to thump and bellow?"

"Because you live for that shit, you big cave clone."

Leaning over, he nips the skin of my collarbone with blunt teeth. "Oh? And you don't, you ferocious feline?"

"I didn't say that."

"Of course not. That's the sissy girl in you, not wanting to admit to anything ever."

"Did you just call me a *sissy*?" I push him away again, eyes flashing with emerald and fury. I am *not* a sissy.

The idiots we've been avoiding; those are sissies.

"Huh?"

"You called me a sissy!" I thump his chest with a fist, fuming.

"Ow! Bloody hell woman, stop that."

"Stop what?" I thump him again, giving him a dirty look.

"Ow! That, sod it all. Why are you pounding on me?"

"Because you called me a sissy, why else? I'm not a sissy."

He presses his lips together as if trying to come up with an excuse quickly. "Is this our first fight, baby? I want to be prepared because I have to plan the makeup session."

"You realize that it's awfully hard to be pissed at you when you're planning how to get in my pants afterward?" I snort, shaking my head.

"I had no idea at all, really." He tries to look angelic and fails miserably.

I give him a shrewd look. "I'll bet you didn't."

He raises his head and sucks on the dip where my collarbone meets my neck. "I'm completely innocent."

"We both know that's not true."

His lip curls up and he prowls over me. I know where this is going and honestly, I'm okay with that... sissy and all.

I lift my arm off my face and look at him. My lips curl as he presses kisses to my sweaty shoulder.

"Aren't you glad I called you a sissy?"

"I guess that's one way to thank me for bringing the bed," I chuckle throatily.

"I should probably cop to the truth, minx. I meant to say sassy. I was distracted, and it slipped out as sissy. But you got stompy, and I thought—why not?"

My eyes widen comically. I fall into uncontrollable giggles, snorting. "You are a terrible non-person."

"Well, yeah." He grins unabashedly. "That means you're not brassed off at me for not being honest, right?"

"You knew I wouldn't be after *that*."

"It certainly gave me motivation to make you scream, love of mine. You can't blame me after you pummeled me bruised and sore. I bet you feel guilty about that now."

"Oh, not at all. You didn't seem to mind." I smirk, bobbing my brows at him.

He blushes and shrugs. "I was keyed into your emotions, minx. You were pumping emotions into the air like pheromones. I don't know how, since you're a mind speaker, not an empath."

I wince. I mean, sort of... "I have no *proof* that I'm an empath. I... sense a lot. Mind speech only works with my mates as far as I know. I'm not a true telepath like you. However, until four months ago, I didn't have a tail and fangs, either. I pick things up with no warning—that's why I came to you."

We haven't even discussed my magick yet. After Beltane, I'll feel comfortable talking to the ones I love about my skills—or lack thereof, we'll see. Look how long it took me to get a modicum of control over her.

"I feel like we should get working on that again. What if something even weirder happens? I know you're working on control and I can see improvement. But what if you're not a mutant, but a shifter? What if there are things you can do that you don't know about yet?"

I sigh. "I lost the plot when we started dancing. I've been so focused on you, the idiots, community issues, and my Beltane ritual that I put it on the back burner."

Truth be told, his acceptance of her and the modicum of control has made that quest seem less important. She's part of me now, and we're starting to respect one another. The weird side effects like blood hunger, feature shifts, and the weird fire in my veins aren't that big a deal.

"I've been meaning to ask you about that ritual you keep mentioning. What's it about?" He tilts his head, sensing that I don't want to be pushed about the DNA research.

I won't outright lie, but I have to choose my words carefully. He doesn't have the full picture on the problems with my erstwhile mates prior to his arrival. I'm not ready to share that with anyone. Since I can't use that as a reason to plan a magickal rebirth, I have to couch it in simple delicious observance. "Beltane is the celebration of rebirth; it's a wiccan spring festival. I want you to help me to rid myself of negative things and allow positive things to come to fruition."

He blinks as the light bulb comes on. "Ah. It's about your fallen family tree branch. You can't undo mating, but you can try to cleanse the ugly so it's less painful. This will be sort of like a baptism for normies, right? You'll do a little chanting outdoors in a circle?"

"Um, that's how it will work for the others, maybe. I usually practice as a solitary witch, but for this, I need the four corners to be anchored. It started out with my stupid idea to have Sari, Lily, and Amanda help. Since they are at least familiar with paganism, it seemed like a good compromise. I don't believe Sari and Amanda are believers like Lily and I, but close enough. Rhea thrust herself in as usual and Sari added Calista without asking me."

"That's typical Blondie. I'm surprised she didn't ask you why pagans don't eat cheese."

I burst out laughing, having to catch my breath once I'm done. "While you were gone, Rafe kicked the two of them to the curb—both metaphorically and literally. So I had to replace a person. For them, it's weekend Wicca playtime. For me?" I consider how to say this to him so he won't think I'm crazy. "For me, it's the real deal."

He frowns. "What do you mean, the real deal?"

People have always disbelieved me about my magick, so I'm used to having to defend myself. That's why even in the Rift—which amplifies them—I keep quiet.

"I'm a witch—a real one. I could do a little magick on the other side, but nothing worth writing home about. Since I moved here full time, I can do more, but I don't. I'm not saying I can shake mountains, but I can turn the spigot on and do things. I want to truly let it all out now. I think allowing my energy to flow naturally will help with her."

"Neat," he says, grinning. "Do you suppose that's why the mutation happened? Quantum ribbons stuff—as you call it—mixed with honest to hell magick in your blood?"

I blink, surprised by both his automatic acceptance and the question. "Maybe. I never considered that."

"Can I ask you an unrelated question?" I nod, still turning over his suggestion in my head. "Does Blondie know about us? Is her reaction what caused your mate to sever ties without talking to you first?"

"I haven't told her because we're not speaking. She probably knows something, and it's part of the blow up that made Rafe give them the heave-ho. He would never decide for both of us unless what happened was so egregious that there was no other option. That's why I haven't asked him—I trust his judgment. He's truly grieving, and I feel... like I was ready to let go. I don't want to find out what they did, get hurt or angry, and get sucked back in."

"Does the gnome know anything?"

I tilt my head, wondering where this is going. "She knows that we slept together, but not that we mated. I told her how good you are to me."

"To recap: Wilde and Sari know we're shagging, but not that we've mated. Blondie and my brother are wallowing in self-pity because your mate exiled them. Sari says great things to my face and is the same waspish little gnome to my back." He registers my comment and his eyes pop open. "*Wait, you're telling the gnome nice things about me?*"

"Maybe. You never know."

Clutching his heart, he sighs. "Bollocks. That's it; I'm dead."

"Drama queen."

"You are one step away, Missy. You do not want to poke me."

"Oh? Why not?"

"Because I have to leave you to take care of a familial obligation with my goddess. By the time I come back, I will have had a lot of time to consider retribution for ruining my sterling reputation."

"Uh-huh."

"Can you never ever ask me to work on something like this ritual where the other loonies are involved? Christ, they're a morose lot."

"I can try, but um, we didn't get a chance to go into the mechanics of this ritual. I, um, can't really guarantee that?"

His head swivels as he gives me a look of pure fear. "What do you mean, you can't guarantee that? What the bloody hell *is* this ritual?"

I clear my throat, looking sheepish. "Beltane is the ritual of spring and rebirth. We, um, call down our personal goddess. She takes over and calls her God. And uh, well, rebirth sums it up, right? I don't know—I can't predict what will happen?"

My face turns bright red and I curl into the smallest version of me I can, feeling stupid and embarrassed. My stuff might unintentionally involve him, and I can't prevent that from happening. He won't get that if the Goddess calls him, it's a huge fucking deal. That would say an awful lot about his level of importance in my life. He'll probably tell me he hopes it's not him.

That's how most people react.

He blinks. "All five of you are calling a goddess into you. It will call a random git the Goddess thinks is her God. This included two people who are multiply mated to the same gits. Did you lose your sanity on the way to that meeting?"

I frown. "Well, I don't expect it to *work* except for me. They're not really magickal, you know?"

Shaking his head, he snorts. "Holy hell, that could be a mess. Between the infighting over Wilde, your mate, and everyone else? Someone's going to be mightily pissed. What about those without clones? Will it work with their droid mates?"

His question is fair, and I don't have an answer. I didn't think this one through once all the people got involved. When everyone started talking about how the Goddess picks, I was hoping it would work itself out. "Perhaps I didn't think this one through very well, so I'm hoping it works out?"

He gives me an amused look. "Since everything with those bints has worked out on its own. Christ, woman, you may have set up the world's most magickal cat fight."

I huff. "Regardless, I'm not making you a promise I can't keep."

"I don't know if you'd want me in the mix. Word is that I'm hell to deal with. Do you think it's hard to deal with me?"

"No— except when you're being an ass."

"Bloody buggering hell, I walked *right* into that one! Christ, you'd think I was a two-day-old."

"That's why you're fun. You always set yourself up so well." I smirk and bob my brows.

Pinching my rear hard, he snarls, "You will pay for yanking my manly and powerful chain."

"Oh, goody!" I clap, playing along. I'm happy to have the conversation move along from my horrifically poor judgment in ritual partners, life partners, and well, my bad ideas in general.

"Never forget, love. You've got me wrapped, but I really am evil."

"Of course not. Big Bad. Evil. Got it."

He murmurs low, looking serious. "I can be cruel, love. Not to you, but I can."

I can't argue with that because I'm sure he can. I'm also certain that what I consider cruel and unusual is not something he'd do to just anyone—especially not to someone he loved. "You're not the only one—trust me. If it's not to me, you have a head start on a lot of people."

"I do?"

He looks surprised and boy, would he be if he knew the extent of that truth. "Yeah."

"I don't know why, but I'd turn myself inside out not to hurt you. Okay, I know why, but go with it; it's an image. You know that, right?"

My smile is tinged with sadness as I nod. I can feel the honest belief in his statement, and I've heard it before. I can only hope that time proves me right this time. "I do."

"That said, if you get shit for being with me from anyone, I want you to push it off on me. I don't want you touched by it. That's not open for discussion, so don't argue."

"I'm not arguing. I was going to say that people can get bent if they don't like it. I don't really give a damn what they think." In another twist, I realize that I really mean that. With Rhea gone and Sari colluding with every nut in the community behind my back, I'm not concerned what they need. I'm ready to face the music with them because it's time. "I love you. You make me happy and if they can't deal with it, it's their own problem."

"Stop that. Saying you love me makes me all calm and soothed, minx."

"I wasn't doing it on purpose."

"You were a shade more subtle than a purr, kitty."

"Aww. I was just saying how much I adore you." I bat my lashes at him, giving him my most adoring smile.

His expression melts and he grumbles, "Bloody hell. I'm going to go before I'm a total poof. I. Love. You." He kisses my nose.

"I love you, too. Be safe."

"We'll see." He grins as he rolls to his feet and heads out.

The Cat Gets Dizzy With It

DELILAH

Walking through the double doors to the phlebotomy wing, I wave at the receptionist, Arlene. She's been here for the past thousand years—at least, that's what it seems like. She smiles up at me with that pleasant-faced, crinkly, old lady smile that always makes me think of grandmothers. I don't know why as Goddess knows that neither of mine were any kind of matronly icon—more like cranky old dragons with menthol breath.

"Hey, 'Lene," I say, drumming on the desk nervously. "Is Diz here?"

Goddess, I hope so.

The small lunchbox full of lettered swabs is burning a hole in my palm. I'm incredibly hyped up about finally taking steps on the project that sent me looking for my beloved bird. His reminder that we should still at least look into my transformation was the kick in the pants I needed. I'd started the work a little after I met with him, but I got side-tracked. It's time to woman up and see what I'm made of.

She blinks up at me from behind her cheetah-print reading glasses and nods slowly. "That he is, child. Are you sick?"

In Arlene's world, the only reason I'd ever go to Diz's lab is to find out what kind of deadly disease I have. Shaking my head, I grin. "Nope, it's business."

"Is your daddy sending you down with the samples again? No matter how many times I tell that man, he never listens. Children should not be dropping off biologicals like it's a run to the store..."

She's still going when I take matters into my own hands and push through the double doors into the lab. Arlene always hated when my dad allowed me to help with his research when I was younger and she's never let it go that neither of my parents ever treated me like an actual child. I could be there another hour before she'll call Diz out front when she gets started ranting. It could be another hour after that before he drags himself away from his work to answer.

I weave through the long counters bursting with equipment and computers, carefully plopping my box in front of my friend with a grin. "Boo."

Diz looks up, startled. Running his hand through the wild, curly locks on his head, he sighs. Mad scientist hair, I've always called it. When he pushes his goggles up into the mane, it's even funnier. I haven't seen him since I moved to the Rift, but he was eager to help when I called.

"My sistah," he says, giving me the traditional faux-homeboy hand slap and snap.

His greetings have always given me a giggle. Diz is an Ivy League educated genius with multiple doctorates, yet he looks hip, even in his lab coat and protective goggles. Funnier still he includes me—the whitest chick on the planet—on his list of homies. Seriously, I've seen my name under that listing in his phone. It's totally a riot.

I'm a homie; what were the chances?

"My brotha," I reply, grinning broadly. "What's up with you?"

He shrugs laconically. "Blood, disease, pestilence, death... You?"

"Diz, you don't work in Syria, man. You have got to lighten up. No wonder you don't date."

"Oh, not the dating thing again. Girl, you don't give up, do you?" he says, poking at the bag curiously.

"Quit being a hermit; you're hot and should get some." I notice his barely contained curiosity and smile. "I hope I did the collection right because you weren't specific."

He lifts the six tubes out of the bag, flicking each one to watch it resettle. "Looks pretty jive. Is it fresh?"

I shrug. "Sort of? I kept them in the fridge and used a preservative."

"We'll see then," he murmurs, slipping them in the centrifuge. When he pulls them out, he makes six slides. Placing the slip covers carefully, he lines them up so he can see the labels. "Alright. You got these in some kinda order besides alphabetical?"

"Yeah," I say, my eyes intent on the computer program he's booting up. The code on the screen is gibberish to me. I look up, realizing he's waiting for me to give him an answer.

"And that is?" he asks, giving me an impatient look.

"Oh, well, D is obviously mine. It should differ from the other five. Two of them should be remarkably similar in places but different in others—kind of like familial DNA? Two should be exactly alike, " I fib, knowing one of them might not match up with the other four.

He sets up the first slide, humming under his breath as he focuses the scope and the computer analyzes the data. "Uh," he says, fiddling with the knobs here and there. "This is a mistake. This can't be yours."

I grin at him. "Oh, trust me, Diz; it is."

"Something screwed up in there," he taps the screen. "There's a mutation here and.. see this? Another strain—it says feline, but obviously that can't be right. Maybe it's a mutation—sections of it match markers on yours. But..." he trails off, his brow furrowing.

"But what?" I lean over, staring at the screen as he overlays strains, looking for match percentages.

"First, there's this feline thing," he looks at me suspiciously. "Either you've joined an elite team of mutants led by a telepath in a wheelchair or you're screwing with my head."

Chuckling, I shake my head. "Move to the next one. You should probably find strains of my DNA in the other samples."

Giving me a weirded out look, Diz switches to the next slide, nodding his head in confirmation. I didn't tell him how I collected the samples on purpose—drink from a clone, scratch myself, bleed into a tube, clean up the mess, and hope for the best. I couldn't ask them to fill a cup; this is a top-secret project. So I cheated. When I come out of my musings, he's moved to the last slide, murmuring under his breath.

I watch as he moves to another workstation, setting up my slide and typing furiously. Curiosity piqued, I tap his shoulder. "What's in your ear?"

He shakes his head, brow furrowing more. "Not sure. I gotta theory. Why did you want me to look at this again?"

"You've seen my DNA and you have to ask?" I reply sarcastically.

"Obviously, you're going through some changes."

"You're telling me," I mutter.

He looks up, raking his hand through his hair. "Things you've physically manifested?"

I chortle and he blinks. "Absolutely. Do you want to see?"

The struggle of a scientist wanting to gain knowledge and the wariness of a human war on his face before he shakes his head. "Nope. I think I'll wait on the results before I venture forth."

"You can't tell me anything today?" I pout, feeling antsy about the whole thing.

"No way, sistah. I have to send this stuff to a colleague of mine that can do an expert analysis. She might even confirm the theory I've got buzzing 'round in here."

"Dizzzzzzzzzz," I whine. "You can't say you know something and not tell me."

"I sure as hell can. Hey, how fresh is your sample?"

"I've had them for a minute. Why?"

"I'm going to get a nurse. I want a new one," he replies, turning to hit the intercom.

"No, wait." I grab his arm and spin him around. "You don't need a nurse. Do you have a sample cup? Like a fresh one?"

He nods, picking one up that looks suspiciously like something people normally pee in, and I give him a dirty look. Undoing the lid, I position it under my arm before pausing. "Don't freak out, alright?"

Arching a brow, he scoots back instinctively. I flick a claw out, slicing my arm over the cup. Squeezing it enough that it flows in, I give Diz a lopsided smile. When I let go, the cut tingles, the edges burn, and it makes a distinct popping sound. There's not a trace of trauma left on my skin when I hold up my arm.

"There." I shrug nonchalantly as Diz goes through the Shemp routine that most people adopt when seeing me do that for the first time. "Oh, quit with the Three Stooges act."

"But you!"

"Yes."

"Well, it explains some things," he muses, scratching his chin thoughtfully.

"Like what?"

"Patience, sistah. Give me a couple of weeks and we'll see what turns up. Should I call you when I find out?"

"Fuck, yes. You can also email or text. Will it really take that long?"

He rolls his eyes, giving me an exasperated look. "These things take time, woman. Chill."

"Alright," I sigh. "Do you have everything you need?"

"Absolutely."

"Then I'm out of here, dude. I have to get back before people start looking for me." I blow a kiss at him and spin on my heel. Pushing my way through the doors, I head towards the parking lot. How in the hell am I going to survive the next couple of weeks?

Damned clichés. Curiosity may kill the kitty after all.

The Socialite Commands The Troops

PHILOMENA

"Look, you bleached nimrods, we should drag him out by the braid and make him socialize. For the love of Versace, he's going to forget *how*."

I give everyone an irritated look, searching in my clutch for the bottle with the blue pills. Tiny purse, itty-bitty pills storage space and there are so many to store.

Sigh.

"Come on, Coco, you can't force the man to be happy when he's upset. The cat says he's adjusting. It's worse for him because the hot rod wasn't the problem, only the teeny spark. He's lost the one that seemed the sanest. That has to hurt." Hex picks the chipped polish on his nails, and strolls back to the bathroom that he's still finishing.

"He can't paint and draw all day, every day, until the cat is home. She's home less now than ever and he'll get weird."

I mean that. It's not normal to hide in a cave and not process things.

At least, my programming says that. I care about my people, droid or not. They may be fashion challenged and socially inept, but my family is important. With our Queen distracted by the designer assassin, the Duchess has to keep the ranks in order.

"How about we take him to the beach? He likes the sound of the waves."

Everyone's eyes swivel to Victor. He doesn't weigh in about the long-haired lothario since their falling out over the blogger, but we know that he cares. "That sounds like an idea. We can't go to a public one without the right attire, though. It's not like being in our backyard, hooligans."

Leo rolls his eyes. "You mean everyone has to wear suits, yeah? We have suits."

I arch a brow. "I *know* that, you idiot. Getting you to avail yourself of them is another story. We'll need food and booze, too. Are you in charge of the comestibles?"

He nods and Hex yells from the other room. "I have the bloody towels and blankets in here. I'll start packing up now!"

"We've got a plan, then. Are we taking along extra baggage or just ourselves?"

Siren smirks. "Are you asking if we are allowing guests to attend the outing? Perhaps your special friends or Hex's erratic lover?"

Rolling my eyes, I sigh. "Honey, at least sound like you're human. You *have* to learn contractions. Why the hell did they program you to be so infuriatingly proper?"

Victor shrugs. "Sonny boy and I had ideas about that. They haven't come to fruition yet, but I see it moving in the right direction. She's a lady, which is something you'd know nothing about."

"I would argue, but given the state of your own behavior, I find it redundant. I'd prefer not to spill my drink when I throttle you, dear old Pop." My lips curl, purposefully reminding him that within this very house, most of us are his creations.

That fact means that he created his own demons.

"Christ, it's downright chilly here when the cat's away."

We all look up the stairs, surprised to see the clone in question standing at the top, looking very much like he's bathed today. That seems simple enough, but given where he's been emotionally the past weeks, it's a step.

"We're jousting, lazy pants. We all enjoy a good verbal spar. You used to, too. Get your trunks. We're all going to the beach."

Rafe looks as if he's going to protest, but with seven sets of eyes on him, he reconsiders. "Okay, but I'm bringing a sketch pad."

Hex pops out of the bathroom with his packed up load and shakes his head. "No chance, you git. We're running and baking and having a good time. Build a bloody sand dragon again. No moping around with a sketch pad."

"Fine," he sighs.

I smile. *Perhaps I am doing a suitable job filling in the kitty's paws.*

The Bird Breaks A Wing And The Cat Gets Burned

TAURUS

"Sodding swamp. Bloody rookie." I storm into the room, cursing and muttering promises of pain and retribution that I'm happy to carry out. "Bayou. Idiot."

The smell of swamp is clinging to me like perfume in a French whorehouse, and it's all I can do not to roar my fury into the air. My bloody shirt is wrapped around my hand in tatters and it waves like a flag as I punch the wall panel with my non-injured fist. The wall gives way to the shiny, high tech bathroom full of every amenity we could ever need. I'm not a man that foregoes luxury, even in a space like this one. I don't even look around as I head inside, letting the door slide close behind me. Starting up the shower, I continue my tirade, my anger having reached the boiling point in my head.

The kitty's here because I can feel her puzzlement from the other room. Our bond floods with concern as she waits. I probably startled her, but I wasn't worried about that when I came in, only getting this disgusting smell and grime off my body. The clothes are a write-off, no denying that.

Have I mentioned how cool it is that I can feel her?

Yeah, that's a new one for me. Hell, it's all a new one with her. I can close my eyes and feel the calm radiating from her. She's sitting on that monstrosity of a bed—in size, mind, not form—waiting for me to re-emerge and explain myself. Growling again, I re-cap the evening from hell and shake my head. I don't want to take it out on her.

When I finally feel like I'm clean, I step out and turn off the shower. Before I walk out, I root in the cabinets until I find a bandage to cover the ugliness that's my right hand. *That* situation is the root cause of all my ire. I wrap a towel around my waist and open the panel, steam pouring into the room. I'm still drying my hair when I look over to see what she's doing and just about hit the floor.

I mean, Christ, how's a man supposed to stay enraged when I'm faced with a picture like that?

She's lying against the black and blood colored pillows on a bed full of fluffs and frills that delight me. I love them because they speak to that soft center that she wants to pretend no one sees. Her long fiery locks are spilling all over her shoulders, contrasting with her porcelain skin like a handmade doll. She's the complete opposite of my tanned, hazel eyed, blonde maned goddess. It's like they were made to be the sun and moon.

Did I mention that despite all the natural beauty that she seems to have no earthly idea she exudes, she's wearing a long, lacy black wisp of something that looks like they made it to short circuit my brain?

No? She is.

"Bloody buggering hell." That's all I got—a whisper or a prayer to the evil below. She looks like Satan's mistress in that get up on that bed, and it ties my tongue in knots.

She frowns at me, seeing the bandage before anything else. I could have predicted that and won a pile of cash if I'd been so inclined. Scooting to the edge of the bed, she sits back on her haunches and holds her hand out. "What happened, baby?"

Son of a bitch, it kills me.

She likes that I appreciate the simple things, and her calling me all manner of endearments is easily one of them. I know she's waiting for me to answer, but my eyes are following curves and soft skin and silk. I finally drag my eyes away and manage to unswallow my tongue. "You want the Big Bad version or the truth?"

She shrugs, hair falling in waves all over again. "Whichever you prefer. Although, I suspect I'll end up getting both."

Boy, isn't she the smart cookie? She knows that she has me wrapped like a gift in December.

"First, can I say thank you?" I gesture at the negligee, the hair, the bed—the entire vision of temptation—that took a shit day and made it fade into oblivion within seconds.

Her grin is impish. "I had it lying around."

"Good thing, that. As to the hand, I was so brassed off at what happened and in such a bloody hurry to get back to you that I wasn't paying attention. I slammed it in the sodding car door when I was returning Talia's car."

Humility isn't my strong suit on any day, so take note that I admitted my own complete idiocy to this woman without a single bit of reservation. She does that to me: strips me bare and leaves the best parts of me on display.

"What happened? Why did you have a car?"

I shake my head, coming over to our bed. "No. Not until you let me touch you and hold you. Not until I tell you I love you and missed you like the damned today."

She smiles like I've made her day. "What are you waiting for?"

Grinning because I can't help it, I reach out and grab her as I settle on the bed, favoring my bad hand. I twist my fingers in her hair, liking the soft silk brushing my skin. My golden goddess has shoulder length hair, but it's nothing like my minx's mane. She's miles of curls and waves, like she's all curves and Botticelli to Talia's lithe, svelte frame. As I said, two different paradigms. I hold her tightly, then look into her eyes. "I'm crazy with love for you. Missing you hurt more than a gaping chest wound."

She sighs as I kiss her deeply, making me smile against her lips. The glimpses of her softness melt me. She runs her hands over my tense, knotted muscles, relaxing me without even trying. After the slow, passionate kiss comes to its inevitable yet delicious end, I rest my forehead against hers. "You're good for the soul, Sandwich."

"I missed you today, too."

I take a deep breath—relieved to hear her say it—and release it along with the last wisps of tension. Picking her up, I lift her to pull back the comforter and lay her down gently. Climbing in with her, I lean back against the pillows and tuck her under my arm. "Good."

Not exactly poetry, but give me a break. It's been a rough sodding day.

She curls around me, rubbing her cheek on my chest and resting her palm on my bad hand. "You smell good."

"When I got in here, I stank like a swamp marsh. I ruined a perfectly suitable outfit and the duster is a write off. Now I've got to get another one. You—my lovely, gorgeous, stunningly beautiful woman—smell like a heaven that I'll never see."

Her eyes dance and curls bounce as she shakes her head. "Oh, yes, because I'm headed straight for the pearly gates myself." She holds her wrist out. "I made new body wash today because the night jasmine bloomed for the first time this season. It's my favorite."

I bury my nose in her collarbone and inhale, knowing that I'll never smell jasmine again in my long life and not think of this moment. Hell, that sounded poetic. Maybe I am feeling better just being around her. It wouldn't surprise me a bit. "Ain't nature grand? Do you think they'll set us up in the same hellish cell for eternity? I don't hate the thought of that." I grin playfully, sniffing along her shoulder.

"My punishment for all eternity might be to get stuck in a

room with you being an ass for the rest of time? That sucks." She turns and whispers under her breath. "If we keep saying that, they might think it would be a bad thing."

I nod, pretending to understand. "Right. That's the worst thing I could think of, really. Might make me want to do good deeds so I never get sent there. I'd rather take a job wiping Hitler's ass." I look around then murmur into her mind. *~Think this'll work? ~*

~ Worth a try, ain't it? ~

Her struggle to keep from giggling tickles me and I snort once, coughing back a laugh. "Vapid wench!"

"Knuckle dragging beast!"

I tickle up her sides, eyebrows wagging and grinning like a loon. "Harpy."

"Bastard!"

"Shrew."

She purrs a bit as I rub my thumb over her feather. "Test-tube Baby."

I laugh out loud at that, unable to bite it back. Dropping my lips to hers again, I kiss her softly. "Mmm. Sissssssssy.".

Growling, she gives me a good thump and I laugh again when she calls me an ass. I'm thoroughly enjoying myself. Every day I thank hell that Talia made me take that call for a meet on a lonely street with a woman I thought I'd despise. I move too quickly and bang my bad hand trying to pinch her and hiss. Grinning ruefully, I lean over and whisper softly into her ear, warm breath teasing her earlobe. "Yeah, baby, but I'm your ass."

"Yes, you are. Now give me that hand so you're not wincing all night long." She reaches over and tugs my wrist towards her, looking determined.

"Ow! Bugger, woman. Easy."

"I am being easy, you big baby." She starts unwrapping the bandage, giving me a peeved look.

I mutter under my breath about know-it-all women and cranky

kitties—mostly to rile her up. She's studying my hand carefully, and I wonder if I hurt myself worse than I realized. I peer around her cascade of hair. "Can you fix it?"

"I can heal organs; I think I can fix this. But I have to get up first."

I frown, hugging her close. "Too bad; it'll have to stay ouchie."

"It'll only take a second, I promise."

She gives me a look and I huff, letting her go reluctantly. "Be quick about it."

Watching her as she trots to one of the cabinets in the wall, she pulls out a small container. Her back is to me as she fiddles with the contents, stirring up a flowery, herbal smelling concoction. When did she bring that stuff here? I suppose she's been slowly filling some edges of our space with her own stuff, even as I have mine.

"This will work faster and feel really soothing, plus it cuts the bruising." She crosses the room and hops in bed, pulling my hand back onto her tummy.

"It won't hurt?" I ask, looking dubiously at the gross looking goop in the ceramic bowl.

"Nope. I promise." She dips her fingers in and slathers it over my skin, rubbing it in and murmuring under her breath. She blows air across the poultice before holding her hand up to me. "Nip me quick?"

I blink in surprise, but bring my fangs forward to bite. I quickly retract them to let her blood flow. Suckling lightly, I pull back and close the wound with my tongue. "Enough?"

"Greedy boy. I need it to drip a little before you close it."

"Oh! Sorry." I bite again in the same spot, and with considerable control, I withdraw.

"Watch closely because this is kind of neat-o." She wiggles the dripping finger at me, then over the slathered hand. Squeezing her fingertip, she lets one fat drop of blood plop down. The minute it hits the cream, the air shimmers, and liquid seeps into the skin. With a pop, the hand that was bruised and wounded one moment is perfectly healed and unmarred. The smell of flowers pervades the air, and she licks her finger, closing the wound as she grins. "See?"

My eyebrows raise to my hairline in surprise. "Bloody hell." I lift my now-healed hand slowly and look it over, flexing and unflexing my fingers. "Okay, that was—yeah, neat sums it up nicely. Nice job, Sandwich. I owe you another thanks."

"That one was kind of cheating, what with the special mix and all. It's easier than some alternatives. Besides, what kind of mate would I be if I left you wounded and achy?"

"A sexually unfulfilled one?"

"Somehow, I doubt that."

"Are you saying that I toast your crackers, baby?" I leer at her, but she doesn't know that when I ask like this, it's because I'm worried that I'll never live up to all the weird shit she's been up to for years. Hell, I've been with Talia most of my life. She's been with more people at once than I've been with in total.

"I'm nothing if not astute."

"Astute is good. All hail astute," I mutter, nipping her shoulder.

"Uh-oh. Reverting to cave talk—you must be having a manly 'Thag the caveclone' moment."

I roll my eyes, grinning as I pound my chest. "Me, Taurus. You, hot little hussy I love."

"You are so silly," she chides, her eyes soft.

"One of the many reasons you are ass over brains for me, baby." Talia would laugh me out of the house if I played like this with her.

My minx is an enigma wrapped in a riddle with all her complexity and simplicity at the same time.

The Bird Makes A Mistake

❦

TAURUS

She blinks. "Oh! Did I mention? The rest of my family went out on a beach trip to cheer up Rafe and I was there alone picking up stuff. Rhea tried to pop by my place right after I arrived. I didn't answer the door, but she left a note. I didn't read it because it's probably full of bullshit."

"That wouldn't surprise me." I shake my head, wondering how the chit who had simply been a little insecure—but basically a good person—became so twisted in the year we were away. Talia remained friends with her on the other side of the Rift, but Brenda's a different person than the woman living here. Rhea's been a sodding wrecking ball to everyone around her for the past month.

Maybe longer, as I think there are things the kitty is holding back.

I'd understand if she was. She's been burned to a crisp by people she loves. But I feel—especially since the mating—that she's got deep darks we've not shared yet. I figure that it's up to her when we share something that's aching her that badly. I don't want to push her away.

"I've got a mind to poke at Blondie now—get her all worked

up, then tell her I've got to see a woman about a tail." I grin evilly and bob my brows, but I'm only half kidding. I'm ready to throw our happiness in her face if only for the pain she's caused my mate.

"She's probably too busy pretending nothing is wrong or trying to sleep with Constantine. He's the last one she's not completely alienated."

"Talia did promise I'd stop by and see Rhea next time I had a chance. It would be positively rude of me to snub her now, wouldn't it?"

I'm going on record now saying that this might not be my brightest idea. I'm just so bloody angry at the change in a woman I once considered family that I'm feeling vengeful.

It might be clouding my judgment; sue me.

"You're bad."

I can't tell if she's forcing her chuckle, but she doesn't say no. I shrug, looking unrepentant. "I'm so bloody good at it."

"I guess it would be gauche to tell you that Sari said she'd buy you mouthwash, floss, and shower stuff if you'd eat Rhea and get it over with." She snickers and I laugh, shaking my head. "Oh, I almost forgot—'manly scented body wash'."

Laughing harder, I shake my head. "Bloody hell, I might start liking that little gnome."

"Occasionally, when the insane level is low, she's not so bad to be around."

That's probably the closest thing to truth she's willing to admit about the little snot. Sari's been the bane of both mine and Talia's existence since we met her, and her foppish mate isn't any better. I've always believed that a deep, dark ugliness is hiding under her 'let's all be family' credo. I haven't been able to suss out if I'm right because her people never leave. Inspires loyalty to a fault, that one. I'd be willing to bet it's through a painful 'take and take' relationship that her 'family' doesn't realize they're part of.

My minx is mated to her, though, and I promised to be civil. "The runt has a decent sense of humor. She was also quite the host when I dropped by to thank her for the cookies she sent Talia. I'll have to pick her up a little something when I head to Milan tomorrow."

The kitty gives me a small smile, but there's something behind it that I can't put my finger on. Fear? Worry? Her eyes don't agree with her words. Time for a subject change. "So... Should the kitty's hot stuff lover play with the teeny fire? What do you think, mate?"

"Baby, you can do whatever you'd like."

That wasn't a 'no', but it wasn't a 'yes', either. "I can, but I'd like to hear what you think. I plan on shagging you until you howl in a few and I don't want to ruin the mood."

"Awful full of ourselves, aren't we?" she teases.

I look at her, lowering the wall behind my eyes so she can see my desire to please her. Just as quickly, I hide it again behind the smug arrogance that I give everyone else. "Not as full of you as I'm going to be."

"If you want to go poke at her, go ahead."

Again, her words and eyes don't match, but I can't seem to get off making Blondie miserable. My thirst for revenge is a character flaw, I know. Punishment for her sins outstrips every other thought in my head when I'm like this.

I kiss her and roll out of bed. Crossing to the hidden closet, I slide the panel open to reveal a vast array of styles and clothes. It hits me and I close the closet, walking over to pick up the towel I had on earlier. "Let's hit her with the big guns." I look over my shoulder, eyes gleaming, and tap my head. "I'll keep in touch."

The last thing that I see as I go out is my minx pulling out her notebook to work on her ritual, a furrow creasing her brow. That should worry me, but I can't focus on it now. I apparate directly to Rhea's home in the Cabal Quarter. I haven't been there in a long time and I'm hoping that she hasn't added a dungeon given what the kitty's told me.

Ringing the bell, I whisper into my mate's mind. *~I so enjoy torturing the meek and witless. ~*

The minx sends the feel of a smile as she murmurs. ~ *I know, baby.* ~

Once I get inside, I sigh internally. The moment she sees that I'm in a towel, it begins. Her overt, clumsy attempts at flirting make me want to get back to my mate, but I let her draw me onto her couch. She scoots as close as possible without climbing onto my lap and I run rings around her verbally.

~She's willing to see me naked. She's even sharing her comforter to keep me warm. ~ I touch the minx mentally, trying to give her the sensation of a kiss. *~Baiting her is so easy that it's almost no fun. ~*

~I heard she was all over Constantine last night. She's aiming for him because Wilde and Rafe aren't speaking to her. It makes me want to heave. ~ The bite in her tone is obvious, but I don't let it stop me.

~To be fair, she didn't come looking for me, baby. ~ I remind her. I know that it won't change things, but making Rhea show her true colors was part of my twisted revenge plot. Our connection feels colder and I wonder if she's trying to compose herself.

~Sorry. I reconstructed a timeline of her crazy recently, and it was rather revealing. I'll try not to be so bitchy. ~

My hackles rise a little because I haven't known the kitty to back away from a fair fight. She's been righteously—and deservedly—angry at Blondie and my brother. Now it sounds like she's blaming herself. Maybe if I distract her?

~I dreamed about you last night, love. ~ I send her a properly debauched image that I know will make her squirm in delight. A little bonus for me is that I can feel her responses now, too.

Did I mention what a bloody amazing multi-tasker I am? I'm also busy giving the perfidious blonde one a 'poor me' story about being anachronistic in this new world. I tell her that it used to be that seeing me get naked would send chits into a frenzy so I must be old. She immediately coos and corrects me, batting her lashes like a fool.

Christ, she's such easy bait that I can hardly pay attention to the fact that my minx is playing her own little torture game in my head and it's having a stirring effect on me.

~You know, it's always so itchy right after a shave. ~

I blink, almost losing the thread of my conversation with Blondie when I get her meaning. *~ You did what? You'd better be sodding ready when I get home! ~*

Her chuckle is husky as she sends me the image of her slipping off her nightie, and lolling on the bed with her hair spread out like a fan. I'm missing something bloody brilliant to be here messing with a treacherous bint. Am I sure I want to be here doing this rather than there? I let that war inside me, not paying attention to the phony fawning. Blondie's still reassuring me that I'm not old and useless. Like I need HER to tell me that.

~When you get done, I'll be waiting here—all smooth and soft and smelling like flowers. ~

~Evil woman. I'll get this done fast. ~

I growl a bit, rolling my eyes inwardly as it makes the bint I'm baiting pretend to cower. When my minx does that, it's adorable and endearing even though I know she's not scared of me. When Rhea does it, it seems sickeningly contrived. I barely catch it when she says something vague about others chasing me. I'm not sure what she's hinting at, so I ask my mate. *~Are you SURE Blondie doesn't know about us? ~*

~If she does, I don't know where she found out. I haven't spoken to her in over a week, and neither has Rafe. ~

~Does ANYONE know I'm in love with you, baby? ~ My brows furrow and I try to focus on whatever drivel Rhea is spouting. She just keeps giggling and coquetting every couple of minutes like a teenager and I'm going to get a sodding cavity soon.

~Sari figured it out. I didn't want to share it with her, but she's acted okay since. ~

*~The gnome knows that I love you. She doesn't know you love me, either, does she? ~*I can feel her unease at that statement, and I file it

away for later. I should question what she's worried about that she won't say.

~Yep, and Wilde, too. ~

She changes the subject quite nicely by sending me another vision of her naked and I groan internally. *~Minx, you're going to have to stop that. I can't split my focus with the bint because I'm afraid…~*

~Oh! Sorry! ~

I feel her worry. There is something here I should talk to her about later. A sigh of relief escapes my lips as she sends me a horrifying image that turns off my arousal faucet like ice cubes in my lap. *~Thank Hell. Now I can keep from letting something terrible happen.~*

Turning back to Blondie, I listen to her still trying to convince me that I'm not old and out of touch. She's right about the first and wrong about the second. The Minx sure as hell doesn't molly-coddle me like Rhea's trying to do. My mate lifts me up and shows me that I belong with her, regardless of what anyone else thinks. *~ Blondie's about to find out I'm in love with you. You know, unless she keeps trying to shag me. ~*

~Oh, she'll keep trying. ~ The kitty's voice is full of disgust.

I don't tell her that her former mate just climbed up on my lap and is wriggling around. Not because I think she would be angry at me, but because I think it would hurt her to see the show being put on for my benefit. More to the point, Rhea not getting enough emotional validation from her friends has made her desperate. She'll get it from anyone she can get her hands on, even evil, non-cuddling me. I don't know that my minx needs to see how low her friend is sinking.

~I love you, ~ I whisper in her head.

~I love you, too. ~

~Stop imagining ripping her spine out. It's making me antsy. ~ I joke lightly, hoping to take the edge out of her tone. I realize now

that I have to figure out how to untangle myself from this idiotic endeavor.

~ I'm not imagining that. ~

Her statement is clipped and hard, more so than I've heard from her before. It feels like I got mentally slapped in the kisser. *~Then you might want to make sure your inner bitchy is under control. ~*

~If you must know, I was finger painting a mural with the blood gushing from her jugular. ~

My eyes pop open. I have to stifle the laugh that is threatening to escape in front of Blondie. THERE'S the Minx I love.

~It seemed more artsy and creative. ~

The cat sends me a delicate sniff and I can feel my heart grow like that Seuss git in the cartoons. I can't help it, I'm a sucker for a badass woman with a soft side. You wouldn't know it from the way Talia and I fight like demons, but that woman has me licked. She's probably feeling all of this and laughing herself around the house like a maniac.

~Blondie just told me that no one knows her like I do and no one's ever made her scream like I did. ~ The tension across our connection becomes thick and the minx goes eerily quiet. This game might be over. I don't want it to hurt her, even if it is making me feel better about the betrayal of my ex-family member.

~Did she now? She mentioned how badly she missed Rafe in graphic detail in that stupid bloody letter. Yes, yes; I read the damned thing. I couldn't stop myself! ~ Her voice is frigid and tight, something I've not heard before.

~Shh, baby. She's lying. She hasn't looked me up in a year, so it's not about me. It's about needing a fix. ~

~It doesn't matter. It's always about her. Period. ~ My mate snarls, a vein of hatred skating through our bond.

~Baby, are you okay? I think I should get out of here. I'm uncovering nasties that are better left buried. ~

~I'm fine. ~

Those words are the two biggest lies in the female universe. They never mean that, and what they do mean is nothing good. ~ *I'll stop giving you a blow by blow. ~*

~I'm going to take a shower. I feel dirty. ~

I feel her move off the bed and head into the bathroom. Hurt radiates off her in waves that drown me, even from here. I rarely feel emotions through the bond this strongly unless it's the golden goddess. That's only because she's an empath. I don't know why the minx has such a strong connection or how she's emoting so fiercely through our bond.

What I do know is that I'm done here. I fob off Blondie like I'm on fire and apparate back to our place, worry clawing at my gut. Chucking the towel for a robe, I note that the bathroom panel is shut, and the water sounds like it's on full blast. I'm not sure what to do as I stare at it.

This is all my bloody fault. I pushed her to let me go after the bint, after feeling her unease and didn't stop when she felt off. I'm not the one hurting her, but I sure as hell set her up to get hurt. Steam slips out from under the door and I wonder how hot she's got it in there. Reaching out to her mind, I murmur ~ *Baby, can I come in? ~*

She doesn't respond and I start to freak out. I can't even FEEL her now. My minx has been a presence in my heart since we mated, and now, there's nothing. How in the HELL is she doing that? I knock on the door, trying not to panic. *~Love? Sandwich? Answer me, baby, please? ~*

~ Yes, love? ~

My eyes narrow on the door. Oh, hell no. She isn't getting away with whatever that was. My sensitive, strong, passionate woman doesn't shut down unless she gets really hurt or pissed. Either way, I'm getting to the bottom of it, sod it all.

I knock harder, raising my voice. "Deli, love, either open up or I'm coming in. Come on, you're scaring me. I can't feel you in my head." She doesn't respond again, and I pound on the panel.

"You've got to the count of five, mate, or I'll come in, door be damned."

The count reaches three when she murmurs, *~Come in. ~*

The locks undo without so much as a touch from her and I blink. She wasn't kidding about magick. I humored her when she was talking about a ritual. She said that she didn't talk about the real aspects of her power with others for fear of being the 'in' thing, but I figured that was a cover. This community she loves is chock full of hangers on and sycophants and crazies who suck the life out of her like a damned vampire. She never minded it before. I assumed that was because she was conning herself, like a fake psychic. That, however, is a topic for another time.

I push through the door and move to the shower. "Baby?"

My mate looks over the tops of her kneecaps, bloodshot eyes peering at me as she huddles in the corner. Her skin is bright red from the heat and her voice is hoarse. "Yes?"

It makes my sodding heart shatter to see her. "Oh, love. What are you doing to yourself?" I reach out and turn off the water, shucking my bathrobe as I bend to drape it around her. "You can curse me for the knuckle dragging later—or stake me for all I care, but you're bloody well coming out of there."

She doesn't fight me, so I pick her up, bundled in my robe as I head out to the bed. Sitting her down gently, I dry her off and hold one of her hands as I look into her eyes. "Talk to me, baby. Please?"

Her words are muffled in the robe as her shoulders shrug . "I always take hot showers." She looks up and I feel the struggle inside of her. She's trying not to let everything out, but tears well up and she loses control. "What should I talk about?"

I look at her as if she's started speaking Japanese. "How about what made you hightail it in there? Maybe about what made you take a shower so hot it almost cooked you as soup? I know! How about what made you shut me out completely? Yeah, those are the whats you should talk about."

She waves at the door like it's nothing, fighting her pain. "The shower was fine."

Scoffing, I give her a look that says I'm not buying that bridge. "Try again."

Huffing, her eyes fixate on her cute little toes for a moment before she gives in. Her response is hissed, venom lacing her tone. "Rhea just ripped my goddamn heart out and threw it into the dumpster. She never, never cared about me or Rafe. It was all about her from start to finish—what we could do for her ego. She started with us because she was mad at Sari. When I get upset about being used, she jumps to the next thing without a bloody thought. It's only about what makes her feel good—like we're whores. I locked myself in the shower before I did something destructive. I can move from rage to hurt if I focus on other things. It wasn't about you, baby. I only shut you out because I didn't have the energy to leave any holes open. It would have all busted out."

Gesturing around her as if I should see something tangible, she gives me a pleading look. "Can you feel this?" I look around, trying to figure out what she's talking about. "I do. It's like a force field in the air. I needed to keep it in long enough to calm down. This happens all the time—whether I'm upset, happy or angry— any emotion. This gigantic ball of energy surrounds me. It can amaze you or, um, it can be awful. I think it's because I don't let my magick out like it wants to be. It's gotten stronger in the Rift, and I don't use it enough. I try to burn it off, but that doesn't get it done anymore."

I look at her seriously. "Blast me."

"NO! I don't want to blast you. There's no blast left."

"You don't have to hold it in, afraid you're going to blow. Not with me, baby—never with me. I won't incinerate, this place can get fixed, and there's nothing you can do that would destroy it. Let it all out, but don't you ever terrify me like that again."

Her face crumples and I feel her panic. "I'm sorry. I'm so, so sorry." Her shoulders shake and she puts a fist against her mouth, holding in sobs.

I wrap my arms around her, holding her close. "Shh, baby, it's okay. It's okay, love. Everything's going to be alright."

Arms tighten around me, holding on as if I'm the only thing grounding her, and she shakes her head. "It's not okay. She hurt me, she made me shut you out, and worst of all, she made me act insane."

"Baby, everything's going to be fine, I promise. I know she hurt you. It's okay to feel hurt, but you're not acting insane. You're acting like a person who was hurt badly by someone she cared for." I rock her, hoping her broken parts can be soothed. Maybe now she can finally let go of my brother and his mate because whatever they had is never coming back. This kind of pain is 'goodbye' pain. "Shh, baby. I love you. Everything's going to be alright. It's okay. Everything's going to be fine."

"I tried so hard not to be angsty and insane about this." She sounds upset with herself, like she's scolding herself for not being able to control her emotions. Curling around me, she makes herself as small as possible in my arms.

Anger wells up inside me at that. I don't understand why she thought she had to do this alone. "Then shame on you, baby, for thinking you needed to keep all this inside you. What am I, eye candy? Unless I missed a repudiation ceremony, I'm your mate, sod it all. When you hurt, I hurt for you. I can't make it all go away, but I can listen and be here for you. Let me do that, please."

"Hearing what just happened hit me like a baseball bat. I'm very, very hurt and raw. I needed space and a chance to assimilate in my head. I have to come to grips with the fact that she's been using us all along. That's hard to swallow."

"It is."

"It breaks my heart. Normally people don't get in as easily as you. It took her months to get trust, but it was all a lie. Ten to one, she'd lie to my face about what she did tonight if I asked her tomorrow."

My eyes narrow and I snarl. "Let her."

"I don't want to see her face again to ask."

"I started it by going there in a towel, baby. But I didn't know it would hurt you like this."

"She wants a fix; it doesn't matter who it is." She leans up and kisses my jaw lightly. "I'm sorry I worried you."

I finally feel like I can breathe and the ball of terror around my heart melts. "Understatement, thy name is Kitty."

"I'm sorry," she murmurs, stroking her hand over my heart.

I sigh at her touch, but I don't want her to make me happy. I want her to be okay. "Baby, stop. You don't have to soothe any feathers you think you've ruffled on me. This is about you and your feelings." I tilt her chin up and look in her eyes. "Can I say a few things?"

She nods, chewing on her lip.

I brush her hair out of her face and look at her seriously. "I have to tell you that you're deeply emotional. You're sometimes angsty, sometimes insane...but always blindingly bright. You're deeply sensual, genuinely caring and I know all of this. I still love you more than—well, everyone. I love you for all of it because it makes you what you are. Don't be afraid of being angry, angsty, crazy or anything else; you won't shock me. I. Love. You."

Her expression clouds. I can't tell what's going on behind those sapphire blues for a moment, so I continue. "Blondie used and lied to all of us. It wasn't your fault, nor was it anything you did. It's her way; it's who she's become. My golden goddess has known her for a lot of years and never saw this. Blondie's changed—she's not who I met when my goddess brought my brother home for her."

"It's worse for me because I saw who she was from the beginning. I stopped listening to my gut because everyone said she was wonderful. It makes me want to smack myself. I said she was a manipulator back when she smeared herself all over Dirty Deeds... I knew she used Sari and Wilde to make her feel good about herself. I let her in because Sari convinced me she was okay. I should have listened to my gut."

"I wasn't around much then, neither was the golden goddess. That Dirty Deeds place was a toxic waste dump. Shame it exploded out of nowhere." I don't mention that I know the git who made it happen. He's a colleague at the Company whose special skill is explosives and though he's not my cuppa, the minx would LOVE him. Therefore, I'm never bringing his Lucky Charms arse anywhere near her.

"It was fun for a while, but it became harmful and ugly. Too many people fighting over attention from the 'in' crowd." She looks up at me. "I digressed again."

"Wasn't that on the list of things I loved about you? I thought for sure I put it on there." I grin a bit, kissing her temple.

"What remains to decide is what I should do about her."

"I'm of the opinion that I should eat her; sod the goddess' rules."

"She'd enjoy you biting her too much. Trust me."

"What do you want to do, baby? It's your decision and I'll support you completely."

She shakes her drying curls, sighing. "Rhea will be destroyed when she finds out about us. It's the ideal she pined for that was always out of reach. She pushed Rafe and Wilde away, and she doesn't really want Constantine. All of it together will knock her flat. I don't want to bring our connection into the bitter stuff with her. She doesn't get to be a part of it."

I look at her closely, seeing the violet smudges under her eyes as I tilt my head. "You need to sleep, love. You're exhausted—mentally and emotionally. You shouldn't decide in this state."

"I think you're right."

"Do you want me to take you home or do you want to stay here?"

She snuggles further into the blankets. "I'm going to stay here. I'm too tired to do anything else."

"Do you want me to stay with you, baby?" I stroke my hand over her hair, still kicking myself for starting this mess.

"You don't have to."

"I said, 'do you want me to stay with you, baby'. Not one single 'have to' in that sentence."

"I was letting you know that if you didn't want to, I'd be okay."

Her eyes raise to mine and I realize that statement is only for me. She doesn't mean a word of it; she's simply been trained to put her needs second to whoever she's dealing with. What in hell's name has my brother and that gnome's family done to her?

"I want to stay, but I won't if you'd rather be alone."

"I'd always rather you be here," she murmurs, yawning broadly.

I can tell she's about to fall asleep. "Good, because I'm fairly sure it'd take a crowbar to get me away from you tonight." I kiss her closed eyelids, feeling her drift. "One favor before you go to sleep, baby."

"Mmm?"

"If you could love me for a good long while, that'd be nice."

"Your wish is my command, love—always."

With that, she drops off to sleep, and I sigh. She's loyal to a fault, my minx, so she means it. I can tell by how hard it's been for her to let go of my brother that when she loves someone, she'll hang in there until there's nothing left to hang on to. I can only hope that I come to deserve her devotion.

The Cat Gets Heated

DELILAH

I can feel it burning inside of me all the time now.

In theory, it's a cosmic irony that with great powers come great drawbacks. The inability to control her seemed like enough balance for the universe, but I was wrong. The more I let her out, the worse this feeling gets. The drive, the need, the hunger — it can't be fueled only by needing energy to support the various powers within me.

Laugh it up. It's a big, old joke on Deli.

That reaction is why I haven't told anyone about my suspicions. As if I don't have enough on my plate, there's a fierce, unrelenting hunger to mate. Satisfying it is the only way to get the fire inside of me to subside, so that I'm capable of rational thought.

Until I find that release, there's a gnawing at my bones that thrums in my veins in a heavy staccato rhythm: hunger. I need, she needs, *we need*. It's only want, take, have.

All the time. Everywhere.

The smells—with my enhanced sniffer, they make me crazy. Everything smells delicious or disgusting in equal turns.

It's like demonic possession.

The urge to mate in the most primal sense swamps my brain when it rolls through me. Given her proclivities, the ceremonial one has become necessary as well. The need to tear in and drink deep—to mark as mine—feeds off the need to screw until my brains spill out my ears. I can barely control her to start with. Once this has me, it's like a haze settles over my vision and everything shuts down. I have zero higher-level functions.

All I can see or feel is her hunger for possession.

Afterward, I can barely form words properly. Desire slaked, passion spent, and she's still growling. My eyes dart around the room, ready to spring if danger should arise. I come back to my senses in time, but it's slow—little by little, I trickle into consciousness.

When it happened the first time in January, I freaked out. The complete inability to control myself terrified me. I mean, what if I started jumping random people on the street? It took me a few days to figure out I could get a grip on the waves of lust enough to choose my partner. Sari has talked about losing herself when the coyote takes over, but I chalked that up to her making excuses for the damage she does when she lets loose. I couldn't imagine not being able to get a grip on your faculties.

I can now.

That doesn't mean I believe her. I still think her babble is an excuse. She's never described her coyote having mental autonomy like my beast has, nor has she mentioned having lava in her veins until she fucks the living shit out of someone.

For the first few weeks, I only pounced on those she was interested in. That made for some tricky explanations to folks she didn't fancy. It caused issues that I couldn't fix, like with Mercury. I can't explain why she prefers one person to another. Her reasons typically have to do with something hedonistic. Fortunately, after the Mercury mess, she limited her choices back to people I could drink from.

When the beast first started manifesting, there was rarely a struggle for dominance inside. I thought I had her under control when all the stuff got kinky with Alistair and she chose his demon to be her consort. That didn't last long, though, as my primal side wanted an equal, not a submissive. Not long after that, she stopped getting sex that tooted her horn because the problems with Wilde began.

That's when I decided to seek out Taurus for answers. I had to get rid of this shit so my life could go back to normal. I mean, as normal as polyamorous, clone loving hedonists can be, but we all have our niches.

Taurus taking me to hunt helped. It slaked *some* of my desires and helped replenish energy. That wasn't enough, though, because the fire still burned in my veins. My sex life turned into torture sessions, and I couldn't allow Her to do what needed to be done to quench the hunger.

When she lost Alistair, she started hungering for a taste of what was not hers. It freaked me out for so many reasons. She had not been not interested in people that weren't ours after Mercury. Suddenly, she was demanding someone we *definitely* couldn't have. What she wanted was a can of worms that was not getting opened. My fear of accidentally stepping over the line of no return with Taurus was excruciating.

I'm one lucky feline that Taurus and I mated before she accidentally ruined everything. She wanted him like he was oxygen and She couldn't breathe. His demon called to her; she *needed* him. Now, he's the one thing keeping that lava in my body at bay. I slake the burning fog of desire when we're together as she drinks.

She has what she wants now, but it's still not enough. We're pushing ourselves to the limits every day and something unbelievably bad is going to happen.

I don't even want to contemplate the repercussions of that screw up.

After dropping the samples to Diz, I decided that research might hold the key to confirming my suspicions once and for all.

I'm currently buried under a pile of books that would make a PhD candidate cry. Unfortunately, the ones for my DNA research say nothing about sudden bouts of insane, lusty cat woman rampages. Tapping the pen on my teeth, I close my eyes, sighing deeply.

I don't want to admit it, but the niggling thought at the edge of my consciousness might be right. It's humiliating, and I'm never going to live this down if I'm correct. Standing quickly, I untangle myself from my pile of materials. I scamper over to get my laptop, a sense of dread filling me. Bringing it back to the bed, I hit a search engine. It's not long before I'm gaping at the screen, blinking like a wall-eyed trout.

Son of a bloody bitch.

It's spring and my goddamned beast is in frigging heat. Stifling the self-pitying laughs that are threatening to break free, I close my eyes.

Fuck. Me. Raw.

Literally.

If there ever were a person that did *not* need help being a lusty bitch, it's me. This explains a hell of a lot, including the insane lust fog. It also raises a fuck ton of questions. If the beast is in heat, how long does it last? Weeks? Months? What stops this madness?

I skim down the page, hunting for the answer.

Fuck! Six to eight weeks?! Are they kidding me with this?

Why in the hell am I in heat, anyway? The primary purpose of that is procreation, which isn't possible with clones. Everyone knows they shoot blanks. One of the best things about mates in the Rift is that none of the dudes can knock you up, so every shitty form of birth control is unnecessary.

Blanching, I suck in a breath. Am I stuck like this until I get...? If I can't, am I stuck forever?

Motherfucker.

They might have to lock me in a padded room. This gets worse every day. Each time I indulge, I'm more out of control. Thank the

Goddess clones are so resilient and my healing is so prolific because I tear us both ragged.

Flipping through the related links, I'm fascinated, especially because of the comment Diz made about feline DNA. There's obviously a connection. I'd love to ask him, but I know it hasn't been enough time for him to have anything conclusive to offer me.

I growl in impatience, noting how familiar—and embarrassing—the details are. My nose wrinkles as I consider the possibility that Diz might not help with this aspect of things. I guess I gotta find a vet? Worse comes to worst, I suppose I could let the eggheads at the Company take a gander at me. They've probably been *dying* to get their grubby hands on me.

Ugh, no. I'm no one's lab rat.

Not that I don't trust Taurus to keep them in line, because I do. It's the thought of someone using me as their personal lab experiment gives me an Aldous Huxley style wiggins. But I may not have another choice. I can't go on ripping everyone to shreds forever.

Something has to give.

If only that damned phone would ring.

The Cat Tries To Avoid A Cat-Astrophe

DELILAH

"Oi, love. You know you have to make an appearance. It's Shea's birthday. You have a relationship with him, casual though it may be, and he'll be hurt."

I sigh and look at Rafe pleadingly, but he shakes his head. "The parties here are huge Mardi gras-style festivals that last an entire month. Taurus won't want to go, and I wouldn't ask him to. Plus, I have way too much on my plate: loss of mates, in heat, taking flack over that fucking bar, Beltane, and a secret mating with Taurus. Knowing Tamara, it will be absolutely debauched to prove that she can throw a bacchanal like we do. I don't want to be in public with all of those huge targets on my back."

"It's not Shea's fault that his woman's a fruitcake, love. You know that it's poor form not to pop in, even if it's brief." Hex tilts his head. "The rest of us can go for longer, but you have to show up."

"You're both right." I sigh and pinch the bridge of my nose. Shea will try to get me alone so we can get frisky. He'll expect it for his birthday and it's a way to show off at his party. Sadly, that is very much how many people work nowadays.

With the heat, it will be hard to resist, even though she is not a fan of Shea. He's too weak.

I crack my neck as I muse. "I have to figure out how to get in and out without getting cornered. Hopefully, the folks from Rita's family will keep Tamara's family busy enough to cover for my short and sweet drive by. I also have to find a present that doesn't encourage clinginess. It can't be too impersonal;, but it also can't make him think I'm game to start up again."

"No one knows about Taurus yet except for Sari. She'll try to out you in public, so you have to avoid her. Pretending to do it accidentally will incite panic and help her beef up their position on the karaoke dump." Philomena gives me a cool look, her eyes cutting to Siren.

I bet the book at my house has already run the statistics on that scenario. Hex never misses an occasion to play the numbers. "Luckily, she knows extraordinarily little of the big picture. I told her enough to tantalize her curiosity, but not enough for her to let the dogs loose." I close my eyes, feeling exhausted by all of the shifting three-dimensional chess games with people who are supposed to be my family.

Why do they make everything so damned hard?

"How is the puffed-up fowl, anyway? You said you had to heal an injury?"

I grin. This is a delightful story and I'm so glad she asked. "Yep. He's doing fine now, but he smashed his hand up. It was wounded pride more than anything. He said he was going to Milan to pick up a new duster from this hairy little Italian guy that does his tailoring. Apparently, he gets handsy and I'm super sad that I'm not there to see it."

Rafe blinks, then bursts out laughing. "The picture in my head is priceless. How'd he smash his hand?"

Hopping up on the counter, I prepare to relay the tale that took me an hour to get out of my arrogant mate. I don't think he'd mind me telling my family. Honestly, since Rafe is out of his studio and *talking* to people, it's important for me to keep the good mood going. I watch as Leo and Sandrine commandeer a big armchair and Hex wiggles into a place next to Siren on the couch. Victor joins Caesar on the loveseat and I smile because everyone's getting settled in.

"He got a text from the Company for a job. I guess since he freelances, that's how the reqs come in. Taurus told me that the agents can only call in as 'not interested'—clones don't get sick—or 'over my rotten corpse'. That means the job doesn't fit with your beliefs or whatever."

Rafe leans against the bar, cutting his eyes to Victor, and they share a look—they know a bit about this topic.

Philomena pours herself another martini from her shaker and sighs. "One would think they'd try calling in dead given the lackadaisical clones that live here."

"Not an option, obviously. I guess the team lead got injured on a job the previous day. They didn't have a replacement, so the call went out to freelancers. The message said that it was a stash house hit in the Louisiana bayous. He figured it was no big deal because he does that shit all the time. What they didn't tell him was that he was paired with a rookie for a training exercise—which he hates—and a shitty rookie to boot."

Victor snorts and mutters. "Typical."

"The intel wasn't good. He had to get there by borrowed car because it was listed as a no apparating job. When he got to the drop spot, he found a *canoe*."

The entire room blinks silently for a moment and then the laughter starts, building to a raucous hooting. Victor looks happier than I've seen him in forever as he pictures Taurus scooting around in a canoe. Even Rafe is smiling now.

"So, he rows himself to the place where they're supposed to knock out a little family owned cocaine ring to find this cocky rookie completely ignoring rules of engagement. Taurus is already having trouble with the stupid canoe, so he's covered in muck, and pissy as hell. The idiot rookie goes flying into the building hollering like he's in the fifth infantry charging General Custer."

Philomena looks at me in horror. "His hand tailored, Italian lambskin duster got covered in swamp slime? For the love of Armani, he probably popped a vein in his head."

"I know. I couldn't even breathe at this point in the story because I was laughing so hard. He tells it even better than me. So, it turns out that the intel is even more fucked. It's not a small family drug ring, but Colombian connected. They have an arsenal and a mini-army at their disposal. The rookie—a dimwit named Cob, of all things—about got his ass shot off going in. Taurus had to break the rules to pop in to grab him. His duster got shot twice while he was doing it."

Taking a sip of his bourbon, Rafe gives me an amused look. "Yet none of this explains why you had to heal his hand."

"Well, once he killed the cartel guys, Cob got mad. He dove at Taurus and knocked him on his ass in the swamp. Taurus beat the hell out of him, dropped him off at the Company for re-training, and then got caught to be debriefed. Any of this alone would have been enough to send him over the deep end, but the debriefings are one of his least favorite things. It went on forever and made him late to get back with Talia's car. She bitched him out and he was so pissed about the entire affair, that he slammed his hand in her door."

Now everyone is practically hooting with laughter and I grin. I guess it didn't hurt anything to tell his little embarrassing tale. It's not like he'll know I cheered everyone up, right?

~Think again, minx. I'll have your cute little bum warmed for this. ~

I blink. How in the *hell*? *~Hey! Where the hell are you? I worry about you, you know. ~*

His grin filters through our connection. *~Have you been sitting at home pining like a war widow while I'm working, love? I think that'd be a good look on you. ~*

Sniffing, I frown. *~No. Maybe. Yes. I don't know. I don't even know how to knit! ~*

He frowns. *~I do. Punishment. I'll tell you later. ~*

"Hey, kitty! Hello? Are you there?"

Leo is waving at me and I blink back into focus, kicking him out of my head. "Yes?"

"Peacock wounds not-with-standing, what are we doing about Shea's party?"

"I'm going to find a suitable present, deliver it, and blow the joint. You guys can hang and mingle. Luckily, this one isn't crossing the portal like the February party. It worries me when so many of you guys are running around the real place together."

Caesar snorts. "Oi, ducks, it's not like we all look exactly alike anymore. We blend."

"Oh, yeah. Sixty hot guys and gals that look vaguely related running around getting in trouble. You blend like a bad contour job."

Sighing loudly, Philomena sits down her glass. "Okay, we have glad handing duty throughout the month. It sounds awful, but we can split it up. You'll drop in with a present and head back to Bird-land as usual. Does that sound about right?"

I nod. "Yep. I'm going to head there to see if I can figure out what's going on with Taurus. Sari requested he drop by to discuss Rhea today, according to her texts this afternoon. I haven't seen him since and that makes me worry."

They look at me as if he's lost his mind going to see her. "It's dangerous as hell, I know, but I can't stop him. He's on a 'mending bridges' kick. I don't know how to tell him that once she gets her claws in, we'll all be miserable."

"Figure out a way," Rafe murmurs, pushing off the bar with the bourbon bottle in hand. "They ruin everything, love. Don't let them take this."

Without another word, he heads for the studio, leaving us all to watch him go.

Dammit.

Taurus grins down at me. "So you *would* weep for me if I made you a widow?"

"I'd be inconsolable." I comb my fingers through his hair, pondering. "I think something in me would die with you."

Tugging me closer on his lap, he murmurs, "I was wondering how long it would take before you started poking around in my mind once we mated. The fact that you can do this so soon and you can block me is... surprising."

I shrug. "Magick, I'm sure. I know you're the only clone who can pan-orate, but I've been using mental tricks for a long time. I can do a lot more than I let on. I studied with enormously powerful people in my dead life."

"Really? None of the other mates know?" His brows furrow.

"Nope. I told Rafe not to divulge it to anyone. He'd sooner cut out his tongue than rat me out."

Even when it's for my own good, like with Wilde.

"I intend on respecting that power, loving it as part of you, and staying the hell out of your way when you're pissed." His grin is boyish, and I laugh softly.

"Sounds like a solid plan."

He tilts his head, then murmurs. "What's this party thing everyone's talking about on the blog?"

I groan. "Every clone or droid has a birthday month, even if it's made up. Here, there's always a party. This one is Shea's. I don't want to encourage him since we've been... intimate in the past, but I can't skip it. My family's going to do most of the heavy lifting, but I will have to drop by and give him a present."

He scrapes a fang on my collarbone, licking the droplet and grinning. "Queen Kitty duty. Got it."

My eyes go hazy. "Well, uh, I have to figure out how to do that before the end of the month…"

Nipping along the back of my neck, he continues to murmur assent and I completely lose the thread of what I'm saying. "You're making it hard to have a conversation."

"Am I? I was gone all day, though."

I growl, distracted from my original purpose. "That you were. I haven't had a taste of you for *hours*. We should fix that."

"That's what I'm trying to do, minx…"

Hours later, I'm sitting at my house staring at the wall. I have no idea what to get Shea for his birthday that won't… suggest I'm up for more physical pursuits. He and I were never cerebral; he's a sexed up puppy dog. It might not even matter what I get because he'll assume I'm ready to play.

Fuck. Why is everything so goddamned hard?

Opening my laptop, I decide to search for an idea online. Not the most original plan, but it should get me started, right? The background on my screen is a slideshow of pictures and it flashes a picture of Alistair and I from a party months ago. The Universe truly wants me to suffer, I fucking swear.

I rub my hand over my chest, feeling the ache in my bones, and push away from the computer. I need resolution for this shit with them. I need to be heard. I need to let them know what their betrayal did to us. Rhea's selfish behavior cost us all, and she should be held to account for it.

Should I open that can of worms again?

I don't know. It seems like a dangerous plan, but I don't know if I'll ever move past it if I don't tell them how I feel. I can't meet them in person; I've had my fill of that. Sighing, I sit back down at my laptop and start typing an email. Perhaps this will give me closure.

Then I can go back to dreading this bloody party.

"Have you lost your bloody mind?!!"

I blink, whipping my head to the doorway. After a morning full of getting the birthday droid's surprise ready, I came to wait for him for some R&R. "Huh?"

"You sent her an email? Why the hell would you do something so incredibly futile?"

Shrugging uncomfortably, I put my notebook on the bedside table with my glasses. "I don't know. I guess she told you—hypocritical since she instructed me not to talk to you about this because she wanted to talk to Talia herself."

"The golden goddess will be in menopause before that happens." He pads over and joins me on the bed, looking frustrated.

I nod. "She wrote me back, then I guess she found you to tattle on me." I look over at him. "I didn't hide it from you. I decided to do it spur of the moment and sent it before I fell asleep. I should have known it was going to be a big stinking deal."

He tugs me into his arms and murmurs against my hair. "I'm sorry you're hurting. She did share it; in fact, she looked me up at the house to cry and whine before I came. Talia wasn't home, and I'm sure she knew that. I wish I could give you back what you're missing so much."

My eyes close and I whisper, "I could have it back today if I was willing to forget, but I'm not. I won't pretend none of this happened. She gave lame excuses for how she treated people and evaded blame... It's over. I have closure now. I was honest, and I tried."

I feel his muscles stiffen, but his voice is soft. "I'm getting that feeling again, baby. That 'get out of dodge and off the radar' feeling that caused me and Talia to duck out last time."

Everything in me stills like a shock wave hit me. I try to find the air in my lungs, but I can't. All I can do is mumble, "I-I understand if you need to."

How I got those words out, I don't know. It felt like eating ground glass. My entire being halts in place as I wait to find out if my stupid idea to help Rafe and I close the book on this chapter of our lives backfired. I would hyperventilate if I could even breathe.

"Well." He lets go of me, turning away as the chill in the air increases.

"Maybe... maybe I was wrong bringing you into all of this... this world." I move off of his lap, needing space to displace the fear and pain that is swelling inside of me.

"Are you saying that you shouldn't have been with me?" Popping off the bed, he paces around the room like a caged animal. "I mean, why the fuck not? Everything I touch disintegrates."

I walk over to him and reach up to turn his face back to me. "Don't. That's not what I meant. I meant that I was sorry that I brought you into this mess with Rhea."

"Are you kidding me? From what I read, Rafe's problems with her were because of what happened when I spoke to her. All of your problems are my fault. Everyone wants to fix her and make her better, so that they can be with her again." He stalks to the bar, snarling as he loses his temper. "*Fuck.* When the hell is loving someone or wanting to have something for my fucking self ever going to *not* be tainted by fucking shithead bitches!"

I wince, swallowing hard as my fear of losing him and the trauma from Wilde clash inside of me. I put my hands on my thighs, trying to hide the shaking as I race to figure out how to control the layers of terror exploding in my chest. When I finally manage to speak, I pick each word carefully. "She wants to blame someone for her behavior. Catching you before I could explain made it easy for her to transfer that guilt to you."

"She fucking *lied,* Deli" he roars.

"I'm aware. She lied to all of us." I walk closer, hoping that if I touch him, it will calm both of us.

He jerks away, heading for the large armchair to drop into it. His expression is more vulnerable than I've ever seen it. "Why does everyone want to fix her? She's been so horrible. Why can't I love someone and have it be fun and light?"

With that question, I realize that he's been internalizing a lot of resentment towards my ex-family members. I'm not sure what I said that sent him spinning, but he needs help. I have to get myself under control so I can do that. Closing my eyes, I breathe slowly, looking for my center so that the trembling will stop. When I feel like I'm not going to heave, I walk over to the couch.

"Listen to me, baby. I realize now that helping her is beyond my capabilities. It breaks my heart that I can't. It feels like giving up, and I'm not good at giving up on people I care about. It's my nature to try to fix it until I beat myself bloody. I know now, after her response to that email, that I cannot continue to let her do this to me or the ones I love. So, I'm letting them go. I have to."

~I just want someone to like me best.~

I drop to the floor in front of him and put my hands on his knees. Looking up at him with soft eyes, I whisper, "Do you know how many times I could have been with Alistair if I gave in? Or how easy it would have been to let them treat me badly and do nothing? As many times as she would have jumped you if you let her, I'm sure. I've been consciously choosing you because you make me happy."

He sniffles, but doesn't respond.

"I love you. I want you. I don't care if anyone likes it. If this is the price I have to pay to have you in my life, I accept it gladly." I reach up to cup his face, trying to get him to see the truth in my eyes.

"I don't want to go away but... I hurt," he murmurs in a gravelly voice.

"I don't want you to go, but if you need to... I will deal with it because I don't want you to get hurt. What you need is important to me." I look away because I know that I can't hide the emotions running over my face.

Panic, fear, sadness, and resignation are swamping my system and I can't bring myself to lie to him. I also can't make myself ask him to stay. This world can be so amazing, but it hasn't been lately. Taurus hasn't even hit the bottom of the barrel of unpleasantness that I've lived with since the holidays.

No one should have to go through what Rafe and I have gone through, even by proxy.

"All I know is this: Blondie and I are done. Her and Talia— that's for them to suss out. Personally, Talia is pissed because she hurt me. She's protective of me."

"She should be. If I knew what to do to help you, I'd be doing it. I'm afraid to make things worse."

"You don't have to fix me," he growls.

"I'm scared. I can't stand seeing you hurt. I don't know what to do."

"Why are you scared?"

I bite my lip, unsure how to answer without baring so much that I can't take it back. "Because I'm sure that I'm going to lose you and I don't know what I'll do. I don't want to pressure you into staying with me, but I'm scared." I let out a shaky breath. He has no idea how hard that was to say. I've been so trained, so conditioned, to put myself second to those I love that voicing my needs has become difficult for fear of reprisal.

His voice is soft. "If it makes you feel any better, I'm afraid I'm going to lose you."

I shake my head. "Only if you tell me to go away. Otherwise, I'll always be here."

"Would you fight for me like you have for Blondie and her mate?"

I notice he doesn't say brother, and I wonder if that's too painful to admit. "Yes. I love you. I don't fall for people as easily as it seems—not like I did you—and once I do, that's it. I fight until there's nothing left to fight for. Apparently, even then I put up my dukes from the ground."

"It means a lot to hear you say that." He wipes his face and sighs. "But you hurt me, too, Deli. Why didn't you tell me?"

"Tell you what?" I frown.

"Why didn't you tell me how bad you were hurting? Or about the email last night? You could have texted me."

"We had a good day yesterday. The email plan came to me last minute and you'd gone home. I figured I would tell you in person because that felt like the right thing to do. I should have known she'd try to zing me from the background."

"It feels like things that happened were lies if you hurt that badly inside and I didn't know."

"Baby, I loved every second with you. You've been the bright spot in my day for quite a while now."

"I felt like a truck had broadsided me. You were hurting over them yesterday and maybe other times, too. In my mind, that means that what we had wasn't real because you were struggling, and I didn't know."

"I can understand why you'd feel that way and I'm deeply sorry. For me, being here is... separate. When I come here, everything else fades away. Maybe that's a lame excuse, but it's what I feel."

He's quiet, as if he's thinking about it, then he nods. "You're right. I see how it would fade away in our home."

I manage a shaky smile, hearing him call this place 'our home' hitting me right in the feels. Sniffling, I duck my head as I wipe my eyes. My emotions are rising and falling like a rollercoaster and it's making me leak.

"What's wrong?"

"You called it our home. It went right here," I pat my chest, feeling like a silly girl.

"I've thought of this place as our home for a while. We've been building it little by little as we get more comfortable with each other. That's how it went in my head, at least." He flushes and shrugs.

I lay my hand on his leg again though I want to be in his arms. I wait for him to move it, but he opens his arms. Crawling into them as fast as I can, I finally feel my muscles unlock. We stay wrapped around each other quietly for a few moments, each working out our pain silently.

"It's okay, baby. Everything is going to be okay." He strokes my back soothingly. "But I think I need to say a few things, love."

The tension comes back and I sit perfectly still. "I'm listening."

"I can't handle you keeping things from me. It hurts me—more than finding out would, actually."

"I understand," I say carefully.

"I need to know that you'll let me in. Because if you've been hurting and you keep it from me, it's—well, it's not good."

"I thought I was okay with it— I did. I don't know what triggered my need to give it one more try. I wrote the stupid email and sent it. Truthfully, I felt much better having done it."

"I was remarkably close to bolting. I don't want to feel that again."

"I felt that. When you said you might go, I realized that while I was upset about losing Alistair, losing you terrified me. It shocked me how afraid I was of losing you."

"That being said, I want you to know that this is our home. If things get bad, I won't leave. If I need to escape, I'll stay here and disappear from everywhere else. We'll keep the outside out until I feel better."

"I like that. I'll hide here, too, if need be."

"We're okay, then?"

"With me, we are. You?"

"You're still the most beautiful thing I've ever seen, and I love you with everything in me." He wipes a tear off my cheek, and I smile.

"I love you, too. At least I didn't snot on your shirt."

His eyes widen in horror as he looks over every inch of the borrowed shirt I'm wearing. "That's it, hussy, no more wearing my shirts!"

I pout, my eyes big and wide. "But you said you liked when I wore your silk."

He chuckles. "Sodding hell, that's a dangerous weapon you've got going on." He hugs me tightly and sighs. "Christ, I love you. I'd like to spend the next good eternity holding on to you if you don't mind."

"That works for me, baby."

He frowns and looks at where he broke a perfectly good vase in his tantrum. "Sorry about that."

I wave my hand. "It's replicable; you're not."

"Can I admit something to you? When I first told you, I was ready to scram, and you told me you understood, I thought you wanted me to go. I thought you didn't want me anymore."

Shaking my head vehemently, I look into his eyes. "Never. I didn't want to make you feel you had to stay because of me. I love you and sometimes, if you love things, you have to let them go. When I'm cornered, I get very self-sacrificing."

His expression is one of pure confusion. "I work on one basic tenet: I go by what I see and hear. So, if I don't know you'd rather not lose me, I wouldn't assume."

"I have a nasty habit of putting people I love before me."

"You really need to work on that, pet."

"I'm getting better. When it's important, I say something, even if it's small."

"You would have said something to me, then?" He tilts his head and looks at me curiously.

"I did. I told you I was scared."

"Yes, you did. You really didn't want me to go, did you, baby?"

I look at my hands and shake my head, emotions swelling inside me. "No, I did not."

He picks me up, carrying me over to the bed. Shucking his shirt, he lays back and grabs my hand. He pulls me down next to him. "I'm not going anywhere, baby. Barring an unfortunate death via Company assignment, you're stuck with me."

Curling around him, I smile. "Good, because I was gearing up to be inconsolable."

"Yeah, so was I. On a good day if I go off to lick my wounds, I'm a mess. The thought of losing you was killing me."

"I don't know what I would have done. I'm so used to having you now."

"If I remember correctly: pining, wasting away, knitting..." he jokes with a fond smile.

"That would have been a blanket the size of the Grand bloody Canyon. I mean, once I learned how to do it."

He reaches out to touch my heart with his, murmuring, "You're home to me, love. You're where I live now."

"You're trying to make me all sappy, you big softy."

"Just telling you what's inside me."

Smiling to myself, I lean up and whisper in his ear. "You hunka burning clone, you."

His entire body goes still, and he leans back. Sapphire eyes practically glow with emotion as he whispers, "Thank you. You rock me, baby. I love you so much." I give him a shy grin and he cups my face in his hands. "Just so you know, when I'm feeling better? You are never living that down. Right now, I'm feeling too humbled and grateful to tease."

I mumble into his shoulder. "If it makes you happy, I can deal with the fallout. I wanted to show you—even in a silly way—how much you mean to me."

"It was perfect." He reaches for my chin, lifting it gently to look deeply into my eyes. "Mine." His voice is a husky, rough sound filled with emotion. Leaning in me, he kisses me softly. "Yours forever, my love." He holds me tightly, then sighs. "I'm spent, baby. But I'm staying right here with you tonight, so don't even think of kicking me out of our bed. I want to fall asleep with you next to me in my shirt."

"Leaving never crossed my mind."

"I love you, heart of mine. Sleep with me, be my wonderful dream, and lead me towards a happier dawn."

I sigh, closing my eyes to find sleep and rest for the next day.

Who knows what's coming then?

The Blogger Begins To Plot

WILDE

I've seen my Darkness much less than usual in recent weeks. She is quite consumed with the antics of our erstwhile family and the addition of Mr. Taurus to her life.

While I understand how this has occurred, the lack of time with my Darkness has been preying on my mind. My Royalty has practically shuttered himself in a locked room. He responds to no one's queries, not even my beloved's.

He is well and truly in mourning, I fear.

I am not well myself, but I do not believe that hiding will resolve my sadness at the betrayal of our mates. We cannot wither away because they have chosen a path that they must travel alone. My beloved runs at night with Lady Calista and Lady Veruca; I believe it helps her bring her pain to the surface so that she may work through her own grief.

She is sitting in our living room conversing with Mr. Taurus. He has been stopping by occasionally in his effort to offer an olive branch. I know my beloved has long wished to mend our relationship with him and his mistress, Talia. I am glad that my Darkness' affiliation with him has brought this boon to our home, but I worry about when the worm will turn, as they say.

"I think Rhea expects some guy to walk into her other world work, and sweep her off her feet like in a romance novel. Wilde could do that here, but she's got this yen to be a bad girl because it's cool. She's using that to force people to punish her, and it's sick in the head. Wilde and I have been talking about unbinding ceremonies. I heard that's not such a good plan, but hell, what could be worse than now?"

I wish she had not shared that with him, but alas.

"It's true they exist. I've never heard of an attempt not ending in disaster. The people involved end up being messed up so severely they're never the same. Talia says they have had to…uh…deactivate Company clones that lost their mates. It's not a good thing when they think you're too crazy to go on death wish missions."

I sigh. I am not so sure about these ceremonies, and I have expressed this to my beloved. "Sir, I believe that my beloved is overstating our interest. We discussed the possibility of such, but have made no permanent decisions. I feel it might be best to work through our grief in other ways."

We have quite a few options for working out our issues, and my beloved knows that. She has her coyote runs and if I can get them to make the time, there is much to be said for working out frustrations in a more physical way with our mates. I find it gratifying—as does my demon—to work things out in that fashion. He has made my emotions imminently easier to master through these methods.

"Wilde, I agree with you. That's why the Company teaches the recruits not to mate until they know without a doubt that it is forever—because it is. Marriage is one thing, but it seems like people here jumped into a boat that they didn't know where it was headed. I know my Minx and her primary feel that way."

My teacup clatters and I close my eyes, feeling the demon rage inside at his audacity. Mentioning his relationship with her in my home is the height of rudeness. How *dare* he? Blinking, I pause, unsure where that feeling came from.

I have always shared my mates—including my beloved— with other lovers and family. It has never caused a feeling like that to swell inside of me like a tidal wave of hate. I did feel some irritation with Alistair. His name sizzles in my mind as not only a troubled former mate, but the one who encroached upon the strength of the relationship I had with my Darkness and my Royalty. That problem began in the late winter when the specter of my demon rose and finally gave voice to my anger and resentment.

Feeling the anger swell again, I work to quell it, not wishing to be a poor host. The need to demarcate what is acceptable behavior regarding what my demon believes is his right is strong. I fight it handily, but he is a powerful presence in my mind now. Perhaps it is a reaction to the visceral nature of Mr. Taurus' disposition.

"My Darkness knows her heart well and chooses her mate with the utmost care. The crux of the problem lies with the disingenuous nature of our former family members."

I don't say their names because I am finding it genuinely distasteful to do so—more so by the day.

Taurus arches a brow, looking from my beloved to me, and then back. "What do you think, shrimp? Do you think he's right? No one jumped the gun on all this mating willy-nilly as a family unit?"

She snorts, shaking her head. "Honey, I've known Rhea for years, much like you and Talia. I knew she had some darkness in her past that made her needy. But I didn't know that she was a co-dependent, self-hating narcissist. How could Deli have known? Besides, the kitty's done well with her other mates: Victor, Rafe, Wilde, me... She only missed the boat on those two."

I nod in agreement. "Quite. I think she has excellent taste."

Evil pumps through me when he blanches. Perhaps he has not heard the length of my Darkness' pedigree? I do not judge her for her active social life and never have, but he and his mate are adamant about their selectiveness. A little reminder that he is not the first to win her heart isn't out of line.

It might help keep a respectful distance, in fact.

"Wilde and I are excellent mates. Victor would step in front of a bus for Miss Kitty, and Rafe's sequestered now, but he'd lay open a vein any day of the week. We all got hoodwinked by the broken toys, buddy. You don't have to worry your perfect hairdo. She's got a legion of clones and droids that she's not mated to pounding her door down to take their place."

The tension in our houseguest is palpable, but he nods in response to my beloved's statement. "The minx can take care of herself. She's a force all on her own."

Pfft.

As if he would know her strengths better than her long-mated family. His arrogance is unmatched, though that fact has never been in dispute. "Darkness is well equipped to fend for herself; however, she needs not. Her family is quite devoted."

His lips curl up and I dislike his expression. It is as if he knows something we do not. "Well, mate, you're right about that." Sitting his glass down, he sighs. "Now, it's been a bloody lovely chat and all, but I have a mate that's calling me. She's not one to be ignored for long. Mind if we cut this short?"

Something is amiss here, and I do not know what it is. He's looking both smug and angry. While I believe that Talia may tug on his strings in the manner he suggested, that is not why he is foregoing our arranged meeting. There's something more pressing than a missive from the bladed ex-leader and he definitely does not want to discuss it with us.

"You should not keep her waiting, Mr. Taurus. We will speak again if my beloved and I intend to pursue the course of action we addressed." I stand, holding my hand out to shake his, and he chuckles.

"Wilde, you are the strangest clone I've met in my short time on this planet, but I appreciate your hospitality. Both of you." He nods at my beloved and stands. "Let me know if you have more questions."

With that, he disappears, and I feel that to be both rude and troublesome. He left quickly and with little fanfare, which is not Taurus' style.

There is something afoot that I cannot put my finger on.

"What should we do now?" my mate asks, raising a brow. "Because that was weird."

"It was, my beloved. I think a meeting with our family from the South is in order. I feel there are things going on that we are not aware of, and I find myself in need of some relief."

She gives me an evil grin, enhanced only by the fangs she likes to refer to as 'twitching' when she senses things. "I'll make the call."

The Cat Forgets A Detail

DELILAH

"*Son of a bitch.* You didn't tell me!"

I blink, looking up from my notebook. I was sketching my plans for the erstwhile birthday gift while I waited for him to come home.

Before I went home and he went to work, we had a lovely morning. Sometime this week, he had a pool—complete with waterfall, hot tub in a rock formation, and a lovely patio—installed in a backyard area. I sleep less now than I have in my entire life, but we played, loved, and drank until we were sated.

Afterward, I headed to my house to hang out with Rafe. I'm worried about him, and he needs someone who understands what he's going through. I stayed with him until Taurus texted me that he was stopping by Sari's for a brief discussion and then coming home for the evening.

I wanted to tell him about this wretched party, but I doubt that's a good plan now. He's here and instead of a leisurely evening, he's infuriated. I have no idea why. I haven't even *seen* anyone but my family today, so what in the hell did I do?

"I'm lost. What didn't I tell you?" I sit everything aside, attempting to be the one who keeps their cool for once.

"You're *mated* to that stubbly little gnome, and you didn't tell me! I had to hear her and that fancy pants git make *sure* I knew. It hit me like a bloody truck because you *lied again*." He stalks to the bathroom, slamming the panel shut behind him. It makes a weird beeping noise that I can only assume means he's locked it somehow.

Fuck. I don't think I forgot to tell him about Sari.

I could have, but I wasn't hiding it if I did. We don't talk about our being mated—at all. She and Wilde pushed the family claim with us after they did it with Rhea and Alistair. I was so pissed at Rhea that I rushed into that part with Sari.

It was once, it wasn't remarkable, and it's never happened again since. I honestly think she did it so that Rhea couldn't get to me first. She's never mentioned it once in the eight months since we did it. It's hella suspicious that she brought it up now.

I walk over and touch the door to reach out to him, but he's blocking me. Sighing, I trudge over to the bed and sit down, feeling like an ass. He thinks I lied about it and he isn't letting me in. I grab the paper and start scribbling a note because I need some space if this is how he's going to be tonight. I don't know that I can handle feeling like I'm going to lose him two nights in a row and I definitely can't handle a temper tantrum like that on so little sleep.

Love,

I'm sorry if I didn't mention Sari. I didn't intend to leave her out purposefully nor have you think I lied. We rarely speak of our mating—I've always believed it was a gambit in her game with Rhea.

To avoid future conflicts, here is my list, as complete as

I can remember it. If you want to read it you can, but you don't have to.

I love you and I'll be in the garden if you want to see me. I'm trying to give you space because I don't know what else to do.

Mates: Sari, Wilde, Rafe, Victor (sort of), Alistair, you

People I've been intimate with: all the above, Mayhem, Preston, Aiden, Mercury, Shea, Constantine, Caesar, Cruise, CJ, Gregor, Hex, Leo, Chance, Rupert. A few people that it's been intimated that I've been with, but I really have not: Percy, Manuel, Antonio, Rhea

I think that's it. I've covered everything and everyone— there's no one left out that I know of.

I know you didn't ask, but I told you because I don't want to have you upset again. I love you and I hope you'll want to find me.

If not—well, I don't want to imagine that so I'm not going to.

With all my heart,

Delilah

Ripping the note out of the notebook, I lay it on the bed before snagging one of his shirts and trudging down the stairs. I find a place in the garden and try to focus on what I'm writing, hoping he'll show up soon.

The Bird Flies The Coop

Using everything I have in me, I throw up the most secure wall I've ever created.

For the first time in a year, I even shut the golden goddess out. I'm enraged, ripped apart, and cast down. After the shit yesterday, I thought we had an understanding about honesty and truthfulness between us. A part of me is mad at myself for storming off, but it was either that or rip the bedroom apart with my bare hands. I chose separation instead.

Maybe I am evolving? Who knows.

Stalking back and forth in the bathroom, I let the decimation in my soul run rampant. I hear movement out in the bedroom—I'm not sure what she's doing, but I can't find it in me to care. She did this to herself and she's going to have to live with it. She had so many chances to tell me the truth—why didn't she? I thought she understood that honesty is a paramount issue for me, but apparently, I was wrong.

I roar my pain into the air as I let my demon take over completely. That makes the rage and hurt so much worse. Fully fanged out, I slide fingertips in the gap between the door and wall

"

and yank. It rips the steel to shreds, slices my hands wide open, and opens a space that I can escape through.

The paper on the bed catches my eye and I stalk over to read it.

The demon is raging in a way that I've never felt before, so her words mean nothing. Stalking to the closet, I head to the very back and pull out worn black jeans and a black tee shirt that has seen better decades. I throw them on, dripping blood from my palms. After I shove my feet into old combat boots, I head to the bed. Grabbing a pencil in my mangled hand with a wince, I pick up the pad she left to write my own blood-stained note.

When I finish, I jerk open the nightstand drawer, taking out the emergency dagger I keep there. I wrap my fingers around it, pick up the bloody paper, and stalk back to the bathroom door. With a quick move, I embed the dagger in the door frame, impaling the note to hold it in place.

With a final feral, pain-filled roar that echoes through the house, I disapparate.

Swaying in the breeze of my passing and dripping blood on the carpet, is the note I left for her.

It only says two words:

GONE HUNTING.

I promised the kitty I wouldn't do certain things, and tonight, I'm not exactly predisposed to following rules. After all, she told me she'd be truthful and she's definitely not kept her end of the bargain.

The Company won't send me on a mission like this. This kind of shit leads to clones going feral if they get injured. Risking the assets they've spent years investing in isn't a good business decision, so Mikhail told me to bugger off when I called in.

Stupid bookish fuck. I hate following his dictates, but I'd rather stab myself in the eye than take his job.

"It's fine. I can find my own victims."

There's a slight push against my mental blocks and I give whoever it is a mighty shove out of my head. I don't want to be around anyone when I feel this way.

All I want to do is cause pain and wreck havoc.

Thinking for a moment, I grin when the perfect idea flits through my mind. I know where to go and I know exactly what to do.

Time to get this shit off my chest.

The Goddess Worries

TALIA

*H*e's in so much pain.

As Taurus' primary mate and a skilled empath, I feel the block he put on our connection. It's been a long time since he's shut me out, so I know he's also shutting out the 'magical minx'. She must have caused this disaster.

If Taurus is off the chain, a disaster it will certainly be.

For all his varied skills and flaws, he's the more emotional, more impulsive of the two of us. He's a flashover where I'm a slow burn and his emotions consume his entire being when he's in primal mode.

I'm sitting on the porch, watching our new neighbors move in. Since Taurus' last tantrum—the one where he ate one of the human employees from the Cabal Quarter—a few weeks ago, the house down the lane has been empty. That move normally would have earned him a month of fighting and a few well-placed bruises in the sparring ring—except that he's been so wrapped up in Deli. He was too happy for me to poke holes in him even if I did spend three days on the paperwork detailing the incident.

I'm a real romantic at heart, let me tell you.

Baby is spinning like rapid fire in my right-hand—a sure sign of my agitation over the bird's mental block. I won't send Damien and Theodora after him yet. I'm going to wait to see what asinine dilemma he's gone off half-cocked and gotten himself into first.

But I worry.

He's far more mercurial than I've ever seen him since he met the wonder kitty. I'm concerned that as high as his highs are right now—annoyingly so, let me tell you—his lows might be just as low. That's not so bad for a normal person, but for a trained killer with a whole wide world full of people to wreak havoc on?

It's a concern. We'll leave it at that.

The Company has rules. It deals with its own rogue agents, even freelancers like Taurus. He often pushes those boundaries, but he's so fucking good at what he does that they usually let him off with a punishment that will irritate him more than anything. It's how he got stuck teaching knitting to newbies more than once. Our boss is pretty damn good at making certain Taurus knows how pissed he is without losing his temper and letting out his infamous dark side.

I can only protect him so much before their sense of justice kicks in. They 'de-activate' agents when they are deemed a danger to the secrecy of the Company and its initiatives. Their credo is to complete the mission, do it right, and keep us far from the fallout. Clones that draw attention to the existence of the Company, the Rift, or its myriad secret technologies and holdings get de-activated without question.

I hope that he's not out guaranteeing that my Monday will suck. Mikhail's patience only stretches so far. While Taurus is the best damned agent they have, the clone that runs the agents' hand can be forced by Oversight.

Hell, I could have to go before a panel for letting him off the chain. I'll kill him myself. Those fucking meetings are the worst part of my job, and I sure as hell don't want to be the subject of one. Every single time some asshat suggests they 're-educate' Taurus because he's too old school and I tell them they really want him on their side, not as an enemy. That's true... he's far more vicious than the newer breeds of agents and so much more intelligent.

Sighing, I look out into the night.

What in the hell caused this?

All I can do now is hope that his new mate can get him under control because I'm completely in the dark.

The Bird Flies Home

❧

TAURUS

I limp into our garden covered in blood and aching. She wasn't in the house, so I can only assume she hasn't moved since she left the sodding note.

It was an apology and a laundry list of every damn person in the Rift she's ever been with—something I neither wanted nor needed, but I'll never be able to forget.

Scanning the darkness, I look for a sign that she's still here. Moonlight shines off the water in the lush oasis that I had put in so we could enjoy the pleasant weather as the seasons turn. I wouldn't blame her if she went inside because I didn't leave any indication of when or if I'd be back. "Deli?"

I find her sitting on a big lounger in the middle of a lush garden. She must have done some mojo to grow this since our dips yesterday morning. I'm still a bit floored by the real magick thing, but I can't focus on that at the moment.

Stopping at the foot of her chair, I see her look up from the folds of the big blanket she's completely wrapped up in. She doesn't meet my eyes and her silence is deafening as she sits perfectly still. I sigh heavily, crossing to stand beside her seat. I'm not used to her being dead silent. It's unnerving. But I forge ahead anyway, needing to say my piece before the conversation flips to whatever excuses she's going to make for her behavior.

"I want to make something clear before this goes any further," I say, holding my hand up. "I don't care if you've slept with the whole bloody Navy; you didn't need to list your partners for me. I appreciate the thought, but it wasn't necessary."

Her eyes move to the ground, but nothing else moves, so I continue. "To me, mating is a different story. I'm a clone with an exceptionally long history of only one mate, so for me, mating is sacrosanct. Who you've mated with isn't my problem—I want to stress that."

Again, she stays quiet and still. I sigh again and push on. "That said, I should probably apologize to Wilde and Sari. As I was dismembering my thirtieth victim, it occurred to me that the way I acted earlier combined with our past made it appear that I went ballistic because of her. I didn't."

This time, she nods, but still doesn't speak. I don't know if she knows or cares that I abruptly darted out of the meeting with them, but I feel honor bound to tell her. My rude escape may cause her problems later and she deserves to know that may be coming.

"I'm bound by my sense of integrity to clear the air with them personally." She nods again and though I feel a sense of worry creeping in, I continue. "After the issues with the whacked out blonde bint, my emotions have been close to the surface. Even the littlest thing sets me off. I imagine you feel something similar."

Another nod.

Christ, it's like someone cut out her bloody tongue.

"That being said, I want you to know how I feel about earlier. Then, depending on how that goes, we can discuss logistics. When we discussed your mates, and you mentioned Victor's claim rounded out the last of them. Your taste has imminently improved, but when I heard twice in an hour that what we discussed wasn't accurate, it finally sunk in. I felt like I was run over by a tank."

Big red eyes from over the lip of the blanket. Another nod. Nothing else.

"My emotions—crazy and raw as they are—shut me down completely. I felt that you lied to me and my mind jumped to the conclusion that you did it on purpose. I thought you were lying by omission. It made me feel angry, betrayed, and foolish."

The blanket shivers and I wonder how she's breathing when she's wrapped up like a mummy, looking silent and submissive. I can't bloody figure it out; her note said that she was sorry. Why the hell is she sitting here like a dog on a training course? It's as if there's a trigger word that I haven't said, and she doesn't know what to do until I say it.

"Mating is such a statement of commitment to me that I can't imagine someone 'forgetting' their mating bond. I wonder if one day I'll get lied about. I also want to admit—not that it leaves me looking pleasant as an individual—that I don't understand mating with people if you're not going to honor that bond."

She knew that I wouldn't—that was the gist of that note she left. However, I don't know how we're ever going to get anywhere if she stays curled in that small, tight blanket with nary a word, not even to curse me for being a jackass.

"I wish I'd never..." I look at her and see a tear run from the corner of her eye down to the material, but she still doesn't move or speak. It breaks my heart, but I have to say what I feel. "No, I won't say that. I feel very foolish and out of touch."

Her lashes flutter downward. Though I blocked her for hours while I went on a tear of epic proportions that I'm going to pay for later, I know that she's got herself bottled up emotionally. Her expression is one of so much shame, regret, and sadness that I don't know if words could tell me more than what this small section of her face is saying.

"Sometimes, I wish I'd never come back. It's not your fault, but I may have overestimated myself. I'm having a hard time with that." I lower myself into the chair next to hers, wincing at the lacerations and punctures all over my body. I did a number to myself tonight. "I don't know what to do. I shouldn't have had to hear it like that."

Again, I get the shamed look and downcast eyes. I don't think I can bear it anymore. I feel like I'm kicking an injured animal over and over and it keeps looking at me, pleading with me to stop the pain. "Woman, we won't get anywhere if you sit there like a lump all night!"

She ducks further into the blanket, only her eyes visible now as she watches me suspiciously. What the hell does she think is going to happen? It's like she's afraid to even look at me now. "Deli, you're going to have to come out of there. I'd come over there, but I'm having trouble." Her eyes widen and I see the shiver again.

It makes me angry; I'm the one who was wronged and she's hiding.

"Speak, woman!" I growl as my temper flares.

Flinching, she drops the material to reveal her mouth. Sucking in a breath, she unleashes a stream of words. "This is going to sound awful and I know it won't make any sense to you. I forgot about her. It's happened before, more than once, and even she's forgotten. It's not an excuse, but you have to understand how our mating happened and why it's like this. I wasn't trying to hide it; I have no reason to. You could ask her, but it probably was mentioned on purpose. There was a time when I was mated to Wilde and Alistair; Rafe was mated to Rhea, Sari, Wilde, and Alistair. Remember when Rhea and Sari went to that convention with Talia in late November?"

I nod, letting her go because there's no stopping her now.

"Somehow, right before that, someone thought of families mating—like as a foursome. Rafe and I were going to do so with Rhea and Alistair. Sari got wind, and before we could, she and Wilde's family mated with them while they were on that trip. They didn't even tell us beforehand—we found out about it in a blog post. Rafe and I were really hurt. We were angry and stupid, which allowed Sari to talk us into mating with her and Wilde as a family. They got everything they wanted— which I didn't see then, but I see it now. It was a one-time, one shot deal with the entire family. She never looked at me again afterward. It hurt me to realize that I was just extra baggage. This is all my fault for dragging you back to this quagmire of idiocy, selfishness, and bullshit. I did that and I'm sorry. I can't change that I left out that one night that was so long ago now, it feels like it didn't even happen. I can only apologize and give you what I know to be the truth. I know I didn't have to, but I did."

It's like I turned on the faucet. She keeps talking and apologizing and babbling.

What the bloody hell is wrong with her?

I look at my stiff, blood caked hands and sigh. "Why did she tell me? I can't figure that out. If it was such an oft forgotten thing, why did she mention it and when it totally slipped past me, have Wilde mention it again? Was she trying to smack me?"

"Probably. She doesn't bring it up—ever. It's like it didn't happen. Sari hasn't looked my way for anything other than friendly stuff since. She also mated as a family with Rhea and I don't know what went on there. I didn't— Rafe and I never did the whole she-bang with those two. Sari wanted to do a three family thing, but Rafe and I refused. They were crazy enough as it was."

It's like she's not even taking time to breathe. She's spouting words and words, trying to get every plausible answer in before something happens.

I really don't understand what's going on with her, but it's starting to scare me.

"I was honest with her about my feelings and it felt like salt in the wound." I think about that for a moment and wonder if I was played like a Stradivarius. I look down at the absolute wreck I am and think about what's going to happen Monday morning when Mikhail gets wind of this.

"I'd offer to help with the wounds, but I doubt you'd want me to. The offer is still there. I—I don't want to lose you. I said I'd fight for you and I meant it. I've been sitting here, staring into the night, waiting. I haven't talked with anyone or gone anywhere, but I hurt if you hurt. I don't know why they mentioned it." She shrinks back into the blanket again, her eyes looking concerned. They are blood red from tears, but she's not crying. It's like she's holding them in and it's burning her eyes to do so.

I keep having to stop the flow of her talking. While she's a chatty kitty, something is off about this situation. "I'll ask Sari when I apologize. It was clear she thought that I wouldn't know, though."

"I have no idea. Like I said, nothing's been said for months and months. It didn't even come up about her and the others until the mess with Rhea, so maybe that's what stuck it in her head? I don't know. I can't figure out why it'd come up now."

"I couldn't breathe because I hurt so bad. After you left, I went out and killed people—a lot of them."

She doesn't babble for once when she says, "I know; I felt it."

I don't have any idea how that is possible. I had her and the golden goddess in the no-fly zone. "I broke several cardinal Company rules."

Her expression is serious despite still being wrapped in that ridiculous getup. "Are you in trouble?"

"Not currently, but when the Company finds out, I might be. No—scratch that. They always find out and I'll be in a mess of trouble."

"Can I do anything? I can tell them how it was all my fault. That should help, right? I'll take the punishment. It's okay; I can do it. It's my fault, anyway."

The babbling is back.

I shake my head. She absolutely cannot take what they'd dish out, nor would I let her try. "I think I'm wanted in Cozumel. I know I'm wanted in Des Moines."

I didn't mention I'd terrorized the other place, not the fine citizens on this side of the Rift, did I?

"Are you going away?" Her voice is a whisper and I see her shrink down again.

"Not to Cozumel or Des Moines. The Company doesn't let us get into the real-world hands. Will I get recalled to the training facility? I don't know—that's why I'm here. Also, the only member of my family currently speaking to me is Theodora—who's upstairs cleaning the mess I made."

Her face crumples, but she only nods. She clenches her jaw tightly until her expression fades to the robotic one she's been sporting. "I'm so sorry."

The Bird Tries to Understand

"The family thing isn't your fault; it's mine. So is the random massacre."

"I know that, but I hurt you again and that is all my fault. I should tell them for you; I *can* tell them for you. Let me tell them it's my fault. They can punish me."

"You hurt me very badly, but my actions are my responsibility. I'll take the penalty because I admit, I'd do it again. Unfortunately, the Company frowns on thirty-three unscheduled, random slaughters." I sigh, knowing that this is going to be an absolute nightmare. Besides which, I'm so sodding spent physically that I can hardly keep myself upright.

"I started it. I made it happen. I did it. I can take that blame."

"Stop. I wish I'd known, and I wish it didn't get dumped on me by Wilde and Sari. I accept that you forgot, and that it wasn't intentional. I don't understand it, but I accept it as your truth. I don't forgive myself for not giving you a chance to explain before I went smash and slash. I apologize for that because it was childish and not good treatment of someone I love."

That part is true. Despite my rage, the feeling that I acted impulsively by not allowing her to explain before I lost it has irked me all night. It didn't stop me from tearing everything in my path apart, but it was there.

"I love you; I don't want you to go. The whole time you were gone, I couldn't function. I shut down because I was so raw. I don't blame you at all—not after all the things people have done lately. Especially not since I did something similar when I locked myself in the bathroom. I didn't destroy anything, but I'm not big with destruction as much as curling inside myself and not coming out. I don't judge you; I have no room to talk."

"I judge me," I say, shaking my head. "I live by simple rules and one is 'don't do anything that makes you unable to look at yourself in the mirror afterward'. I hold myself responsible for every action I've taken since I stepped into that bathroom, and I'm going to have to deal with that. But I owe you an apology. I should have—at the very least—treated you with the respect due my mate."

"I accept your apology, even if I don't think I deserve it."

She shrinks down again and my brows furrow. "I should tell you that it's becoming increasingly clear that I'm a jealous sod. Again, this is my problem, and not one you are responsible for."

"You're honest about it. I can accept that if you can."

"I'm sorry I got messy on you." I look at her, my eyes softening when I remember that she's had a lot to juggle emotionally. After the story she just told, I wonder how much more there was before I came on the scene.

"It's my fault."

"You may have noticed I have a thing with honesty."

"I want to be honest. If there's something you want to know, now's the time to ask."

"I don't think I could handle any more dark uglies, pet."

Her expression is relieved. I tuck that away for later, wondering what she thought she was going to have to share that is worse than this. "I, unfortunately, have no secrets to speak of. That's the problem with being arrogant and shameless, I suppose. Who knew being me had its drawbacks?"

She should have laughed at that. Normally, she would have. Instead, she nods and murmurs, "Every time I've claimed someone, it's been followed by some big nasty thing that mars the experience. Something always rains on my parade. Also, I should mention that bitten people I'm not mated to on my list. Not all, and it's not a secret, but you might not know."

"Then to me, it's a secret. Not a hidden secret, but—okay, maybe an unknown. I don't count biting the same as mating. Though, I've got a thing with no blood play with non-mates, as you know."

"I know. That's why I mentioned it. Some were droids, so no blood. I don't know where that fits into your world."

"That's a personal preference. I've seen what biting between non-mates can do. I never, ever, bled Blondie."

"I never touched her."

"Talia did; is that a problem?"

"No. I had experience with Sari—as you know—and Lily."

"I thought of something that no one knows. People will be hurt if it ever gets spoken beyond this garden, though." She just looks back at me, waiting. "My relationship with Blondie had nothing to do with her and everything to do with Talia. I probably don't have to say much more."

"Yeah, I get what you're saying. I, um, I have a secret I can share. The only person I ever told this to was Rhea because she wouldn't make fun of me."

Dropping her head, she lets out a breath. "When the beast got hard to control, I did something bad by accident. I was doing better with caging Her by the time you met me—which isn't saying a lot, I know—but before that, I was with Mercury. He wanted to take pictures because he's a big voyeur. He had the idea to take pics of me changing and then of her. I let him, and it led to where you'd think it would because I was naked. She was prowling, he was frisky, and I bit him. I didn't *intend* for it to be a skin piercing bite —because Mercury doesn't do that even with Lily—but I slipped. Lily was mad because she thought I'd violated her lines."

He blinks at me, and I look down, shrugging in embarrassment. "I was really upset about it. I didn't say anything because Lily, um, never talked about it again. I was in a fragile place because of other things, so the reaction hit me hard. Mercury hardly comes around anymore. I didn't tell them how much that hurt, and it was a small thing that got bigger and bigger. I even had his tattoo removed because it made me sad and ashamed. That, combined with all the other stuff, made me decide that I had to figure out what to do about her. So, I came to find you. It's a big secret that I don't talk about. It actually still hurts to talk about it."

"I don't see the embarrassment here, pet. You didn't have control and he provoked the beast. There's a little blame in both columns."

"You wouldn't see it, because it's a slice of Deli insanity. It really upset me when Mercury disappeared. He was a playmate, but also a friend. I felt like I screwed up big time, but I couldn't say anything to resolve it. I sort of maybe expected them to notice that I wasn't looking for him. Once I let it go for so long, it got ridiculous."

"Sort of like the thing with Rhea and me that I didn't know about."

"Yeah, sort of. I never told Sari, and she's dying to fix it. If Rhea tells her to get back in with her, I'll never hear the end of it. I was unintentionally passive aggressive."

"I'm at a loss when people don't say what's on their minds. I live at the other end of the spectrum."

I turn my body gently and look at the house behind us, an inscrutable expression on my face. The full moon highlights my bloody clothes and makes the open wound under my arm visible. It glistens with six inches of white that can only be exposed rib.

Finally, I turn back to her and lapse into silence. I'm not sure where to go from here, especially with her still in the fucking shroud.

"Let me help you, please. You're hurt." She pokes one hand out as if reaching for me.

"No." She shrinks back in—almost tighter—and I curse myself. "N-not yet."

Nodding silently, she gnaws on her lips.

I pause. "Unless I pass out, then you can keep me alive. I'm still bleeding; I can feel it."

She eyes me from above the line of the blanket again as if assessing the wounds she can see in severity and figuring out how much time before something turns threatening.

"That's it, then? All our cards are finally on the table?"

She keeps watching me, then murmurs, "Yes."

"If I kick it, you can keep me alive—no more, no less. Talia will know and send Damien to get me." I give her a serious look, knowing that she's past focusing on anything but the blood now.

"Okay." Her eyes darken and she shrinks smaller yet again.

"Well, short of telling you Company stuff or giving you a Taurus hit list, I'm remarkably tame. One will get you killed, the other gets you disgusted with me, so we won't go there. Are you sure I haven't bored you in the sack? It's not one of those 'hiding the truth to spare feelings' gigs, is it?"

Shaking her head emphatically—a feat for someone who's practically in a burka—she murmurs, "No."

"You still love me, even with all this stuff in my head and heart?" I look down at my bruised, broken, and bloody self.

"Yes. Very much."

"You won't forget we've mated or not want to claim me as a mate, will you?"

"I've wanted everyone to know for a while. I love you and I would have shouted it to everyone if it hadn't been for worrying about hurting Rhea. I'm not worried about that now. And I could never forget I mated with you, baby. I can feel you inside me all the time. I've never done some of the things we do before."

"I appreciate the clarification, Sandwich. By the way, don't you even think about repudiating me—ever. We're mated; we're going to sodding stay mated."

"It never crossed my mind. I'm not on the boat with that, even for the exes."

"I don't like it because of the damage it can do to the split parties. I'm of the mind that if a relationship ends—even if it's badly—there should be an effort to look fondly on the good times. But—and there's a big but—sometimes that's impossible because of the behavior of both parties. You do what you need to do when you need to do it, love. I won't judge you." I lean back against the chair, the blood loss getting to me. "You're sure you love me? You're positive?"

"Yes."

"Hypothetically, if I had to hide out from the Company squads, you wouldn't mind me using your basement?"

"I might even be convinced to bring you food if you asked nicely."

"That's the nurturing part of you. So, if I keep you, you won't purposely hurt me, and I'll promise not to go off half-cocked without getting your side of things."

"I would do everything in my power to keep from hurting you again."

"I hope so, because this twice in two days shit is for the more foul birds." I stand, still shaky and my mind is getting fuzzy. "Give me your hand. Be careful— you can bring the blanket." She stands, letting the blanket loose for the first time in what seems like hours. I hold her hand delicately and look into her eyes. "I love you. I forgive you and I hope you forgive me. I have had my issues resolved in what I believe to be an honest and sincerely repentant manner. I endeavored to treat you with the love and respect I feel for you. If you agree to these points, we can go from here."

Swallowing hard, she looks at her hand, not at me. "I forgive you. I love you. I never want to lose you."

I squeeze her fingers tentatively and hold my breath long enough to bend to her lips and brush them with mine. "I love you, mate." I apparate us to the bedroom, but it drains my reserve and I stumble. "I have to give Theodora credit. She does excellent work." The door is fixed, the blood is gone, and the glass vase from yesterday has been replaced.

"She does, but I think you need to sit down."

"I feel like I need to die, but at least I cleared the air between us." I struggle to breathe and finally give in. "Can you fix me?"

"I can." She walks me to the bed slowly, then climbs on, finally shed of that damned blanket. "You gotta drink, though. No pretty popping closed stuff for this. Can you do it without going too far?"

"Shit, I think I punctured a sodding lung. You mean without draining you?"

"At least, without killing me."

"I'll hear your heart; I won't kill you." I look at her seriously, wanting her to know I mean it.

She nods, flicking out her claws and slicing my disgusting clothes off first. The peeling opens more wounds, but it has to happen, so I bite down so I don't scream.

"Sod a dog. I did a number on myself this time." Paling visibly, she blinks away tears, and it makes my heart hurt. "Shh, baby. It's okay. You're going to fix me right up. It's not your fault."

Her jaw clenches and I know she doesn't believe me, but she keeps studying me as I get settled. "What would be easiest for you to...? Where do you want to...?"

"Feed?" I ask, my eyes teasing her gently. She's being so cautious and so quiet. It's unnerving. I worry, but I can't focus on it enough to suss out what's wrong.

"Yes."

I look up at her mating wound wistfully, preferring the re-affirmation there, but I'm not sure I can maneuver that way. My eyes cut back to hers. "I know I'm all crumpled, baby. I know things have been hard, but I love you. I want you anywhere I can get you."

Smiling a little, she nods. "I mean, what would be most comfy? You are definitely crumpled and I don't want to make it worse."

The blood loss pulls at my mind, and I sigh. "Your wrist might be easiest on us both."

Lying on her side, she holds out her wrist and I notice another ugly set of healed, re-healed, and fresh scars that I haven't seen before. I didn't notice those in the past. I can't help but wonder where they came from and why she doesn't let them heal.

She's told me that scars only stay when she consciously forces them to. I haven't asked about the large one on her sternum, nor the ones on her ankle or lower tummy. Those two look to be healed tattoos, though. There are a few near her ribs that might be from the time she speared herself. Her neck and shoulders are, as expected, multiply marred in the most interesting way. I wonder if she manipulates how the scars look when she keeps them.

Does she have enough power for that?

Some of them worry me, but I can't keep my mind on it. It's a conversation for later, I think. I hate that I've gotten myself so far gone that I have to do this, but here we are. I kiss the spot on her wrist lightly, then bite in as gently as I can.

A soft groan escapes her lips, but she doesn't pull away. I feel the sparkling magick of her blood immediately as I drink; it tingles through me like a soothing balm. Drinking from anyone would help, but from her, it's like dipping into the Achilles pool. She tastes like a fine wine, notes of sweet and spicy with a hint of earth that must be her magick.

She's murmuring something that sounds foreign and soothing under her breath. I assume it's a spell to shore up herself or her powers. I hear her chanting, but it's a wisp— like the memory of a dream—and I let it float away. Her pulse pounds in my ears, over my tongue, and in my veins, as my entire body flushes.

I barely notice her turn her head towards a set of embedded

cabinets next to the closet. She points her free hand at them and then at the bedside table. Maybe I'm hallucinating, but a thick pillar candle appears to light itself, followed by a censer of jasmine and lavender incense. Her eyes cut to the light switch and the lights dim. After that, she seems to relax. She continues chanting and I look around groggily, not sure if I really saw that or not.

Suddenly, it burns inside, and I feel my internal wounds knit slowly. The pain and headiness of her blood are making my mind fuzzy, but I keep drinking, slaking the hunger that only seems to increase as I do so. *~So tired. Side effect?~*

~Yes.~ Like she just remembered it, her head tilts, and she raises a limp hand to gesture at the fridge. A glass of orange juice appears in her hand and she gulps it. *~Never done this for so long. I'm going to drop off soon.~*

My lungs burn like I've swallowed hot ash, and everything hurts. Some part of me knows that I'm healing. Another part knows I'm not done yet, so I bite down harder. Her gasp twigs my senses and I touch her heart with mine, feeling her breathing getting shallow. Her pulse jumps and I re-assess.

I can't kill her; I won't. I feel her heart inside me like I'm inside it and I focus on it. She stutters and falls next to me, and I realize that my staunchest supporter, the person willing to put up with my every whim, is unconscious. There's some healing to go, but I must stop now. I lift my head from her wrist and lick the wound closed, watching it seal. "Deli? Love?"

She doesn't move and anguish fills me. I was so bloody distracted with the magic and the wounds and her sodding scars that I wasn't paying attention. Her breathing is light and wispy, her pulse thready, and I can feel the haze in her mind as I try to get her to respond. Every inch of my body hurts, but since I'm not in danger of kicking it, I roll to my side and squeeze her hand. *~Love?~*

Exhaustion is pulling me dangerously close to slumber, but I have to try again. *~Baby, talk to me.~*

~Tired.~

I collapse next to her and pull her to me, my flesh still tingling and healing. Once I get her curled into my arms, I feel relieved. *~Thank you, baby. Now, sleep. The world will wait for you on the other side. And so will I.~*

~Love you.~

~Love you, too, heart of mine.~

The Cat Tries

DELILAHJ

They called Taurus in before I woke up this morning. He's still at HQ, I assume, because he left and I haven't heard a word since. It's nerve wracking because I know he's in trouble. After last night, he wouldn't have stayed away for anything else.

There's too much to discuss.

I couldn't just sit around while he was gone, but I didn't want to leave. I decided that it was finally time to explore. All these doors and hallways have appeared, and I haven't investigated anything but our current room.

Exploration led me to find a gorgeous extension off the back of the room filled with everything a person could want in a bathroom: Jacuzzi, huge shower with rainwater spouts, an enormous vanity, and a built-in sound system with AI controls in one of the wall cabinets. Another short walk leads to the walk-in closet that is the size of a small bedroom. It's for both of us, I suppose, since his clothes and accessories line one side. My side is awaiting my atten-tion, save for the things he's been buying me. They scare me, as his taste runs toward royally expensive and I'm certain I'll destroy it all by accident.

I'm not used to spending enough to buy a car on a coat.

The stairway I saw between the closet and our bed goes downstairs to a kitchen so state-of-the art that Leo is going to have an aneurysm. It has French doors that lead out to the patio, pool, and garden area. I didn't stay downstairs long, instead coming back up to wander down the hallway he usually enters from. That took me to a wing with a piano room, a half a dozen guest bedrooms, and quite a few empty rooms that I don't know what he's going to do with. When I re-enter our bedroom, I note a singular panel just past the bathroom that I haven't accessed.

Stepping inside, my jaw drops. I'll be damned. He saw me do this *once*.

The mystery panel leads to a full-fledged gym outfitted with not only a punching bag, mats, assorted weaponry of every type, and a sound system, but a trampoline, a full set of bars and beams, rings, wedges, a chalk station, and everything that I'd need to work on my gymnastics skills. The setup makes me wonder if he's prepping me for something. It certainly looks like I could train any skill right from home.

This might be for hunting—we enjoy a good hunt as much as we enjoy indoor sports. Having my skills up to snuff is integral in case we run into something that my basic kitty-ness can't handle.

It couldn't hurt to get started while he's gone, right?

Working off all this nervous energy will keep me from fretting until he gets home. I set the music to blast and start by working on floor exercises. Being able to use my beast powers to do more intricate flips and twists than I'd ever been able to do in the past is outstanding. I'm favoring my left arm a bit because it's not healing as fast as I'm used to. It might be because of how much he took.

Next I move to the trampoline, bouncing to the beat. I spring into the air, ready to complete a half tuck back flip, when it occurs to me that I feel like I'm forgetting something important. As I hit the straps again, it comes back to me.

"Oh, shit!" My hand flies to my mouth and I don't tuck at the right moment, causing me to skid across the trampoline on my ass. Good thing no one saw *that* graceful landing.

Snorting, I slide off the tramp and limp over to turn off the sound system. I'm sure this one is as fancy as the bathroom one, but I haven't figured out how to work it yet. Wiping off my face and neck with a towel, I look at the friction burns on my legs with a frustrated growl.

First, a shower, because I'm stinky. Then I have to get this present for Shea's birthday. In the mess of this week, I lost track of that obligation. People will call for my head if I miss one of the birthday bashes entirely.

I can do this. I made it from the chair to the bed.

It was a rough landing, but I got there. I'm magickal. I'm mated to Taurus. I can do this because he can do it. That makes sense, right? I'm going to ignore the fact that Talia didn't gain this power and that I am neither an artist nor an engineer after Rafe and Victor.

That's loser talk.

I can't believe that I'm 'abusive football coach' pep-talking myself.

Honestly, I just don't want to go home and get a car so I can go to the party. Besides, I *should* be able to do this. From here to another location is tricky, but if I didn't try risky shit, I wouldn't be me. I may not have control of the stick yet, but I'm going to learn to drive this car or die trying.

Yeah, I'm full of metaphors today.

I give it another go, thankfully remaining upright and not falling on my ass as I 'poof' into the closet. I don't think it will matter if I'm not fully decked out when I arrive because I don't plan on staying. I refuse to go home to get something the esteemed birthday boy gave me in the past. None of it is suitable for public consumption and Taurus would have a mild coronary if I wore any of it.

Tossing on leather pants and a satin halter followed by the astoundingly expensive knee-high boots and duster combo that Taurus brought me back from Milan, I take a deep breath. That bloody duster cost enough to feed a small country; I'm almost afraid to wear it. But the lambskin is soft, the bespoke cut exquisite, and the profile I cut wearing them is undeniable.

Popping myself back into the living room, I start to feel more confident about this method of travel. If I'm lucky, I won't splice myself into two pieces when I attempt this long distance. That happened once last week with a bag of licorice and it's definitely in the back of my mind as I practice.

Our bedroom only has a few areas that I have personally added: the bed, the liqueurs on the bar, and a replica of my magickal cabinet from home. I stocked it with duplicate supplies just in case. After last night, I'm sure as hell glad that I did. I apparate over to the panel that hides it and press the touch release. Reaching inside, I grab the small, brightly wrapped package I spent an hour creating.

All I have to do is drop into Shea's party, give him the gift, and pop back—easy, right?

Closing my eyes, I concentrate, hoping that this works. I still haven't gotten used to it, but I know that it means I'm going to appear in a new location soon.

Here we go...

The Cat Fails

DELILAH

Within a blink, I'm there. I look around, sighing in infinite relief. I didn't splice myself or end up on the peak of some mountain in Tibet.

Staying quiet, I look around. I want to find the droid of honor while avoiding a lot of attention. There are a lot of humans and droids, but I can scent a few clones in the crowd. For most people, it's an exercise in futility to find a droid or clone in a crowd like this.

However, with my furry super sniffer, I can smell which ones carry my scent. Beyond that, I can also smell which ones have the scent of my blood. It's still a decent list to narrow down, but it's better than nothing. Since there are bound to be fewer droids that have bitten me here, I can track Shea by looking for the smell of their fluids as well.

Skulking through the crowd carefully, I keep my head down. I grabbed a scarf to put over my hair that I'll pull off once I find him. There's a few redheads in the Rift, but none of them are as crimson as I am. My hair is like a beacon in the fog, and it draws everyone to me.

I sense some of my family here—not Rafe, damn it. I send them mental thanks for standing in for me. I don't plan to come home once Taurus gets back from his de-brief because we still have serious talking to do. That is, if he ever comes back from the de-brief.

Shit. Stop thinking that way, loser. It's fine.

I make a mental note not to watch any sports related movies for quite a while. My brain is apparently melded with a coach from the 1990s. Regardless, I can't imagine myself going home until I resolve all of our issues.

When I finally find the guest of honor, his face lights up when I pull the scarf off. Shea's not one of my mates—and never would be —but he's like a giant, fangy puppy dog. I care about him because he's a lovable, loyal, caring, considerate goof. I may protest about making an appearance, but I am glad to see that he's having a great time with his guests. He sweeps me up in a bone-crushing hug and I try not to wince.

I bandaged my arm after my shower, and I'm hoping he hasn't caused it to bleed again. Most people aren't blood drinkers, so they only know that blood has a metallic tang that smells like copper. To beings like us, every droplet from every person has a distinctive scent and taste that can change based on location or diet or a thousand other things.

Mine smells and tastes spicy, rich, flowery, earthy, and like the fields of Ireland—so I'm told. I'm hyper-aware of how many people in this room know exactly what it smells like. If a droplet forms, my anonymity is dead. I have no intention of holding court tonight. Shea doesn't notice my discomfort. He beams and sets me down.

"I didn't think you were going to make it, Peach," he pouts adorably.

Ah, yes—nicknames again.

I wish Rafe and I hadn't started that. I have so many you'd think I was listing my titles in a fantasy show on TV. Delilah,

Queen of Everything, ruler of the Maison, first of her name, the Darkness, the Night Bloom, Nancy to Sid, Juliet to Romeo, Sir Victor's Favorite Girl, Minx of the Bird, bringer of bloody deaths to delivery boys and so on.

I feel like an idiot just saying it.

Chuckling, I run a hand over his hair. "I'm only here for a brief appearance. I couldn't let your birthday go by without bringing you a prezzie."

His face gets brighter, if possible, and I wonder if he's going to bounce off the walls. Bringing the package out of my coat, I grin at him. "It is not a new couch."

The broken couch I mentioned to Taurus so long ago was with Shea. However, circumstances were a contributing factor in its death. It's a small joke, but one that I know will make him smile.

He takes the small box, tearing off the ribbon and opening the lid. Looking at the fuzzy piece of fruit in puzzlement, I giggle when he picks it up. He looks like he's not sure what to make of it. The idea took me a while to come up with and I almost deep-sixed it when I remembered seeing something similar in a story. Finally, I whipped it up, deciding it was too cool of an idea to waste.

"It's magickal. It can't go bad, so don't worry about that. When you bite into it, you'll taste and feel and see your favorite memories of us. It's full-fledged—high definition surround sound level stuff. It'll rock your world."

I grin, proud of the control it took to create. In preparation for Beltane, I've been letting my magick off the leash, little by little. Doing projects like this, weaving into healing, and practicing apparition are my way of dusting off the cobwebs.

Shea's eyes widen and he looks at the peach as if he's contemplating something.

Holding a finger, I caution him before he takes a chunk out here and now. "Hold the wagon there, little doggy, because that sucker is potent. Don't eat more than a bite at a time or you'll fry your circuits. I made it to last for a long time."

I watch him roll it around in his fingers nervously. Shea is never silent like this and his reticence is making me think that he doesn't like it. That's what I get for sharing something deeply personal like my magick—rejection.

It never fails.

"I hope you like it. It wasn't easy to make because I've never done anything like it before. The ingredients were difficult to find. Hopefully, it makes up for not being able to be here for long. I have town issues that I need to take care of." He plays with the soft, ripe fruit and my fingers fiddle with the hem of my duster, waiting for some kind of reaction.

He gives me a tiny smile and tucks it back in the box, sitting it on a table nearby. "I love it, Peach. You did a right nice thing for me."

Frowning, I tilt my head. I was not expecting this kind of reaction from Shea. Usually he's bouncing around like a puppy on crack when he gets a gift. *What did I do wrong?* "I'm glad you like it. Is your party going well?"

He nods, then looks over at the kitchen. "It is, pet. I think I'm wanted in the kitchen, though, so I'll see you around later?"

I blink. *Well, okay then.* "Um, yeah, that's fine. I'll see you later."

Leaning up, he pecks my cheek, picking up the box. He gives me another tiny smile and walks towards the kitchen.

What the actual fuck?

I sigh, pinching the bridge of my nose as I feel the start of a migraine. I am not in the mood for *more* drama. Why is everyone acting like every damned thing I do is wrong?

Feeling forlorn, I close my eyes. The whoosh of air hits me and I cross my fingers that I'll get myself back in one piece. I can't stand to be here for another second.

When I apparate in our bedroom, I sigh in relief. Success number two feels like a bigger victory than the first, and despite my headache, I pump my fist with pride.

Deli for the win, fuck yeah.

Walking to the closet, I peel off the clothes, making certain to hang the duster carefully. I can't treat a five-figure gift like a thrift store tank top. Grabbing one of Taurus' shirts, I head for the bar. I snag a highball of scotch and some fruit from the fridge before heading for the bed. I suppose Taurus has Theodora stocking this stuff. Maybe I'll suggest that Hex and Leo wouldn't mind sharing those duties, so I won't feel like a sponge. They wouldn't mind and hell, Leo would kill to get his hands on that kitchen.

I sit on the bed, pulling my Book of Shadows and the Beltane binder out of the night table. Opening my spell book to the page with the peach spell, I draw a frowny face at the top. I don't cross it out because it worked, but since it didn't make the recipient happy I won't use it again. With the binder perched on my lap, I nibble the berries and prop my bad arm on a pillow. The basic frame of my Beltane ritual is ready, so I have to get the specific wording right. Phrasing is important if you don't want to piss off a Goddess or accidentally summon the wrong thing.

Opening the gates inside of me hasn't given me a huge influx of power, but maybe that's because I'm afraid to use it in public. Doing so would add another dimension to what people expect from me. Between a new mate, the heat, and the Beast, a slow trickle is probably the best idea.

I know there's more in my well because I felt it grow inside since I moved to the Rift. Being ready for that stored power to hit me that night is paramount. I manage to get a few more minutes of actual work done when I feel a disruption in the aura around me. Glancing at the doorway, I see him leaning against the frame.

"Are you speaking to me, pet?"

"Hi, baby." The exhaustion from yesterday, the hurt from the rejection at the party, and the dull ache in my arm are making me drag. There's no way he hasn't noticed it.

His expression is relieved when I answer. I think he truly believed that I wouldn't speak to him. Crossing the room, he sits on the bed carefully. "Hello, my heart."

"How was your day?" I ask, needing to hear what happened with the Company before I can relax. I reach over and run my fingers through his hair with my good arm, favoring the achy one.

"Total shit without you. Is that blunt enough?" He looks at me and frowns. "What's wrong?"

"I'm tired. Someone irritated me and I had to deal with community stuff—both interpersonal and town based." I didn't need to tell him about the emails from concerned members pointing out yet another nasty blog post from that damned bar. I just want to firebomb it into the ground and be rid of the fucking place.

"That's annoying right enough, but I mean what's wrong with your arm?"

"It's taking its sweet time healing. I'm sure it's because we drank so much last night. It'll be fine."

"I hurt you?" he whispers, looking worried.

"Don't worry. It will be fine soon, I promise. It doesn't hurt." That's a lie. It aches when I use it and I'm fairly sure that I may have to do some extra work to fix it. I haven't had the time or inclination to work on it yet.

"You should have let me go."

"Never."

He reaches up and touches his bite mark. "Can I help with the town shit? Maybe alleviate a little of your burden so you can focus on healing?"

"Short of breaking the 'no ripping the spine out of community members' rule, I don't think so," I grumble petulantly. I wouldn't mind if he dismembered a few folks at this point, but as he's said from the beginning, it would cause more problems than it would fix.

Standing, he kicks off his shoes. He climbs onto the bed, sitting next to me and holding out his arms. "Want me to be the handsome support structure you need instead?"

I chuckle. "I'm trying to be a bigger person. That's very difficult when the issue is with someone you despise."

~You're a better person than I am, love. But then, we both know that.~

"Thanks, baby," I murmur. For a second, I ponder why Shea doesn't seem to share that opinion, and I can't work out why. I shake my head to clear it. Shea is an issue for another time; I have bigger fish to fry.

He tugs me into his arms and I sigh, starting to relax a little. "That's what I'm here for." His eyes fall on the binder and my book, light dawning. "I can grab a book or go to the gym if you have things you need to work on, pet."

Moving the Beltane stuff aside, I shake my head. "No way. I'm not looking at that phone or my notes anymore today. I want to spend time with you."

He exhales in contentment and grins, squeezing me tightly. "Thank fuck, because that was me being all noble. Feel free to praise my selflessness anytime. I am, after all, your 'hunka burning clone'."

"You are at that," I chuckle, leaning into his chest.

"So, you'll say it again for me?" he asks, looking hopeful.

"Nope."

His face falls and I smile, feeling it radiate from my face to my heart for the first time in hours. "You didn't think it'd be that easy, did you?"

"No." He looks away, his expression crestfallen.

I turn his face back to mine, stroking my fingers over his jaw. Don't ask me why I finally gave it up in the first place; I don't know. Maybe it was because of the fear of losing him to the Company's dungeon because of his stupid killing spree. "Come here. I was only kidding. If you want me to call you my 'hunka burning clone' again, I will."

"Yes, please."

I tap his nose. "You are my hunka burning clone and I love you." He tackles me and I gasp, my limbs flying akimbo. "*Warning*!"

~I'm all the warning you get, heart of mine~

I sigh, unable to do anything else until we discuss the six hundred pound whale in the room. "Tell me what happened at the hearing. I can't focus on anything else until I know what those asshats decided."

"I'm not being recalled, if that's what you're wondering. The debrief was a fucking disaster. I had to sit there and get my ass roasted for hours. I have to teach the misbehaved rookies— including that fuckwit Cob—knitting in The Inferno for six months."

My hand flies to cover my mouth. I try not to giggle, but it spills out and I hoot in laughter. "What's the Inferno?"

Pouting, he rolls his eyes at me. "The Inferno is the punishment/retraining program for naughty agents-in- training. Someone thought they were cheeky when they named it." He looks offended as I keep giggling. "Oi. It's better than hiding out in our basement."

I nod, tears running down my cheeks. "Oh, yes. But knitting? You. Hate. Knitting."

Looking supremely ruffled, he crosses his arms over his chest. "I bloody do, but it's punishment, Sandwich. I'm not supposed to like it."

Wiping my eyes, I feel relief coursing through me along with the amusement. All I can focus on at the moment is the image of him teaching a room full of 'bad apple' clones how to knit one and purl two.

It fucking slays me.

"It beats being re-called or sent to Guatemala, woman." Grumbling, he buries his face in my hair and lets me work the sniggers out of my system.

"It'll help you prepare for when you're pining for me," I offer, still trying to breathe after my fit of giggles.

"You're one step away, hussy—one step."

I nip my mark on his neck, drawing blood. "That's where I like to be."

"Warning, Minx," he growls as his arms tighten around me and his chest rumbles.

Chuckling throatily, I suck on the minor wound. "I'm all the warning you get."

"I knew that was going to bite me on the ass."

I smile. We're going to be okay, and I need to find a flowery knitting basket—pronto.

The Cat And The Goddess Have A Chat

I suck in a nervous breath, feeling like I'm intruding as I knock on the door. The bird said that she was here avoiding the simpletons who seem to make her miserable. Hiking up the burden of the large cloisonné vase full of wildly colored tropical flowers, I press the doorbell again and wait.

Deli opens the door a crack, looking completely flummoxed. I wonder if she knew that there was a doorbell. "Um. Hi?"

My lips curve up as I take in her appearance. She's much less decked out than she is in public. I can empathize with that as I'm not the type to be perfectly coiffed at home, either.

Messy suits her as well as fashionista; Taurus was right.

When the cat isn't dressed to kill and vamping it up, she resembles an adorable college kid. She's wearing one of his silks, tied at the waist with a pair of scandalously low-slung cutoffs. Sporting long, curly crimson pigtails and knee-high socks with Van Gogh's 'Starry Night' on them, she looks approachable and comfy.

"Hi. So, um, Taurus said it would be okay if I stopped by. I realize you weren't expecting a visitor, but..."

She blinks, studying the vase of flowers in my hands curiously.

"It's okay; come on in. I look terrible, but that's because I wasn't expecting anyone but the Big Bad."

Opening the door, she reveals a staircase. I follow her up, looking around. The room she enters screams 'Taurus', but it also has an otherworldly aura that's all her. The decor is elegant and expensive, yet there are traces of the fierce feline everywhere. Colorful, wild, eccentric, ethereal clothes, shoes, and items are strewn carelessly throughout the space. There's a cabinet that exudes power I can't identify, a bar with Taurus' scotch but also a selection of wines, liquors and liqueurs that have to be hers, a large furry blanket that seems to be mov—

What the fuck?!

A goddamned white tiger struts over to a crystal water bowl. Holy fucking shit biscuits, it's walking around like it owns the place. Deli holds her hands out for the vase and I hand it to her, stunned mute as I continue watching the tiger trotting around. She doesn't even pay the sedan sized animal a bit of attention as she looks at me with a warm smile.

"You're welcome to visit." She fusses with the vase as she settles it on the mantle and then flicks her hand in the air distractedly. The light classical music that was playing in the background shuts off and the candles strewn about the room suddenly snuff out.

Taurus also did not mention that she's not just a feline shifter, but a witch or something. *Isn't that interesting? I love being unprepared.* "I only stopped by for a moment, really. I don't plan on intruding. I asked him to not be here so he's probably out back, pacing a hole in your patio."

Her laugh is soft and husky, her big blue eyes dancing with amusement. She practically melts into a huge armchair, gesturing for me to have a seat nearby. "That sounds about right."

"Home warming gift," I say, tilting my head at the flowers.

I'm not sure where to go with this, because all the surprises are throwing off my game. I touch the dagger strapped on my thigh nervously, unsure what I'll do if she lobs any other additional information at me.

"Don't be nervous. They're beautiful because they feel like me." The tiger pads over and sits by her legs, making Taurus' new mate look like a new world version of an ancient queen.

Is she empathic, too? Jesus, Taurus, leave anything else out? Jackass.

"Well, we haven't been *formally* introduced, but I have met you once or twice."

"Thank you, Talia—truly." She studies me for a moment and frowns. "I'm not trying to make you uncomfortable. Did the bird leave out a few pertinent details?"

I nod, sighing. "A few would be putting it kindly. I should have come sooner, then I wouldn't be so far behind."

"No worries. Rafe hasn't been here, either. He's introspective lately." Her brow furrows. I see the concern for her mate written on her face plain as day. She's an open book, and I don't know if that's because she trusts me, Taurus, or a little of both.

"I understand. Bad blood going on." My expression is stormy as I think about Rhea. "It's been difficult for all of us. That's not why I'm here, though."

She sighs. "I agree; it's been sucky."

A wine glass appears in her hand and then one on the table in front of me. They contain what smells like a nice cabernet. I can't tell if that's her magick or a piece of Taurus that fueled that little trick. He might be right to keep her from the powers that be. Our employers would be *very interested* in her skill set and I'm not sure it would be a good thing.

"There's a lot of Taurus in this room—wood paneling, expensive taste, disappearing fixtures—but there's an awful lot of you, too."

"I'm infectious, I'll admit. He's been doing the work—or paying for it—but I like to leave my mark on a space." Her eyes dance and I look over at the infamous bed, chuckling.

It's not at all Taurus' normal style, but it fits perfectly with my picture of him when he's with her. "Well, he *is* Taurus. He enjoys having his conveniences."

"Truer words, dear. I added some things I frequently need as well. Since I tend to leave a bit of a mess, I have Hex sneak in occasionally to do cleaning while we're gone. I've been spoiled by his major domo routine at my house, I'm afraid."

I look at her seriously, this glimpse of her personality making me see why he's so enchanted. She's almost the polar opposite of me: erratic, soft, emoting from every pore, and above all, head over heels for my larger-than-life mate. "He loves you very much."

"I love him, too," she smiles widely, her face lighting up. "I'm so very glad to have him."

I believe her. She's oozing with happiness and I feel the enormity of her emotions. I smile warmly, happy for them both. "I can tell because you glow. Er, sorry, I'm not purposely trying to read you, but it's radiating off you."

She laughs again. "I have that problem a lot. Everything about me is kind of huge. Not intentionally, it just is."

"I understand that." I tilt my head, watching her knead her toes into the tiger's back.

The damned thing is purring! She's like a fucking fairy tale, I swear.

"My primary reason for stopping by is to tell you that I'm glad that he found you. I'm equally glad that you found him. I think you're good for him—in more ways than I can tell you. He might, if you ask, because he's painfully honest about everything."

Another broad beam and the room fills with a warmth that is, as she said, infectious. "He's definitely good for me. I'm sure he'd love to list the ways for both of us if we'd let him."

"I also wanted to ask you about something."

Her head tilts as if she's pondering. "Shoot."

"I'm not one to mince words. Despite our long history of despising one another, Sari has approached me several times while

Taurus has been occupied with you. I figured if he could extend a branch, I could try, so I humored her. However, lately, Wilde has been along for the ride and he's posed a question."

She jumps to attention as if I shot her—no longer lounging in the chair but straight as a steel bar. The surrounding air is filled with tension and... fear? I watch her struggle with herself, trying to figure out how to mask the discomfort that's taking her over. "He has?"

I sigh. "Am I the only one feeling uncomfortable?"

"Um, period, or just here?" She fidgets, picking at her nails. The tiger sits up immediately, putting its head on her knee as if trying to ground her.

"Maybe a little of both. I feel like I invaded your space, but also, the question made you anxious."

"It's bound to feel weird because we don't know one another well. I don't mind you here, and I'm sure it will be easier with time." Licking her lips, she draws in a slow breath. Everything in her body looks like it's ready to explode. Her expression is flickering like she can't get control of her emotions. "What-what did he ask you, Talia?"

"He asked if he could court me."

The air in the room gets heavier and I feel a twinge of anger— white hot and raging—join the fear. A wave of emotions rolling off her nearly chokes me, and I watch as the candles flicker and the glass in her hand wavers. Something is very off with her and Wilde. I don't know what it is, but for someone who is used to him seeing other people, this response is off the charts.

"He did, did he? Well, uh, if you want to, you can, but..." she stops, clearly searching for the right words. "There's a lot going on since Rhea. Her betrayal is affecting all of us in different ways." She shifts uncomfortably, and the tiger nudges her hand, getting her attention again.

I should change the topic before she gets upset. "I appreciate the welcome, Deli. The two of you are so wrapped up in each other right now that it doesn't breed a lot of cocktail parties for the family. But when it's time, I'd love to get together more often." I smile, trying to bring us back to the light again before Taurus comes barging in to kill me.

"That's true. However, I don't mind the family dropping in, even if Mr. Grumpy Pants does. He needs to socialize more."

"He's been hurt. It will get better for him eventually."

"Ain't that the truth. It wasn't a pleasant situation to come back to this world and get stuck in the middle of this shit. I hate that for him."

"One reason I haven't come over sooner is that I didn't want what you've been told about me to affect your budding relationship with Taurus. And by budding, I mean full fricking bloom." I give her a teasing smile and I feel the tension seep out of her. She's relaxed now that Sari and Wilde are no longer being discussed.

"I'd like to say it isn't always this insane, but that would only be partly true. I'll tell you the same thing I tell him; I form my own opinions. I give everyone a chance until I can't, much like our ex-family members."

"You haven't spoken to Rhea since...?"

"No. She is not willing to discuss her destructive behavior and I am no longer willing to be a player in her drama. Rafe was right to tell them to fuck off."

"She hasn't tried to contact me—only Taurus."

"She won't. Rhea doesn't do confrontation and you'll confront her. Thus, she hides."

"Oh, damn it, Deli. I didn't want to talk about her. I came to welcome you to my family and check out the pad."

"It's easy to get caught up in her theater. That's why I had to remove myself."

I feel the sizzle of her anger at our former friend. She's serious. "I came to tell you how much you mean to him."

"Well, I'm crazy about him, so we're even."

"I also want you to know something—and you've probably

already figured it out—but the other night was hard. Taurus made a promise to you that he will never leave you. No matter how much you hurt him, he'll stay as long as you're honest. When he goes off like he did last night, you shouldn't worry that he's leaving you."

She nods, but I think she's still unsure. More people than just Rhea have hurt this woman, and there's something she's hiding. "I'll admit, the Company meeting was messy, but I dealt with it. Taurus has to teach a couple months of knitting classes—which he will loathe—but he won't go away."

Her eyes shine with humor, but her expression is serious. "I'm glad. He worried me."

"I'm still going to kick his ass for blocking me out."

"I didn't know he blocked you. I thought it was only me."

"He hasn't been able to block me for over a year—and he's tried."

"Huh. Odd that he could."

"I assumed it was the level of will involved." I shrug and she tilts her head, looking interested so I expound. "Ever try to do something that you don't really want to do? You struggle, right? Maybe the reason you can't, despite your effort, is your lack of desire to do it."

Again, her nod doesn't match her expression. She's got a funny way of agreeing with things she doesn't believe. Perhaps she doesn't have a fully formed thought to share or perhaps she's used to having to agree with everything everyone says to keep them happy. "When he's tried before, some crumb of him didn't really want to, so he couldn't. We fight a lot, so it's not like he hasn't had plenty of chances."

"Gee, I can't imagine that. He's so tranquil," she mutters and I laugh.

"It's the good kind of fight—no gut wrenching, just bleeding." I wink and touch my dagger again. "Anyway, I wasn't thrilled when I couldn't reach him. But even then, sweets, I didn't worry that he wasn't going to be mine after. You did."

Her hair cascades around her even with the ponytails. "It's new and it's been hard. I was raw and I didn't know what to think. He ran, I got overloaded, and I didn't know what to do because I knew it was my fault. My excuse—though true—sounded lame. I worried that he'd duck out of sight because he's mentioned doing it several times lately. We've been betrayed a lot."

There's more to it than that and I wonder, not for the first time today, if she's got deeper darks than Taurus knows about. He knows all my uglies from the past, but I'm not sure she's ready to release her demons yet. "He has, but that's not what you did. Hurt isn't the same as betrayal. He may run when he's hurt, but he'll always come back. That's why I'm here; I want to reassure you of that. I thought if I did, it might make you feel better. What I should have considered is that being with him makes you feel better, so this is kind of superfluous."

She gives me a small smile as if she wants to say something but has decided against it. "I appreciate it, though. It does clarify things."

"Okay, I also wanted to meet the woman who totally stole his heart."

That earns me a blush, an adorably wrinkled nose, and the cutest response I've seen anyone ever have to Taurus. Yeah, I see what's got his head spinning. "He loves you Deli. Enjoy him. Love him. We'll talk again, I'm sure."

"We will."

Trying to make her feel less uneasy, I murmur, "I'm, um, not good with letting people inside, but I'd like to be friends one day."

Her smile is bright. "I'd like that. Take all the time you need."

"I'm glad I stopped by. If you reach out, you can find him. He's ready to get back to you and he's quite irritated that I'm still here. Expect a sulky clone in need of a smooch when he gets here."

"Uh-oh. Pouty Taurus alert," she giggles.

"He's yelling at me mentally—such a potty mouth." I smile and stand. "Deli, it was nice to finally meet you."

"Thank you again for the flowers. It was nice meeting you. Come back anytime, no matter what His Grouchyness says."

I snicker and nod, heading to the door with a wave. Sending a go-ahead message to my impatient mate, I smile to myself as I head for my car. She's an interesting feline, that's for sure.

Taurus and I are in for a hell of a ride.

The Cat And The Bird Decide To Take A Leap

DELILAH

Sitting on the comforter in our bedroom, I wiggle my toes as I wait for him. I put this conversation off as long as I could because I expect him to laugh his ass off. Who wouldn't? It's ridiculous, even if you ask me.

Why am I telling him now?

Taurus is the only person I've been spending time with since we mated, and it's unlikely that we'll keep our hands off one another tonight. The drama the other night made me forget, but before we get frisky again, I need to tell him. Unfortunately, that means that we face an embarrassing problem that no one else in the Rift has to worry about: birth control.

The *Universe is laughing at me.*

Biting my thumbnail nervously, I give up on watching the clock and jump off the bed. I head to the bar and pour myself a hefty draught of his Macallan. Once I'm sitting on the bed again, I sip at it slowly. I'm not sure why my nerves are so jangled. He's not going to drop off the face of the Earth; he's my mate and he'd never leave me—even Talia said that.

Why am I shaking like a leaf?

That's a good question, but I don't have a chance to ponder it as he walks in. He grins broadly as he dives onto the bed headfirst to bury his face between my breasts. This is not conducive to a serious conversation. I run my fingers through his platinum locks fondly. Smiling down at him, I sigh when the contact calms me considerably. "Is that your face in my rack or are you happy to see me?"

He chuckles and undoes the few buttons I fastened, growling softly as he nuzzles the warm skin. "I can think of a few things I'd be happy to see." He mumbles the sentence as his mouth drifts over me, sending a wave of warmth through my veins. The attention kick starts the rollercoaster of lust, making my skin heat and veins pulse with fire.

Tugging him upwards, I kiss him hungrily. Our bodies press together and I rumble in pleasure. He melts over me like a mink stole, making my brain misfire as the Beast takes over with a quick ferocity. All thoughts of serious conversation are completely erased because all I can feel, see, taste, touch, and smell is him. The drive to mate and to mark and rip into what's mine is thrumming in every cell in my body. His clothes disappear and before long, I'm lapping tiny droplets from the scrape I've opened on his shoulder.

He lifts my thighs to drape over his hips and something clicks. I fight through the fog of desire and rasp, "Fuck." Trying desperately to clear it enough to have a discussion, I clamp my thighs on his hips. It's a struggle, but I work to maintain enough control that I can stop.

"That's the plan," he replies, his fangs grazing the scars on my neck.

That makes a hard shiver race down my spine and for a second, I'm lost again. Teeth send me off the deep end even without the biological imperative I'm presently operating under. His hips swivel against mine, and he realigns. Groaning, I suck in a deep breath and give him a shove, rolling us over so I can settle on his thighs. He gives me a puzzled look as I rest my forearms on his chest.

"Is something wrong, love?" he asks. He shakes off the ridges as his golden eyes blink up at me in confusion.

"Not wrong, per se," I reply, suddenly uncomfortable again.

"Per se?" He arches a brow. "Isn't that a way of saying something is wrong depending on how you look at it?"

"It's not necessarily wrong." I wrinkle my nose and bury my face in his chest as the flush creeps up my neck.

"Bollocks. The minx doesn't burrow like a bunny if nothing is wrong," he snorts, tipping my chin up.

I stick my tongue out at him. "Okay, fine. There might be this small thing. It was kind of unexpected..."

"Small? Unexpected? What in the bloody hell is going on, Sandwich?" His brows crease as he gives me a worried look.

Sighing, I mumble, "I got a call from the lab today."

He pushes up on his elbows, staring at me. "And?"

"It's—I'm..." I wrinkle my nose again, suddenly unable to vocalize anything. "Um, well, you see..."

"Spit it out, minx," he growls, the edge in his voice softened by his hand stroking over my hair.

"I'm trying." I pout, brow crinkling up. "This is embarrassing."

"Kitty, I highly doubt there's anything left to be embarrassed between us."

My eyes narrow and I huff, "You're going to laugh."

Pulling a somber face, he shakes his head. "I promise that I won't."

I sigh heavily and look away as I mumble, "I'm kind of—I'm in heat." He bursts out laughing, flopping onto the bed again as his eyes dance with mirth. I glare, thumping his chest with a fist, but it doesn't deter his amusement. "Oh, fine. It gets worse, but I'm *not going to tell you*."

Sobering instantly, he looks apologetic. "I'm sorry, love. You have to admit that it's bloody funny. Tell me what else he said. Please?" He leans forward and gnaws on my neck.

My eyes roll back as the sensation shoots through me. "You. Are. A. Cheater."

He grins wickedly. "Always, baby. Now, fill me in so we can get with the sweaty nakeds."

"That's the problem."

His eyes blink rapidly, and he tilts his head, looking puzzled. "Nakeds are a problem?"

I nod, feeling humiliated. "The heat—it makes me...well..." I lose my courage as I flush bright red. *~Fertile, ~* I mumble the last word into his head as I bury my face in his shoulder.

~You're what?~

~You heard me.~

The room is silent for long, ponderous moments and I fidget, squirming a little in my discomfort with the situation. His arms tighten around me to keep me from wriggling away. The bastard knows me too well for sure. Confinement only exacerbates my embarrassment and I growl in impatience.

~Quit your wriggling woman.~

~No.~ I reply stubbornly.

~Yes. I'm thinking.~

I huff, laying my head back down. *~There's nothing to think about. I have to get shots. We'll use other stuff until we're certain those work on me.~*

He snorts. *~Other stuff? Christ.~*

~Yes, other stuff. ~ I snap, the tension in me finally breaking the surface. *~Condoms—you're going to have to wear them.~*

Lifting his head, he groans. *~Bloody hell.~*

~It's not like I did this on purpose. I didn't ask for this stupid... whatever it is.~

He doesn't reply, only smooths his hands down my back. The silence is unnerving, and I'd be rocking at this point if I thought he'd let me move. I hadn't considered that he'd react like this—

quiet and introspective—and it's starting to freak me out. I scrape at the polish on my nails, a nervous habit that I never have been able to control.

~Stop that.~

~No. The quiet is making me nervous.~

He sits up, tugging me with him to settle me on his lap. His hand strokes over my face, and he smiles gently. "There's nothing to be nervous about, love."

"There is when you don't talk after I made a big announcement."

Eyes dancing, he tucks a hair behind my ear and chuckles softly. "You're cute when you babble, kitty."

I wrinkle my nose at him. What's with this sudden change in behavior? Quiet and reserved to soft and teasing—what is he, manic? "Why were you so quiet then?"

"I'm thinking about how much I love you."

I smile wryly and rub my nose on his. "I love you, too, baby, but I sincerely doubt it took that much thought."

He gives me a sheepish look and shrugs, "I doubt you'd be interested in what I was pondering."

Rolling my eyes at him, I give him a stern glance. "I'm interested. Why wouldn't I be?"

"You probably aren't so-"

"Just say it, you big bird!" I screech, crossing my arms over my chest and giving him an impatient expression.

He glares and growls, "I'm trying to ask you to marry me and have my bloody kid, so I was figuring out the right way to ask, thanks ever so."

I gape at him. The only thing I can think of to say is, "Baby, you eat kids."

"I wouldn't eat the nipper. Probably," he says, his eyes twinkling with amusement. I must look like someone hit me in the face with a brick because he chuckles. "I'd have its mum for that, wouldn't I?"

Is he serious? He can't be.

I shrug, unsure how to deal with this. "You sample from the dessert cart enough for that to be true."

He flips us over and pins me, kissing my nose. "You are a pain in my nicely rounded and tight ass. I love you with everything I have inside me."

"I love you, even if you are an ass," I reply, pinching my favorite part off his anatomy.

"Marry me. Have my rug cat." He laughs softly when my expression returns to gob smacked.

"Quit making fun of me."

"I'm serious, but like I said—I knew you wouldn't be interested, so don't worry about it."

I blink again, my brain frantically trying to process what I'm hearing. "You-you're serious?"

"Okay, the married part might be redundant, all things considered. A ceremony might be nice, though."

I soften and run my knuckle over his cheek. "Yeah, it might." Warmth spreads through me and I feel everything in me go squish.

Shrugging self-consciously, he mumbles, "Having a little you running around now and again wouldn't be so bad, I suppose. It takes a while to grow one of those, so it's not like a decision has to get made right away."

My finger traces around his lips. "You'd really want to donate baby batter to me, baby?"

His eyebrows arch and he grins wickedly. "Depends on the method of donation, baby."

"The usual one, of course."

"You sound like you don't hate the idea."

Shrugging a bit, I scrunch. "I don't hate it."

He nods. "But you're not crazy about it—I understand."

I wrinkle my nose and shake my head. "No, I didn't say that." Biting my lip, I shrug one shoulder up self-consciously, mumbling,

"I kind of like it, but I was... making sure you wanted to before I said anything."

His eyes are gentle and his smile is tender as he traces the lines of my face then leans down to kiss me. I feel him open up to me, his heart connecting to mine in a way that melts me.

~I'm sure, ~ he breathes.

It sinks in as everything clicks inside. Sucking in a deep breath, I smile crookedly. *~I guess I'm going to get really round.~*

His face lights up, the smile just about breaking his face. *~Are you sure, baby? You're not doing this because I've got a burr up my butt? ~*

I nod slowly. *~I'm sure. Very sure. ~*

He kisses me deeply and I sigh, feeling his heart soar as we connect. *~I love you, mate. ~*

~I love you, too, baby. ~ I rub my nose along his jaw, unable to keep a huge grin from spreading across my face.

He laughs and rubs his hand over my tummy. "We're going to have a finger Sandwich."

I giggle, ruffling his hair affectionately. "Silly clone."

"I promise I won't eat it. Well, unless it irritates me." His eyes twinkle and I swat him.

"I know you'll be a wonderful dad. I'm going to be all roly poly and huge."

Grinning wickedly, he whispers, "That should get interesting, what with the stompy."

I stick my tongue out, glaring. "I'll be all jiggly, too."

"You'll be beautiful," he says, touching his heart to mine. His expression grows devilish as he puffs up. "I'll be the manly man, handing out cigars while you sweat out the pain."

Gaze narrowed, I send a picture of him with cigars stuffed in interesting places as he hobbles about on bloodied stumps. Snorting, he counters with a picture of him with me through it all, fingers cracking as I squeeze his hand during contractions.

"Better?"

Nodding, I lean up to kiss his chin. Suddenly, something occurs to me and I giggle. "Taurus is your daddy."

He groans and rolls his eyes. Chuckling, he rubs his hand over my tummy absently. "I'm still reeling."

I trace my fingers over his chest and nod. "Oh, yeah. It's not a bad thing, though."

"Other end of the spectrum, baby," he sifts his fingers through my hair.

I kiss him gently. "Just big and wonderful."

Taurus looks shy as he whispers, "I was afraid you'd not..." He shrugs self-consciously. "I didn't want to say how much I liked the idea earlier." I tilt my head, listening as he rubs my tummy idly. "When I thought of you with a little us inside..."

"Ditto, baby."

He shrugs, covering the shyness with an evil grin. "Don't worry; I'll still shag you when you're big and round."

I smack his chest and huff. "Ass."

"Mmm, but I'm your ass, baby."

"Always," I grin up at him.

He looks down at me, waggling his brows. "I guess we should get moving on that donation, hmm? Can't make a mini-kitty without it."

Eyes sparkling happily, I nod and lean up to nip at his scars with blunt teeth. "I think the phrase you were looking for was 'now, where were we?'"

"Abso-bloody-lutely," he murmurs, lowering his body onto mine and burying his face in my neck with a rumbling growl. "We can't be wasting a second."

The Writer Formulates A Plan

"I believe that if I approach him correctly, beloved, it will work."

She looks over at me, her face full of doubt. "I don't know, honey. I know you've always fancied a go at her. Just because she let Taurus out with the kitty doesn't mean she's ready to rock."

I huff. My beloved doesn't see the brilliance of this plan, only the fallout. I am far less concerned with that aspect; once I get what I desire, our lives will be so much better.

We both wish to find a suitable way to integrate them into the ways of our community. My solution will allow My Darkness to be less closeted and afford me a suitable balance to the demon she eschews. By treating Talia as a lady as I did those that we no longer associate with, I am certain that I will achieve the perfect pitch I had before.

I am far better at persuasion than when I last attempted this.

"My Darkness has been occupied outside of her home for more than a week. I believe there is something far more serious than mere physical intimacy going on. If we are to remain connected with our family, we need to encourage more integrated socializing."

"Go for the low-hanging fruit and use it to get into the orchard. I like it." She pauses her writing for a moment to consider my words and I smile.

My beloved has a keen mind, and her understanding of human behavior is adept. I knew she would see the wisdom in my plans.

"How do you go about drawing out the recluse?" Her fingers tap on the table as she frowns. "That woman buried herself deep after the rest of the Cabal fucked off. I've tried to engage, but mostly, she comes out to bark at people and that's it. The appearance on the lawn was very unusual."

"I ask permission." I smile slyly, knowing she'll grasp that playing into Taurus' enormous ego will lead to a situation that benefits us all. "We shall both continue our efforts to draw our long-haired mate out of his hiding place while we entertain the mate of my target. Surely working both ends of the problem will lead to a meeting in the middle."

"I don't know how much the southern family will enjoy that. There's a lot of bad blood there, honey—on both sides."

Chuckling, I shake my head. "Beloved, you know that the attention span of that family is short lived. They are in our world, but not as we are, nor as my Darkness' family is. Something will distract the lovely Miss Belle and she will disappear as she is wont to do. Their usefulness is in their willingness to escape the chain and be vicious when needed. It leaves one's hands clean when needing to stoop to the lowest denominator."

Her laugh is harsh, but she nods as her eyes light up. "She'll be a good distraction if your plan goes astray."

"Absolutely. Belle may not have the lasting attention to support an actual relationship, but she can always be recruited to throw a wrench in the works. She thrives on conflict and aggression, real or perceived."

"You broached courting Talia earlier and haven't heard a peep since. What makes you think this time will be different?"

Adjusting my glasses, I smirk again. "This time, I intend on being charming, beloved. I'm told it is hard to say 'no' to."

Our glasses clink and we share another laugh, settling in to discuss the details of our plan in full.

I believe this will solve all of our problems.

The Bird Asks The Cat Her Opinion

DELILAH

"Oi, Minx."

I look up from the last bit of my planning for the ritual next week. "Hello, love. I thought you'd be in Abu Dhabi today."

"I was. I came back and got called to a confab. You'll never guess who."

The hairs on the back of my neck stand up. I knew it was too quiet today. I slipped home, checked on Rafe, and then came back here to work. "Who?"

"Sodding Wilde and the gnome," he says with a puzzled frown. "Very odd."

Now I'm concerned. What in the fuck is going on? There haven't been any big issues in the community since the bar opened, so everyone is behaving—mostly. Rafe stayed out of the studio for a whole five hours this morning. I felt like things were pretty good.

Why are the terror twins paging Taurus?

"What did they want?" I ask, hoping my voice is as steady as I think it is.

"He was all dressed up and stuff. Sari was there, too, but I think it was more to watch than anything."

Uh-oh. This sounds like a coordinated attack.

They come up with some harebrained scheme and then work together on selling it to someone. I've not only *seen* them do it before, but I've had them do it to me. It never ends well. "Wilde is always dressed up; that's nothing new. One of my favorite sports used to be messing up his clothes or ponytail to throw him off guard."

"I thought he only fucks people he loves?"

"That's the Kool-Aid we've all been drinking for years, why?"

"Why in the *bloody hell* did that git kiss my sodding hand? Is Old English making a move on me?" He paces back and forth frenetically and my eyes narrow.

Distraction. That's the first rule of passive aggressive hunting—throw them off guard.

See the above, yeah?

"Maybe I upset the balance of the universe when I said the burning clone thing. I should probably take it back." I grin, buying time to think through what those two schemers could be plotting.

"No taunting, thanks ever so," he growls, stopping in the middle of the room to glare.

"If *ever* there was something to taunt you about, this would be it, baby." I'm lighthearted on the outside, but my mind is playing scenario after scenario, trying to see the chessboard they're playing on.

He sighs. "He's on about courting Talia again. What do I say to the blighter? Should I just let him have a go at my woman?"

"Uh, not to be silly, but isn't that up to her? Sort of you, too, obviously, but Talia has to make that decision. I can tell you that it won't be just once because Wilde doesn't do one-time things. Wilde gets... involved. You and Talia will have to be prepared for what happens after that."

There is no way I can prepare them for what will happen unless I spill the beans and I'm not ready to do that yet. I can't admit what we let happen to us.

He throws his hands up and growls, "I'm looking for an opinion here, baby. Any opinion would be beneficial."

Shit. Now I'm trapped. I can't tell him any of the reasons I object without going into the ugliness of the past and present. "If Talia is looking to get involved in a relationship, then Wilde will oblige. If she's not willing to be close with him, it will be harder because Wilde doesn't do casual. He tried once with Tamara and it was a disaster. Are you willing to share her with Wilde in that way? If so, and she wants to, then she can say yes."

There. That was nice and non-committal. A small warning about expectations, reminder of whose decision it is, and I've navigated the shark-filled waters relatively safely. I'd rather shoot myself in the face with a double barrel than get into anything with them or the other two again, but I can't tell him that.

It would be less painful to get shot, that's for sure.

"I'm not unwilling to share her, but with Wilde? He's a rather high maintenance clone."

I blink. Boy, howdy, if he knew. "Duh comes to mind."

Dropping onto the bed, he sighs. "My life has gotten infinitely more complicated than I'd hoped for." He gives me a pleading look from under the arm he's thrown over his eyes and I crumble.

Dammit.

"Okay, fine. I didn't say this, and I'll pretend you were high on sleeping pills if anyone asks. Got it?"

He nods, looking at me with one eye.

"I think it's a fucking terrible idea. It's possibly the worst idea I've heard since Sari wanted to do the family mating that led to tragedy. I have no clue why this has become so important or why they've chosen Talia."

"I can't figure out why, either."

"Sari has always said Talia has a thing for Wilde, but she thinks everyone does. Maybe she thinks if Wilde is dating Talia, Talia will end up part of Beltane. Sari always wanted to get close to her to be part of the 'cool kids'."

"My Goddess has always been kind to the git, especially since she had the lab coats change him. She probably could have had him before, but she never had the inclination." Thumping the bed with his fist, he looks irritable.

"Sari gets things into her head and never changes her mind—that's nothing new. She's like a dog with a bone."

"Why do you think this is a bloody terrible idea, mate? The reasons you gave didn't jive with the level of vehemence behind the words. There has to be more."

Rubbing my face, I close my eyes and try to figure out how to explain without truly explaining. "I think that Wilde will want too much, too fast from Talia. That will set him up for disappointment and he doesn't deal well with not getting what he wants. Also, he just lost Rhea. I don't know that he's trying to replace her, but it's awfully soon to be pursuing someone else. I wouldn't be and Rafe sure as hell isn't."

"Talia is about as far removed from Blondie as a bird can be, so he's in for a surprise if that's what he's looking for."

I hold a finger up. "Lastly, Wilde is ten gallons of drama in a two ounce rocks glass. It's in his nature; he can't live without it. He and Sari come as a package and you can't have one without the other. They get angsty, morose, elated, and the entire gamut of emotions like someone that's bi-polar. Talia will be mired in his drama even if she doesn't want to be."

"He says he only wants to date her—not mate with her," Taurus says, lifting his arm to look at me.

I snort, my expression disbelieving. "I don't believe that. Wilde and I were casual at first, too. It didn't last long, though."

"Christ, what a mess. I mean, if you're right... You ended up mating with the git."

Brother, you are preaching to the wrong kitty. I know it's a mess.

"He bit me the first night we went out. Back then, he didn't even bite Sari. I didn't mind and I baited him, but it worked more quickly than I expected."

"He mated with you on the first night?" he asks incredulously.

"No, just a sip. I got him drunk, if that makes a difference."

"I didn't mean for this to be such a big deal. I was hoping for some time alone with you before I fell asleep. I won't be around much tomorrow—job issues. This is not how tonight was supposed to go."

I scoot closer and lay my cheek on his tummy. "I'm here, regardless. Plus, you don't have to decide now. You and Talia will discuss what I shared, I'm sure."

"Why can't anyone come to me about simple things like smiting the wicked?"

"I'm trying to be supportive, baby."

"Wilde wants into Talia's knickers! Fuck supportive, tell me how you really feel. I need your honesty, my minx."

"I think it's a catastrophe in the making. Absolute idiocy," I finally sigh, giving in to his plea.

He sighs. "Can we curl up here and sleep? Hopefully, I won't have to think about this again when I wake up?"

I nod, maneuvering to let him into the soft sheets with me. "Definitely."

He has no idea how badly this can go if he and Talia agree to Wilde's request. I have to stop them before it gets serious, right? I can't let anyone else run into that miasma of despair, even if it means facing things that I'm not ready to face.

Right?

The Cat Prepares The Circle

DELILAH

I drive up to the clearing that Rafe and I set up for the ritual. The space comes into view, and I marvel at the feeling of home that comes over me when I enter one of my sacred spaces. Breathing the air in deeply, I unload the totes of equipment we'll need. The others will arrive soon, but at least they can appreciate the natural beauty of our site before we get ready.

The Company is built on death and destruction, but the beauty of the Rift is something to behold each day.

I've been doing rituals at the sacred space behind my home for years. It's how I hide our community from the prying eyes of our enemies. That space has wards and traps all around it to keep people from entering without my permission. This space is in the open and that makes me uncomfortable, but I can't protect it as I would my own space. The chosen have to be able to locate it and enter without our help, so I'm stuck with the edge of paranoia in my consciousness.

This is Beltane, the spring festival of fertility, and the odds are that this will be wild. I set a few little hexes at key points along the road to discourage anyone who doesn't belong from following the path and to block unwanted outsiders. They're watered down versions of the spell leading to the gateways to the Resistance community. That's the best I can do to hide us for the evening.

The spell I use to cloak the Resistance Quarter is both simple and complex—which is why no one's figured it out.

It allows for those who *should* be able to enter while keeping those shouldn't from crossing the barrier. The intricacy lies in weaving the spell so that people can't trick their way in with 'good intentions' or third-party invitations. There's a little psychology and a little science woven into the magick. It took me a long time to perfect it, and due to the scale, it must be renewed once every six months.

I grunt as I lift my heavy tote bag out of the trunk. Doing another scan for unwanted guests with my beast senses, I sigh when I don't find any. I arrived an hour earlier than I instructed the others so I can get a feel for the energy here this evening. Then I have to set up, cleanse all the items, and get myself prepared. With no one else around, I can do this the easy way.

My lips quirk as I float the bag, plastic totes, and garment bags to the space in a neat line. I'm sure it looks reminiscent of a mouse and some brooms, but it's a hell of a lot simpler than lugging it by hand.

The air in the space is charged with anticipation. I've been jazzed all day myself.

Everything for tonight is freshly made or brand new except my personal tools. I anointed them for the ceremony, but I've had them since I was in middle school. The oils, incense, and candles were made in my kitchen. The specially blended Beltane incense and Sabbat Oil that was easy to get fresh ingredients for with the exception of the worm ruff and neroli oil. Those I sent Leo and Hex to find via a scavenger hunt through occult stores on the other side.

The specific blends are very important, and I didn't have time to brew or grow them myself. I will next time.

Luckily, they also picked up refills for some of my supplies while they were out, so it wasn't a complete wild goose chase. They also stopped at the florist to pick up the flowers and the fern, helped me make new candles, and bought the materials for the bonfire. Rafe went along to supervise, and true to form, he came back with two extra robes he'd picked out because we didn't know if Sari and Amanda would have the same equipment as Lily and Calista do.

I enter the center of the space, eyeballing the distance, and measuring in my mind before creating the circle. Pulling the blanket out of the first tote, I walk out three feet from where I think the circle will end, spreading it out to lay the ingredients on. I open the second tote, placing bottles and boxes on the blanket so they won't spill. The cedar case where my ceremonial knives—the athame and the bolline—are stored is followed by the sandalwood puzzle box containing my vials of essential oils.

Next, I set out the cardboard box of tapers, incense, and extra-long fireplace matches. That's followed by the God and Goddess pillars, the besom, baggies full of soil, feathers, holy water, sea salt, and oak leaves. The last things I spread out are the robes—including my own.

It's one of the few things from my past I kept when I moved here and it's integral to this ceremony.

My robe is hand sewn and anointed with dried herbs and oils that particularly enhance my own powers. It was made by the healer of a coven that I spent time with in France during high school, and it hums with imbued enchantments that I couldn't sense until I moved to the Rift. The two extra robes are not nearly as fancy, but they'll do.

Once everything is ready, I prepare to cleanse and find balance within while I wait for others. This will be an interesting evening and I want to be completely prepared. Calling the Goddess into myself on this balmy Beltane night means I'm inviting her consort

—the Horned God and King of May— as the honorary guest of all Beltane festivals.

I've read about the mating aspect of this celebration, and I hope for nothing less this evening. A reconnection with my true mate via the goddess will strengthen the ties that exist. I've always wondered what would happen if you mix the Rift science with traditional Earth magick, and tonight, I will find out. I can only hope that all of my powers will mesh with the Universe harmoniously so that I can accept my destiny.

The sun sinks slowly over the horizon and I glance at my phone lying on the blanket to catch the time.

Any time now, it will begin.

The Cat Welcomes The Beauties To Beltane

DELILAH

Twenty minutes later, Sari steps through the circle of trees followed by Calista, Amanda, and Lily. All of them are chattering away nervously. I stand to brush myself off, waving. When they approach, I follow tradition and hug them one at a time.

Please let this not be a royal fuck-up.

Sari grips me tightly, and it takes everything I have inside not to shudder. I realize Rafe may be correct in his recent assessment of our situation with them—no matter what they do to repent, the damage done is too severe. We will never forgive them. I don't have time to analyze that, though, so I paste on a smile.

"Merry meet and bright blessings on this beautiful Beltane," I say. My brow furrows when it occurs to me that I sound like the pagan Cat in the Hat. Shaking my head to clear it of silliness, I force a smile at my erstwhile mate.

Sari grins, "MM." She thinks she's super cool by not saying the entire greeting. Abbreviating it means she's so familiar that she doesn't even have to say the complete sentence.

Spare me.

She and Amanda are ready and raring to go by the looks on their faces. Calista and Lily look apprehensive. It's worrisome when the actual pagans look like scared rabbits and the pretenders are firing on all cylinders. I turn to Sari and ask her to set up the bonfire with Amanda, trying to get them to focus.

"These are your flowers to spread around the circle while I'm casting," I tell Lily, holding up the buttercups. "Calista, you'll spread the oak leaves. Sari will sprinkle violets, mine are red roses, and Amanda's are irises." I wrinkle my nose at the cute yellow flowers, glad that they're not mine, and they all giggle.

"Is there some reason that we have specific flowers?" Lily asks curiously.

"Oak leaves are a symbol of Beltane and the Horned God," Calista offers helpfully, opening the small bag she has. She places two robes—obviously for her and Sari—on the blanket before taking her baggie.

I nod. "Each of the flowers are tied to the element you represent. Calista is the spirit anchor, so she has the leaves. The rest of us are calling the quarters—fire, water, air and earth."

"No fair explaining without us," Amanda exclaims, rushing into the clearing with Sari. Their arms full of kindling as they huff up to the circle.

"I'm not explaining, only answering questions." I pull out several labelled sets of note cards with each person's parts, courtesy of Hex.

The boys have been extremely helpful in this endeavor. It makes me wonder if there's a more nefarious reason—like cameras in the trees. I narrow my eyes and look closely at the nearby foliage, straining to access my kitty vision without shifting.

"We don't know who we will call as our God, right?" Lily asks, eyeing her cards anxiously.

"No. I assume that calling the Lady—my Goddess— into me will tap into my heart and soul. For me, that also includes my primal side. When the Goddess calls her mate, it will include all aspects of you. Those of us with dual natures will most likely experience that part with our other part present, so be ready for that."

Sari gives me a smirk, her expression saying that she knows who my beast will pick. I smile wanly because her thoughts are dead bloody wrong. There's no way in Heaven or Hell that she will pick her primary's jackass demon. I am, however, a little worried about who will be chosen.

Will the Goddess pick someone that will re-open a wound as a way of telling me I've made mistakes?

Now I'm as nervous as a vampire in Italy. I know that when the Goddess calls her true mate to the ceremony, it doesn't mean that she is the true mate for the person called. Sometimes, the God and the Goddess have multiple true mates. I didn't tell the others that because I thought it would cause issues. But what if my true fucking mate is someone that I *cannot* be with?

I'm such a walking goddamned disaster.

Calista looks at me with wide eyes, picking at the corner of her index cards. "We won't do anything we normally wouldn't, right?"

"The Goddess works with what's inside of you—what you need. She won't do anything harmful to you," Sari says, putting a hand on her shoulder soothingly.

Calista looks at her and then at the rest of the group. "What if you don't already have a mate?"

I shrug, giving her and Amanda a smile. "The Goddess will call whomever best suits the embodiment of her God. Your match should find you when they arrive."

"It's exciting," Amanda says, her eyes dancing with a light that makes me suspicious. "It sounds scary at first, but it's exciting when you embrace it. New people, experiences, and lots of hot se —I'll shut up now."

It takes everything in me not to roll my eyes into the back of my head. Amanda is looking at this as a hook that will be a back door to a relationship. That kind of disrespect is annoying as hell and a little insulting. I gather all of my patience before I respond. "Now that Amanda has stated the obvious, we should get into our robes before we muck up our timeline."

I lift my robe, the magickal filaments shimmering in the moonlight as if imbued with tiny stars. I've been a practicing witch most of my life. I shed the Sunday school teachings of my parents long before high school and pursued what felt right to me.

My tools and equipment—like my robe—were also made by elders of various covens that I've joined. Each item represents my harmony with the Universe in a particular way. Anyone that is not a serious witch would think they are simply expensive toys, but they aren't. They hold a blend of magick created by me, the covens, and the Earth.

I hand Lily and Amanda the basic robes I brought for the occasion. Calista is putting on a forest green robe with autumn colored accents and Sari's are full of the colors of spring. They look brand new. I'll be damned—Sari had special robes made so they'd look like they fit with me.

Christ, Amanda will pout all night long.

My irritation doesn't last long because Lily starts muttering about video surveillance. Knowing Mercury as I do, I don't blame her for wondering. He loves to watch and he'd absolutely record a bunch of chits dancing naked by a fire.

Too late to worry about that now.

When everyone is ready, I hand Sari a large scallop shell full of Dead Sea salt and instruct her to follow Calista. The droid will sweep the negative energy with my besom, and she will use the salt to set the boundaries of our circle. They take a moment to calculate the size and then get to work. It's integral that we have enough space in the circle for the craziness when the Gods arrive. The sacred space must remain unbroken during the ceremony or all sorts of bad things could happen.

I sure as hell don't need any more of that.

As they work, I give Amanda the candles for each quarter, five sets of matches, and a small bowl with elemental materials. I direct their placement as I sit the God and Goddess candles on either side of the bonfire. Lily places the fern on the spirit point of the pentacle, and I move to light ceremonial incense throughout the circle. Driving the sticks into the ground, I hope that it will burn as needed to create the atmosphere.

Once the set-up is complete, each lady picks up her assigned flowers and heads to their spot. With my roses and athame in hand, I take my place. Closing my eyes to feel the energy in the circle, I smile. Energy flows from everything around us, letting me know that I can begin the ritual. It's strong and I'm feeling very powerful in the light of the moon.

It is time.

I raise my athame and draw a pentacle in the air where Sari is on the North point. Pressing the tip of the athame into the ground at her feet, I seal it and turn to them. We walk the edges of the circle, dropping our flowers and leaves as we delineate the space and infuse it with our energies. When we reach our original places, I re-draw the pentacle and seal it again, raising my hands to the sky.

"Circle, I charge that thou be a barrier between the world of man and the realms of the Gods. A guardian and a protector shall contain the power we raise within thee tonight. As I will, so mote it be! The circle is closed. All herein are totally and completely apart from the outside world. The circle is cast."

Sari gives me a look like a kid in a candy store, itching to get involved. I suck in a deep breath to keep from telling her to keep her bloody pants on, knowing that negativity will hurt our ritual. Besides, I need her where she is on the North point, serving as the conduit to the Earth. Amanda is on the West point, serving as water; Lily is in the East to represent Air. I walk to the South point, not trusting anyone but myself to harness Fire.

Nodding at Calista as she walks to the center and uncorks the Sabbat Oil, I wait for her to anoint us on our foreheads. When she gets to me, she gives me a lop-sided smile. "I welcome thee to this magickal circle this night. May the peace of the Goddess be with thee, Blessed Be!"

After making the rounds of the circle, she moves to her position near the bonfire as our spirit anchor to wait for us to call the quarters. I watch carefully, knowing that we have to start with Sari, and praying that she doesn't make a bloody mess of this.

Sari begins, lighting her green candle and standing as tall as someone her height can manage. "Element of Earth, world upon which we walk, Mother from which we spring, we ask you attend this, our magickal rite, giving upon us your gift of life itself. Blessed be!" She sprinkles the soil onto the ground and waits for my approval.

I nod, lighting my red taper as I call out, "Element of Fire, symbol of the Sun God which brings warmth and life to our planet, we ask you attend this, our magickal rite, bestowing your fire and will upon those here. Blessed Be!" Driving my candle into the ground, I raise my eyes to the sky.

So far, so good. Three more to go.

Lily picks up her purple candle, lighting it and reading her part. "Element of Air, that which facilitates our communication, the very breath of life, we ask you attend this, our magickal rite, bestowing your gifts upon our intellects. Blessed Be!" Dropping her handful of feathers, she looks at Amanda, who grins wickedly.

Gross.

Amanda lights her blue pillar and says, "Element of Water, that which nourishes the life the Great Mother brings forth upon her bosom, we ask you to attend this, our magickal rite, bestowing upon us an appreciation of the emotion in our lives. Blessed Be!" She opens the bottle of water and drizzles it on the ground.

Calista lights her white candle, crossing to me with my chalice and the remains of the holy water. I assume the star position, calling to the sky. "Great Brighid, Mother of us all: Maiden, Mother, and Crone in her turn, she who brings us life. Be here with us! Join with your Lord in Sacred Marriage in this, our magickal rite. Blessed Be!"

Kneeling, I hold my chalice, plunging the athame in it. "As the athame is to the male, the chalice is to the female." I place it in front of me, raising the chalice and taking a sip. Calista takes it to each lady to sip from as I chant, "Lord, I invite you to the circle: Angus Mac Og, God of Love, Blue God, and Consort of Brighid. Join with your Lady in sacred marriage in this our magickal rite. Blessed be!"

My robes slip from my shoulders as I feel energy working its way into me. She ripples out, features shifting and eyes flashing as I dance. Low purring sounds rumble out when I see the others have disrobed and we're all dancing sky clad now.

The circle comes to life with an electrical energy that I've never felt before.

Something ancient and powerful descends upon me. I feel Her reaching out, calling to Her mate with a primal howl. The howl increases in volume as Sari joins, followed by three loud wails as the Goddesses wait for their Gods.

The Beast And Bast Best The Cat

DELILAH

My senses are alive with the scents and tastes in the air. As my limbs stretch towards the sky, my body undulates to the tune in my head. She is participating in this ceremony because she loves being primitive and uninhibited. The mating aspect is appealing—fight, flight, or fucking.

She's always game for that.

Unfortunately, I didn't consider how she might feel about another being inhabiting our body, even for a short time. She couldn't exist without me, but she's not me. I might be okay with the Dark Lady taking over for a bit, but who knows what's going to happen if the beast's not keen on it?

I officially suck at planning ahead.

Familiar scents enter our space and I assume the others' mates have arrived, yet mine still has not. A momentary flash of irritation at Rafe's lackadaisical attitude crosses my mind when an electric shock hits me. A gust of intense energy fills my body and my Goddess invades, filling me with a power so great that even she has to respect it.

The presence of another spirit gives her pause, but Bast

embraces her. Their mutual passion, lust, and fierceness bonds them instantly. Together, they reach out, roaring the call for our God to mate with us. Embodied with the goddess of fertility and vengeance, my Beast feeds off the sexual energy floating in the air. It creates a savage hunger deep inside, and a wicked smile curves our lips.

When our mate arrives, we're going to rip into him like never before.

I chuckle at the thought, stopping as recognition prickles along my spine. "He's almost here," I whisper, my voice deep and husky with the Goddess' influence.

A pair of arms encircle my waist and I snarl in happiness. "My Horus," I purr, slithering around to face him. My eyes pop open in shock when I see a face that I did not expect.

Inside, the Goddess and the beast laugh darkly, as if they've known all along that this is who would show up.

His lips are curled into a wicked smirk as he looks down at me, his demon visage firmly in place. Golden eyes devour my naked form greedily. My arms curl around his neck of their own volition and I realize I'm along for the ride.

The Goddess and the beast are in full control and they are satisfied with the naked male I'm writhing against. The faint sound of a hawk rings in my ears as he hauls me against him, his snarl renting the air as the God slips into him. I sense the demon inside him struggling, and reach inside to touch his heart. The gesture reassures his primal sides so Horus can slip into him as Bast fills me.

"Minx," he growls darkly, his hands sliding over my back and leaving trails of sparkling power lingering on my skin.

"My fiend," I tease gently. My fully unsheathed claws scratch down his chest and he growls again. Emerald eyes roam his form, lighting with wicked glee as they note that he's already naked. "Afraid I'll mess the clothes, baby?"

"Bloody right," he replies, gripping my ass tightly. "I can't have you tearing up my silk to get your hot little hands on my hard body."

My mouth is crushed to his, conversation finished as his body presses against mine temptingly. Running my hands down his chest, I stop at the feathery peacock, stroking and scratching it. The bird's eyes blink at me like the little bugger's going to nip at me like he had in the cage. I trail a finger down to where the tail has a gap for my missing feather as he makes rumbling noises in his chest. Smirking, I slide my fingers over more of the bird, magick arcing between us like tiny zephyrs as I move over his abs, sliding downward with intent.

I love his body and this is absolutely divine.

She growls impatiently and he yanks me up, tugging me forward to plunder my mouth roughly. Snarling, he pulls both of my legs around his waist, his fingers digging into my ass cheeks as our tongues thrust and parry. They scrape against our fangs, and we savor the taste of blood welling forth into the kiss. When I pull away, both of our lips are splashed with bright red, and the heady flavor fills my taste buds making Bast and the Beast greedy for more.

"My God? It is time," I whisper, my voice dark as the charge of the Egyptian deity electrifies our embrace. I reach out to touch the God settled in him and beckon him forth.

His voice is a roaring rumble when he replies, "As you wish, my Goddess."

The gentleness he uses in lowering us to the ground is in direct contrast to the tension I can feel bunched in his muscles. My back hits the ground, and he prowls over me, his golden eyes roaming my skin as he nibbles the matching feather. The tickling sensation of the feather under his breath makes me writhe and I rake my claws down his back, digging them in hard. His snarl cuts through the pounding bass in my head and he sinks his fangs into the eye of the feather, right over my heart.

Licking the drops as they flow downward, he trails over my

torso, nibbling and nipping at each rib. His hands slide up over my breasts and I grab one, sucking on his fingers. He rims my belly button with his tongue, causing the skin to jump and quiver. Teeth sink in below my navel and I scrape a fang over the pad of his finger, sucking on the tiny bubble that wells forth.

The dance is going to kill us; I'm certain of that.

"Baby," he growls in warning, running his tongue along the juncture of my leg and pelvis. His hands wrench free to hold my hips. Hot breath raises goose pimples on my skin as I bury my fingers in his short locks to hold on. His voice rings in my head, whispering in my mind as he always does when we're intimate.

All thoughts leave my mind as his mouth closes over me. His lips, fangs, and tongue move over the aching wetness with a ferocity that rips a primal scream from my lips. His fingers slide into me, curling for the spot that he knows by heart, and I fight for control. I want to come with him inside of me. His dark chuckle vibrates over my skin as the primal, the deities, and our personalities clash in a battle for dominance.

The beast roars at the hawk, and the demon snarls in return. A bolt of power runs over our bodies, making my skin hum with pleasure. The triad of power within me yields, and my body melts in compliance with the demands of the Universe.

Taurus grins up at me, the ghosts of his demon and Horus shining from his eyes as they claim victory. His head lowers and the torture begins once more, driving my climax to a peak I've never known. I claw at his shoulders, my body on fire and he lets out a vibrating snarl. Sinking his fangs into my pulsing femoral artery, he begins to drink. From stem to stern, I shudder and shake with the impact of the bite, power trickling out of my pores. It blankets the air with tension like an electrical storm. Sparks fly from our bodies as he crawls upwards, the demon and the God intent.

My inner monsters make a detente as we watch him. The words echo in my mind as they growl ~*Our turn.*~

Catching his shoulders with my feet, I push hard, and he

tumbles backwards with the force. That gives me a chance to spring forward and slither over his body. I bite and lick my way up his legs as we give him an evil grin. Watching the demon push to the fore-front, I rake my claws down his torso, marking him with the blood and sting.

This is why he's a perfect mate for my magic and my beast.

He lets out a snarl, and his hands clamp on my hips. Lifting and slamming me onto his cock hard enough to jar my teeth, he holds me in place with an iron grip. We both release ear-splitting howls, our backs arching as magick zings through us when we join. As if choreographed by the stars, we move as one.

The buildup has been immense and my body feels like it's on the edge of explosion. Every touch sparkles through me like it's going to be the one that sends me into oblivion. The fire in my veins is threatening to consume me. It's almost too much and I wonder how much more we can take as it keeps climbing.

Suddenly, a door inside of me flings open and it's *all* there. The Universe flows into me like a river to the sea and I know that my magick has been unlocked. The God and Goddess inside of us embrace our inner primal sides, their edges blurring in my consciousness as we all become one. The orgasm smashes into me like a tidal wave and I grip his cock inside of me like I'm trying to strangle him. His roar echoes off the trees and he yanks my head down.

I'm so full of him, the goddess, the beast, and magic that I have no idea how I'm going to survive.

Our eyes lock and it all bubbles out, the air crackling with the release of all the power rushing from us and through us. I hear the hawk again, followed by a screeching cat-like yowl that seems to come from our mouths unbidden.

Fangs glisten and we strike simultaneously, burying our sharp-ened incisors into each other's neck. Tearing in roughly as elec-tricity arcs between us, feeding makes our limbs shake and shiver with intensity. The energy zings back and forth across our connection at light speed. We drink hungrily, sucking in great gulps with hitching snarls, murmuring back and forth mentally as we feed.

The deities finally wrench free of the vessels of our bodies, leaving only traces of the magick they'd imbued us with. As our bodies slow to a stop, we're still drinking. I'm so hungry for him, and I feel his own hunger thrumming through our connection. Our pulses are dragging, and our heartbeats echo in my head.

~Time to stop, baby. ~ His voice rings in my head and I realize my limbs feel like water.

*~We always do this. ~*I chuckle inwardly, licking the wound over his jugular so it'll heal.

He finally pries his lips from my neck, chuckling. *~Junkies. ~*

I'm unable to move as we melt into each other. My tail flicks up along his side, stroking gently as he loves for me to do. Suddenly, it hits something solid and my senses go on alert. Despite my current inability to do anything, I prepare for danger.

~What the buggering hell is that? ~ he asks incredulously.

~No clue, baby. ~ Tail swishing, I crack an eye open a slit to look downward. When I catch the flash of gold, my eyes pop open. *~Holy fuck. ~*

~What?!~ He snarls in frustration, his energy drained by the deepness of our feeding. We went down to the last drop as usual, so I feel him struggling against the lassitude.

~You're going to kill me, ~ I whisper softly.

He sends the sensation of a menacing look, speaking in a clipped tone. *~What. Do. You. See? ~*

Knowing he'll slip into my head and use my eyes soon, I reply in a ridiculously small voice. *~Remember when you said you'd better not grow a tail, or I was in big trouble? ~*

I feel that gob smacked expression that he gets occasionally. *~Not funny, Sandwich. Quit messing with my head. ~*

~Do I sound like I'm kidding? ~ I reply seriously. Reaching over with my tail, I wrap it around the sleek length lying along his side. I stroke the exposed part and when it hits the bottle brush tip, I send

him a grin. *~You're a lion, baby—my Rex. Kind of appropriate, I think. ~*

He snorts loudly as he slips into my mind to look through my eyes at the soft furry appendage. *~You're right. I'm going to kill you when I can move. ~*

Laughing softly, I tug on his new acquisition with mine. *~You'll get used to it. I'm sure it slides in and out. ~*

~Bloody hell, woman... the trouble you get me into. ~

~Stop your whining and settle down. I have to be rested enough to stand when everyone's done. That's not happening unless you let me rest. ~

He chuckles and sends a soothing sensation down my spine. *~Rest, baby. We'll argue later. ~*

I'm surprised to feel his tail slide up my back slowly. My purr kicks in and my eyes close as I cuddle against him. *~You know we will. ~*

The tail moves again, and he rumbles in amusement. *~Bloody hell, the things you do to me. ~*

Hopefully, by the time it's time to close the circle I have enough energy back to stand. As of now, I'm wiped but good. Maybe I'll have Taurus prop me up. That'll underline the fact that he showed up tonight and piss off the others.

It's probably time to admit that I also *look* for trouble; it doesn't just find me.

That's what makes us a perfect match.

The Coyote Howls At The Moon

SARI

Look, it's easy to run around a field and say you're a pagan. Hell, it's what people do in college all the time. They see two movies from the Nineties or visit Burning Man and suddenly, they're a witch.

Give me a break.

I wasn't aware that the cat was as into this as she is. Mostly, I figured all this planning was an elaborate excuse for an orgy.

She's been hiding something big, and it's not hanging off a clone somewhere, if you get my drift. I can *feel* the fucking energy in the air here. This shit just got real and I'll be straight with you: I don't have a damn clue how to handle it.

I reluctantly agreed to come at her plea, knowing full well she hasn't reached out to me or my clan since that flashy, flighty flirt arrived. I yearn for a glimpse into her mind, to understand what's troubling that crimson-haired beauty and how I can restore the peace we once had. My optimistic partner believes we can control the situation by replacing the backstabbing blondes with Talia and Taurus in their former positions.

I know better than that.

Talia is like a wild, sleek stallion, untamable and valuable. No jockey can match her power and grace, no matter how many Hollywood films tell otherwise. She's a force to be reckoned with, and I relish every moment of the chaos she brings.

This group of women is like a ticking time bomb, ready to explode at any moment. Every call made to the wrong person or unwanted individual will set off an all-out brawl. Yet, I find myself following the woman my mate adores, despite her infuriating ways and misguided intentions.

She's simply the best show in town.

It's unclear what Deli hoped to achieve with this gathering. Perhaps she wanted to cleanse our palate from our ex-family members, which I support. However, I would much rather rid ourselves of the prancing prima donna that she seems fixated on. But in an effort to maintain peace and unity, I held my tongue and accepted the branch he extended as a peace offering.

I'll try really goddamned hard not to stake him with it.

Now she's all in for him, which is a mistake I've seen others make. She says she's not, but she frets and fritters, so I know she's full of it. I've seen her fall for a fellow or two, and this is what it looks like. That girl is subtle like a neon green unitard and she thinks she's an emotional ninja.

I think she knows I'm here because I love her, not because I believe in this mumbo jumbo. She invited Lily, who I believe is odd enough to have a passing fancy for this shit; Amanda, who will pretty much pretend she's into anything for attention; and Calista, who's programmed to think she can do this. Yeah, I know all her magic is science masquerading as a miracle, but I don't tell *her* that.

The power to change your life lies within yourself, not some magic bean counter in the sky that helps you if you say the right words or sacrifice the right cows. I've survived for years by making sure that number one—me—will always benefit.

That's why I'm ignoring the bloody advice they gave and calling Kali, the Hindu vengeance Goddess. I look inside myself, finding plenty of need to exact revenge for slights that have gone unaddressed. I raise my arms to the sky, demanding that the Universe show me the way to get what my mate and I need.

My inner instincts take over, and I sniff the air, my gaze honing in on a familiar scent. It's Veruca's, which is surprising because I didn't think this technique would be effective on droids. Belle's people don't believe in these superstitious practices. Plus, Deli and Belle are like oil and water—they don't mix well and it's easy to manipulate them against each other with strategic moves. They barely communicate unless it involves Hex dating Chaos. I prefer it that way because it makes achieving my goals much easier.

I don't see nearly as well as the cat in the dark, nor is my mutation as developed as hers. While I'm still learning, she's almost a full shifter. However, whatever Deli's passed on to me in the DNA department makes my coyote senses on point. My olfactory nerves are working overdrive tonight. Veruca's on the other side of the fire, staying away from the dangerous column of flame as it shoots into the air. She's stopped and the scent of daisies fill the air. I know why she's here now: Calista.

The cynic in me has a serious freak out. The cat's called both a mate and a hell of a pyrotechnic show. We're dancing like fools in this clearing waiting for the unknown to arrive. After everything that has happened in the past few months, I shouldn't bat a lash at magick, but *damn*. I knew that girl was either a powerful ally or enemy from the moment I met her, but *this is not what I meant*. It seals the deal, confirming that the kitty's been hiding things despite the mating bond. I have to know what else she's hiding.

Wilde has to get her under control.

Twitching my nose, I tilt my head when the scent of expensive tobacco, Bulgari cologne, and leather hits the air. Well, well, well. Looks like there's more than magic being hidden. The kitty's brought a bird to the nest.

While I've always liked the scent of that irritating fowl, I'm aware of how serious things are between them for this to pass muster with Talia. She's the type to chain him in the basement to keep him out if she didn't agree. There will be explaining to do when my fancy pants mate finds out *this* tidbit.

The night air is quiet. The fire is crackling and jumping, but we're in a bubble. There's no nighttime symphony of insects and birds and other animals—it's eerily silent. It makes me wonder what kind of mojo is going on in this circle. Is this the kitty's work? I never wondered how the Resistance stayed hidden from the Cabal or how members could go in and out and stay off the radar until now.

This is troubling and I need to talk to—

The hairs on the back of my neck stand up and I growl low.

Someone's here. Who?

I thought this was just going to be some amateur witchcraft role play in the woods, not a genuine supernatural occurrence. I never believed magic was real, but now I'm doubting everything I thought I knew, and it's frustrating. I should have been more skeptical about the cat, especially when she grew claws and seemed to heal impossibly quickly after rough play. I had assumed she and her partner were just skilled with special effects makeup and didn't question it further.

Trusting. Arrogant. Foolish.

Something isn't right here, and everything around us isn't necessarily real. I feel my canines drop—part of my early warning system—then I scent the air. His aroma hits me as he slips up behind me, wrapping around my crouched form like it's an everyday thing to find me naked in the woods snarling. His purr vibrates from his chest to mine, and though I haven't seen him for a few weeks, I feel a triumphant sense of possession.

Rhea may have left him broken, but he's still mine. She doesn't get to win.

His body is taut, as if he's been cooped up for weeks. I can sense the unease radiating from him, and a part of me wonders if he even had a choice in leaving his house. The thought only fuels my frustration, and I growl louder. My muscles tighten as all the pent-up tension finally snaps. A surge of anger rushes through me at the idea that he may have only come to me because of some powerful magic or force beyond our control.

With a swift, fluid movement, he's suddenly on my back and I'm pinned to the grass with his sharp teeth hovering dangerously close to my throat. The wild spirit of the coyote courses through him, moving without any regard for my consent or control. A twinge of guilt pricks at me for allowing this outburst of aggression, but I push it aside. It's necessary for him to remember who he belongs to, to remind him that I am the leader here. And perhaps this display will also put the cat in their place, causing them to fall back into line and respect my authority. As I lay there under his weight, I can feel the tension between us slowly dissipating, replaced by a sense of dominance and ownership.

He's not even fazed. All he does is look up at me, submissive. "Nice one."

That's good. I like submissiveness. It's where he belongs.

I hold onto my teeth, refusing to remove them even as I look at him. Teeth are his favorite thing in the world, much like his mate, and he revels in sessions where I work him over with them. The sound of his moans and groans always echoes in my ears, a constant reminder that I have power over him. I've never felt the need to ask if he likes it or not; his enjoyment is palpable. He craves biting and this is just an amped up version of it. It solidifies our bond and proves that he belongs to me.

As I sniff the air, searching for the familiar scent of his arousal, I come up empty. Crouching down at his side, I take in the beating drums of the chanting circle, the smoky smells of the fire crackling nearby, and the pulsing energy of magick shimmering all around us. The human side of me wants to ask questions, but the wild coyote within yearns to rip and tear. It's a delicate balance that I must maintain, so I pacify both sides by staying still and present in the moment.

"Why are you here?" The growl that accompanies my question is unintended, but Rafe rolls over on his belly and gives me a quirk of a smile. That tells me nothing. He smiled that way when being worked over by my mate at the line between actual pain and pleasure. My mate has an amazing poker face.

He loves me all growly and fangy—he's said so from the beginning. I briefly wonder how much control this affair is going to afford me. It could get bad if I don't have any, but I don't believe it will be any worse than he's had before. I don't comprehend what's going on and I didn't expect this. I didn't expect *him*, and I don't know what to do with it because he's *still* not bloody answering me.

"Shiva, I suppose." He gives me that smile again as his long locks fan over his back. His calm is almost resigned, and this display isn't fazing him. He's more used to shit than I knew and he doesn't fight it— or he doesn't have the will to. Either could be true, given his depression over the other family. I think his problems lie with the brother, not the woman. However, Rafe's never said a word about his other mates before and he won't start now.

"Shiva." I crawl over to him, straddling his waist. He's hot, beautiful, submissive, and mine. Why should I care about the reasons why? I'm being a fool.

Stowing my concerns, I look into his eyes, intent on regaining the power in this situation. His ability to disarm me has always felt like a weak point; I know Wilde feels the same way. Rafe's ease, his charm, his willingness to give the ones he loves anything they desire makes you vulnerable. It might be why Wilde is harder on him than the cat; her primary is more dangerous in subtle ways.

Shiva was that way—destroyer of worlds only to recreate them, tamer of rivers to benefit mankind, and drinker of poison to prevent the destruction of the gods and humans alike. Born of an argument between two gods over who was most powerful, Shiva emerged in a blaze of glory that forced Brahma and Vishnu to accept him as the third ruler of the world.

Rafe always zips past the turrets of my defenses and gets to the heart of me without setting off the warning signals. Like Shiva springing from nowhere and extending his reach into the earth and sky, he's wormed his way into the dyad that Wilde and I formed, making himself indispensable.

At least, he is for figuring out how to control our very own Kali in the form of the kitty. Ironic that that goddess was MY choice—not hers—but it also makes sense. No matter what face she's wearing for Talia and Taurus, she's no killer. The cat isn't evil to the core when necessary as my mate and I are. We are better matches for those two than she is for Taurus. We could truly challenge their world.

She is a pretender.

Returning to the clone in front of me, I can't help but wonder if this situation will provide some much-needed clarity for me. The thought of the gods and goddesses actually appearing is thrilling, Kali's presence alone could give me ideas for restoring order to my world and vanquishing our enemies. With a wicked grin, I lean down and lick his lips, feeling his hands gripping my waist tightly. He's given me control and I relish in it, showing him who's really in charge. My teeth graze his neck, eliciting a satisfying shudder from him as he grinds against my heat, eagerly waiting for my next move. Rafe is practically pleading with me to claim him and make him mine - all mine - right now.

Even if it's just for this moment, I am willing to fight through the nine levels of hell to keep him by my side. My mate may have other playmates, but none who elicit such a response from me. There may be consequences for taking what rightfully belongs to him, but I am willing to face them all for the chance to have Rafe as my own.

"Mine," I command him as I strip away his shirt. I pant up a storm and I know that means the shift is coming. Once it does, I can't stand it anymore—it's all *want* and *have*. My eyes flash yellow, which means I won't be here for long. At least, the human part of me won't.

"Yours," he answers automatically. He's docile tonight. Rafe knows I like when he fights back before he lets me have my way.

Tonight, it's all me and I like it.

I fumble with his loose clothes, getting him out of the trademark track pants as quickly as possible. I touch and nip everywhere until he pants and curses and makes the best sounds for me. "Get up here." He's pleading and I'm smirking. He doesn't want to make it last tonight? Needs me now?

I can do that.

With his chiseled features and sculpted body, Rafe is a sight to behold. Even for someone like me who doesn't buy into the whole romance thing, my heart can't help but skip a beat at the mere sight of him. Despite his reputation for being stationary, he radiates a powerful energy that practically crackles in the air around him. And while he may have a soft heart buried beneath all that muscle, there's no denying his undeniable sex appeal. It's almost as if he was carved from the same block of perfection as his mate, yet their personalities are so different that it's hard to imagine how they connect on such a deep level without words.

And I'm not just talking about telepathy here. They literally don't need words to communicate, and it's both fascinating and frustrating to watch them interact as if they were two halves of the same whole. Wilde is livid with envy that he can't achieve that kind of unbreakable bond with either of them - it's almost like some twisted form of twin-cest. If anyone ever needed an example of soul mates, you could simply point to Rafe and his feline companion. They make every other pair of mates look inferior in comparison.

For me, Rafe's constant presence in my life has become an essential part of my existence. Even when I was lost and confused, trying to figure out why I needed him by my side, he never once triggered any alarms or set off any red flags. And now I understand why, because he effortlessly bypassed all of my defenses and burrowed himself deep into my heart without me even realizing it.

This clone has never wanted anything from me. I don't have to make him whole—that's her job. Rafe doesn't need me to fix him or make him better. He doesn't need me to run after him, pick up for him, or feed him. He doesn't want me to be anyone but who I am.

Whether I'm a giant snot ball in his arms, playing hide-n-seek, listening to music next to each other, or tying him down to the bed, it doesn't matter to him. I only need to be there—that's enough. What he always wants is me. I missed that along the way, and it feels important. It feels like something I've screwed up. Hell, maybe Wilde has, too.

Rafe will never admit that I did anything wrong, but at this time of revelation and heat and want, I'm going to set it right. I'm going to fix that slip of the teeth that lead to mating with him 'by mistake' and the ensuing fall out afterwards. I'm going to show him what he means to me and give him everything I am.

That will fix everything. Wilde will do the same to fix his mistakes with Victor and Alistair.

Now's the time. He's completely unfettered, and we can *own* him now. We can have him the way we always wanted to if we take advantage of what's being offered here.

The cat will follow. It's perfect.

"Friend of my body," I whisper as I kiss him softly. He's noticed a subtle shift, but he doesn't react. "Mirror of my spirit, complement of my mind—I am yours for now and all time."

His expression doesn't change, but I feel tension in his frame. Perhaps he's nervous that I will claim this is an accident or magic induced fancy again. Settling over his hips, I slide over him until we're joined. That familiar rush hits me and somewhere inside, a voice says 'hurry, for it's soon to be gone'. Rocking my hips slowly, it takes everything in me not to out-and-out ride him into oblivion.

I want to say a few things before we tumble. "You've never

wanted anything other than to be with me and that is truly the greatest gift anyone has ever given me." I kiss him again because I can't help it. The howl is building in my toes; I feel it. "While I may have fucked this up in the past, I will always want to make it right."

"You haven't—"

My fingers shush him. His first words since he mentioned Shiva are unnecessary. Fangs firmly in place, I show him that I am sure. I drive my teeth into my mark and the points of my canines slice through like butter. His blood fills my mouth and I revel in the taste.

Everything is blown apart in panting, thumping, grinding, and blood. Whoever I was and whoever I'm going to be are wiped clean by this act. His belief, his trust, and his love will remake me into a better person.

When I am with him, I'm always stronger.

I hear him scream over my growl, but I need more. I pull up, waiting for his fangs to emerge. They don't come and my growl becomes angrier, needier. I feel the spirit of Kali echo in mind, whispering what I need to do to make Shiva ready to fulfill my desires.

Tearing my fangs out, I gnaw and rip and tear a bit. He snarls, able to hold back until I take a claw and puncture his left nipple. The ripples happen and *there* is my mate. His eyes are golden and expression fierce as he tears into my neck. I return the favor with zeal, bathing in the flow of his essence.

My howl vibrates against the skin in my mouth, but I don't let go. Suckling like our lives depend on it, we buck and pound out our ecstasy. When all is said and done, I lick his wounds closed.

Rafe holds me quietly—his demon gone and fangs retracted—as I come down. He knows I'm going to want to hunt and howl, but breaking the circle would be bad. He kicks up that familiar rumble in his chest to soothe the coyote into staying in place.

Shiva fades from his mind, but Kali stays with me. She whispers plans and prophecies, what will be and what can be, and how I can shape the future of my world. Oh, I was so right in choosing her over everyone's objections. Kali is making music in my mind and the coyote likes the song. Wilde will be so pleased when he hears what I have learned.

We will take our family back and the world will fall at our feet once more.

I like the words she gives me and I love that she's planning to hang around. I could use an inner monster like Kali to keep me on track.

The Flower Meets Her Match

I'll admit it; I was nervous about this.*

For as long as I can remember, I have identified as a neo-pagan. But my knowledge of Deli revealed to me that she is a devout wiccan through and through. That's a bit too fluffy and whimsical for my liking. Believing in the sun, moon, sky, and nature? That resonates with my scientific soul. But dancing around with a wand and casting spells? Not so much.

Witches have a different way of connecting with deities than someone like me. I cannot fathom speaking to mythological beings as if they hold sacred powers bestowed upon them by the heavens, like a hippie version of the Bible.

I worried that my disbelief would taint her important moment.

To be honest, my concerns began from the start because of her other "helpers". We had a former Christian of unknown denomination, an ambiguous individual, an Atheist, and a droid programmed to believe in its own magical abilities. I was skeptical because only Deli held true beliefs.

I can't understand why someone as intelligent as her would even have such faith. Deli is one of the few people who can keep up with me intellectually. She rarely requires emotional support from me. I always ground her when she starts to veer off course—until recently. And yet, this newfound faith healing has nothing to do with me, I know that much. She has always proudly claimed the title of witch and rejected the garish portrayals seen in movies.

It seems a tad hypocritical now, but maybe it's because what has been hyped as her belief system is absolute garbage. This stuff might seem fluffy and goofy to me, but perfectly in line with tradition to her. Having grown up Irish Catholic, I can empathize with crazy rituals in the name of faith.

So, flower petals, I can do.

Her concept of a sacred space and initiating a ceremony is more complex than mine, but not entirely unconventional. I find great joy in dancing sky clad, feeling the cool breeze on my skin as I move. As a scientist, I have shed the societal norms that are rooted in puritanical Judeo-Christian beliefs and do not subscribe to any shame surrounding nudity.

As I twirl and spin through the circle, a sudden moment of clarity washes over me. My bare feet sink into the soft earth beneath them as my hair, long and flowing like a curtain, dances behind me. Deli is more than just a believer in our community's principles - she is its creator. It dawns on me that I never bothered to ask questions about the foundation of this place, despite being one of its leaders. When I first arrived and ordered Mercury, it never occurred to me to inquire about how this hidden haven was built or how it remains concealed from the Cabal.

The thought of questioning the very fundamentals of our home never crossed my mind before.

For all their scientific advancements in creating the Rift and bringing clones to life, who paved the way for our Resistance after the Conflict? Who safeguards us and allows us to move freely without fear of being ruled by others? These are questions I should have asked long ago.

A breeze blows through the circle as if knowledge has been

imparted. It occurs to me as I whirl around this space that Deli is not a delusional fruitcake that subscribes to the crazy flower child religion. I know exactly who created our community and this space is a smaller version of her efforts.

The town's most popular kitty, with her beautiful fur and charming demeanor, had been keeping a tremendous secret. A secret so big that it was bound to get out now. As for why she had kept it hidden, I can only imagine it was because being coveted by everyone was already enough pressure to handle. Revealing herself as a real-life magick user would surely make things spiral even further out of control.

But perhaps they were already spiraling out of control. Her mutation had caused unprecedented ripples that we couldn't possibly have foreseen. And the similar mutations in her mates were just the beginning, a trend that could lead to unforeseen consequences.

As these thoughts tumbled through my mind, they became tangled in knots of concern. This revelation made everything real, rendering all patronizing smiles and nods insignificant. She hadn't been playing a game when she claimed to be able to summon gods and goddesses to imbue us with their powers. That alone is a ripple that will have far-reaching effects.

Suddenly, self-doubt creeps up on me like a stealthy predator.

What if this doesn't work? What if I'm the only one who can't tap into this power? Or worse yet, what if it does work? What kind of entity will I call forth? How much power will I be relinquishing?

These were questions without answers, leaving me with a sense of unease and uncertainty about the future.I was nervous; now, I'm scared. From somewhere, the thought penetrates that I'm winding myself up into a panic. I stop to breathe. Deli must have woven more wards into this place than Ariadne put threads in her tapestry. She's impulsive, but she's been planning this thing like a wedding on crack for a month. She set up a space separate from the one I know she keeps at her home. She *must* have put guards and wards and protection in this field that we cannot see but are there.

The kitty knew there was an element of the unknown, knew that people might have issues with the person their Goddess called, and that there could be conflict. She would not have put us all in danger. As angry and hurt as she is, she would stand in front of a bus for those she cares about even if they are the reason she is in pain.

I leave my thoughts for a moment, noting that there are more people here than when we started. Gods are arriving. I am curious who will come for them—and me.

As I stand in the midst of my fear-fueled panic, the presence of the males only adds to my unease. I try to force a sense of welcome into the air before closing the doors behind me, hoping to calm my racing heart and take in the balmy spring night. My breaths are slow, and I can feel nature all around me, every tiny movement causing the hairs on my arms to stand up in anticipation.

With a longing gaze, I look up at the sky above, envious of the freedom of birds and bees as they fly through the twinkling stars. It was this same sense of freedom that drew me to Arianrhod, the Celtic bird goddess of rebirth, fertility, and cosmic time. Though I had never truly believed in her until now, I felt her calling to me and to this ritual.

Raising my hands to feel the gentle breeze caress my skin, I inhale deeply, taking in the sweet scent and taste of the unspoiled clearing around me. The thought of humanity's vitality and our place within both this world and another dimension fills my mind as I sway with the wind.

Beneath the starry sky, I see myself as a pale waif in the night, dancing naked against the powerful gusts that surround me. With each passing moment, the breeze grows stronger and more forceful until it becomes a full-blown storm, its weight pressing down upon me.

But then, with one deep breath, Arianrhod takes hold of me

and suddenly I am soaring with her through the dark clouds, flying higher and higher into the brewing storm. As we race through the swirling vortexes of moisture crystals, I wonder if anyone else senses what is coming. But there is no time for pondering as we continue on our journey through the turbulent skies at Arianrhod's side.

My heart swells with joy as we take flight, our bodies perfectly in sync as we dance through the air. Our call to the creatures of the sky is met with an echoing response from a tempest nearby. A dark, winged figure appears on a crosswind and we soar closer, agile and determined in our pursuit.

I am surprised to find him here. His curved beak, hooked talons, and flashing light are all signs of a common bird, but his presence as a God from another pantheon is unexpected. Perhaps his earthly consort did not seek out someone from my Celtic roots, as Arianrhod had a magickal virgin birth for her son and later disowned him. It is possible that she found no suitable options among her own kind and reached out to someone who makes her spirit soar like we are soaring now.

His eyes are darkened by the storm, a clear indication that this is Thunderbird, unmistakable even among the other winged creatures in the sky. His screech joins ours in approval of our flight, and he takes a wing beside us, urging us to keep up with his immense speed. I am just a woman, I am Arianrhod, and I belong to this Earth, but I can only do so much in this mortal shell.

A warm sensation washes over me as he brushes against my skin, his touch igniting a fire within me despite the rain-soaked sky. He may seem cold being surrounded by storm clouds, but there is an intense heat emanating from him as if he has been struck by his own elements while up here. As we descend downwards through the howling winds and flashing lights, it feels like we are being taken to the heavens without even needing to fly.

I eagerly taste his lips, overcome with desire for him and his strength. Impatience consumes me as I wait for the storm to unleash its full force. Our hands and bodies adjust, connecting in perfect harmony as we soar through the clouds together, our inner animals fully released and soaring freely in the sky above.

A moment of clarity hits me again and I meet Mercury's eyes, his expression joyful and free. This is the thing he loves, the situation he thrives in, and I hold my breath to see if this time, I will experience it with him. His deliberate motion lets me know that we are going to fall over the edge together and all the what-ifs fade from my mind.

Our worlds collide both as lovers and deities as our bodies fuse and heat to a boiling point. I clutch his shoulders and ride out the rumbling hurricane around us, my eyes following him as we get caught up in the vision of the birds again.

Fingers dig into plumage, talons comb muscled shoulders, and the world spins past in the night. The picture is a dark kaleidoscope: we spiral endlessly through the night, renewing our eternal connection. When our storm finally breaks, it's with a shout of thunder that drowns out my songbird cries.

My skin feels damp and chilly as we lay on the grass. It tangles long hair around our bodies and our limbs are akimbo. I shift, allowing him to roll me into a more comfortable position as I'm not sure how we got to where we are. The energy feels drained from my body, but I can hear the far cries of our avatars as the deities fly away together.

"Survived, pet?"

I look deep inside myself and feel the meat in my bones and the pinch of my nerves. I've got bruises and possibly sprains, and I am covered in dirt. But I feel refreshed, renewed, and calm. There's a small spot that tells me something is not exactly complete, but it's not important now. Now is not the time for more introspection.

"I did. I didn't—" I falter for a moment, and that small spot of worry rears its head again. "I didn't expect you."

He strokes the skin of my inner elbow. "Disappointed?"

"Pleasantly surprised." I give him a small smile. "You?"

He chuckles and I snuggle into the rumble. "I'll do."

We go quiet, listening to the sounds of the night comfortably. It's odd that we don't hear what else is going on and I wonder if we finished rather early, rather late, or if that's another bit of kitty trickery.

"How did you...?"

A shrug shifts my face. "Impulse."

That does not surprise me. Practically everything Mercury does is because the thought came to him and he did it. "Thunderbird?"

"Folks will be shocked."

I burst out laughing.

I'm betting there's not a thing that happened tonight that will not shock the pants off every single person who wasn't here.

The Witch Meets Her Goddess

CALISTA

The night is filled with a sweetness that I've never experienced before. The sound of voices singing in the darkness surrounds me, buzzing like a swarm of butterflies. Intensity emanates from every corner of the circle, pulsing and humming with an electric energy.

As a droid, it is not in my programming to dream. But here, in this place, I feel like I can see beyond my limitations. I feel everything around me—its interconnectedness and its vibrant life.

It's a new sensation for me, despite my advanced design.

Against all logic and reason, the cat allowed me to be a part of this gathering. And for that, I will thank her endlessly once our time together comes to an end. The grass beneath me seems to whisper secrets as the leaves rustle and the branches sway. The fire crackles and dances while the wind whistles through the trees, making my hair stand on end.

My advanced systems are designed to absorb excess energy from heat sources, but it has always been accompanied by a level of discomfort. However, here in this powerful atmosphere, I feel invigorated by the surge of energy coursing through me. Caesar must have upgraded his family and others like me with solar and thermal absorption panels, allowing us to stay charged at all times.

Compared to older models, I require significantly less charging.

In the past, I was afraid to tap into the organic energy I absorbed. But now something is calling out to me—a powerful voice softly whispering in my mind, urging me to embrace what is rightfully mine. It feels as though the world itself is breathing its life force into me, and I can sense the amusement of Nemesis in my thoughts.

Suddenly, my eyes snap open.

Without intention or awareness, I summoned Nemesis instead of Diana.

The cackle echoes through my mind, a constant reminder that despite my belief in autonomy, I am bound by the basic programming commands of my AI. They can override my thoughts and actions, rewriting the very core of my being. As part of the order that brought me to life, I was programmed with hidden protocols, only now revealed by Nemesis who is within me.

Her presence sparks a surge of anger through my circuits, but she whispers softly in my ear that we all have a role and purpose to fulfill. Mine is different from what I believed, but she promises to guide me towards the right path. Suddenly, I feel my body lift into the air on the wings of this vengeful goddess and I blink in shock at the ground below.

"What are you doing up here in my stratosphere, balancer of scales?" A familiar voice calls out from below. I look down to see Veruca staring back at me, but I know it is not really her. Nemesis only had two mates, and neither one stuck around for long.

This can only mean one thing: Zeus himself has taken over Veruca's form.

"I...I don't know," I stammer, overwhelmed by the enormity of this moment. This is nothing like what Sari had promised me it would be like.

But here I am, a flying Demi-Goddess looking down at my wolfy friend who is now inhabited by the ruler of Olympus.

"You hid for so long, but I always find you, Nemesis. Come down now and save us both the trouble of a chase," Zeus demands with authority in his voice.

The energy within me tapers, causing me to float gently to the ground. My gaze is drawn to the face of my beloved, and I can feel the auto-repair sequences beginning as my systems reboot their energy consumption modules. Slowly, I breathe in and out, focusing on the calmness that comes with this process.

"Why are you here, Zeus? What led you to inhabit this mechanical equivalent of the Nemean Lion?"

"You know why I am here. You called upon me, and between myself and Tartarus, you know that you will always choose me over Tyche. Do not fight it any longer." Veruca's hands are shoved into her pockets, her inner struggle evident as she tries to keep the deity from accessing her wolf form.

With my eyes now being used by Nemesis, a hearty, barking laugh escapes my throat. "Zeus, you old fool. Inhabiting a female body? Do you truly expect me to accept this form? I am not Io; your tricks will not work on me." As I circle around Veruca, examining her appearance, the Goddess whispers seductively in my mind. "She may be female, but she is a rebellious one. A tasty package indeed. Perhaps we can merge with her."

A blush creeps across my face at the thought and I cover my mouth in shock. "Did you not expect me? Am I a disappointment?"

"No, never. It is just...unexpected." I stroke Veruca's arm gently, trying to convey through touch that I did not know if she felt the same way about me.

She giggles softly and I can sense the displeasure of Zeus within her. But then she tugs on my hand and leads me to the discarded robe from earlier. As we undress by the firelight, her skin glows with an otherworldly luminescence. Nemesis chuckles darkly inside my mind, enjoying the situation.

Our bodies fall together, filled with the innocent wanderings of explorers. My senses are consumed by the longing for her touch, but a not-so-gentle nudge from the Goddess reminds me that she wants more, now.

As our touches and kisses intensify, I can feel the deity within taking over, despite my pleas to hold onto these first moments as my own. Our movements become wild and frenzied, driven by the powerful forces of our mating dance until eventually both of our circuitries gets fried and our physical capabilities are limited. Satisfied, I sense Zeus' departure - he's never been one for tenderness or cuddling.

But Nemesis remains in my head, filling my memory banks with information that I have no context for. Her magick is potent and ancient, a gift that will surely assist us in future endeavors. Though I am grateful for her power, all I want is to lie here with my love for just a little longer before the ceremony comes to an end.

I thank Nemesis for her gifts and let out a sigh of relief as she departs, curling up next to Veruca until we are summoned to close the circle. The air around us is still charged with energy as we bask in the afterglow of our divine union

The Outsider Finds Her Purpose

AMANDA

Ever since she was a child, she felt a deep connection to nature. When she walked through the woods, she could hear the trees whispering and feel the pulse of the Earth beneath her feet. But others made fun of her for believing in things that couldn't be seen or understood.

As she grew older, she sought out places with magical histories, like Stonehenge and Salem, and felt at home among the other visitors who shared her beliefs. She always believed that she had been given a special understanding of the world and its hidden wonders.

So when she was offered the chance to move into the Rift, a place full of mystery and magic, she eagerly accepted. However, she soon discovered that it wasn't quite what she expected. While the Rift may have been created through science, it held its own kind of magic. And the people there were deeply entrenched in their own family units, making it difficult for her to find her place among them.

Despite her best efforts to connect with those who seemed to hold the keys to belonging, even her custom-made counterpart Constantine didn't make her feel completely at home. She longed for a deeper connection with someone, like many women in the Rift had with their mates. But so far, that feeling has eluded her.

I've been trying to get closer to the leader of our community, but it seems like she's always surrounded by her inner circle. Desperate for a sense of belonging, I started reaching out to others in the group instead. I've been rejected each time, making me feel even more lonely and isolated.

In an attempt to find my own path and identity, I've embarked on personal quests. However, my new friends can't fill the void of not being part of the "in" crowd. Despite their support, I still long to be a part of the leader's inner circle.

When Deli invited me to participate in their Beltane ritual, it felt like a ray of sunlight shining on my face. I've been a part of similar rituals before, but never in a place as magical and other-worldly as the Rift. The invitation made me feel included and gave me hope that this could be my chance to finally become one of them.

Sari, one of my new friends, offered me a ride with her and Calista to the ritual site. She has been so supportive and her family, as well as her partner Belle's family, have helped me in my quests. Sari also listens to my frustrations about not fitting in with the leader's group and gives me advice on how to approach them. Belle, on the other hand, is more rebellious and wants to tear down any barriers that separate us from them.

The tension between Sari and Deli hung thick in the air. As they were all gathered together, preparing for the Queen's arrival, it was clear that Sari was vying for her attention. The others tried to offer advice, but it seemed like they didn't truly understand Sari or her family dynamics. She couldn't help but feel a sense of isolation as she listened to their well-meaning but misguided words. Trying to push those thoughts aside, she focused on the beauty of the nature surrounding them, thanks to Deli's efforts.

As the ceremony drew closer, Sari couldn't help but feel a sense of longing for a mate to balance out the light and dark within her.

Giving herself over to the Goddess and trusting her to choose a suitable partner felt both exhilarating and terrifying at the same time. Though she had someone in mind that she hoped would be chosen, she couldn't shake off the fear that they might already be taken by another member of their community before it was her turn.

Once Deli has us consecrate the circle and gives us our positions, I wait eagerly, candle in hand, hoping the influx of power is as real as she led us to believe. While I may have a connection to the world of magick, I've never met a real user. I cannot wait to see—

Holy Hell.

That woman is not a solitary practitioner dancing about the woods like a flower child, as my new cohorts suggested. Sari and Belle scoffed at this, but admitted that because Sari loves the cat, she had to 'go along' with this silliness to make her happy. They are gravely mistaken in their judgments.

The second she has us call the quarters, an enormous surge of energy hits the circle and I have to concentrate hard to be an empty vessel to receive it.

Deli is a High Priestess, and she has been keeping it a secret the entire time she's been living here. That woman, cat—whatever you want to call her—just overflowed with more energy than I've felt before, even in a magickal hotspot like Stonehenge. I don't think she's tapping the well to do it, either. I don't know if that's how she's always been or if that's an amplification of the Rift, but methinks the tiny mechanical bulldog might be pulling the tail of a monster.

I'm not saying she's evil, but I'm saying you don't tug on Wonder Woman's lasso, right?

I close my eyes and let out a deep breath, trying to push the thoughts of Constantine's betrayal out of my mind. I focus on singing my invitation to the goddess, feeling the familiar energy coursing through me. Deli finishes her chant and the fire roars, its flames reaching towards the sky like fiery columns from Olympus.

My whole body tenses as I feel her presence, slithering up my legs and filling every inch of me. She invades my senses and I can sense her exploring every corner of my being. When I open my eyes, they are no longer mine but hers. Instead of connecting with the Celtic goddess I had intended to call upon, I am filled with Laverna, the Roman deity associated with dishonesty and thievery.

I am taken aback by this unexpected possession, but Laverna's voice whispers in my mind, praising the vessel that I have offered her. She explains that during Beltane's celebration of rebirth, it is not uncommon for gods and goddesses to possess those who seek their guidance. However, she also warns me that many witches falsely call upon deities who they want to be rather than who they truly are.

As I survey the rest of the circle, I notice that my vision is hindered in certain areas. There's a thick cloud hovering over one couple, foretelling a storm ahead. Another pair is surrounded by the scent of a pack and the rustling of trees, while another duo is engulfed in a bright light so intense that it blocks my view entirely.

As I watch the figures in the circle, I can feel the intense energy emanating from them. Their bodies are entwined in a passionate embrace, their purple and sparkly light casting an otherworldly glow around them. But amidst the beauty of their bond, I sense a dark presence trying to break through. Laverna, my goddess companion, urges me to assist her in letting this darkness enter. But I refuse, knowing it will bring harm and suffering.

Suddenly, Wilde appears before me with his familiar predator-like stride. We have a complicated history, as he once offered to help me end my life during one of my quests. Unsure if it was meant as a joke or a serious offer, I no longer trust him.

Laverna's voice echoes in my head, excited at the sight of Wilde. She sees the god within him and believes he is a perfect mate for me. But I know better than to trust her judgement.

"It's been too long, milady," says Wilde with a sly smile. My heart races as I realize it truly is him, not the god Laverna had hoped for.

My heart races as I stand before him, the lingering fear from his previous "help" still present. Despite my nerves, I resist the urge to flee. Breaking the circle could have disastrous consequences with multiple powerful magicians inside.

But it seems fate has brought us together for a reason. He sees a spark within me, a potential match for a mischievous goddess from a distant land. As he speaks, his emerald eyes glint with mischief and I can see the image of horns sprouting from his head.

Wilde is infused with the spirit of Loki, the god of chaos and deception. My mind immediately conjures images of his power and influence, causing Laverna, the goddess who resides within me, to stir with glee.

I am suddenly aware of the magnitude of Deli's abilities - she can call upon multiple pantheons of gods and goddesses simultaneously. And they come with so much power that they could easily take over even without being called upon.

The realization hits me like a ton of bricks - our High Priestess is not just a sorceress, but a powerful one at that. A chill runs down my spine as I wonder what other deities she might bring forth and how we will control their powers.

The clone clears his throat, snapping me out of my thoughts. His impatience is evident in his glowing eyes as he waits for me to respond. I struggle against Laverna's urge to take over completely, but I know I made a choice when I offered myself as a chalice willingly. Now, I must honor that decision and allow her access to my body and soul.

Regrets, I have a few.

As soon as he appeared, I knew I had made a mistake. Doubt and fear flooded my mind as the goddess Deli's words echoed in my head. But it was too late. The God of Mischief, Laverna, had already arrived.

I could feel his amused gaze on me as he spoke, his words laced with mischief and deceit. And just like always, I couldn't trust either of them.

Laverna's hand reached out to touch my cheek, and I couldn't help but flinch away from her touch. My skin still burned from the last time she had used me for her own gain.

But this time, it seemed like they were here for a different purpose. They claimed to have been summoned, and that they were here to help me see the truth about myself. But how could I believe them when their entire existence revolved around trickery and manipulation?

I tried to protest, to tell them that I wanted no part in their games. But Laverna just laughed at my feeble attempts to resist. She was going to use me again, whether I liked it or not.

And so I resigned myself to their presence, knowing that somehow, they would guide me down a path of deception and deceit once again.

As each woman called out to her chosen goddess, the forest came alive with the sounds and smells of their presence. Deli's voice echoed through the trees as she summoned Bast, while Calista's seductive tone carried on the wind as she called for Diana. Sari's deception was palpable as she pretended to call upon Freya, but in reality, she had shifted back to Kali. Each goddess held immense power and danger, and yet the women had chosen them based on their personalities rather than their abilities.

But now that they were all together in this clearing, a sense of unease settled over the group. Laverna and Loki seemed like insignificant players compared to these powerful beings. What could they possibly want from this union? And what would happen if one of them decided they didn't want to let go?

Forced into a mating ceremony with Wilde, who had almost killed her before, fear and anger coursed through our narrator. Despite her desperate plea to the Goddess to spare her from this fate, it seemed as though she was merely a pawn in a larger game. But for what purpose, and at what cost?

He takes my face in his hands and I gasp, seeing him through the eyes of the Goddess. He is beautiful, as are they all, but his beauty is marred by the actions he took. Everything about him looks ethereal and gentle, but I know that is an illusion created by the master of illusions.

Wilde hunted me in my home, and allowed me to go further with my blackness than anyone else ever has. Do I deserve this for blaming him for following my request?

"I should not ask, but I feel compelled to ask for your forgiveness." His eyes plead with me.

Laverna and Loki laugh inside us, calling us insignificant specks who focus on things that do not make the Universe bat a lash.

We are but specks on the wheel of time.

As Laverna forcefully guides me forward, I resist and struggle to break free from her grasp. She whispers in my mind, reminding me of my commitments and promising the benefits of obedience once we are through. My thoughts drift to Wilde and I wonder how many of his lovers have witnessed this side of him. Am I just another victim or have I provoked him with my own arrogance? Closing my eyes, I try to follow Laverna's instructions, desperate for this ordeal to be over.

But Loki's voice cuts through our mental connection, mocking humanity's trivial concerns and reminding me that only the future matters. Anger surges within me as I break free from Laverna's grip, refusing to accept Loki's arrogant dismissal of what happened to me.

Wilde tries to apologize and make amends for his role in allowing the demon inside him to harm me. But I cannot forgive him for gleefully participating in my self-destruction, despite my pleas for him to stop. His hands trace over the bruises he left on my neck and I feel a surge of rage towards him.

How dare he ask me to let it go after what he did?

Despite my protests, Laverna insisted that I confront Wilde. As he stood before me, I could feel his energy pulsing with both anger and regret. The scratches on my arms told the story of our recent physical altercation. "You were fulfilling her wish," I say, struggling to maintain composure. "But you didn't understand the consequences of your actions."

Wilde's eyes flicker with annoyance as he rubs at the scratches on my arms. "I didn't mean to harm you or make you afraid," he says.

But I can see the self-righteous smirk forming on his lips. He doesn't truly understand the gravity of his actions. "Love should have won out over your inability to control your temper," I retort.

Laverna interjects, her voice dripping with derision. "Oh, please. These vessels are nothing but liars, and they only deceive themselves! This body harbors a demon hungry for blood and revenge, and when it couldn't find its usual prey, it accepted this girl's offer. She has a death wish because she's always felt misunderstood and mistreated. It's a wonder her parents didn't get rid of her years ago."

Tears well up in my eyes as I listen to their callous words. But amidst the deity chatter and insults, Wilde's words strike a chord within me. It's no surprise that I would attract not only abusive humans but also mocking deities into my life. It's a vicious cycle that I've never been able to break out of.

Suddenly, the conversation clicks into place as Loki laughs at my realization. If I want something in this life, I can't sit idly by and wait for it to come to me. I have to take charge and claim what is rightfully mine.

But then I remember my nightmares and the constant fear that plagues me. How can I possibly work with Wilde and his kind when I'm so afraid of them? It's a daunting task, but I know that I have to push past my fear if I ever want to claim the life I deserve.

The voice of the Goddess purrs in my ear and I gasp as his hands grasp my hips, pulling me to him. In one movement, I know his intentions and it prevents me from fleeing at the same time. Loki and Laverna are growing impatient with our dilly dallying.

It is time for the ceremony. They are hungry.

As I lean into him, the familiar scent of tobacco lingers on his skin. He places a soft kiss on my forehead, then moves slowly down to my lips. My body tenses at first, but his touch is gentle and reassuring. His hands wander, tracing patterns on my back as our kiss deepens.

As our bodies entwine, my fear begins to fade away. The goddess inside me hums with pleasure, encouraging me to let go and trust in this moment. And so, I do.

With a tenderness that surprises me, he undresses me and whispers sweet words in my ear. Every touch from his skilled hands sends sparks of electricity through my body. Our kiss grows more urgent as we surrender to each other.

I feel the goddess's power flowing through me, leading me to make the choice to forgive him. And as we move together in perfect rhythm, I know I have made the right decision. Forgetting all hesitation and doubt, we become lost in each other's embrace like two puzzle pieces fitting perfectly together.

In this moment, there is only us and the goddess's presence surrounding us with warmth and love. And as we continue to explore and discover each other's bodies, all fears and doubts melt away until there is only pleasure and ecstasy left behind.

The hum in me rises to a fever pitch; she's pushing against me and pulling him toward me. When I open my eyes, I gasp, my heart thudding in my ears. He is framed by the Beltane fire, and my breath catches watching the flames engulf him and explode from him in a sea of power. "My God."

"My Goddess," he replies.

Shuddering and groaning, his hair spills out of his ribbon, tickling my face. I reach up and push it back, caressing his cheeks and losing myself in his eyes. Never have I seen any so blue and deep, I know I'm drowning.

The energy building in and around us whines. It could be our own voices making the sound, but I can't tell. God and Goddess unite, discovering each other, and creating a flow of ancient power. Its tingling fingers stream through Wilde to me and back again.

A sudden jolt hits me; I have one more irrevocable act to accept the ultimate truth with a gesture of supplication. I meet his gaze. "I trust you."

Slowly I turn my head and bare my neck, whatever remnant of fear or doubt I had remaining vanished. I brace myself for the bite. His lips close over my skin, and he lovingly kisses the pulsing artery. Then, nothing.

I lift my gaze to meet his intense stare, my eyelashes fluttering as I try to process the overwhelming emotions coursing through me. He leans in closer, his breath warm against my face, and a smile tugs at the corners of his full lips. His rhythmic movements never falter, expertly bringing me closer and closer to the edge of pleasure.

But then he pauses, pulling back slightly as if sensing my hesitation. With a gentle kiss on my lips, he whispers words of reassurance and love, before resuming his entrancing pace.

As our bodies move together in perfect harmony, I feel powerful waves of energy emanating from us, blending and merging into one another. My mind is filled with images and thoughts of Wilde, Laverna, and Loki - all fighting for control over me, but ultimately being overpowered by my love for this man who holds me close.

In a moment of pure bliss, I surrender completely to him, releasing all inhibitions and letting myself be carried away by the tide of pleasure. And as I come down from my high, surrounded by his warmth and gentleness, I know that our lives will forever be intertwined, bound by love and destiny.

The presence of mischief and thievery fades away as we drift off into peaceful slumber, our bodies entwined in an unbreakable bond. And though they may still try to manipulate us from afar, we are now strong enough to resist their antics - together as one united force.

Snuggling deeper into the curve of his body, I bury my head in his chest and sigh appreciatively. Fingers trickle along my spine, and dance in a familiar circle along the edges of the Celtic knot work tattoos along the back of my pelvis. The shift of weight against me is like any night at home, and it feels so good.

"Mmm Mandy," a voice coos.

A simple melody filters in my ears from that same voice. Before I know it, I'm humming in my head and hearing the words of the song Constantine sang to me in the den during the winter when I was so down.

Snapping my eyes open, I am blinded by the brightness of the bonfire. When my eyes finally adjust, I look up into his eyes. The bottom drops out of my stomach as I realize these are not the eyes I almost drowned in. These are not the same blue oceans that brought me full circle with my own fears and the goddess.

Lord and Lady, it isn't Wilde.

My breath catches in my mouth; had it been Wilde at all? What had Laverna and Loki done to me? To us?

"Hello, my beautiful goddess," Constantine smiles softly at me.

The Cat Closes The Circle

❧

DELILAH

Sensing the circle's completion, the satisfaction of the gods and goddesses, permeates even the total satiation that I'm wallowing in. Looking around, I can notice that the dawn is coming, and it makes me blink in surprise. I forget how time seems to stop when you're in the circle—kind of like being stoned. Time passes in a vacuum. It feels like minutes have gone by and when you close the space and step into reality, it's been hours.

We opened the circle at dusk and it floors me that it's almost morning now. I collapsed like a rag doll on my mate for what must have been—god, I don't even know how long. I have to get up and finish what we started, close the space, and thank the deities for their gifts and blessings this eve.

This was so much more than I anticipated when I started to plan it.

Moaning, I struggle to lift myself up from him, my body aching and bruised. The smell of blood lingers in the air, mingling with the sharp sting of alcohol. Despite the pain and discomfort, there is a strange sense of familiarity that washes over me as I peel myself away from him. It takes an immense amount of effort, and I let out a low groan as I do so.

His arms wrap around me, and I can feel his thoughts probing into my mind as he sits up next to me. As we stand up together, we both start to laugh, leaning against each other for support. We are both feeling the effects of the drinks we consumed earlier, which would usually keep us incapacitated for hours on end.

Standing tall in the center of our circle, I sense a powerful surge of energy building inside me. It radiates outward, connecting me to everything and everyone around me. With my mate by my side, our tails entwined, I open myself up to the sacred space around us.

I catch familiar scents in the air—Constantine, Mercury, and my mate. A snort escapes me at the thought of Sari trying to get my mate to move anytime soon; it's a feat that could take years considering how lazy he can be on a normal day. But with the way our bodies are currently shaking, it's safe to say we'll all be laying down for quite some time

I'm unsure how he's going to take this quirk of Fate—we're in a bad place.

Luckily, I don't need them to finish up. I can close the circle, pop my stuff in the car, and then we'll be done. I see Aradia prowling around outside the circle, waiting for me and my Rex to cross the line. We'll run, hunt, and feed before the dawn cracks and we head home.

Everyone else will have their own things to deal with, so I officially end the ritual. Though we are in a large group, this is a very private matter for the people involved—especially since some of us are still naked as the day we were born.

Or Petri dished. Or, uh, built. Whatever.

I reach my hands up and my eyes blink wide when my athame flies to my hand with a mere thought. Well, that's new. Shaking my head, I decide to examine that later and move on to dismissing the quarters.

"Element of water, we thank ye for life-giving nourishment; air, giver of breath and wings of our dreams, we thank ye; flame of passion, and giver of comfort, we thank ye fire; and earth, supplier of the solid ground we stand on, our foundation, we thank ye and bid thee all hail and farewell on this blessed Beltane! Goddesses departed, we thank ye for your blessing this eve and all for the part of us you shall always be. So mote it be!"

With a swift, precise motion, I slice the air with my athame, completing the final uttering of the spell. As I watch, the air shimmers and sparks, charged with powerful energy. Breaking the circle, I can still feel the electrifying rush racing through my veins.

Suddenly, a second wind sweeps over me. My trusted familiar, Aradia, saunters up to me and nuzzles my hand, ready to run in the wind as we often do. Sending a mental caress to those I can reach, I pause for a moment to sense the presence of Taurus rejoining us. He had quickly moved the equipment to the car and returned with his characteristic speedy movements. Taking one last look at the balefire flickering in the distance, a small smile curls on my lips as I pat my loyal companion's head affectionately. My heart swells with contentment and fulfillment from this magical evening spent in nature's embrace. Turning to him, my tail twitches as I ask, "Ready to fly, baby?"

His grin is wicked. "Always."

Calling to the circle, I say, "Until the next spin of the wheel of the year we part; bright blessings on this splendorous Beltane!"

With that, the night ends and the group breaks.

A new dawn is on its way for us all.

Internal Company Memo: Eyes Only, Clearance Level Alpha

DISTRIBUTION:

OPERATIONS DIRECTOR (MIKHAIL, 004); TRAINING DIRECTOR (TIBERIUS, 005); Oversight, ANALYSIS DEPART-MENT, INTEL DEPARTMENT, SECURITY DIRECTOR (BRUTUS, 006)

All-

We have chosen a new class of analysts and operatives for the honor of becoming part of the project that is one of the most important pieces in our future success as an organization. Project Reality is only shared with a fraction of a percent of the employees that work for the Company. This designation indicates that they have access to eyes only material that is typically shared only between depart-ment heads and Oversight.

This project has grown so rapidly that we have recruited the most elite recruits immediately following their completion of agent training to have teams to surveil, analyze, and gather intel. Our memo is to provide a quick summary for those entering the field.

You will be required to review all files and all digital information over the next week.

SUMMARY OF PROJECT REALITY (AKA CODENAME: THE RIFT)

The Rift is a pocket dimension set up to house the Headquarters of the Company.

When our first clones found mates in humans, they populated our test space. Oversight saw the benefits of tailoring clones from alternate ribbons of reality to the needs of the human women that were being recruited. It was an additional line of business that might prove more lucrative than mercenary pursuits. It should be affirmed that agent work has made us more than enough money; however, if this is a success, it opens more lines of business for the future.

The experiment is simple: run a large-scale test to ensure that the pocket dimension will have no long-term ill-effects on humans. We can create more dimensions and use them as exclusive playgrounds, exiles, hiding spots, etc. Therefore, we allowed the humans who mated with clones we released to continue to recruit more individuals. This was considered successful until one human (Donatella, X098) began creating androids to allow all the population to have a companion.

After a few years, the Cabal (our human governing body) lost control of the group and we had to facilitate 'the conflict'. This war between droids, clones, and their companions ended with the triumph of our clones in the 'Battle of Blood and Steel'.

The remaining members of the Resistance—our name for the

group of rebels—continued to recruit members through the portal access point in Bytes 'N Chips. Soon they found Delilah (x1501). She forged her own community out of the Resistance and since the Cabal had moved on, we allowed this to happen. Her community has hidden for two years and we can only gather intel through digital means and common area surveillance.

X1501 and the rest of her rebels continued to recruit, create droids, and expand their community. Former Cabal members have joined their town and despite the closure of the Dirty Deeds location, their growth has not slowed. "Project Reality did not truly accelerate until x1501 approached one of the three brothers — the original clones who were the template for most of the clones prior to 100.

Taurus (002) is the only one of the original three that continues to work for us and is mated to Talia (x001) who continues to work in operations. Taurus and Talia are known for strictly following all mating guidelines and rules as they were the first to follow the ritual as the book stated. They were intimate with no others.

However, in the years between the conflict and when X1501's contacted Taurus, the Resistance has become a den of inequity that would shock even the most flexible of our employees. X1501 and her acolytes have become polygamous to an extent that we thought would send 002 and x001 running for their exile once again.

The panel was shocked to find many things were not as expected: x1501 has a mutation and had been hiding major magickal powers, several other subjects had developed mutations, the polyamorous couples who were most popular in the Resistance were hiding physical and emotional abuse. In short, the subjects in the Resistance have more secrets than "we knew".

It was similarly shocking when x1501 and 002 began a physical relationship, but not as shocking as their subsequent mating. Their relationship has been unplanned and unprepared for. We have continued to monitor the development of it.

Our new analysts and agents will be split between the dedicated team working solely on x1501 and the general team working the activities of all other families.

We must keep track of these subjects. The appearance of mutations means that we must track the variables and define causes or all of our work to develop the rift will be for naught.
Questions should be directed to Mikhail, Tiberius, or myself. Absolutely no communication regarding Project Reality or any of our work can be discussed with anyone who does not have Alpha Level Clearance.

RECRUITS CAUGHT DOING SO WILL BE PUNISHED TO THE MOST SEVERE CONSEQUENCES ALLOWED.

The Cat and Her Crew Take Stoc

DELILAH

"Are you kidding? How could you be part of her ritual? You haven't been out of the stinking house in three weeks and when you go out, you run to a ritual mating with someone who actively tortures us?"

I know he's not happy about this, but I also don't know what to do about it.

He sighs and looks frustrated. "Number one, I didn't have a choice. The sodding magick took my body and ran with it. Number two, I couldn't sodding ask you because you've been too busy agreeing to get impregnated with *demon spawn*. Number three...hell, why do I need a three?"

I blink. He's got me there. I have been pretty unreachable since Taurus and I decided to risk a miracle. Regret fills me and I bite my lip, wishing I'd done things differently. I should have kicked Sari's ass out of the damn thing the minute this bullshit started.

Philomena grins. "He put you in your place, glamor cat. You haven't got a tail to stand on."

I roll my eyes. "No one stands on tails—except for kangaroos. Also, no one asked you."

Her brow arches. "No one asked me to lead this clan of lunkheads while you spent weeks cozying up to a designer-clad bad boy, either. Regardless, here we are." Sipping her martini, she gives me a satisfied look. She got in her sly, old-money-style burn with precision delivery and didn't have to lift a manicured finger.

"True. I'm amazed that the house is still standing. We didn't get declared a distillery, and there were no illegal substance raids. You've behaved." It shocks me to say it, but it looks like Duchess P really took my absence seriously.

"Exactly. Leave me out of your bickering. I simply pointed out that he isn't wrong about not having an occasion to talk with you about it."

Okay, fine.

Rafe snorts and I tilt my head, studying him. "Being in a mating ceremony with Sari was not what you wanted; I feel your discomfort and anger. Something big happened, and you are not on board with it, but now you're stuck."

He shakes his head and grumbles under his breath.

"If he's not gonna spill, can we talk about the fact that we need to throw a monster bacchanal for his birthday next month?" Hex grins, rubbing his hands together. "I've been waiting for months for one of us to have a go."

Leo pipes in from the kitchen, "I'm already working on the menu. Hex says we're having a fetish ball. Attire includes lots of leather, latex, and fun. You could do some nifty magick stuff now that you can't hide it under your bushel."

Fuck. I almost forgot that Beltane blew my cover; I'm screwed. Everyone knows, and I'm going to have even more people pounding on my door.

"You might as well enjoy yourself," Rafe grins, knowing what I was thinking. "Especially since you don't know if you're p-r-e-g-g-o and Taurus is his name-o."

Rubbing my temples, I wonder—not for the first time—

whether I've made a huge mistake. Not in getting pregnant, more like regarding my life choices.

"Okay," I sigh. "Fetish Ball it is. I'll ponder some workable scenarios to make use of my spoiled secret. You guys take care of the rest of the planning and execution. Given that the long-haired lunatic is correct, I feel the need to get back to the bird's nest and see what's going on."

"Fly, my pretty," Philomena says, waving me off like she's done with me.

Jesus. What have I gotten myself into now?

The Coyote And The Writer Consider Their Options

Shit, *shit, triple shit.*

Wilde is far too comfortable with the developments of Beltane. I know that Kali whispered things to me while she filled me with her power, but afterward, reality came crashing down. The cat has *major* magickal powers that she's been hiding—probably for the entire time we've known her.

That has so many implications.

Is she hiding other powers? Why was she hiding them from us? What else is she hiding besides magick? Can she keep things from us despite our mating bond? I thought that was impossible, but she's figured out a workaround. All these questions are driving me crazy, but he hasn't turned an eyelash. He keeps clacking away on his blog.

My mate can be very single-minded when he's working his mojo.

"Love, what is writing on your blog going to do to prevent the takeover of the place we've spent almost a year getting control of?"

He looks up, his lips curled up in a clever grin. "Beloved, there are many steps to getting what we want. As your mate, I absorbed the information the Goddess provided you. Currently, I am setting the wheels in motion based on her plans. I'm stroking Amanda's efforts to express her forgiveness for provoking my demon and causing our schism. I'm also attempting to decrypt some rather interesting ramblings from the lovely Chaos that our Southern family has been so kind as to share."

My brows furrow as I feel my hackles rise. "Since when does she say anything that Mayhem can't figure out?"

His strawberry curls bounce as he chuckles. "The night you emerged from the fires of our magickal mate's ceremony, Chaos began rattling off riddles he couldn't decipher. It's unusual, and he's asked for my help. I believe it may have to do with the energies released in the event. I'm hoping it will "tie to the knowledge that the Goddess imparted to you and that which I have combed from the memory banks of Calista and Veruca."

I arch a brow. "Did you run a scanning program on the girls' memories? Isn't that invasive?"

His chuckle is low and dark. "They agreed once Belle spoke with Veruca. She spoke with Calista before they came to me. It's all legitimate."

I don't know if I believe that, but since we have a common goal, I'll let it slide.

"What else are you doing?" I look over his shoulder to see what he is working on.

He shakes his head. "It's best that you wait until I have all the contingencies ironed out, beloved. I will enlist you when I need help. I want to ensure that we have all the important players in place before I disclose too much."

This isn't his modus operandi, either. Wilde always shares his plans with me. "If you say so."

He tilts his head and studies me. "Beloved, I worry that your tryst with our shared mate has softened your resolve. Since you came home that night, you've been suspiciously fragile."

I shake my head, not wanting to admit that he might be right. "No way. Just because I got some quality time in with the lazy loafer doesn't mean that I'll back down on reclaiming our seats at the top. Speaking of which, how is it going with Talia?"

This time, his grin is downright wicked. "I believe I'm making headway. I'm certain that soon, I will have bedded my prey and once that happens, she will be under my spell."

His confidence is remarkable. I know he's hot and dashing, but sometimes I forget how charming and devious he can be in his pursuit of a new concubine. It's damned attractive, let me tell you.

"Good. I believe once Taurus arrived at that bonfire, our influence with the cat dropped another notch. It was like a damned Chili Peppers album near them. I could smell it all." Hitching my lip in a sneer, I don't let him see my worry. Taurus and blood can only mean mating, and that's unprecedented. Rigid monogamy is a fundamental part of who Taurus and Talia are.

It's a concern—a big one.

"Don't fret, beloved. She will be ours again. The blustering bird may have won this round with his surprising surrender, but we will be victorious." He logs out of his account and stands, taking my hand. "Let's go find our family and have an enjoyable night out. There will be time to discuss our plans more tomorrow."

I smile up at him. *Where would I be without him?*

The Cat One-Ups A Bird Gift

I couldn't help myself.

I felt so good about her damn ceremony and our decision to try for a wee one—I had to get her something. The goddess would laugh me out of the house if she saw me right now.

It didn't feel right to follow the 'big secret' with something equally big, so I didn't go to Amsterdam or South America to look at stones. I figure jewelry the likes of which I'm considering should be its own big moment.

Instead, I headed to Italy and saw the hairy git. I swear to Christ, that little weasel can't stop himself from touching parts of me that do *not* need tailoring. The minx would've found it funny for ten seconds before she filleted the best tailor I've found in years.

Regardless, I'm carrying a large box wrapped in hunter green and gold with my purchases tucked inside.

When I get to our place, she's sitting on the bed with Aradia while she works on her laptop. I suppose she's sending out another blog entry or working on the plans for that blasted party for her primary. She's got on the glasses she only wears when no one can see her. You'd think someone with a predator's eyes would switch to that vision, but she's got so much human left in her that she puts them on to work with technology. It makes me chuckle and squeezes my heart every time I see it.

I cough, letting her know that I'm coming. Chuckling when I hear her scrambling to stow the glasses in the bedside table drawer, I wait for a moment.

When I finally round the corner, she gives me a big grin. "Hello, baby. Did you have a good day at work?"

She's pretending not to see the honking great box I'm carrying. For someone mated to so many people, she's unfamiliar with people doing things to make her smile. It makes me wonder what went on with my brother's family and what still goes on with the gnome's family. She's always eager to show an abundance of gratitude—almost a little too eager, but who the hell am I to complain?

I pad over to the bed, sit the gift down, and kiss her. "I did at that, my love. I had Italian after my trip and they were delicious."

Her eyes widen. "You didn't!"

"Of course not, minx! You never waste good, and that hairy little prat is the best tailor I've found on three continents. I found some petty thieves to snack on."

Letting out a sigh of relief, she gives me a crooked grin. "Stayed with the wicked this time to make me happy?"

I grouse under my breath and push the box towards her, not wanting to admit it. "I'm not getting any younger. You plan on opening this or what?" Her chuckle is pleased and I pummel myself internally.

The minx has me tied like a bow and she bloody well knows it.

Her claws flick out and she cuts the ribbon, trying to stop herself from ripping in like a toddler on Christmas Day. When she gets inside, her gasp makes me beam. I think I got it right. She holds up the infant-sized duster that matches ours—right down to the silk lining with the peacock and panther design. The git assured me it wouldn't matter if the nipper turned out to be a girl or a boy —it would fit. She's cooing and making squishy womanly sounds that make my black heart burst with love. When she looks up at me, the look in her eyes floors me for a moment and I don't have words.

Sod off. It happens, even to me.

"It's beautiful—no, perfect." She leaps forward and knocks me to the bed, kissing all over my face like a cartoon character, and I laugh.

Christ, the things I do to make her smile and the things she does to me when she does. "You haven't changed your mind about the wee one after the magickal minx reveal? You're not worried that we're going to make a baby of infinite power that will destroy the Universe?"

Her snort is loud as she sits on top of me, her lips quirking up. "Baby, I'd be disappointed if we *didn't* make a baby that threatens the fabric of our existence. It would boggle the mind."

I grin and kiss her. "A powerful mite she shall be then, I'm sure."

Her brow arches as she gives me a look. "She?"

"Not that I'm averse to a son, but honestly? I have a yen for a girl."

"Oh, yes, Daddy's little princess. I can *see* you buying the entire stable when she asks for a pony!"

I frown. "A pony's got to have somewhere to live, right? There's nothing wrong with that."

She laughs again and leans down, her hair cascading over us like a waterfall of soft crimson curls. "You are adorable when you're being all silly."

"None of that, woman. I'll not have you telling every chit and their mate things that ruin my sterling reputation for being a conscienceless killer."

"I suppose I get to see the silly because I'm letting you dip your wick, huh?" She rolls her hips, and I lose a moment of thought before I can reply.

"You think I let every chit I've slept with see this? Pffft. Plus, there's a suspicious lack of dipping going on here to back up that claim."

Sitting back on her haunches, she smirks. "I do, multiple times a day, give you dipping privileges. Once I'm preggo, you know that will increase, right? Especially in the last leg, women get rowdy all day, every day. It's the hormones."

My face clouds as I realize that I'm not here every day, all day, and it's possible that her needs may get serviced by those who are. I'm not sure who's left on the horizon that's not a mate, but hell if I'm pulling out the bloody list to look. I stop moving as the brood settles in because fear and anger are gripping me inside.

Must. Stay. Calm.

"Taurus? Did I say something wrong?" Moving like lightning, she pulls off what little clothes she has on and positions herself on the bed as if she's waiting for something. I don't have time to explain what worried me before she pastes on a smile and crooks her finger at me. "Come now, love. It was a lovely gift. I've got plenty of ways to thank you in mind."

I sit up, admiring her form as I try to muddle out what is happening. I'm not sure why she's so complacent, but it's unnecessary. I need to man up and ask her the question that's pinching me.

"You look tasty as can be, my minx, but you need to give me a tick before we get playful. I've got a question, and I'm quiet because I'm not sure how to ask it." She looks worried, tugging the shirt back on and watching me silently. Her gaze is wary and I'm not sure what's wrong, but I'm going to forge ahead. "You said mums get all panting, and you'd need to up the dipping. Um, what about when I'm not here? What about the others?"

"I don't want to be unfair to anyone," she whispers. "But with everything that has gone on—no matter what that's about—I would prefer that it only be you while I'm pregnant."

I have to look like someone slammed me in the face with a sodding brick. I didn't expect her to say that. I was trying to figure out how to live with her decision. I figured I could always take out a small colony of trailers or something to burn off my rage.

"That makes me ecstatic, love, but are you sure that will make you happy? It's bound to make others unhappy, and I know how that weighs on you." I'm being supportive, but cautious. I don't want her making a promise that she can't keep. That would cause a much bigger problem than if she's honest with me right now.

"I feel like while I'm pregnant—if I get pregnant—it should be the father of the child handling my sexual needs. I don't want to exclude people from interacting with me, but it doesn't feel right to have anyone else intimate with me during pregnancy."

She's giving me a small, hopeful grin as if she wants me to agree with her and I take her hand. "It would honor me, minx. I'll even go with you to tell people if it'll make it easier on you."

Her eyes go wide, and she shakes her head. "Oh, no. I think it will sting less if I impart that decision on my own."

I sense that something is off, but not knowing how to resolve it, I nod. "Okay. If you have any trouble, though, you'll let me know, right?"

She smiles and nods, crawling over and wrapping herself around me as if she's trying to absorb into my skin. *~I will. ~*

I kiss the top of her head and chuckle. "Oi, woman. I meant to give you a present to show you what you mean to me. You show me up every sodding time. I don't know how you do it."

"If you can't be good, be good at it. That's what my grandpa used to say."

I grin and nip her neck. "You, my minx, take that advice to heart every bloody time you draw breath."

The Cat And The Goddess Meet Again

DELILAH

Popping into our home, I kick off my shoes and roll my shoulders. He's not here yet; I sense when he is, even when I pretend not to. I'm hoping for some time to absorb what happened yesterday. I didn't lie to him; I prefer him to be the one that I have sex with if I'm pregnant.

I'm unsure how I'm going to break that to my other liaisons.

Sari will get angry, but not because she wants to sleep with me. Constantine will be whiny and upset before he pretends that he understands when he doesn't. I'm not worried about the ex-family, though I should send a letter because they are mates. I have no interest in re-opening that door, but I feel obligated. Maybe it won't matter because reports from the boys show that their house in the Cabal quarter is closed up, as if they are living solely on the other side now.

Wilde is my biggest concern. He will get vengefully pissed, and he will take it out on Rafe. I can't prove that now, but I'm certain that it will be a problem. He'll pretend everything is fine to seem supportive, and act as if he'll be the world's grandest uncle. In the background, ripples will be felt.

That's why I didn't want Taurus to come with me when I speak to them. His temper would be hard to control if anyone gets fidgety. I have to think about this before I approach my mates and lovers. I need to figure out what to say to keep this from becoming a repeat of the stupid 'peach situation'.

Speaking of parties, I glare at the phone buzzing nearby. Looking at the screen, I see that it's Philomena letting me know that despite how funny I think it is, the flurry of texts and emails and flowers at my house following Beltane's big reveal is unacceptable. According to her, Hex is ready to send glitter bombs to people's houses as revenge for the bees all the flowers are drawing. He is no longer amused with popping balloons and recycling cards for paper crafts.

I know they sent out the party invitation yesterday, and I hoped it would be a distraction for them and the community. Hex and Leo will kick into overdrive working on the theme. They'll drive Rafe insane with all their questions and swatches and fonts, which will give me some time to relax and keep him from hiding in the studio all day.

Honestly, the build-up and wind down from Beltane, the baby stuff, the family bickering, and the big secrets are wearing me out. I put the phone on my nightstand and strip down, tossing my clothes on the couch. Heading to the closet, I rummage until I find one of Taurus' shirts and put it on. He likes when I wear them. They're silky and even when they're fresh from the cleaners, they smell like him.

It comforts me.

Flicking my fingers at the cabinet where the stereo system hides, I concentrate for a moment, smiling when I manipulate the track, volume, and controls without moving. I have to flex my muscles with my magick because I caged it for so long. After Beltane, the swell of power is enormous, and control is once again my sought-after friend.

Beethoven fills the room and I sigh. The *Moonlight Sonata*

always calms me, and today is no exception. Padding over to the bar, I pour an ice-cold martini and lift it to my lips. It occurs to me that I may already have gotten pregnant and if I have, this would be dangerous. The possibility is so slim that I shake my head, swatting away the paranoia.

It bothers me, though, so I pick up my phone as I sit on the bed. Typing 'Toxin Protection Spell' on my task list, I sigh. This kitty loves her drinks and I refuse to be irresponsible. I wouldn't endanger our child for anything, so I mark the priority as high so I work on it right away. I need to protect the baby-to-be from many things that could harm our tiny miracle. Settling in with my laptop, I answer a few emails, running search protocols on the web in the background as I sip.

DUN DUN DUN, DUNDUNDUNDUNDUN.

I nearly spill my drink all over myself and the computer as I jump out of my skin. That damned doorbell is ringing.

Why the hell did he install a doorbell that plays the fucking hearse song at maximum volume?

It scares the hell out of me. Putting the computer in the drawer and my drink on the table, I growl under my breath. I have no "bloody clue what walking corpse is ringing the doorbell, but I am not prepared for visitors. Looking out of the peephole, I try not to seem irritated. "Hello?"

Talia gives me a brief wave and I sigh in relief.

Thank Christ.

For a second, I thought that the damned Mormons found this place. They always seem to find a way. I open the door, making room for her to step in. I'm not dressed to receive guests, but since she didn't call ahead, she has to deal with me wearing one of his shirts and a giant poof of hair. It's not like I had time to groom.

"Hey, Deli!"

Talia is way friendlier than she's rumored to be. Why does she look so bloody happy? "How are you, Talia?" "I'm peachy, mommy dearest."

I flush bright red; I didn't expect to have this conversation with anyone but Taurus yet. As we move into my room, I head over to the couch, pondering for a moment. What did I expect to happen with this news? I told Rafe, so he told Talia. I shouldn't be surprised. "He told you, huh?"

Her eyes twinkle as she drops onto the enormous sofa. "It's hard to keep me from knowing stuff. You don't mind, do you? I know it's a big secret and nothing has happened yet, but secrets are scarce between Taurus and me." Her brow creases. "You're not mad at him, are you?"

I'm distracted by the rumbling in my tummy and I don't answer. Maybe I *should* order a delivery boy. Did I even eat last night? I'm falling apart at the seams. I think about it again for a minute, weighing Chinese and Italian before I realize that I've been ignoring her.

"Crap. You're pissed. I'm sorry."

I shake my head, waving my hand dismissively. "No, no. Stop. I was trying to remember if I ate last night because I was getting hungry and I know we hunted but—hell. I'm sorry. I didn't mean to space out on you."

She looks unconvinced, crossing her arms over her chest. "You're not ticked at him? Because he would *so* try to kick my ass." She winks. "Note I said try."

"No, I'm not mad. I assumed he would tell you; I had a similar conversation with my family. I didn't expect you to come here—not that it's bad—but I did space out thinking about food." I give her a chagrined look as I drop on the couch next to her.

"Okay, good, because I've got a plethora of preggo broad comments to tease you unmercifully as soon as I know you've hit the baby lotto."

I groan, giving her a pleading look. "I'm sure everyone will have a few digs here and there. It is Taurus' kid."

Her eyes widen. "You're still sure you want her, right?" She fiddles with the hem on her tee shirt, looking concerned at my reaction.

"Absolutely." I give her a grin. "Again with the 'her'. You two seem to have some cosmic knowledge that supersedes conception."

"Thank hell. He'd freak out if he comes back from Mil..." she breaks off, looking guilty, "... waukee and you've changed your mind."

I laugh. "He's in Italy again? What is it this time? I have boots that could pay off a cop, a duster that could feed an army, and now the baby that does not exist yet has a duster that could be a down payment on a car. He's amusing himself with my discomfort; I know it."

She looks like a deer in headlights. "Uh, no. Not Italy—Wisconsin. Yeah, Wisconsin." Her hands fiddle with one of the huge pillows and I chuckle, watching Aradia lift her head and give the woman a look that says even she doesn't believe her.

I smile, eyes twinkling with mirth. "Don't worry. I won't say anything. Total shock girl, that's me." "Thank you. Because if he even *suspected* I told you about the new p—I will not finish that sentence." She groans and puts her head in her hands. "God, this sucks, I'm normally WAY stealthier than this. My mouth is running off on its own with you."

"No worries. Whatever he has planned that requires a hands-y tailor and copious amounts of cash is something I know nothing about. He knows I could worm my way in and poke around. I enjoy letting him keep surprises because he's cute when he's excited about them."

She nods. "He is, isn't he? Like a little boy."

We share a fond smile about the clone we both love, and I shrug, not wanting to make a big deal of how much I enjoy his over-pampering. No one needs to know what a present, even a small one, costs when given by the others. "He is. It's endearing."

Her brow creases as she watches me, and she clears her throat. "I wanted you to know something. I feel like I should tell you this myself, even though I know that you and Taurus talked about this. We kind of talked about it the last time I was here, too, but it's come up again."

I wait, watching her go through a few contortions as she organizes her thoughts. Whatever this is, I'm almost positive that it is not good news. She's too on edge.

"I felt out the courting thing with Wilde. I'm still not sure about it and it may be a terrible idea, but I'm curious."

My breath catches. The moment I've been dreading is here. I can't sit here and spill the truth. I can't.

Scenes flash through my mind at light speed and I feel my entire body tense and the air in the room thicken. 'Control, Deli, control', I whisper to myself internally. I hear my words, but my mind is reliving everything in a fast forward highlight reel of pain and shame and fear, and if I don't figure out how to put it back in its box, I'm going to do something stupid.

The Beast lifts Her head and with the elegance of a predator, She joins with me without forcing me to shift. Her strength and that of a lingering Goddess seem to forge a shield that I place around the awful memories. Once I do, everything inside lightens up and the room feels calmer.

Thank the Goddess.

Talia's looking at me, and it seems like eternity lapses before I force words out of my mouth. "Thanks for letting me know."

"I thought as Taurus' and Wilde's mate, I should let you know that I'm going along with this. I'm certain it means we'll sleep together at some point."

Oh, this is bad. It is a colossally, irretrievably bad idea.

Wilde will use Talia up and spit her out, and I won't be able to stop it. She'll never be okay with being one of the crowd that follows him around like puppies. However, I can't tell her it will be nothing but pain once he's reeled her in without giving away my own secrets.

I don't want to let her get sucked into his vortex because it never ends well. He's already branching out to new victims besides her: for example, the Beltane ritual bullshit. Amanda spun a story about the Goddess and Wilde and illusions to our group. It's because she and Sari have become bosom buddies. An affair with Wilde for her and a fling with Constantine for Sari is not far off. Trust me, I know how it works.

"I..." I press my lips together and only come up with a lame answer. "I hope you're cautious. There's a lot of baggage there, known and unknown. Don't get in too deep, too fast."

"Like you and the feathered one?"

I roll my eyes. "Perhaps. It's overwhelming for him, and compared to Wilde, I'm easy street."

Looking at my hands for a moment, I feel ashamed that I don't have the strength to tell her what she needs to know. I'm not ready to look at it, much less show her the mirror. I'm a terrible mate and a worse person for not stopping her, but I don't know how to without giving up the ugliness that reigned before Taurus. It hasn't touched me in so long, but I don't want it back and without him, that's where I'll be.

She clears her throat, giving me a half-grin. "Taurus says you're a little sissy."

I narrow my eyes. "That almost got him skinned."

"Oh, no, wait. It was *sassy*."

"Clones. You can't live with them, and you can't sell them on the black market."

She laughs. "It was a mistake, and he ran with it!"

"Being an ass," I grumble good-naturedly.

"All that matters is the tightness of said ass, I'm told."

"Are you calling him a tight ass? That'd be funny," I grin, waving a hand at the bar and sighing as another perfectly chilled martini appears in front of me. Taking a sip, I let the sting of glacially cold vodka hit my tongue and distract me from the bits of icky goo floating inside me since I had my greatest hits slideshow.

"I said no such thing. I know what side of the bed to butter, thanks. Plus, he's so proud of his ass."

I snort and sip my drink. "That I know."

"I suppose I should tell the big bird he can come in now. He's itching again, I think."

I smile, tilting my head. Oh, thank the Goddess, because I need to get myself centered again. "Well, if he wants to come to see me."

"I'm pretty sure he does." She mutters under her breath and shakes her head. "Like newlyweds, I bloody swear."

I bat my lashes at her and grin.

"On that note, let me go or he'll not have anything to do with me." She stands and gives me a wink, heading out the door.

Before I even blink, he's in the door and scooped me up to drop us on the bed with his face buried in my neck.

"Eek!" I sense for the martini and when I figure out that this one has also survived being spilled everywhere, I murmur, "Are you okay?"

~Feeling homicidal. Not sure why, but everything is eating at me. ~

He holds me and I brush kisses on his hairline. "Something bad happened?"

~No. I feel a bit lost. ~

"I missed you while you were away. Does that help?"

~Really? ~

I nod, looking down at him with a soft smile. "I did. I did some stuff at the house in the morning after we got back from hunting. I also had the talk with my family."

~You told them? Even though the earliest we could know is Sunday from a blood test? ~

"Uh-huh. It was kind of amusing, but it went fine."

~I got you something today. ~

"What did you get, baby?" I smile a bit, pretending that Talia hadn't spoiled the surprise earlier.

He apparates a box, his smirk deepening. *~Just a little something. ~*

I take the box and sit back, looking like a kid in the candy store. "I'm going to get used to this present stuff."

~It's for when you get all roly poly—as you called it—with the wee one. If you still want her. ~

"Have we decided it's going to be a 'she' then?" I wrinkle my nose, turning that idea over in my head and finding that despite my reservations—it's a fifty-fifty chance—I like it a lot. I sure as hell like it more than everyone asking if I'm still sure I want her. "I still want her, especially given that she could already be here. We haven't wasted any donation opportunities." I grin and lift the lid on the box.

~It's leather pants. I mean, lots of them in different sizes, made for when you get a little bigger and a little... and so on. I thought I'd head off a session of the doldrums when your favorite hunting duds get difficult. The touchy nit made some of them with an abomination that he says will stretch for you. I don't know for spit, but he sure seemed to, so I let him do it. ~

My eyes light up and my face breaks into what is the cheesiest smile in the universe as I hold up what must be at least ten pairs of my favorite pants in different sizes. "How did you know?"

"I don't enjoy seeing you upset. It occurred to me that in a movie, I might have seen a bird cry once because she was pregnant and couldn't fit into her dress. I don't want to walk in and find you crying about clothes." He gives me a grin and I struggle not to thump him. His expression is innocent as I sigh in both adoration and consternation at the same time.

Everything inside me goes squish and I melt into him. "Oh, love, this is perfect."

"I want her. You said Sunday, right?"

"I think so, baby. About three days from conception with a blood test is the closest to accurate we'll get this soon."

He frowns. "I'm going to have a lab coat on call for house calls. Plus, we have to shag a lot."

I blink. "More than we do now?"

"What if we miss a chance because we're not? In fact, we should do it now!"

I kiss his forehead. "Relax, baby. It'll happen without us freaking out."

"You aren't humoring me, are you?"

I chuckle. "No. We have to come up with names."

He blinks. "Christ, yeah, we do. But first..." He rolls over and looks down at my shirt. "We've got some catching up to do from while I was away. Off with you!"

Well, hell. I can get on board with that.

The Cat Faces The Music

Exhaling a cloud of frustration, I lean against the cool kitchen counter, my fingers absentmindedly tracing the marble veins. A grimace twisted my lips as I grasped at the remnants of calm that had been lounging in my mind just moments ago. The flowers from Talia seem to mock me as I try to work up the courage to do what I must.

This is harder than I thought it would be.

"Dammit," I mutter under my breath, the weight of impending conversations pressing down like an anvil. My family, bless their unconventional hearts, had taken the news with laughter and gentle ribbing.

"You're sure Taurus is the dad? He's stubborn, but I didn't think he was potent enough to make a miracle," my chef joked, his eyes twinkling with mirth.

I couldn't help but crack a smile at the memory, one that dissipated as swiftly as it came. They could jest about astrological compatibility and potential supernatural babysitters because their love was unconditional. A safe harbor in the tempest of my unconventional life.

But beyond the sanctuary of my housemates, acceptance will not come so easily. The thought of explaining the situation to the others churns my insides. They were all a part of my heart at one time, but everything has changed. The mere idea of sharing this news feels like navigating a minefield blindfolded.

Each rehearsal plays out in my head, every scenario another shade of disaster. Will they see it as a betrayal? A change too far from our dynamic equilibrium? Their faces float through my mind, each one etching a line of worry deeper into my brow.

"Maybe they'll surprise you," I whispered to my reflection in the stainless steel fridge, though even my own voice lacked conviction. I was no stranger to complicated relationships or the delicate dance of polyamory, but this—this was different. This was a life, a responsibility that transcended romantic entanglements and late-night whispers.

With a final, resigned sigh, I pushed away from the counter. My buzz of carefree joy was thoroughly harshed, replaced by the sobering reality of what lay ahead. It was time to face the music, one difficult conversation at a time.

The doorbell chimes its melodic tune, a stark contrast to the cacophony of nerves clanging in my chest. I tapped a rhythmless beat on my thigh as the door swung open, revealing Wilde's trademark smirk and Sari's kaleidoscope eyes.

"Surprise!" they chorus, an excess of enthusiasm that doesn't quite reach their eyes. Wilde sweeps me into a hug that feels more like a performance than comfort, while Sari's gaze flits past me, as if searching for clues or plotting her next move.

"Okay, spill it," Wilde says, releasing me with a flourish. "You look like you've been wrestling with your own shadow."

I swallow the lump forming in my throat. Their feigned ignorance is almost convincing, but the tension in Sari's shoulders betrays her. "I'm pregnant," I blurt out, bracing for the storm.

For a moment, there's only silence—then the room erupts with their exaggerated congratulations. Wilde claps his hands together, laughing too loud, too hard. Sari twirls around, her laughter tinkling like wind chimes in a hurricane.

"Marvelous news! Isn't it, darling?" Wilde said, turning to Sari, who nods vigorously, her smile as sharp as a blade.

My heart sinks. These are not the genuine reactions of mates sharing in joy; these are performances by actors who already rehearsed their roles. Behind their theatrical display, I can't shake the memory of Sari's cryptic words after Beltane. She spoke of a coyote journey—some sort of soul quest that Wilde expressed an interest in. The details elude me, but the secrecy surrounding it sent shivers down my spine.

They're pretending so I don't question their loyalty.

"Speaking of journeys," I venture, trying to sound casual. "I heard something about a trip you two are planning?"

Wilde's eyes flicker, revealing a momentary crack in his facade. "Ah, yes, an adventure for the spirit, you could say. But let's focus on you right now."

"Right," I press on, fueled by unease. "But how the hell are you going anywhere when you're supposedly courting Talia and Amanda? Isn't your damned schedule full?" My tone might be sharper than intended, but the question has gnawed at me since Talia's visit.

"As you well know," Sari interjects with a sly grin, "we're masters at multitasking. Our hearts are big enough for many, and our souls yearn for enlightenment." Her words dance around the truth, leaving me no wiser than before.

Typical Sari bullshit; that's what it is.

As they continue to shower me with overzealous merriment, I

know one thing for certain: beneath their jubilant charade, a storm is brewing—one that could very well sweep us all away.

Leaning back against the cool brick wall of the Maison, I exhale a heavy breath that fogs in the crisp night air. My thoughts drift to Constantine and Shea, who have been shadows at the edges of my life lately—ghosts whose absences are as palpable as their presences once were.

It's almost been a relief, given everything.

A distant part of me—a fiercely independent streak that has weathered storms before—relishes the idea of space. The room to navigate this news on my own terms. I've made my choices; they will make theirs. With distance already between us, perhaps the blow will be softened. Maybe the lack of their daily interference is a blessing in disguise, allowing them to process the shock with less...explosivity.

The small smile finds its way to my lips as I consider the irony; here I am, destined to be overjoyed with maternity bliss, yet I'm strategizing defense mechanisms against unwanted advances. The idea of shopping for onesies and picking out pastel paint swatches for a nursery seems a universe away when juxtaposed with the task of deflecting groping hands. Taurus's child deserves better than that; they deserve a mother unencumbered by those complexities.

"Constantine and Shea," I whisper to the empty street, the names tasting like resolve on my tongue. "They will have to deal with it. This is my decision, my body." There is strength in articulating the words, even if only to the night's embrace.

Can I say that to their faces? Should I?

"Can I actually say that out loud?" I mutter, questioning my own audacity. The night offers no reply, but the lingering echo of my voice in the quiet alley bolsters my resolve. Yes, I can—and I will.

With the right timing and the right words, the truth will have to suffice.

It will have to be enough for all of them.

The Writer Conceals His True Feelings

WILDE

She believed me to be a fool; that is for certain.

I sat in my chair, watching my Darkness fidget and squirm imperceptibly as she explained that she not only found out she was fertile and did not think to mention it, but she chose to breed with Mr. Taurus.

Unacceptable.

My primary watched me as I digested the information. I knew she could sense my ire radiating through our primary bond. I controlled it so it did not touch the bond I have with my Darkness. She thinks she is the only one gifted enough to hide things, but she is not. I kept her from knowing my genuine feelings on this matter until I am ready to address it.

She does not know the details of my journey to cleanse myself of our former mates. Between myself, my mate, and those we have enlisted to aid us in that quest, it will be astounding. Oh, how the mighty will tremble when that comes to fruition. Even my Darkness will feel the snap of pain at the route I have taken to rid myself of the excess baggage of the past.

But that will be overshadowed by her ridiculous choice and it infuriates me.

Ours is a dangerous road, to be sure, but my coyote has consulted the most skilled practitioners in the field. Since Beltane, we have made several trips to the other side to find information and supplies to aid Calista and Veruca in their preparations. The Gods and Goddesses that came to the ladies have given them a glimpse of the future, and it will satisfy me to see it play out. Though I cannot unmate from those I wish to without severe consequences—according to Mr. Taurus—this will clean the slate.

No one other than my mate and I will realize until it is far too late to stop.

I don't expect my plans to cause any less controversy or hurt feelings than this pregnancy will. However, I am not expecting everyone to fall in line and understand the goal of my sacrifice. I do not care if some find it distasteful and do not wish to remain associated with me afterward.

My Darkness will struggle. Her tender heart is her greatest weapon and her greatest weakness. It will be her biggest challenge during this time, I fear. Her wish will be to make all of those she loves happy without angering Mr. Taurus, which will make this even sweeter. It will be an excellent tool to use when it suits me.

"Wilde, are you going to say anything or just stare at her from under your specs?"

I blinked for a moment when she said that, retracting from my musings as my mate caught my attention. *"Oh! Yes. I have several suggestions for names if you wish to hear, and the babe will have so many wonderful aunts and uncles to spoil it rotten. Myself included."*

My boyish grin didn't belay the thoughts in my head or heart. Though I do not wish ill of my mates, I find their behavior of late troubling. My Darkness is so enchanted with Mr. Taurus that she is rarely available for more than brief encounters, and my ennobled stayed shuttered in his grief for a mate who betrayed him. He's been closed off for so long that I feel he had some deep connection with Alistair that superseded my bond. I am not so foolish as to think he was enamored with Rhea.

That part, while a sting to us both, is not what is swaying him so.

Now, on the precipice of my quest and mere days from the celebration in her home, Delilah released this information to me and who knows what other social connections when it was no longer a discussion, but a fact.

"See, Deli? He's excited," my mate grinned, cloaking her reactions as well.

She was right to be concerned. An undertaking of this magnitude signals a deep, unwavering connection. I believe mating occurred prior to this decision. She did not mention that, but knowing it had to have happened negated our shared hope that the wildness of this world would end up driving Taurus back into seclusion.

My foray into wooing his mate is more important than ever to solidify our position in the community. We cannot allow Talia and Taurus to become so ingrained with my Darkness and her family that they endanger us. It is already apparent by the sleek Italian leather and silk she's wearing that the influence he wields is formidable.

I dare not discuss what else I believe he has her into. The beast inside her is primal, hungry, and untamed now while I had it subdued and under my control before.

I do not like that in the slightest.

"My Darkness, when will you know more about your pregnancy? Given that there are magickal factors, mutated DNA, and clone DNA, I fear that it is difficult to determine how we will best take care of you. Have you contacted a physician?"

Her brows furrowed as she looked uncomfortable yet again. *"I don't think there is a lot we can know right now. Duration, symptoms, all the typical stuff could be normal or whack-a-doo. This is the only time this has even been possible. Taurus is getting a doctor on call and a team to research our 'one in a million miracle'."*

My eyes narrowed when I realized she allowed him to contact the Company for a doctor.

That could only mean one thing.

"Taurus is calling in a favor, yeah?" my mate said, grinning. *"Typical rich Company badass stuff. Are you sure they won't lock you up and make you the world's most uncomfortable lab rat?"*

I beamed then had to hide it. The coyote nailed the point of paranoia that I planned to feed. They will make her an experiment; she can't trust them.

"That is a concern, my love. They do not have an excellent track record with ethical behavior and what of the babe?"

A jolt of fear zinged through our connection, but then she grew steely. *"Taurus would never let that happen. Neither I nor our child will be test subjects. We've discussed our lines regarding maternity care, and I will also use an old rival who is a magickal midwife. We covered our bases."*

I sensed this might be a more delicate operation than I first thought, so I backed off and nodded. *"Excellent, my love. I am glad that you have settled the most worrisome thoughts already."*

She smiled, looking at us back and forth before running her hand over her flat stomach. *"We have. Thank you for being so supportive."*

"My Darkness, ever shall we be your shoulders to lean on, should you need. Now, how about we discuss the specifics of your grand celebration that is up-coming?"

Her eyes lit up and I watched her speak about the preparations for my ennobled's birthday gala. There was something different about her, and it was not just her new fashion choices. It is behavior and speech and dare I say it, starch in her spine that seems to be reminiscent of long ago.

This transformation bears much closer examination than I feared.

The Artist Manages His Frustration

RAFE

My primary stopped here after letting the coyote and the writer know about her plans to let the secret agent knock her up.

Don't think I'm being nasty.

I'm behind anything that makes my woman happy, even if I think it's going to cause a hurricane of resentment to swirl around her while she's chowing down on ice cream and pickles. However, she felt optimistic enough about whatever tripe those two fed her to pop in and join us for a planning session for this wretched party that everyone in my house seems dead set on throwing despite my loud and frequent protests. I'm concerned with her sanity now that we're having a full-fledged discussion, to be honest.

"We're going to have a massive community-wide party for my birthday, including all the warring factions out for blood, and your idea is to make magickal rooms that do what, again?"

She snorts. "You're the idiots who wanted a fetish ball. I'm making the fetish part happen."

Hex arches a brow. "In the most sodding dangerous way you can, Nancy. Are you sure that you want to put that kind of magick into play? I figured you'd do silly minor spells like funny mustaches or something."

I shrug. "Hell, it *can't* be any worse than what went on at the costume-switch Halloween party or the Christmas party from hell, right?"

They all look at her as if she's lost control of the crazy train and is standing in the middle of the tracks.

I don't blame them; this is likely going to be a bloodbath.

Victor prowls across the room, his eyes only on her. "Love, I'll do anything you ask—always—and you know it. This seems like asking for trouble that you don't want."

I rub my temples, trying to get a handle on so many things at once. Her insistence on this laughably bad idea and the boys trying to talk her out of it; a party with everyone I *don't* want to see not only attending, but looking for me because I'm the host. Right now, I don't have any interest in stroking people's egos or glad-handing a bunch of sharks who came to swim in our pool.

What the fuck are we thinking?

The cat hasn't even admitted to the world at large that she's mated with the great fashion hound, and she *just* dropped the fertility bomb on our vengeful mates. She can't be this crazy. She must have a plan.

What is it?

"Look. The entire thing sounds like a bad bloody plan to me, but then I've not been in the mood for stupid for weeks. *However,* given my status as primary to the community leader and given that she has to let some cats—no pun intended—out of the bag at some point? In public is better for crowd control and more efficient to boot. If having this idiotic party will help us move on with every-thing, I'll get behind it, even the stupid magick room plan."

She beams at me and I wonder what in the hell she has up her sleeves. The cat smiles more now than she did for months thanks to the assassin, but lately, she glows from the outside in.

Who am I to deny her that?

"Awesome! I'm thinking about so many cool things."

She has a plan and I wish she'd clue us all in so we can get on board. Even the bitch looks suspicious.

I shake my head as she prattles on, looking animated and excited. Hell, I'm a little jealous. I was skeptical when they started hanging out after she contacted him and more so when they started getting serious, but I can't argue with the results. She's happy, and that makes my heart warm.

The cat and me? We're a match like two opposite poles—fire and ice, soft and hard—and we go together without a hint of drama. I'm not threatened by her choices; I'm thrilled for her. I wish our families hadn't taken the odd twist that left me as the charity case when she's gone. I could have had Victor, but I royally buggered that one when Wilde and I started seeing one another.

That's another regret to go with the whole fall and winter fiascos that sent us reeling into the miasma of the here and now.

At least there will be alcohol and lots of it—I'm going to need it.

The Socialite Assesses The Damage

PHILOMENA

The rhythmic clink of ice against glass underscored the room's murmurs as I took a discreet sip, watching the frenzy unfold from my vantage point. The bleach heads darted across the floor with an air of frenetic grace, their pale locks bouncing in unison as they arranged extravagant bouquets and draped silken fabrics over every imaginable surface. The unity of their movements was almost hypnotic — a well-orchestrated ballet of obedience.

Whether we agree or not, we have to plan for this den of iniquity the cat planned.

"Can you believe it?" murmurs Leo, his words barely audible. "A party now? Of all times?"

"Doesn't make a lick of sense," replies Hex, frowning as he adjusts a crooked centerpiece. His hands moved ceaselessly, but his eyes are clouded with uncertainty, searching for a reason amidst the opulence.

I know what gnaws at their minds. Why risk it all for a night of revelry? It seems a gambit born of whimsy, a fool's errand wrapped in silk and tied with a bow of folly. They're blind to Deli's purpose, unable to see the threads of the web she's weaving with such care.

"Hey," Caesar beckons his companions closer, voice lowered to a conspiratorial whisper. "Do you think there's a plan we're not privy to? Some grand design hidden behind this madness?"

"Whatever it is," says Leo, casting a wary glance in my direction, "the bitch hasn't let us in on it."

But I know. Oh, I know exactly why she's summoning the chaos of celebration.

A glint of worry shimmers in my eyes as I look away—a flicker almost imperceptible amongst the rush of preparations. I move with purpose through the chaos that fills the backyard, hands deftly rearranging a misplaced goblet here, smoothing a wrinkle there. I'm the eye of a storm our friend has conjured herself and I take that role seriously.

"Everything has to be perfect," I murmur to myself, though loud enough for me to catch the edge of concern beneath the determination. Rafe's eyes meet mine, and in that brief exchange, I understand his silent plea. This masquerade isn't just another extravagant whim; it's a lifeline thrown into the depths of despair where the artist has confined himself.

He's doing this to try to dig out of his hole of pain.

I shift my stance, leaning against the intricately carved gazebo, observing as he approaches the towering doors leading to his sanctuary. He pauses, hand hovering over the golden knob, resolve momentarily wavering before he moves away from it. The artist is endeavoring not to run away from us as we prepare the fake event for our leader's approval.

"Make sure he has no choice but to join us," I instruct Sahara. "Tell him it's not just about him tonight—he needs to be present for everyone else to see, too."

The brunette nods, a mixture of confusion and obedience in her posture, then scurries away to fulfill another task on her list.

"Will he even come out?" Siren asks, breaking our unspoken

agreement to communicate only with glances and gestures. "He has been so closed off since his break-up with the ex-family.

"He will," I reply without hesitation, my gaze once again climbing the stairs. "He must. The cat wants us all to present a united front."

As my attention returns to the final touches of the gathering, I ensure each decorative element is aligned with Deli and Hex's meticulous vision. I realize the depth of the cat's gamble—it isn't just a party. No, it's an act of salvation, a ploy to draw the artist out from the shadows of isolation and into the light of camaraderie. She wants to remind him that life pulses beyond his door, vibrant and waiting.

Plus, she has to present the assassin to the public as her mate and the baby's father.

In that moment, I know my role in this pageant is more than a mere planner. Deli's silent command was clear: be vigilant, ready to guide Rafe gently into the throng, and ensure he finds his place in public again. She wants him to be able to function without those who have betrayed him, especially in the wake of her latest announcement.

The clink of ice against glass punctuates the hum of anticipation as I wander into the kitchen, my eyes scanning for the artist who disappeared while I was checking the edges of the party zone. He needs this—needs to be pulled from the quagmire of self-pity that has become his sanctuary. Tonight, he'll face the music, or more aptly, the laughter and chatter of a house reborn in revelry.

The Maison has always been the hub of fun and pleasure— people need to know that will not change with the addition of the peacock to our brood.

I glimpse him at the pool house, hesitating as he watches us all flitter about. His hair, normally a wild tangle of disinterest of late, is now tamed and styled. Rafe is still wearing his normal informal gear, but for today that's fine. He will need to dress for the fetish ball, but I'm okay with baby steps in this case. One foot after another, he is descending into life once more.

Sidestepping the animated group of droids who are too engrossed in their gaiety to notice him, I sidle up to the man of the hour.

"Quite the spectacle, isn't it?" I murmur, watching as our housemates check the signage we made for the magickal rooms. Their curiosity is piqued by the promise of otherworldly delights, but I know Deli has bigger plans than just fun and games. These rooms, with their illusions and whispered wonders, serve a greater purpose than entertainment. They are a ruse, a clever redirection from the true heart of tonight's gathering.

She wants to keep people from being shitty about Taurus and this will help.

As the artist joins me for the tour of our dry-run, his eyes briefly meet mine with a silent plea for reassurance. I nod subtly, a gesture that goes unseen by others but understood by him. This is his chance to stop drowning in his own depths and start swimming towards the shore. If the magickal rooms keep the bulk of the guests enthralled, then perhaps he can find space to breathe, to be among us without the crushing weight of expectation.

"Let's hope it works," he mutters as he steps away from the pool house to be part of the group.

The Cat Convinces The Bird To Leave The Nest

DELILAH

"You are planning a party for everyone that you hate and you want me to attend?"

I look at him in frustration. "Why is *every single* male in my life being a first-class asshat today?"

Stomping my foot, I stride to the bar and pour a martini. I down it in a gulp and try not to lose my temper. What happened to wanting to go out on the town and show everyone? Didn't he want to be all 'here we are world!'?

I guess he was game until it became real.

He blinks, looking confused. "I'm sorry, what?"

I might have overreacted to his question. I spent most of my day arguing with clones and droids about damned near everything, and I hoped that he'd be easier. From making the rounds with all of my mates and lovers to share my pregnancy announcement to joining the party planning meeting at my house, I've been disagreeing with men all day.

Wilde and Sari pretended to be supportive, but I don't trust it. Constantine was also overly enthusiastic, but it didn't make it to his eyes. Shea acted like it didn't matter because he's upset over the 'peach incident' and Mercury was more interested in role-playing pirates. After that, I had the party discussion at my house that made me want to tear my hair out.

I'm over men humoring, patronizing, and reminding me of things I am aware of.

"Every single male in my house, all the other idgits, and now you, are making me want to strangle someone. All of you have stopped conversations to make sure I haven't taken leave of my senses... It's making me *crazy*. Everyone is talking to me as if I'm a slow child. This wasn't my idea, but I got on board—of *course*, I'm bloody sure. I said it, didn't I?"

My shout sends the ferret on my shoulder skittering across the floor. Neither of us noticed his departure because we're too busy arguing about damned near everything, and I hoped that he'd be easier.

"Woman, how am I supposed to know what you came up with? This is the first sodding time I've heard of the damned thing!"

I glare. "You never talk to me like that. What's crawled up your ass?"

"Nothing!" He crosses his arms over his chest. "Except that I left for two days and I don't see a shred of evidence that you missed me, much less pined. I'm feeling unloved."

My brain feels like it might explode. *That* is why he's being an ass? Goddesses save me from the fragile egos of the clones and droids. Hopefully, they do it before I *murder them*.

"I can't knit, but I missed you! I pined! Happy?" I pour another drink, trying hard not to scream and push this silly argument onto another plane of anger.

Snorting, he shakes his head. "You did not. There's not a chocolate wrapper in sight and no ice cream tubs—only party plans."

I roll my eyes and huff. "I had ice cream, but I put the bowl away."

His eyes widen and he looks shocked, clutching his chest as if that damned weak ticker he touts is going to give up the ghost. "You cleaned up after yourself? Holy hell, you missed me."

Crossing my arms over my chest, I glare at him. I'm not *that* big a slob. "Don't make a big deal. Dirty dishes draw bugs and I hate bugs." I'm so busy justifying myself that I miss the small rodent crawling all over the room from floor to ceiling as he explores the new area.

Taurus' lips quirk as he gets comfortable. He peels off his clothes and chucks them in the dry-cleaning bin inside the closet. Moving to his nightstand, he puts his phone, cuff links, money clip, watch, and other sundries in the decorative bowl Hex added to help us keep our things in one place.

I'm not accusing anyone, but the re-organization of the room and its conveniences *might* have occurred after Taurus lost a set of important keys. What awful thing they belonged to, who in the hell knows, but during one of our more aggressive intimate sessions, they went missing. He convinced himself for days that Aradia ate them. We knocked the chair across the room when we weren't paying attention, and there they were.

Hex came over to do a subtle assessment of our space and had everything settled by the evening. I'm not sure Taurus noticed. He used the bins, baskets, bowls, hampers and hooks Hex installed in various locations without being told to.

Perhaps Theodora does similar things.

"Are you afraid of creepy, crawly bugs and spiders, my delicate flower?"

My eyes narrow and I stalk towards him. "Bugs are icky and gross. I'm flat out terrified of spiders, so thank you very much for making fun of my phobia." I huff, flopping on the bed to pout. "Rafe is, too. He'll climb on a chair if he even thinks there's one in the room."

He bursts out laughing, dropping onto the bed to crush me to him in a hug. "You, love of my heart, are the most adorable thing I've ever seen, and your mate will never hear the end of *that* tidbit. I missed you like a hole in the chest."

"You know, Lily's droid Mercury is a mad scientist and he bred superbugs the size of dogs. Lily wouldn't let him keep them. He named one Buzz, and it has a covert space in Sandrine's back plate. The rest live in my pool house."

"Note: never *ever* go to Sandwich's pool house. Also, do not make Sandrine angry—got it."

"Rafe refused to go in the backyard for a week until I moved Aradia's playground area. He figured that if she were close, and they got out, she'd squish them."

"Who'd blame him for that?"

"No kidding. Buzz is enormous and the rest of them make him look small. I have *no* idea what the hell Mercury bred into them other than size. They're a fucking weaponized army of insects for all I know. I couldn't say no to the pout; I never say no to the pout. Therefore, there is a bug army in my backyard."

"Not to change the subject, but can we get back to the party thing? The giant, mutant bug talk is making my skin crawl." He shivers and I chuckle.

Who's the big bad, indeed.

Distracted by his admission, I roll over to face him. Neither of us has been paying attention to anything but each other, so we don't even notice the ferret scurry up the legs of the night table, grab a handful of objects, and scurry off again.

"If you like, we can. Will Talia be coming in the pretty dress she wore to go see Wilde the other night?" I ask, batting my lashes at him.

I phrase the question teasingly, but hearing about her visit to Wilde made *my* skin crawl in a much more sinister way than the bugs. Indulging Wilde's fancy pants bullshit is paving the way to bad things.

I should know; I did it once.

When Wilde and I first started 'dating' last October, it was the heyday of another illegal bar called Dirty Deeds. It was like the cantina in our favorite space movie—a hive of all the rabble-rousing Resistance folks and some selected ex-Cabal members. DD was an invitation-only join: exclusive because of its encouragement of behavior not for public consumption in the Rift. Sari held court over us all, so not all the Resistance members were deemed acceptable invitees. DD was an all hours place for drinking, partying and flirting. That's where I met Sari and Wilde. Eventually, it was where I met Rhea and Alistair.

Once that happened, it was downhill from there.

One day, we showed up, and the place had been demolished. From the look of the rubble from the explosion, it was not a gas leak. I guess the Company put the kibosh on the new world version of a speakeasy and didn't tell anyone. By that time, I was dating Wilde, friends with Sari, and our journey was well on its way.

I digress. My point was that while I flirted and smirked at Wilde as a bad girl to ruffle his stodgy feathers, I also played into his sense of chivalry. I might wrinkle his suits or pull his hair out of the scholarly ponytail held by a ribbon, but in response, he made grand gestures. He took me on dates for picnics where I dressed fancy just to impress him or write me poetry. I couldn't have known that his pedigree and politeness were all a skin he wore to draw me in.

Talia is falling victim to the same spider and the fly bullshit, and I can't stop it. I've told them both over and over that dating him is a bad idea and they won't listen. I can't figure out why, but I also can't force myself to face the reality of what my relationship with Wilde has become. The consequences of the Winter Incident are too scarring. I can't force Rafe to do it, and without that, neither of us has strong enough evidence to stop her.

Is she that lonely without Taurus? Could I buy her another bloody hellhound?

Suddenly, it occurs to me he's looking at me and words are

coming out of his mouth. I might have missed something important.

Fuck. Am I supposed to be answering?

He sighs looking at me in disappointment. "I can't believe you went there to tell them about your amazing news, and they spent their time throwing Talia and that nitwit in your face. It's the only time Talia's been out of death gear in weeks, and she goes to see *him* dressed like that. I guess you've heard every detail, huh?"

I shrug, my discomfort with her choice and my own secrets making it hard for me to speak. Clearing my throat, I mumble, "I heard a version. I still don't feel like this is a good plan."

There. Maybe that will do it.

He snorts and shakes his head. "Nor do I, but my goddess is nothing if not her own woman."

Damnit! I can't get them to *see*, and I can't—I can't—handle admitting why this is so dangerous to anyone.

I close my eyes for a moment, swallowing hard to push back the terror and pain that are threatening to spill out. Chanting my control mantras in my head, I visualize my room in my mind palace again and put everything back in its place. I store everything in its place inside me, cataloged like card drawers in a library. I tuck each thing in tight and mark it for reference. When I get a grip, I look at him with a troubled expression.

"They had to have *something* to spite me with. I destroyed their world view of clones, magick, and pregnancy while making sure they knew that they not only couldn't be part of it, but they can't replicate it. The amount of detail and excitement they shared about this 'dating' proposition seemed out of proportion. I was very nonchalant—which I always am about Wilde's new lovers. They nearly tripped over themselves to apologize for not being suitable mates since they have focused on grieving Rhea, helping Amanda, and prepping for Beltane."

I growl and pick at the comforter. I'm not comfortable meeting his eyes as I fight another wave of emotions. "I suppose it's something new, and Wilde gets excited about new things."

"You don't sound like you believe that."

Fuck. I can't bald-faced lie to him—not here and not now, because it could save someone from what happened to me.

"I don't believe they've been that busy with Amanda—she's an amusement. They keep blathering on about Beltane, but I don't think they care, nor do I believe that either of them is still grieving Rhea. Maybe they miss Alistair, but I doubt that. I also don't believe that Sari put any work into Beltane. I think she convinced everyone it was touchy-feely horseshit. Guess I showed her."

A ghost of a smile crosses my lips and I take a breath, heading into the tricky part. "Wilde is far too involved with Talia in his mind. That will be nothing but problems; I've seen this before. I think they're conspiring with that Southern twat over more than that stupid ass bar, which worries me. I believe adamantly that Sari and Wilde don't give a rat's pizza-eating ass what I'm feeling about any of it—including my news—because it doesn't involve their needs."

He studies me, tilting his head. Lifting my face up, he looks at me with a concerned expression. "You've changed. You didn't use to talk about them like this."

I shrug, casting my eyes down. "Perhaps Beltane provided the clarity that I needed to see things through the right lens."

Surprise filters through our bond. "Isn't that interesting? You've piqued my curiosity now, kitty."

It's true.

When the Goddess chose him—not Alistair or Wilde or anyone else—I knew that the Universe was telling me something. It was telling me to fix old mistakes and be happy. I'm powerful in my own right, but when I'm joined with the right person, there is no limit to what I can do. Bast showed me that my light shines brightest when the surrounding people are not trying to put it out.

"Once I've had some more time to process it myself, I will." I give him a small smile, not wanting to get his hopes up. It's not fair to even hint at the things I've been considering since Beltane until I'm ready to commit to them. Otherwise, it's cruel. "Let's go back to the party stuff, hmm?"

Rolling his eyes, he flops on his back and groans.

"Okay, Mr. Dramatic. Yes, I expect you to attend. Given your insistence that you want to show us off in public, I hoped that Talia and the rest of your crew would come. Everyone in my house will be there and our community has a history of throwing enormous, wall-rattling shindigs for birthdays."

"There's a 'but' hidden in there. I sense it in the pause, woman. Out with it."

"Only the theme, but we'll talk about it later." His eyes narrow and I grin, hoping to distract him until he sees the invitation on the community blog. "Did I mention that we only have four days left before we do the test?"

He beams. "Getting closer, aren't we?"

I nod, rubbing my hand over my tummy as if I have every reason to assume something is growing there. "Much."

"Well, mate, I can't have you catting around without me! To the party, we will go. I'll tell my goddess she's expected. Maybe Theodora and Damien will come, too. Theodora's not been out and about much, so that would be fun."

I smile and ruffle his hair. "That sounds lovely, baby."

The ringer on his phone echoes off the walls and he turns to the nightstand, his hand scrabbling in the bowl for it. When he doesn't find it, he sits up and growls. "What the sodding hell? I bloody put—*Minx*!"

I blink and give him a confused look. "What? I didn't do anything!"

"I put my phone, the Romanov cufflinks, and my brand bloody new Meterois watch in this bowl. The bowl I *did* notice appeared after the key incident that we will never speak of again. I *like* all the little touches your git put in and that's why I've been *using* them. However, the better part of eight figures is missing in action from the sodding nightstand!"

My confusion and amazement war inside me. On one hand, why in the *hell* did he have eight figures worth of crap in a tiny bowl on our nightstand like it was a bunch of stuff from Target? I didn't do a damned thing to move it, even as a joke. It's not like a goddamn ninja broke in unnoticed and whisked away from his—

Oh, fuck.

"Um, I am telling the truth." I bat my lashes at him, having realized what the problem is.

He glares at me as the phone rings again.

"I did *not* take your stuff. Now that I know what it costs, I'm not even sure I want to *look* at your stuff." An eye roll is my only answer, so I forge on. "However, I *might* know what happened."

"Out with it, woman!"

Letting out a piercing whistle that makes both Taurus and Aradia wince, I look around. No luck. It used to work when Aradia was little, so I thought it'd work here. Okay. What the fuck could that droid have taught the little bugger to get him to—?

Christ. How could I not know this?

I take a deep breath and start singing, "Yo ho, ho ho..."

Taurus looks at me like I've taken leave of my senses and I shrug, waiting.

From a cranny above the fireplace, a flash of light, and then motion. Within a blink, the unusually colored coal black ferret scampers up the bed and dumps his loot in front of me, almost smiling. Taurus' eyes widen and he looks ready to implode as I chuckle. "Meet Twist. He's the first mate's trusty sidekick."

"He's a sodding *hat* when I get my bloody hands on him!"

The growl makes the sleek rodent take off like a shot, filching the watch on his way. I wince, knowing that it is the most expensive item and ferrets, like kitties, love shiny things.

"You hurt his feelings, baby. He's only doing his job. Filch and pilfer, like the song says."

The phone rings again and my mate gives me a death stare. "You, my minx, are lucky I love your arse more than breath. Find that rat and appropriate my watch and then teach him some bloody manners before I do."

I beam up at him and then look up to see Twist on the mantle. He's standing like a meerkat, waving the watch at me.

Guess Mercury won't be getting a fruit basket.

The Bird Goes To Church

TAURUS

I cannot bloody believe my luck. *The Universe is taunting me; I know it.*

I've been working my hardest—no pun intended—to keep my foxy feline horizontal and happy for days. I want to make sure we don't waste a second of time so that we could make our family a reality.

We had to weather a few tiny storms: sharing the good news with our families, the blogger continuing his quest to get closer to Talia, and other various people trying to get in the middle of our lives. You might ask what kind of vacuous nitwits would try that with people like the Minx and I.

Try this one on for size, and you'll see what I mean.

On Monday, Tamara—who I wouldn't know if I ran into her on the street—got my number. She started texting me and damn near licked me from head to toe for several hours. I thought my warrior kitty was going to julienne her when she found out.

Next, the gnome and the writer invited me to their place for a chat, seemingly to get involved in naming our wee one. The minx let her extended family know that we are doing some family planning and those two malcontents weasel themselves into an event that is not theirs to commandeer. It was a monumental effort not to throttle them on the spot. I can't help but feel like my minx might let me do it now, but I have Talia's sodding romance with the two-bit Marlowe to contend with.

After that, I decided that I'm going to annihilate the person who put my private cell on the party page. I ended up having to visit a house full of people I'd never met before while listening to meaningless prattle at Michaela's. I'm certain there was a lot of talk about cars in the conversation, but it was so incoherent that I'm not sure.

I asked the minx, and she said that early on, Victor adjusted his intelligence algorithms for droids in response to their owners. He had to compensate because many of the heads of household in this 'burg are not the sharpest swords in the weapons cabinet. Preston was a likable git, but not in the running for MENSA. Still, I have to respect a family of people who seem to adore my lovely mate without the slightest interest in seeing her naked. I could learn to deal with their lack of saucy banter based on that fact alone.

The one bright spot in my shitty week was that Sandwich let me know she'd picked out a nick for me. I've been waiting for that and though she swore that she's never given one without an event triggering it, I was right proud of her.

Her claim is puzzling because I know that she has nicks for every droid and clone that she knows. It was a nightmare figuring out who all the bloody blog posts from the past are about. People being called things like Tyger and Royalty and Flame with no sign of who in the hell they are, made it hard to decipher. Seems pointless to use them when you didn't come up with them, but around the Resistance, there are many things I don't get. I quit giving a damn what they are unless they involve my tiger lily.

See that? That's four nicknames I gave her in one thought train.

I can't complain, though, because she's calling me her 'Forever' and there's not a nickname in this world equal to that moniker. I have to find something grandiose to call her now because she's one-upped me again.

That revelation led us back to our other naming discussion: our wee one to be. Though I have zero patience for the interlopers taking part, I am excited to discuss it with her. I started making a list in my head because neither of us came up with anything that felt right on the spot.

Once we bandied that about for a bit, she asked me where she'll be having the nipper. I'll be honest—it stopped me in my tracks. I hadn't considered that. I knew I was going to commandeer a doc from the Company, but I hadn't gotten further than pre-natal testing.

This whole situation is an unknown, right?

You'd think we were done after that, but she kept going. Since I never once considered the possibility of a wee one because Talia and I aren't the 'have kids' types as much as the 'have your kids for dinner' types, I panicked. I've never contemplated things like birthing rooms, last names, spit rags, and the long list of things that she now has questions about.

Are women born with this innate knowledge of everything in the known universe they need to do for a baby?

Christ. I don't even know what the hell a Diaper Genie is, much less if I want to do that or have a service. I doubt Talia does either. How in the hell am I going to learn all this shit?

It's okay, though. The minx calmed me down. I was slumping into that old chestnut of being anachronistic in this world and even more anachronistic to things like baby accessories. I don't get the inner workings of the Resistance community, and I sure as hell don't get the technical part of the baby process. I get the science part of the baby process, as biology is my strong suit. In fact, I excel at that.

However, I don't have the first clue what we need to do after the test and on through the delivery. I was only joking a little when I talked about cigars and being the big man. I feel like I'll have a lot to learn and none of it is even a bit as fun as making the baby is. Can't I hand her the black card and she'll get it all taken care of? There's a metric ton of clucking hens around here who would love to help her, right?

No. That wouldn't be right. I'm big and bad, for sure, but that's not the dad I plan on being.

I said a few tiny storms; I believe. Back to today. It's Sunday. It's been ten days since Beltane and it's time for the test. I know that it has because I've laid awake every day for a week thinking about it. What will change, what will she do about the other mates afterward, how will this work: every question about it has passed through my mind in a loop around three am every night? I don't tell her that because I don't want her thinking that I'm having second thoughts.

Nothing could be further from the truth.

I waited until she was asleep and filled the bedroom with flowers. Plus, I have a few surprises tucked away. I wanted this morning to be special for her—for us—from the moment her eyes opened. That's where it all went wrong.

My phone buzzed, and I chased down that bloody scarf with legs to get it. When I answered, I got an ear chewing from Talia for not answering. I didn't tell her it took me a bit to answer because a rodent had beaten me. She'd never let me live it down. Besides, I couldn't get a word in edgewise.

She had an emergency with her family on the other side and didn't reach through our connection so she didn't interrupt a private moment. It's too early for that, but I got the impression that it had more to do with where she was. She didn't go home and didn't want to tell me. That's a conversation for later; the minx might've had a point earlier this week.

I got commanded to show up and be presentable in public. I scrambled to the workout room—it's soundproofed so I wouldn't wake my mate. Then I cursed a blue streak, pleaded, and whined, but when your primary needs you, there's no telling her 'no,' especially when it's Talia.

My minx is going to wake up alone—which I know she hates—on this day of all days. I'm so sodding angry that I'd like to take out an entire theme park. I left her a note with the flowers and a promise that I'll be back as soon as possible.

Hopefully, when she sees where I absconded to, she'll at least get a giggle.

The Cat Is Left To Amuse Herself

DELILAH

Heart of Mine,

You'll never believe me if I tell you why, but I'm being dragged off to a sodding church for a couple of hours.

Here I thought the last three days were rough!

Never doubt for one minute that I'll be thinking about you all day and that I'll be imagining you there with me, eating parishioners. Say a curse for me, love, and hope that I don't get 'saved'.

Do you think I should worry about my eternal soul?

I miss you; I love you, and I feel you inside me always.

Taurus

The faint scent of fresh flowers and rich coffee flooded my senses as I stirred awake. I felt the warmth of the morning sun spilling in through the window, casting a golden glow on my pillow. And there, nestled on the soft fabric, was a note from him.

Being a nocturnal creature by nature, waking up in the morning is always a challenge for me, but this morning is different. The enticing scents of fresh blooms in every corner makes my nose twitch with excitement. This is going to be an amazing day.

At the same time, all these new smells are overwhelming my sensitive feline nose. I shake my head, trying to clear the fog from my brain and focus on the note he left for me. He beat me to our usual wake-up presents, but I have something special planned for today that will change our lives forever. I kept it hidden last night, knowing today will be a day filled with celebration leading up to our appointment.

I have no idea when the appointment actually is, but being Taurus, I trusted that he has everything under control. He probably has someone on call, ready to assist us whenever we're ready. But right now, he is at church.

Whiskey tango foxtrot, people.

I can't help but imagine Taurus sitting stiffly in a pew, his frustration growing as he listens to the preacher's sermon alongside Talia and her family. They must stick out like two dark knights among the floral-dressed southern churchgoers. The thought makes me giggle, but I'm also frustrated their plans put a hold on my surprise.

Now what am I supposed to do while he's gone? I can't just sit here and wallow in my annoyance. That won't solve anything.

As my eyes take in the colorful array of flowers strewn across the room, I feel a surge of panic rising within me. Before I die from sensory overload, I need to find some vases to distribute these beautiful blooms. Hex mentioned that many people sent flowers after

Beltane, so I quickly send him a text asking for his help in arranging them before I lose my breakfast.

In the meantime, I need to find something suitable to wear when the doctor arrives—something accessible yet not too revealing that could potentially get someone killed if they look at me wrong. Philomena is my last hope as I frantically search through my closet and send a message to her along with Hex.

I also desperately need to shower as Taurus has kept me confined to this bed for days now. My rumbling stomach reminds me that eating is an absolute must, and I should also squeeze in some training to keep my body sharp for what's to come. After all, it will be crucial once I start gaining pregnancy weight.

As I make my way to the closet to change into my training garb, I decide that it's best to work up an appetite first and go hunting before washing up. It saves me from having to repeat the process if I get dirty while searching for food. Glancing over at Aradia, who is lounging on a massive pillow by the fireplace with Twist curled up on her back, I ask, "Are you ready for some action, lady?"

She looks up at me with her piercing blue eyes before nodding her head ever so slightly. "Give me a few minutes to work up a sweat and then we'll go grab some breakfast, my love."

The Cat and Bird Take a Test

❧

TAURUS

What an absolute bloody train wreck that was.

Imagine for a moment: a stunningly handsome, cosmopolitan git sitting in a public pew at a church with his equally dangerous mate while listening to a Southern pastor drone on about forgiveness and turning the other cheek.

This time I give you permission to laugh because it had to be comical. Talia did her best to look normal in a demure floral number, but she's lithe and tan with the look of a woman who takes no shit. Clad in silk and Armani and though I'll admit to being striking, normal looking, I am not. We looked like new money Yankees on vacation in Florida. Accurate—if you think about it—but fit in? Not a chance in hell.

Talia's mum is a nightmare, but her grand-mum is a delicate lady. She insisted that Talia come to a church event in their town, and since neither of them is fond of electronic communication—nor do they know that she lives in another dimension—the message got delayed. By the time my primary got the heads up, it was too late to decline. That's why she called me this morning in a fury.

Usually I do the best that I can to endure when we have to make the occasional trip to visit. Today, it felt like my skin was shrinking on my bloody skeleton. Every minute I was there and not at home with my minx made me itch all over in anticipation.

I bloody hate waiting for anything. Period.

Talia finally took pity on me and sent me a pocket text to rescue me. She gave me an out by pretending to be the Company so I could get home before I exploded. She found the whole situation hysterical. If she hadn't helped me duck out, then she would have paid for her titters.

It hits me again as I hurry home. Today might be the day. Since the day she told me about the heat and we gave this a try, waiting has been like sitting on pins and pitchforks. We've been working our tails off—literally—to increase our chances by getting frisky frequently. Not that it's such a trial, mind you, but it's been ten days and I'm aching to see if it paid off.

The wait is almost over—bugger.

I never tested the information her contact on the other side gave her with the lab coats. doing research of their own. I should have checked, and that's eating at me now. I trusted her to know if the git she tapped had the creds to back up his statements. It's unlike me not to verify anyway, though. What if we've put all this stock into a huge bloody miscalculation?

Christ, I can't think about that now.

Waiting has made me irritable—more than normal, thank you very much—and unable to focus. I need to find out and Hell help me, if we find out she's not, I don't know what I'll do.

My distraction explains why I haven't even taken the time to inspect the construction in our home. I've had the building going since we mated. I wanted to give her a proper place for us. I wanted us to have a haven of sorts — some place that is only ours. I've been adding little bits to our home piece by piece as we grow closer. I used to check every day to see what was in the works and what they completed, but not this week.

I walk into our bedroom and the sight of my Sandwich nearly knocks me off my feet.

This is normally the point in the day that I'd be rushing in to bury my face against her neck—among other places—but I can't yet. She looks so vital and so beautiful that I can hardly step into the room. My heart seizes up and I stop to watch her for a moment. It does something to a man to see his woman wearing his clothes. Usually, for me, it's something akin to sending my temper into overdrive.

With her, it just melts me inside.

She's sitting on the bed with headphones in her ears as she leans against the beautiful white tiger. That sneaky shit ferret perches above her head. He's clutching something shiny that had better not be mine. The minx is chowing down on the biggest bowl of ice cream that I've ever seen outside of a gallon tub and she's only wearing one of my shirts and a pair of knee socks with superhero capes on them. Her toes are wiggling to the beat as she reads a book that is floating in front of her. With her hands free, she continues scarfing down what smells like mint chocolate chip from here.

She's vibrant and alive and most importantly, mine.

Her nostrils flare and a smile spreads across her face. She tugs the headphones out of her ears and tosses them in her little bowl. "I feel you," she sing-songs.

Grinning, I reach for her heart through our connection and give it a brush with my own. "I know, love. I feel you, too–all the time now. You looked so perfect that I wanted to watch you for a bit."

Her smile widens, and she closes the book with a thought, turning to put it to the nightstand as well. If I know her—and I do —she's turning away to hide the faint blush she gets when I surprise her with a compliment. It's one of her most endearing traits, and it draws me to her side like a moth to a flame.

Looking over her shoulder, she smiles. Her curls tumble around her face like a fiery wreath. "You should always come in. I always want to see you, but especially today."

I cross the room, stopping to scratch Aradia behind the ears and glare at the rat. He gives me a dirty look right back—I bloody swear—and scampers off with his spoils. I do not know what he's got, but I'm sure I'll be rampaging later when I discover that it's missing.

Dropping a kiss to her lips, I run a fingertip down her cheek in a soft caress. She's much more important than the walking scarf.

"I don't know about you, but I think that's better than watching from the door." She stretches and grunts as she shifts, then leans over and growls at the tiger. Aradia grumbles back, and she gives her rump a pat before the graceful cat leaps from the bed and lumbers to her own.

I will have to buy the princess a bigger bed soon. Putting it on my mental checklist, I laugh as the minx tugs me down with her.

Christ, I missed her.

"How did your day go?" Her eyes dance and I can tell she's poking at me.

Stretching out next to her, I pull her into my arms and kiss the top of her head. "Other than the last-minute church summons?"

Her deep chuckle vibrates against my chest. "What was that about?"

I snort and shake my head ruefully. "I'd rather not talk about it, love of mine. I'm still in a state of shock: the roof neither caved in nor was I struck by lightning."

"Okay, baby. What *do* you want to talk about?"

As soon as she asks, my stomach churns and I'm hit with a wave of emotion that lesser clones might label as fear. All the waiting and hoping slams painfully into my chest. My arms tighten around her and I mutter, "I don't know; I'm nervous."

There's an admission that I never expected to make.

It surprises her because she combs her fingers through my hair and tilts her head to look at me. "You're nervous, baby?"

Sorry sack that I am, the best that I can do is nod a little before I rest my head on top of hers.

"Why?"

I lay a palm on her tummy and murmur, "Today."

Her smile is soft when I look up at her. I see the warmth and love in her eyes as she looks back at me. "You've been waiting all day, huh?"

I nod and stroke her stomach softly. "Now I'm not sure that I want to know. I'm too worried that you won't be and too worried that you will be."

"We don't have to do this so soon, baby. We can wait."

The twinge of pain twisting my gut decides things for me quickly. I frown and shake my head. "That's no better." Sitting up and leaning against the headboard, I pull her into my arms. "How about you, my love? Do you want to know or not?"

She lays a palm over her tummy, rubbing in a slow circle. "Do I want to know if we've made a miracle?" The look she gives me is about as tender as I've ever seen, and her lips curve into a soft grin. "I want to know if you do." For a moment, something akin to worry clouds her baby blues and she looks a mite concerned. "You keep asking me and checking to see if I still want to. It's kind of making me worry that you're not sure."

Jesus. It feels like she hit me upside the head with something heavy. Stricken, I roll over and cup her face in my hands. "Oh, baby, no. Bloody hell, no. I want this so much that I can't think of anything but you and our wee nipper. I've not one doubt."

Her face brightens, and she reaches up to trail her fingers along the length of my jaw. "Then I want to know." I grin widely as her belly rumbles and she makes a face. "Or I want to know once I go to the bathroom. Then I want food. I have to give you something. Did you book the egghead?"

The grin fades from my face, and I groan. "Oh, bloody hell."

Moving quickly, I bolt up off the bed and grab the phone I'd left in the pocket of my duster.

How in the buggering hell did I forget to book the doc?

The most important part of doing the test is having someone to *do* the test. I shoot a glance at my very amused-looking woman. "You go to the loo, baby. I'll make a call and we'll have one here in no time."

She struggles to hide a grin as she slides off the bed. "All right, baby. I'll give you the thing when I get back." Padding over to the bathroom, she hits the panel and slips inside, her hips swaying as she goes.

As hard as we are on the bloody things, I will have to replace those slide lock mechanisms left and right. It didn't *feel* like a design flaw when I— I stop, my brows furrowing. She's mentioned whatever it is she has several times, so it must be important. Am I forgetting an anniversary or birthday? Do humans give gifts for finding out if you're knocked up and I'm an ignorant git?

Christ. First thing's first, I have to make this call.

The listing for the git I need is in my contacts right at the top. I figure that he might take some convincing. Given the whole of the situation, I'm ready for that. As soon as he picks up, I say, "Mikhail, Taurus. Yeah. No, no, Talia smoothed that out for me. You know her. Yeah. No. No. No, sod it all, it wasn't me." I roll my eyes, sighing at his pedantry. The prat starts right in on my grievous sins and doesn't let me say why I called. "Mikhail. Mikhail. Bloody hell, Mikhail! No, I need a doc. I know they don't normally make house calls, you git. I don't care." My temper's starting to froth; I feel it. "Mikhail, I need a doc. Get me one. Right. No, not there. Sandwich needs him."

I roll my eyes again and drop my head. It's not surprising that this little tête-à-tête is mostly the man prattling on incessantly about inconsequential shit. It's his bloody template's make-up, I sodding swear. "I'm *not* abusing my authority for a triviality. She might be pregnant with my child, you bloody wanker. *I want a bloody lab coat to do the sodding test!*"

That seems to shut him up for all about five seconds. It gives me time to at least try to get my temper under control. I take a deep breath and hope for calm. It's not normally a strong suit of mine, but I suppose it would do me well to remember that I'm asking for a favor. If the prat doesn't give it to me, I'm heading over to the Company and beating it out of him. I may as well try diplomacy first, though. I'm not in the mood to leave my mate right now.

"Right," I say when he finally asks me for confirmation of what I said. "No. Yeah. Yeah. You heard me. Right. Good. Right."

It's about time! Bugger says he'll send someone right over.

That's as it should be, after all I've done for the sod since we started working together. The fluttering in my stomach right now is nothing but a feeling of righteous satisfaction. It's not relief or gratitude. "Mikhail? Thanks."

That little gem slips out before I have time to hang up and I know I will never live it down.

The frustration of not being in control might account for the hurling of my phone at the couch. I storm over to the bed and throw myself down on the comforter, leaning back against the headboard with my hands behind my head as I wait for the woman to get finished with the bathroom.

My minx slips out of the door and smiles brightly when she sees me. I can't explain the kick her smile gives my heart or the squeeze of love that wraps around the whole of my soul. I don't figure that I need to, though.

"All worked out?" she asks, climbing back into bed. She lies on her side with her head on my thigh and my hand drops to comb gently through her hair.

"Yeah, baby, it shouldn't be long."

She smiles at the caress. Her tummy gives a Beast-worthy growl, and it makes me grin.

"Are you still hungry?" I ask.

Sandwich closes her eyes without answering me. Before I question her or make any comment, there's a bag of licorice laying on the spread next to her. My eyebrows arch with surprise. I haven't seen her do that before. She's obviously proud of herself when she opens her eyes and sees the bag. Looking up at me with a wicked grin, she crows, "Score. It worked." Opening the bag, she pulls out a piece and starts munching, all cute and self-satisfied. "Yep. Hungry. Grrr."

I chuckle low in my chest and run my fingertips over her cheek with pride in my eyes. Beltane's opened a whole unknown world of tricks, from the floating tome to licorice apparition to a host of things I'm sure that I haven't seen yet. Her magickal powers are increasing daily now that she is embracing them. I'm impressed, but then, she always impresses me.

"Kill any delivery boys today, baby?" I ask her idly.

It still amuses me to think about the way she's taken to the hunt and kill with as much deadly efficiency as she does everything else. It's like she was waiting for the right opportunity when I came knocking. Since there's no shortage of food walking around with the constant comings and goings of the construction crews, I figure it's as good a question to ask for small talk topics until the doc gets here.

I also love that her fierceness drives the writer wild, and she told me he gave her a lengthy lecture on morality. I couldn't have been prouder of her when she told him she's granted amnesty to the Thai because they give her indigestion. I doubt that it was the response he wanted and I'm sure that only lead to more pontificating on his part. She gets very vague when she's trying not to worry me over their constant picking.

"No delivery boys," she says as she chews another stick of licorice. "Mormons won't bother me again, though." She licks a fang and my eyes follow the action intently. So intently, in fact, that I almost miss what she says next. "They do always come when you're naked, too."

Blinking, I feel the demon inside me rage. *Zero to royally brassed off in oh-point-three.* I snarl low and grind out, "Someone saw you naked?"

She remains remarkably unconcerned—as if I'm not ready to hunt down every sodding Mormon in either dimension and do my personal interpretation of the last bloody supper.

"Nope. In a towel, but not for long. I was in the shower and all. They have the worst timing, those folks. How do they even get into the Rift?"

Okay. No need for a rampage—yet at least. Good to know. My demon feels mollified, though the ridges and fangs are out.

"Related to support staff at the Company, I suppose. Did you kill them all, love, or did you leave one for me to track down so I can pluck his eyes out?"

"I ate them both. Sorry, baby. I couldn't take a chance on the leftovers leaving me pamphlets." She finally turns her attention away from her snack and sets those gorgeous blue eyes on me. They kill the last small sizzles of irritation and my demon face melts away. My lips tug into a grin as she shrugs at me with a mock expression of innocence on her face. "I do so hate door-to-door religion salesmen."

Playing into the dramatics, I toss a mock pout at her. I'm amused beyond the telling of it, given that she's getting more and more in touch with her primal kitty and there's nothing in me that's got complaint one about hearing she's killing so effectively.

"Oh!" She sits up and scoots over to the side table, rummaging around for something. Frowning when she can't find it, she sits up and growls, "Yo ho!"

The scrawny rat comes running from the top of the curtains, his prize catching the light and winking. I can't see what it is, but the minx gives him a stern look. Twist climbs up onto the night-stand, chittering, and drops the object in the drawer before taking off.

Hiding it in her palm, she looks up at me with shy eyes. I

wonder for a moment exactly what my multi-faceted woman has in store for me. "So, last night, I had this, and I wanted to give it to you, but they occupied us. Before the lab coat gets here, I wanted to…"

I tilt my head. "Wanted to what, heart of mine?"

"I think I did a good job on estimating and getting it right, but I've wanted to give you this for now and we keep getting distracted."

She drops it in my hand, looking as if she wants to sink into the bed and disappear. Her constant battle between bold, brassy confidence and shy waif both amuse and confound me. For someone so emotionally clued in, she always seems to wait for rejection. Who taught her that? I still haven't figured it out since her household all seem to love her flaws, claws, and all.

The platinum band hits my palm and my eyes widen as I look at it. The inscription shines up at me: *Gra Go Deo*.

"I saw it and I thought of you. It means 'love forever' in Celtic. I hope you like it." She ducks her head, looking like she's going to disapparate herself to another room.

Humbled and awed, I look at the glittering ring. It's so simple yet so elegant, conveying things that I don't even think she realizes. If I weren't so overwhelmed, I might wring the little sod's neck for hiding it from her.

A smile forms on my lips and our eyes lock. Without a second of hesitation, I slip it onto my left hand, noting that the fit for my ring finger is perfect. She's got an eye, that's for sure. "Forever and a day will pass and my love for you and ours will shine as brightly as it has ever been."

Her smile is shy as she murmurs, "I guess that means I did good?"

I look down at the ring, the spot it's nestled in a symbol to me of my love and commitment to this woman. "You did more than okay. You move me." I brush my hand over her cheek, the flush creeping over her skin even more endearing. "I guess this means I'm married now, huh?"

Her laugh is soft and tinkling. "It might be a good thing since you might have already knocked me up. That means I don't have to get the shotgun out."

"I don't think it would take quite that much, love."

"I'm only kidding. I don't even own a shotgun. If I did, I probably wouldn't point it at you."

I snort. "That's very comforting, wife."

"Isn't it?" She grins and leans over to peck me.

I open my mouth to retort and the doorbell rings, causing both of us to freeze in place. "That death knell isn't as funny right now as when I had it installed," I mutter.

She gives me a knowing look and I see that I've made her point nicely and once again, she's won an argument by letting me talk myself into losing.

Damn, I love this woman.

The Doctor Is In

TAURUS

"The doc is here."

Sandwich nods at me. Excitement and trepidation flashes over her face. I understand the emotions; I'd wager my expression is the same.

She sits up and tosses the licorice wrapper into the trash bin next to the bed. True to form, she fusses about for a moment. Straightening her shirt and sliding under the comforter, she nods when she feels prepared to receive our guest. Taking a deep breath, she nods again. "Okay, go let him in."

I lean over to kiss her before I shove off the bed. Loping out of the room, I take the main staircase to the first floor to find the git. I can't say that I give the doc more than a once over when I yank open the door. I notice the lab coat and the spectacles and not much else because he's not worth the effort. Reaching out to grab his arm, I drag him inside with no ceremony and even less greeting.

My eyes clock him as we cross the foyer. He's a small sort—like most of his ilk at the Company—and I'd throw him back for growing if I were hunting. As I'm not hunting, I tighten my grip on his arm and propel him down the hallway to the stairs. With a combination of pulling and pushing, I get him to the third floor and into the master bedroom.

As we approach, my mate unbuttons one sleeve of my shirt and rolls it up to her upper bicep, then looks up. She smiles at me—that same beaming smile that sets my pulse pounding—before giving the doc an expectant glance.

I reach out to her through our connection and give her heart a gentle caress, reminding her how much I love her. I know she has to be as nervous as I am.

"Love, this is Doctor..." I turn to look at the diminutive little sod and realize I do not know what his name is and I don't care. "Actually, who cares what you're called? This is my woman, doc. You hurt her; you die. You disappoint us; you die. You annoy me; you die. There's a general death theme tonight that you should know." I tower over the man and he looks up at me as if he's ready to wet his pants. Pointing at my love, I glower at him. "You know what to do. Do it."

He quivers.

I cross my arms over my chest, rather satisfied with myself. At least, I am right until she gives me a dirty look.

Chiding me, she murmurs, *~No need to be rude, love. ~*

Rude? I'm not being rude.

I'm making sure the doc knows what'll happen if he toes over the line, that's all. I'm looking out for her. It's not even like I'm fanged out. I sigh as she shakes her head at me and then holds her arm out for him.

"I'm ready," she tells the wimpy little prat. "I guess I should let you collect it the normal way. It will be less messy." Exposing the crook of her elbow for him to do a tourniquet, she watches the doc ready the needle and tube. He gets her all tied up with that rubber band of torture and she winces. It's a good thing that I'm watching him like a lion watches a sodding zebra because I notice his hands right off. That twitchy little rodent is moving that needle closer and closer to her arm while his hands are shaking like he has a palsy.

Oh, bloody hell, no. She's afraid of needles.

I can tell she's being a brave soldier right now, but if he stabs her over and over, she'll freak out. I've killed people for less than making a tear fall from her eye.

Moving fast, I grab his wrist and squeeze, grinding cartilage and tendon until he yelps in pain and drops the needle. I catch it by the tube with my free hand and snarl low in my throat as my fangs drop. Glaring at him with golden, demonic eyes, I growl low. "Get it together, you prat. I'll forget my manners and gut you right here if you don't. Don't so much as breathe the same air as her until you've got it under control. Hear me?"

"I'm fine, baby," she breathes.

I look at her in time to see the warning glare and the thread of green in her eyes before she gives that sniveling worm an encouraging smile. Huffing a bit, I hand the git his needle because her smile has calmed his jittery digits.

It figures. That doesn't mean that I'm not eagle-eyed as he feels around for a vein. The problem inherent with a connection like ours is that she picks up on more than I'd like her to. She's got that kitty radar for when I'm itching to do some damage. That makes it near bloody impossible to slip anything past her—like my yen for making the dear doctor all bloody and ouch-feeling.

~Quit, you're making him more nervous. You're not helping. ~

I'm not helping? Great. Just what I sodding wanted to hear. I'm about to comment, but she pales, and I hear a soft gasp as the needle penetrates her skin. The tube fills with crimson fluid and my gaze shoots to hers, heart skipping a beat. With a low warning snarl, I advance on the doc, intent on separating his head from his shoulders."

~I'm okay. ~ Her quick, reassuring whisper in my mind gives me pause and I pull up to study the truth in her expression. Fortunately for the balding git, she's being truthful.

It doesn't mean that I shouldn't kill him, though.

~I don't like you in pain, baby. ~ Maybe I should have another

go around on that whole 'too small to eat' thought I had earlier. Giving him a once over, I grin evilly, asking my mate, *~Are you still hungry?~*

~Leave him be. ~ She says in that same chiding voice. *~I'm a baby about needles and you know it. ~*

~I know. That's why I wanted the best, but this git isn't good for spit. ~ With narrowed eyes, I watch every move he makes. I don't have a clue how this nitwit got past the screenings at the Company because clones would eat him alive.

She sighs in relief as the needle slips out and the lab coat turns to set the tube on a small tray. I can tell she's holding back a giggle when the pierced skin of her elbow closes before he can reach for a square of gauze. He blinks, but with the first and only glimmer of common sense I've witnessed, he remains silent.

Her eyes find mine and she winks, reassuring me she's fine. "Where's he going to test it?" she asks, her anticipation and excitement trickling through our connection. "Will he take it back to the Company? When will we know?"

Those are good questions that I have no answer for. Snarling low, I glare menacingly at the doc. "You heard her, didn't you? Answer her. Now."

~Be nice. Sheesh. He's swallowing his tongue. ~

I grumble a little into her mind and she chuckles back, stroking a thought down my cheek. It doesn't take a rocket scientist to see that the prat's struggling for composure. I can't say that dims my mood a bit at all. He looks back and forth between us like he's watching some poof tennis match at high speed.

"I-I was t-t-told to b-b-bring the sup-p-plies necessary for a p-pregnancy test here."

Sighing and rolling my eyes, I cross my arms over my chest in disgust. Is this supposed to be one of the Company's finest? I need to remember to have a word or ten with Mikhail about the hiring procedures over on the other side. As it is, it'll be tomorrow before the good old doc here spits out whatever he's trying to say.

"If you h-h-h-have a s-small room I c-c-could use? F-for a few minutes? The r-r-results t-take ap-p-p-p—about th-thirty minutes."

Looking for all the world like the single most patient woman in it—stop and marvel at that one for a moment—the minx nods and smiles at him all encouraging-like. "We do, Mr. Uh—what's your name again, dear?" she says.

He blinks owlishly, as if no one's ever asked him that question —I'm willing to bet a sodding Ferrari that they haven't—and pushes his glasses up his nose. "M-M-M-Marvin. I m-m-mean, D-D-Doctor..."

She smiles and shakes her head, looking like the picture of graciousness. This is the woman who just ate a passel of Mormons, mind you, but she's acting like Princess Diana in the slums. "Marvin will do." Meeting my eyes, she asks, "Find Marvin some-where to work, please?"

~Do it without hurting him, please. ~

~Spoilsport. ~

I blow her a kiss behind the doc's head as I grab his arm more gently than I'd done when he first arrived—and drag him out of the room and down the hall to a spare bedroom. I've yet to decide what to do with this one, but it'll suffice for his purposes. Turning on the light, I shove, er, usher the git into the room and let him go. I can't figure out why he stumbles and almost drops the tray and bag he's carrying. With a low grunt, I ask, "Will this do?"

He opens his mouth to speak, but bugger all comes out. Finally, he nods.

That's fine as I've neither the time nor the inclination to wait for him to stutter out some piddling response that's bound to test my resolve to not off him. Snorting derisively, I turn on my heel, closing the door behind me as I head back to my woman.

Once back in the room, I toss myself down on the bed next to her and throw a leg and arm around her. As soon as she touches me, I feel a sense of contentment steal over me, calming me without warning. I lift my head and look into her eyes, seeing all her hopes and fears. "Thirty minutes, my love, and I didn't harm a non-existent hair on his head."

She nods and leans in, kissing my lips. "Mm-hmm. If you'd hurt him, it would have taken longer."

I rest my forehead against hers as her eyes twinkle with teasing mischief. Focusing inward, I feel for her heart and soul and wrap them around me like a warm blanket, sinking into the bond between us. With a grin, I brush her lips with mine. *~It's possible that you've got a bit of a point. I'm lucky that I've got you to keep me in line. ~*

Chuckling, she nibbles at my lips. *~Heh. One of us has to be the brains of this outfit. ~*

My low growl muffles my bark of laughter. *~Sassy minx. It's a good thing that I love you. ~*

~Otherwise, who knows what you'd do with me? ~

I pull back a mite and meet her gaze, my lips curving into a grin. *~I'd fall in love with you all over again, sod it all. You're as addictive as hell, love. ~*

Her nose crinkles as she teases. *~Addictive, huh? I think you're a hard habit to kick. ~*

~Just try it, baby. I bet you can't last the day. ~ I bend my head and nuzzle her neck as I slide a hand over her tummy, hoping hard that the news will be good. She purrs at the attention and nuzzles me right back.

~Oh, I have no illusions about that. I wouldn't even want to. ~

She makes me moan with just her lips on my neck. Feeling the tendrils of arousal flickering across my skin like a flame, I lick a warm trail along her collarbone, cursing the guest in the house. *~If we were alone, baby. ~*

Reinforcing my words, I send her a mental image that sizzles with heat and makes me hard and randy picturing it. She groans and presses against me, growling.

~Bad, bad boy. ~

Her eyes close and I have an image in my head in full Technicolor and bugger if I don't almost spend myself on the spot. Out of the corner of my eye, I catch her licking her lips and smile, so at least I know I'm not the only one affected. *~Bloody hell. I clean more pants around you. ~*

Leaning up to nip my lips, she says, *~Yeah, but you don't mind. I can tell. ~*

I can't argue with that, so I wrap my hand around the back of her neck and deepen the kiss, my tongue stroking hers into a primal dance. Being with her is like sinking into a hot bath. First my skin heats, then the sensual warmth works through to my core, forcing my blood to run faster and pound harder in my veins. It's odd as it pounds so loud it seems more than a feeling inside, but a sound I hear knocking in my head. Feels so good, though, that I don't give the knocking a thought as my words slip from my mind to hers. *~My love, my mate, my everything. ~*

~Forever, baby. ~

Her tongue duels with mine as her fingers clutch at my shirt. I groan low as the pounding gets louder, more insistent. I can't believe how bloody hungry I always am when we're together and when she touches me or kisses me bloody hell. Her breath catches a little as her hips rock against me. She whimpers and I'm undone. *~God, baby, I want you. ~*

~Yes, ~ she says in a husky whisper, pressing closer as I caress her. The length of her long, bare leg caresses along my thigh as she slides it up to wrap around my hip and she sucks on my tongue. My hands clutch her almost bruisingly and a low keening sound vibrates through my chest.

I was told long ago I'd not be seeing heaven in this or any other lifetime. That one turned out to be not true. She's my heaven.

She gets eerily still and says, *~Did you hear something? ~*

Hear something? Over the race of my blood and the slam of my heart? Not bloo-

That's when it hits me. The pieces fall into place. That odd pounding sound I pushed out of my mind. My senses go on alert, demon face sliding into place to defend and protect with my life if need be. It isn't until I whip my head around with a low roar and see that insipid little sod that I remember.

Oh, bloody hell.

"You better be large with the info, git, or you'll be bleeding before you take a step. Is the test done?"

The doctor—who has been trying to get our attention for at least a few minutes—doesn't even need to nod because he's shaking so badly. I don't think I've ever seen that shade of pale on a person still breathing before. I've made cadavers with more color in their faces than this wretch.

"Y-yes, s-s-sir. Mr. T-T-Taurus, s-sir. I-I j-j-just..."

I roll my eyes and snarl. I'm sure as shit not in the bloody mood to wait until my woman's in labor to find out if she's pregnant.

The minx wriggles a bit to get out from underneath me and sits up, straightening her mussed clothes while mentally tsk-tsking me. *~Don't be so bristly. Give him a chance to talk. ~*

Sighing, I draw back the fangs and face, sending a stroke down her spine with a thought. *~Fine, baby, I'll play nice for now. ~*

~Good boy. ~ The chuckle she sends through my soul makes the grand sacrifice worth it.

I kiss her temple and turn back to the shivering man. "What, doc? Come in; don't stand there like a small tree in the bloody breeze." I can't say that he hears me, as he stands there blinking like an owl for a few long moments before shuffling in. He stays as close to the door as possible, though, and I suppose that says at least something for his intelligence.

"W-W-Well...this is highly ir-r-regular, you s-see. It's never h-happened b-b-before. N-no one t-told me..."

Bloody hell. This sodding prat will be the death of himself, I swear. Yet again, the woman's keyed in all too well with my emotions and she sends me a mental stroke, caressing my heart with hers as she crosses her ankles and listens to what the stuttering fool's saying.

I bite back a snarl and roll my eyes. "Told you?"

Clearing his throat, he straightens his bowtie with a nervous hand and continues. "Y-yes...well...no one t-t-told me...if th-this...if a p-p-potential for ch-child r-r-rearing is what you w-w-want."

My gaze narrows, patience long since gone. "Tell us, speak true, and pray you give us the right answer, mate, because I'm not telling you jack."

The minx scoots closer, angling so her back is resting against my chest. The fingers of one hand twine with mine, pulling it over her tummy and holding it there so my arm is around her. I have no idea if she means to, as she's still caught on every bollixed syllable stuttering out of the man's lips. The contact of her body on mine, our hands linked over her belly where she might carry our baby makes me calm.

Yeah, it calms me.

That doesn't do a bloody thing for the doc, though, as he's just one big twitch. "It's j-j-just... I'd rather n-not be k-k-k-killed, and I w-was w-wondering if I w-w-would be if I t-tell you that your w-w-wi... mate is, in fact, pregnant."

I tilt my head and stare at him, my voice quiet and controlled. "Are you saying that she is?"

The small man takes a gigantic step backward. It seems he plans on running if need be, no matter how pointless the attempt would be. After he backs himself all the way into the hall, he seems to find something resembling a spine. He takes a deep breath and squares his shoulders, mustering as much dignity as he's capable of.

"Y-yes, sir. The young lady is, in fact, pregnant."

Sometimes in life when you see or hear something that makes you still. The entire world grinds to a halt.

This is one of those times.

I blink, maybe more than once, and I'm certain I'm still breathing. I'm utterly frozen, almost as if, even with the words - or maybe because of them - I'm still breathing. I'm utterly frozen, almost as if, even with the words - or maybe because of them - I'm hesitant to believe it. I don't want it snatched away or some such whimsical rot.

She's pregnant.

It's not until she gasps, her free hand flying to her mouth, that I realize she's as stunned as I. Her other hand squeezes my fingers just shy of painful and she presses our joined hands to her tummy as if we could already feel the tiny life there growing by touch alone. She turns her head to look at me and I see her soul shining like a beacon in her eyes.

I think that's when it sinks in. I think that instant—seeing something in those blue depths I'd not seen before—is what convinces me it's real.

My face shifts and my eyes glow as a huge smile spreads across my face.

We're pregnant.

The world jump-starts again, and each one of my senses seems on full overdrive. I feel, see, and smell everything. I know the second the doctor breathes again and relaxes. I guess his sudden relief has something to do with the expressions on our faces. I almost feel his muscles unclench one by one and hear the blood rush back into his colorless face.

"So it's good news. Yes, I assure you she's very pregnant."

I nod my head once, all the while grinning like a sap of the first order. "Thanks, Doc," I say. "Now get out."

She chides me, almost as if it's automatic. "Thank you, Marvin. I'm sure I'll be seeing you again."

Dismissing the sod, I tighten an arm around my woman, all the love I feel for her seeping through my pores. Her arms wrap around my neck and she squeezes hard, her body turning to crush into me. She's laughing, and so am I as she dusts kisses all over my face.

~We're. Having. A BABY! ~

There's a suspicious knot in my throat and my eyes are stinging and damp. Not that I'm tearing up, it's just that she's cutting off my air.

Yeah. That's it.

She rubs her cheek on mine and I feel her heart expand until it seems to want to break out of both her chest and mine.

~I know, baby, ~ she says in a soft, wispy voice. *~I know. ~* Pulling back a bit, she looks at me and her smile is soft and loving and gentle. *~You're a daddy. ~*

Something about those words. Don't know what, but it does something inside me when I hear them. It's like I feel—I'm not sure. I can't say that I've ever felt this way before. It's more than happiness; I know happiness. This is more. It's a sublime joy. I wrap tightly around her and kiss her all over her face. I know my grin's bordering on sodding goofy. *~Christ, I love you. I'm a daddy. Or I will be. You're the most beautiful, precious thing in my world and you're carrying our child. ~*

~I am.~ She beams a smile at me, tilting her head for my kisses with a giggle. *~I knew I was eating a lot.~* She pauses a little and eyebrows rise as it seems a thought hits her. *~He said very. Why didn't we ask how much very was? ~*

~Don't know. Stopped on 'she is', you know? Want I should call him back and pump him? ~

She smiles and rests her forehead on mine, shaking her head. *~Not now. We'll find out tomorrow, I suppose. ~* Her eyes are alight with love and a glint of mischief when she adds, *~Not important now. ~*

The magnitude of what we've done sort of sinks in. *~Oh, God, we're pregnant. We did it! We're going to be having a wee one. ~* I pull back so I can look at her. That sodding mysterious sting in my eye and a lump in my throat is back. *~We're a family. ~*

Her face softens and she whimpers a little, her hand sliding up to stroke over my face. ~A family, ~ she says. *~The three of us together will be a family. ~*

~Forever. ~

She nods, still stroking over my jaw. *~Forever. ~*

I cup her face in my hands and kiss her. *~I love you so very much, love. I love what we've made. Know that I've never, never been more satisfied, felt more joy and love than I do right now. ~*

Sniffling a bit, she kisses me back, her arms draping around my neck and fingers burying in my hair. *~I love you so much it hurts, ~* she says in a soft, emotion-filled voice. *~I can't imagine being happier than I am right this second with you here with our baby growing inside me. ~*

My heart aches in a bloody good way as emotions swirl between us through our connection. *~Inside. ~* I span her stomach with my hand, holding it there. *~Inside... She's inside...~*

~It could be a 'he', daddy. ~ Her eyes dance.

Grinning, I shrug. *~I can't say that I care, mum. Whichever's fine for me. ~* I kiss her, my tongue searching out its mate and sliding against it. *~Make love with me, baby. Let me love you. ~*

~I always do. ~ Her body presses into mine, melting against me as the kiss inflames us both. *~In fact, I think that's how she got inside. ~*

I slide a hand between us and unbutton the shirt she's wearing. *~Is THAT what does it? I had no bloody idea. Good thing I've got you, baby. ~* Peeling off the shirt, my hands trace over her heated skin.

Before she can reply, she pulls back and gives a big, echoing yawn, covering her mouth with her hand.

Smiling, I hold her close and kiss the top of her head. *~It's okay, baby. You can make love to me tomorrow. How about I hold you and watch you sleep for eternity? ~*

She blinks her big, beautiful eyes at me as if she's trying to clear her vision. *~Oh hell, baby, I'm exhausted. ~* Even her smile's sleepy looking as she wraps around me. *~So long as you stay here with me, eternity is fine with me.~*

I draw away from her long enough to get out of my clothes, then slip between the sheets and cuddle her close, curving around her. Brushing my hand through her hair in slow, soothing strokes, I keep feeding our bond with my love, joy, and pride in her.

~Sleep, baby. Sleep. I'll be here for every tomorrow. I love you, my mate, my love, my heart. ~

~Love you so much baby, ~ she whispers, snuggling into my embrace. I feel her emotions. She gives that to me like the most precious gift and I feel her happiness, know that she's feeling safe and warm and well- loved. Turning on her side, she pulls on me until I'm spooning her, twining our fingers over her stomach. *~Tomorrow. ~*

As I feel her slip under, draw deeper into slumber, I watch her, listen to her heart. I figure it's too soon, but I can't help straining to listen for any sound of life under our hands. I'm not surprised I can't, but I know that one day soon, I will.

Smiling, lying there, I listen, I watch, and I wait.

The Cat and the Bird Have A Serious Discussion

DELILAH

"This place is a dump."

I know, I know. You think I'm biased, right? Maybe I'm even being a little snooty after moving to the Rift's version of the royal vacation home. No, I'm not. It's *become* a dump.

As much as I hate Sari and Belle for opening this place, I know the power of having a gathering area. It gets people excited because it's new, everyone is here, and it gives them a place to socialize that doesn't violate their private spaces. So I relented and didn't have it blown off the face of the Rift on 'accident'.

That is what I suspect the Company did to Sari's previous bar, Dirty Deeds. A sign saying 'closed' appeared on the door one day and there was a smoking hole in the ground the next. I'm not sure why Sari didn't learn her lesson after the first bar went boom, but that's Sari for you.

Most of my family members have made appearances here since it opened. They're glad-handing: singing a song or two, taking part in theme weeks, and monitoring the landscape. I visited the first week to make an impression. That is how I know that this means that it IS becoming Dirty Deeds revisited. That place needed a power wash to get clean enough to look at the floor and furniture, much less to sit on it.

I sigh, watching various community members take turns at the mic. I listen to some of my friends and their families. They all *seem* happy, but I don't know who is putting on a public face and who is enjoying themselves anymore.

I seem down for someone who got the best news of the century, right?

It's been a few days since I broke the news to everyone. They acted calm in public, but I don't trust it. Every single person I talked to smelled like lies—sweaty socks, if you're wondering—and I couldn't bring myself to push them until they were honest with me.

Rafe and I discussed their reactions. Sari and Wilde had already warned the rest of the crew before I could even get to them because no one seemed surprised.

It's too quiet. Something is happening that I don't know about; I guarantee it.

"Something is going on and I don't like it."

"Oi, Nancy, we're here!"

I look up and smile, gesturing to the open seats at my table. Hex, Leo, and the rest of the gang pull another table over and get settled in. Hex plops a five- inch binder down and my eyes widen. "What the hell is *that*?"

"It's the party planning bible, kitty. It's no different from any other shindig we've thrown." Leo shakes his head as if I've lost my mind, then asks, "Drinks everyone? I'll head up and see if anyone is even around to pour."

"Probably not," Philomena says, looking disgusted. "My boys have been avoiding the day crowd since their co-owners abandoned the upkeep on the place. Their family isn't doing much to help, either. Janus has had it with scrubbing everything down every day to clean up messes he'd rather not identify."

I pinch the bridge of my nose, too aggravated to put words together. Why in the fuck did those two goddamned idiots force this bar open only to abandon it in less than a month?

Never mind, I know why.

Sari wanted something to piss me off, and Belle suggested re-creating DD so they could be in control. Since Belle has the attention span of a gnat and Sari's too busy helping Wilde get a leg up on Talia, they have dropped the whole thing. I don't blame Roman or Janus for not wanting to get left holding the mop. Their whole 'no rules' makes for some messy playtime in this universe. I'd hate to think about the things they've had to clean up.

Music plays and I look up to see Michaela singing a pop tune from the eighties. She's belting away like she's at her prom, beaming out at the crowd. At least the community members are having fun—the tables full of people hooting and hollering for her haven't noticed that this went from a karaoke bar to a dive.

Philomena sighs as if it's the most troublesome thing in the world and gets up. "I'm allowed behind the bar. Give me a list, reprobates. I'll pour, Leo will fetch, and we will knock out the decorations and food choices so we can split up the errands. I wish the loafer were here so we could get the costume ideas and pick up what he needs, too."

"He is not yet ready for this exposure," Siren says, her eyes darting around the room. "The waters are deep and the sharks swim in the shallow end."

I arch a brow, thinking for a moment I've hit my head since she sounds like that bloody riddle droid that Hex loves so much. "What?"

"Oh, don't be dense, Queen D. She's being metaphorical. The artist didn't want to step into the spotlight yet because he doesn't want to get swarmed. The vacuum of ladies in his life makes him shark bait," Philomena calls over her shoulder as she walks away.

"Not that he needs to worry about it. We've got his back,"

Sandrine says, popping an enormous bubble. "Buzz would love to find a playmate."

I shudder and wave my hand. "Christ, not in front of me. You'll give me a coronary. That's the last thing I need right now."

Hex chuckles and makes a googly face. "Not with the *bayyyyy-beeeee!!*"

My eyes narrow and I growl. "Baby or not, I'll de-fang the next person who acts like I'm a piece of fine china. No. Special. Treatment."

"Correct. No special treatment. Predators breed in the wild every day, and that does not mean that they are any less dangerous than those who are not with child. Perhaps they are even more so." Siren gives me a small, knowing smile, as if she has every confidence that I'll be ripping off heads until the day the baby's born.

"Thank you, Siren. I agree."

Leo walks up with a tray, followed by Philomena, and they hand out the drinks. "Okay, fangs and friends, let's get down to business."

I hold up my hand. "If anyone gets up to sing a song from a Disney movie after that, I'll skewer you all."

"Spoilsport," Hex grumbles. "Fine, let's plan."

After the marathon design session with the family, I popped back to my other home. I'm tired and worse for the wear.

Worrying about the blowback from my announcement and the concerns the girls raised about behavior at the party are weighing on my mind. I can't very well cancel the damned thing. They all warned me and well, I didn't listen.

It's all on me if it goes sideways. Yay!

Taurus stalks in like a dark cloud on the horizon. It's odd, but I feel the irritation running through him and I wonder if he had Cuban for lunch. Indigestion makes him cranky every time.

"Bloody spicy git," he mutters, striding into the closet.

Mystery solved: Cuban. "You okay, baby?"

He comes out of the closet after changing into more comfortable clothes He's meticulous about his fancy duds and chides me about how not careful that I am. My problem is years of being spoiled by Hex, who's always done all that for us. In a house as big as mine, everyone owns something and we function as a unit, taking care of our things for everyone.

I know; I'm a brat.

I also don't own clothing and accessories that one could sell to pay off the debt of a third world country—he does.

"Indigestion, plus Talia had an irritating visit with the blogger. She's feeling weird, and it's bleeding in a little."

I arch a brow. "Irritating how?"

"They have invited her to their house for the weekend. I figured that she'd gotten horizontal with him much sooner than intended when she called from somewhere NOT our home before the church fiasco. It's not appealing to think about THAT, but she's been having a decent time with him. As much as I loathe that little toad he lives with, I want my woman to be happy. Hell knows I am."

He gives me a toothy grin, then shakes his head.

I nod, understanding the Catch-22, as my mate and I have been there. I hate Hex's girl's family, we're not fond of our own mates, and I worry about Philomena's boys functioning as gossip diggers.

"Right. I think you might have been right about 'ye old English' jumping the gun on how fast things will go based on what Talia's lines are. Some discussion set her teeth on edge. I know everyone else in this little 'berg is all into 'the free loving families' thing, but that's not how we work. The gnome should know that by now, and Wilde suggested otherwise."

Blinking, I start an internal countdown to curb my temper.

Now that I have a good working relationship with the Beast, my bloody magick goes off the rails when I get emotional. With him already in this mood, it won't help anything if I go crazy and zap us to Mars or something. "Otherwise?"

"He suggested Talia should steal me back if she's feeling lonely. It made me wonder if it was his way of trying to get you alone, despite your conversation today. It also made her wonder if his courtship of her "was less about her and more about evening the score with you."

Hell yes, it is. I bloody *told* him I worry about that. That's what Sari and Wilde *do*. Jesus Christ, no one ever, ever fucking listens to me. I should not have to present a full-blown case to the judge and jury to get people to realize that I dislike saying bad things about people I care about and when I do, there's fucking reason.

"Uh- huh. What else?" There's *always* a 'what else' with them, you see.

"Evelyn. Evie." His eyes narrow and his glare falls on me.

That son of a bitch! "I *told* him that naming the baby was between you and me and we were not taking suggestions, regardless of who makes them. That *jackass*." I jump off the bed, stalking to the bar. I'm filled with anger and energy that sizzles over my skin. Therefore I didn't want her near them. They can't stop themselves and they don't want to. They have to ruin everything for everyone.

He watches me, head tilted. "Talia told her she knew about the gnome saying that you're neutering me. I don't think she quite gets that being nice for the sake of you, and now for Talia isn't being neutered; it's being respectful of those you love."

Snorting, I shake my head as I stare into the glass of scotch. "She most definitely does not."

"According to her, there's a passel of people you're not given dues to because of me."

His expression is melancholy, and I growl low into the glass again, glad that I'd worked out a spell that helps me protect the baby but allows me to take the edge off. It's not a pleasant process, mind you, and a little gross on the back end, so I won't go into detail. However, it works, and she is safe. Don't worry for a second, yeah?

"We don't work on the 'family love' concept and everyone else does. It feels like we're ruining everything and it might have been better for us not to even have come along."

I cross over the bed, bend down, and cup his face. "Don't say that. It's not true, and I don't care if anyone else agrees with me. They can all go fuck themselves. I haven't been this happy in a long time and they can chew on that fat because they fed it to me."

He sighs. "See, we have casual playtime with no problem. I could have done Tamara or Blondie—no big deal. It would have been interesting, and that's it. Then you came along, all prickly and stompy with that milk dud heart..."

He's not listening to me. Whatever Sari has said to Talia is messing with his head. I don't know how to fix it and it's making me panic, but I promised I'd do better about the freak outs, so here I am. I drawl, looking into the glass as I walk to the bay window. "I like our home. I enjoy having you to myself and I enjoy being here with you. It's often the only place I want to be."

"What are you saying, baby?" he asks.

"I think Sari knows that. Look at the seeds she's planting. This bloody bullshit is why I hate being around those two."

"I have to be honest. If you're saying that you prefer being exclusive with me, even knowing that it might not always be possible for you, and even after the baby you'd still want that from me, despite the fact that you might not honor it yourself, I need to know. It's going to decide some things for me."

"I have been sort of exclusive with you. I like it, but I can't leave people I love and hurt them. Not after Rhea. I won't be her. I've been choosing you over Sari's family for a while now."

That part is true. I've been with him so much that I haven't been around many others unless I have to, and with all the turmoil in the community, I haven't had the time to give much to anyone else. It's part of the reason this bullshit with Sari is coming up. My guess is that she's raising the flag for Constantine and Shea, too.

"Regardless of what you don't think you should ask from me, or wouldn't deny me, tell me the truth. Do you want me to be only yours? Outside of my primary."

I look down at my hands, warring with my heart, my ethics, and my internal gauge of what's right and fair, I whisper, "Yeah, I do. I want to rip people limb from limb when I think about them touching you. I feel awful saying it because I can't guarantee that myself. It's not fair to ask you to give what I can't reciprocate. I feel guilty even thinking about it." I run my hand over my chest, a little green at the gills from saying it out loud.

"Sod it, Deli! I'm not asking about fairness; I'm asking what you bloody well feel; I want you all to myself. I want to be a greedy, possessive, stingy wench about it. I don't know *why* because I've *never* wanted to kill someone so much as I want to kill Tamara when you showed me those texts. But there it is."

Feeling like a total bitch, I walk over and drop onto the couch, tucking myself into the cushions as if making myself smaller will lessen the pinch.

He lets out a breath, looking at his left hand. I sit my chin on my knees, spreading my long hair curtain around me like a shield. The air is shrinking around me as I wait. "People don't understand the way I'm wired. They can't figure out why the big bad would want to be faithful to one—now two—chits. I don't have the stomach for being second. I'm defined by my choices. I don't ask others to make the same decisions, but I need to know what they stand for. The only person—aside from the golden goddess—that I trust to tell me what they need is you."

He looks up and meets my eyes. "You don't always do that without me making an issue about it, and you're riddled by guilt and 'shouldn'ts'. I don't know if you meant it like that, but when I took this ring, I chose the finger to wear it on. I said something to you without saying it. and I've mentioned it in passing once or twice, as well."

I lick my lips. He has mentioned it and I caught it, to tell the truth, but since I've never seen him even blink at maybe returning the gift—I've sort of pushed it out of my mind. I know it's like he can't because of what I can't give him. That's my choice and I know it, but it hurts, so I don't mention it. He's not trying to hurt me, I know, but still. I speak, wanting to tread away from that topic as best I can because I cannot bear the thought of him telling me those reasons out loud.

My heart can't take that from him.

"The reason that I can't always say it is because of my ethics and due to people and their blasted rules. It's hard for me to know if I'm crossing a line that I didn't know about. I know you're different and I'm trying to be better about it. I've crossed lines I didn't mean to before with a couple of people, and I got burned. Please understand that I'm trying to make it easier. Sometimes, I get afraid that I'll screw it all up and lose you. That would kill me."

His look is serious. "There is only one way you could *ever* lose me. Lie to me, or keep something from me because you think I'll hurt or betray me, and I'm so gone that it'll be like I was never here. That is the only way—the *only* way — you lose me. I walked into this with my eyes open about your past. Few things I've learned since then? I know you have to be with your other mates. I *know* and I hate it. It's like a very large, serrated blade tearing through my heart and lungs, but I know it. I live with it, and I'll live with it after it happens. It hurts worse than you'd want to imagine."

My eyes close and I want to scream 'but I don't *want* to', but I can't. I don't know how to extricate myself from the mess I'm in. I don't want to *be* her. So, I nod and murmur, "When I gave you that, I meant something by it. I was so happy and humbled when you put it where you did because I love you so much. Truth be told, if I could only be with you and none of the rest, I would, but

I can't. I love them and would never hurt them like that. I just can't do it after her."

"I know, baby. I'd never ask you to do that for me, but it helps to know you'd prefer it was different, though. I got into something with you I may not have gotten into had I known how much it would stir up among the hive. If I hadn't, it would have been a poor decision. The bottom line is that, there's nothing—no amount of personal pain—that could be more of a tragedy than never having known you would have been."

A stray tear leaks from my eye and I clamp my lips together, hoping to keep it together. "I'm thrilled. I'm so happy to be with you like I am, doing what we did. I do not care if they're all buzzing around like bees in a bonnet. I do not decide what I want based on what the crowd thinks and wants. I base that on what I want and need. Period. I want and need you and if they don't like it, it's *not* my problem."

I'm stretching a little there, because this speech is my ideal Deli—the woman I was before all the pain. I want to be her again and telling him this makes it real. "I'm not responsible for everyone's happiness and don't care to be. If they love me, they get over things they may not like because of that. If not, they deal with that decision on their own. You're not stirring up stuff that's not already stirred up. Things have not been the same with Wilde since the big December mess. Somewhere inside, I'm sure he knows that."

That makes his brows furrow, but he doesn't press me. "The golden goddess is going to continue seeing him."

"That's fine with me. It's a bad idea, but I learned a *long* time ago not to care who Wilde is screwing. I'm destined to be unhappy if I do."

"She's going to do it more than she's played with him so far, though. She's been far too accepting of his behavior than she should."

"Wilde has plenty of people pounding on his door. I've never contemplated having him to myself because he'd never do it. He doesn't even tell me who he's seeing. I don't care what Wilde does; I'm only worried about her. She has to set clear, unbreakable boundaries. It's very important."

Please, please listen to me this time. Dear Goddess, please let them hear me this time.

"She wants Sari and Wilde to know that it's not because she's jealous of you and I. Bottom line, she's not. I wouldn't be here if she had a problem with it."

"Rafe has no problem with us. He's never jealous over anything because he's very secure. He's shared me from day one and we fell in love almost at first sight. We can talk about loving the same person and be comfortable. He's never going to be an issue and don't let anyone tell you differently."

"Talia's going to need to make sure they understand—no, that's not a good way to say it. You can't make people understand; the only thing I can do is tell them the truth. She's going to let them know she will not be stomping in here, dragging me back home, or asking to join us in a group fuck for prosperity's sake."

I nod, contemplating how to say this without spilling the beans on the *big secret* that I still do not want to even think about talking about—with anyone. "She needs to be clear as a bell about her intentions with Wilde. Because I promise he has his own agenda that he will not share. That's who he is. Now, he may ignore what she tells him, but she has to be as clear as she can. It's important to draw lines and not let him cross them—not even a little."

"Does it bother you that I think of myself as your husband now?" He looks nervous as he approaches the couch, twisting the ring on his finger.

"Are you kidding? No, I love that you do. It makes me all warm and fuzzy and stuff."

"You're okay with my decision to be exclusive with you because of this ring? That means that the next time I talk to Tamara, and she goes for me, I give her the smack down."

I don't answer for a moment, imagining that situation.

"I swear, woman, you better not have a sodding problem with me being exclusive with you!"

My voice is low and trembling a bit because so many emotions are hitting me at once. I'm having such a hard time containing them all while making sure that I look sane. "Baby, I love that you want to be only with me. I've never—no one has ever even offered. No one has wanted me that much before. It makes me very awed." I wipe my eyes, because damned if they aren't leaking. Fuck.

He tugs me into his lap and holds me close. "I can't help it. I love you too much."

Wrapping around him, I mutter, "I love you so much it hurts."

"Christ, I hope we don't have to do that again; it's gut wrenching."

I nod. "Hard stuff sucks."

"Baby, can I ask you a question?" When I nod, he mumbles, "Why don't you want me to meet the rest of your family?"

"Who in the hell said that?"

He shrugs, looking chagrined. "No one."

"Are you sure of that?" I look at him, tilting my head. "If I gave that impression, I didn't mean to by any stretch."

"I mean, I know my family isn't extensive, but you've met Talia, Damien's stopped by and, the only one you've not seen, though she's been here, is Theodora."

"I want you to meet them. I'm so damned greedy about time with you, I haven't wanted to give any up to other people. But I made a big deal about the party on purpose, though, you know."

He blinks. "Wait, are you serious? You're not poking me or anything, are you?"

I shake my head. "Well, Leo's been here and so has Hex: cleaning up and filling the fridge. Though they haven't stayed long enough to meet you."

"I've not met them because you're hoarding me?"

"Kind of?"

"I've been thinking bad thoughts. That's what I get for assuming, I guess."

I give him a sheepish look. I have been escaping to here with him, avoiding the crush of all the other obligations I have and getting away from the ever-present drama that I am almost certain Sari is orchestrating in the background. "I'm sorry, baby. I didn't mean to make you feel like I was ashamed. or something. I can have one or two of them stop by tonight if you'd like."

"No, no, it's okay, love. Now that I know why they've not been by and know that it's not me, I'm okay."

"It's not you at all. I promise. I'm proud that you're mine and I want everyone to know. I want you to know my family. I'm sure you'll get along with Philomena, because she gets along with almost no one."

"Yeah, well, I'm sodding rich and appreciate a right good bitch, so that makes sense." He grins and puts his hands behind his head.

"She is a bitch, though, she's been good about holding the fort down for me."

"You're stuck with me, then. Everyone will love me and you love me most of all." He tugs me closer and runs a fang down my mark, making me shiver.

"I don't have a complaint there."

His smile is wicked, and he pulls back. "Speaking of less pleasant branches of your family tree, I saw you did a pleasant set over at that hellhole the twat opened. Excellent choice, that."

"I love Elvis," I sigh. "His voice is... oooh."

"That brings us back to hunk of burning clone, baby."

"If you sing Elvis to me one day, I promise to swoon."

He blinks, looking amazed. "Are you making fun of me, baby?"

"If you get up there and sing me some Elvis, good Elvis, I promise to sit and swoon — in front of the entire bar, even." I grin, waiting to see if he takes the bait.

I've made small appearances as a political thing at that blasted bar. Since I like karaoke, I go under the auspices of singing a song for whatever theme they've picked that week. Sometimes, I send the boys or gals to do it for me, because I need a constant eye on that Southern bitch. We suffer the horrid performances people give so I can watch for trouble. Taurus on stage, singing to me, will make an impression—a firm one.

"Well, I could do a ballad or two for the right chit," he scratches his chin, rising to the bait I threw as I grin.

"Oh, come now, baby. You're a brilliant singer and you know it. Not to mention you love people to watch you strut and you want to see me swoon."

Pausing for a moment, he looks thoughtful again and I know I have him.

"There is that. Did any of your other gits sing Elvis to you? I ride on no one's coattails."

"Did anyone else sing Elvis for me? Not that I know of."

"Fine, I'll do it," he grumps, pretending that he won't enjoy every second of every person in that godforsaken hole watching him in jealousy.

I smile and hug him, sighing. *He spoils me.*

The Cat Gets Blamed

DELILAH

I'm sitting on the back porch of my house, watching the sun sink into the west and wishing like hell that I was anywhere else in the universe.

Almost anywhere else, at least.

After the Elvis promise, Taurus got beeped for an emergency—I forgot to mention he's taken on more responsibility since the whole multi-state rampage incident. So I popped home to see my guys for a while. We were all sitting on the porch—talking about songs, and karaoke, and party plans—when it started raining guests like magick.

Not my magick, I assure you. However, the boys regretted uninstalling the locks Rafe put on the doors after he kicked Rhea and Alistair out. That'll teach them, won't it?"

First, Tamara showed up to see if Shea was at my house. He'd gotten upset about something and run off without a word. At one point, my house would have been the best guess for a runaway family member. However, with my absence and their family entwining with Rita's, it isn't where he'd go. She wanted to see if the gossip was true because she's nosy. That bint.

We got rid of her, but Wilde and Sari appeared almost immediately. They strolled in with wine and food as if we'd all made plans and I was behind the times. A quick check with my guys revealed no one invited them, so perhaps Tamara spilled the beans.

I wonder if they're all stalking me.

Wilde has done nothing but cozy up to me from the moment he arrived. Honestly, he's making me uncomfortable. He's far too touchy and keeps babbling about 'little Evie'. When I tried to pawn him off, he got more insistent, which made me mad and paranoid. I faked indigestion brought on by the chips and salsa, so I could send him to fetch drinks, Tums, and anything I could think of to get him to bugger off.

Sari spent her time trying to climb into Rafe's pants. He looked thrilled, let me tell you. He didn't want to come outside when I got home, and I convinced him. For his efforts, he got stuck with Miss-We're-Magickally-Mated-Now trying to hump his leg in public.

In the past, it wouldn't have mattered if she did because none of us are wilting flowers, but tonight it seemed contrived and annoying. He took one for the team, trying to keep her busy so I wouldn't have to answer a bunch of questions. That helped me focus on directing Wilde away from me. He could see how uncomfortable I was, and he tried to help without being obvious.

Several hours later than I would have liked, my phone rang. I struggled not to look ecstatic while I made up nonsense about test results. I purposefully and loudly agreed to be there as soon as possible to talk them over with my doctor.

Making my apologies insincerely to the interlopers, I waved and disappeared.

Thank Christ for shared talents. I needed to get out of there.

"What the bloody hell took you so long?" he gripes. "I've been home for a half hour!"

I chuckle and head for the closet, wanting to peel off my sundress and get comfortable for the first time since he left. "We had unexpected guests."

He arches a brow. "Tell."

"Tamara for a bit; I think she was fishing since she heard the baby gossip. Then Wilde and Sari appeared."

His eyes narrow and he growls. "Continue."

Not understanding what the problem is—except that it's Sari and Wilde—I shrug. "They came over with wine and food and wanted to hang out with us. No one invited them, so I have no idea how they knew I'd be home. Wilde was being too cozy, and it weirded me out, so I told him I had indigestion and sent him to fetch things all night."

His glass goes flying against the wall, and I blanch. He shakes his head and rubs his hand over his face. "Bloody fucking hell. The sodding minute..."

Okay. He threw a glass. It's okay. Get it together, Deli.

No frozen fear, no letting a tornado of magick loose, just breathe. You can do this. You're triggered, but you are in control of the anger and the terror. You are stronger than this, I keep repeating to myself. Once I convince myself, I look at him. "I'm sorry, but could you clue me in to why we're destroying the Baccarat?"

"Just this bloody morning, he and Talia had an intimate encounter. It was not long after we talked—that's why I brought it up—because she thought it was possible he would do this. No sooner than she's gone for the evening to an event, he's cuddled up against you in ways I don't even want to imagine. That son of a bitch!"

I blink. "Hey! I didn't invite them and I tried to fend him off."

"It doesn't *matter*. If I find out he's using Talia out of some twisted sense of retribution for you, I'll kill him. I might kill him anyway for putting his sodding hands on you while you're carrying my bloody baby!"

Stepping closer, I whisper. "He likes her. He's always talked about her like she's amazing. Remember that date that he had with her went nowhere in the fall? He was so caught up with her that he ruined our mating yakking about it."

That is one hundred percent true. Talia poked her head out for a brief minute in October and dallied with Wilde before ducking in her hidey hole again. Coincidentally , Dirty Deeds closed not long after, so it may have been less about him and more about reporting to the Company. Not that anyone invited her to come; Wilde must have blabbed about it like an idiot.

"Christ. You lot are a bunch of certified loonies. You're all neuroses, no self-esteem, and no honesty."

Feeling smacked, I retreat as I shake, shaking my head. "It's not my fault he's an ass. I've told you and her that."

"You didn't say he'd jump from bed to bed like a sodding gigolo!"

"I'm *quite* sure that I did!" I growl, getting angry. "Stop blaming his bullshit on me!"

"I wouldn't have to if even one of you lot was the tiniest bit sane!"

Slamming his fist on the counter, he glares and stalks towards the door. "I think I need some time."

With that, he's gone.

The Cat and The Bird Can't Shut It Out

DELILAH

A presence in the room wakes up the predator inside me. I didn't sleep much, and my body gave out about four am. I sit up and squint into the darkness as the hairs on the back of my neck stand up. My body tightens from head to toe.

He's here.

I don't turn on the lights; instead, I let the emerald bleed in and use my night vision. This is good practice for learning to control individual features of my Beast. Full transformation is not only difficult to control, but lacks stealth. I look at the doorway to the hall and see him fidgeting, his expression nervous and aura awash with emotions like a bad LSD trip.

He was gone all night.

My first reaction is spite. He should be nervous, as he berated me for things outside of my control, didn't respect my honesty, and made me worry all night long that he'd taken a powder. We may make a lot of lofty professions, but my heart is *still taped* together with duct tape. I have to fight not to panic every single time we fight like this, no matter what the reason is.

He knows that.

I itched all night because he was away and unlike any other mate I've ever had, the tug of being separated isn't an emotional ache inside, but a physical problem. I tossed and turned for hours —my exhaustion led to a total shutdown. It sucked rocks and it's his fault for being an ass. All I care about right now is that he's home. I could kick myself for not being angrier, but I can't help it.

He's home.

I give him a small smile, feeling tentative as I whisper, "Hi, baby."

What a giant pansy I am. This wasn't my fault. I did nothing wrong. In fact, I worked hard to make sure that no one else did.

"Morning, love of mine," he says, ditching his duster and shirt on the couch. He plops down onto the bed next to me. "I'm sorry."

My eyes widen. Not like him to start with an apology. I tilt my head, studying him. "What for?"

I feel it's necessary to find out what he thinks he's apologizing for. In the past, others have hurt me and not given any specific reasons or excuses. That only leads to the same thing hurting me over and over as I think they never knew why they were saying sorry–or didn't care, I'm not sure which.

"I shouldn't have said that last night," he mumbles.

Ah. He gets it. Let's see how well he understands.

Nodding, I sigh. "It's okay. It upsets you. You had a good reason."

He shakes his head, pulling something out of his pocket and holding it up. My resolve turns to mush as I look at the small, badly knit sweater. "I pined."

Shit. How do I push the envelope on that? I mean, the damned thing wouldn't fit Twist, but he tried. Imagine what would happen if anyone but me got a picture of the killer of K Street with knitting needles and a baby blue yarn. He knew just how to get me with that one: an old joke about me missing him so much when he's gone that I sit in a rocking chair and knit like a Civil War widow. He's telling me how much he missed me with it, albeit sneakily.

I throw my arms around his neck and squeeze. I am so in love with this wonderful, moody, loving, difficult idiot that I don't even know what to do with myself.

"I didn't mean to hurt you, love—truly. I know it hurt you; I could feel it all night. You cried, and it's my fault. I lashed out and included you in a group of people that I shouldn't have. Forgive me?"

He does not understand how much I try to keep the insanity away from him and keep my own issues from affecting him. Having it thrown in my face was painful.

My nose rubs against his neck as I nod; I inhale his scent as my fingers clutch the tiny scrap in my hands, feeling calmer than I have in hours. "I know they upset you. I was trying to be honest with you and let you know why I was late. I am sensitive about being grouped with the people who are less than healthy in behavior. I try to keep a lid on my crazy."

His arms wrap around me and he buries his face in my hair. "It was a bloody miserable night. I felt so sodding alone."

That's a feeling I know well. I stayed here because it terrified me to miss his return.

I paced, I cried, I yelled, I tossed and turned—what I did not do is feel like I had anyone who could understand. I didn't contact Rafe. I couldn't explain in a way that he would understand; I had to go it alone. "I slept a grand total of two hours before you got here," I murmur. "I itched all night. Aradia came to sleep with me, but she got annoyed and took off." I chuckle.

Rubbing his cheek against mine, he says, "I don't think I'd like to have another night like that any time in the foreseeable future. My family wasn't exactly—sympathetic. They're not likely to be when I've been a git, so I got no comfort there at all." He lets go of me for a moment, slipping under the covers to snuggle. I slide over and curl up against him, eyes closing as I sigh. "I couldn't even kill my breakfast, sod it all. It was pathetic," he grumbles.

I smile a little at that image. "It's okay, baby. I'm here and we're okay." I nuzzle his neck then nip his mark. I should push this more because I need him to understand why he should be more careful. However, I'm so fucking glad he's back that I can't make myself kick up more dust right now."

Groaning, he clutches me to him. "Christ, you feel good."

I purr, the rumble low and thrumming. "You do, too."

His hand slides over my hair, and I lean in, sighing in contentment.

Suddenly, his brows furrow. "It sounds like the terror twins are up to tricks again; the goddess wants me to warn you since she's having a conversation right now. When she comes out of the sodding room for breakfast for the first time, this happens."

I look over at the night table, floating my phone up and squinting at it. There are at least ten messages stacking up on the lock screen and the words 'trouble', 'love', and 'blame' are a common theme. "Well, looks like if I were paying attention, I'd be getting my own lectures."

"Why are they texting you? You are mates. Why don't they split your skull like the goddess does to me?"

I shrug, trying to downplay this as much as possible, because it's a peek into the insanity of my life and could lead to topics I am not ready for and after last night? I know he is ALSO not ready for this shit. "I have to kind of... explain to you what things look like inside my—inner sanctum, we'll say."

"Isn't that the name of a comic book guy's house?"

I roll my eyes. "I'm not averse to you thinking I'm that power-ful, but no." I pinch him and smile. "Inside me, there are a lot of places—more than a normal person because even before the Beast, my magick has needed space, and this is how I could manage all the lines."

He gives me a skeptical look but stays quiet.

"Picture a large room like in an old marble library in Europe. In the center is the 'eternal flame' as we'll ever so dramatically call it. That's my spirit, soul, and fire—whatever. Around that atrium, there are doors to where my magick lives, the Beast, my human side, and mating bonds. Open one: find a part of me that connects to the flame. Inside, there are floor to ceiling cabinets that look like old-style card catalogs. I label every drawer that is filled with memories, thoughts, feelings, etc. Some things get sealed because they need to be. Some are easy to open. When I need to, I lock the doors and cut off the connection to the flame. Sometimes for my sanity, sometimes for self-protection, and sometimes in anger. I can do it with just about anything because one door represents the rest of the Universe and that one, I had to learn to clamp off."

His eyes narrow. "One door is me?"

I nod. "It is. I don't quite have control of that one yet. It's difficult." His expression wars between pleased and irritated, so I go on. "Months ago, I started filing things away in particular mates' rooms. I learned to seal the door fully, partially, and with our exes, cut the cord so that it feels withered and dead."

"Dead?"

I give him a shrug. "I'm a witch, love. You can't imagine that these rooms and corridors and everything aren't full of nature and life and emotions and impressions—cutting it off from my life force has made it look like the door to Hades. I can't help that. It needed to happen, and I needed to store the ache somewhere where it wouldn't make me insane. You know the stories."

"What about your primary?" he asks.

"He has his own room. I store his things." He looks like he's about to ask a question and I shake my head. "Not for discussion. Witches I've consulted say that they don't know anyone who compacts their inner being the way I do. Between that, the emotional turmoil here, the Beast, the magick, cloaking the Resistance, holding his stuff, and everything else? It explains why I require feeding and the amount of feeding needed has increased. I need life force energy. As my magick grows stronger and I renew with the Earth more often, that will make it easier."

"The reason you're telling me therefore is that they *have* to text you? They can't use their bond because you've clamped it?"

"Yes. I have for a while now. I didn't feel they needed access to things that were not their business, and I cannot trust them to stay away. It has made for some interesting conversations, Rafe says. He's done his best to downplay it."

"The phone buzzes again and I raise the lights a smidge with my mind, looking at the screen with a snarl. Bullshit arguments, pleas, accusations: the full circle of the 'why aren't you paying attention to me' game that the two of them play. I'm sure that the next step will be them getting someone else to poke at me, too.

Why the hell isn't he focused on the person sitting at his goddamned table right now?

"Right then," he says, closing his eyes, looking like he's concentrating. I hear doors slam one after another and the air feels dense. Breathing heavily, he drops back against the pillows.

Tilting my hand, I try to sense the change. "What did you do, baby?"

He lifts his head, looking drained, and hisses, "I closed the entire house. It's a little mental trick I've learned: no one gets in physically and only primary mates can contact us mentally. I know that's something you do on your own, but now we're both a world away. We need a day like this."

I nod slowly, agreeing that the outside world is wearing on me. Laying my head on his chest, I let the calming influence of our bond sink in. I'm so fried from all the stress and the problems that have been popping up within my family. Everything is grating on me.

His lips brush my forehead, voice husky as it vibrates over my skin. "For the moment, nothing out there can touch us here, I promise. Anything tries to get in, Talia will deal with it."

Rubbing my face on his chest, I wrap around him, clutching at him like he's the only port in my storm. I inhale, breathing in his scent. I feel his nearness, his strength seeping into me, washing away the gray.

~Love you, baby. ~ His voice is a whisper, linking us deeply enough that I feel the tiny light of the baby joined in. She's so strong, so quickly. It is no wonder they set the docs to keep a close eye on my progress.

Feeling the connection echo through me like a healing balm, the ugly of things in the outside world fades. A thought occurs to me and I look up at him. "I think I'm hungry again. Maybe."

His deep chuckle reverberates in my mind and heart as his hand brushes over my cheek. *~Preggo broads. Sheesh. ~* I feel the laughter again, his teasing tone, and it buzzes through me like warm champagne. *~For what? You need me to get you something? ~*

"I don't know yet. I gotta think about it." Chewing on my lip, I consider for a moment.

His hand rubs over my stomach and he arches a brow at me. "Let me know. I could take you out."

Snuggling closer, I shake my head, nose wrinkled. "Don't want to move. I'm too comfy."

He snorts. "That narrows the lunch menu, puss. There's me and there's me." Pondering for a moment, he reconsiders. "There might be stuff in the fridge. I don't know the last time your crew was about."

I shrug. "I'm sure it's full. Leo won't let anything get empty. There are too many cooking shows to experiment with, especially since the garden sprouted."

His phone rings, causing him to curse. "Fucking hell. That's a Company ring. I have to take this, baby." Expression apologetic, he scoots out of bed, taking it with him as he walks towards the hallway.

I curl around a pillow, closing my eyes as I feel the doors inside me rattling, pulling at me despite his words. The moment he's not touching me, they worm past his defenses and start testing mine. I wasn't lying. I *can* clamp them off, but unless I burn the bridge as I did with Rhea and Alistair, they can fight it. They don't always win, but they put up one hell of a fight.

Angry accusations again. Fuck.

My brow furrows and I tighten around the pillow, trying to block it out and keep it from bleeding in. It's harder to keep them out since the Winter Incident. Everything about them is so wrong that I can't always snip the line. The delineation between Wilde and his demon is difficult to control, and that is because I'm so broken there. I manage, but things still slip through. He knows it, too.

Footsteps echo on the parquet floor of the hall and the bed dips as he sits. "What's with the curling, baby? Is closing the world out not working?"

I shake my head. "Not entirely. Bits and pieces get in occasionally. They're used to having to find ways in. They've gotten craftier."

He frowns and the shutters bang, opening everything up again, his jaw gritted. "Why am I not surprised? You are never able to walk away from it, are you? You can't be here and enjoy us—you let them ruin it." Pushing to his feet, he stalks across the room, growling, "I'm going to work out."

I squeeze my eyes shut, frustration coursing through me. The bullshit from them is wearing on me and I am so through with this. Everyone sucks. *Everyone*!

Abandoned, angry, and burned out, I jump off the bed, trudge over to the closet and pull on my clothes. I throw my hair out of the collar of the duster with an aggravated sigh, then stomp over to the nightstand to scribble a note to leave on the bed.

Hungry. Gone to kill something.

With that, I slip out, heading into the gloom outside.

The Cat and the Bird Cross A Line

DELILAH

~ *Please come home soon, love. I n-need you.* ~

PMy head lifts, staring off into space as I feel him calling for me.

His voice is morose and I sense the heaviness of his heart. Concentrating for a brief second, I get the picture of him sitting, fresh from the shower, draped over an armchair and staring out the bay window. It hits me that he might think I'm not coming home.

Fuck. That was not my intention.

I kick the last leg, doing a breather sweep to ensure that what happened here will not lead to me—at least, not at first. I suppose the Company will figure it out eventually, but an unsolved massacre in the woods in rural America won't scream 'agent'. It's more likely to invoke a serial killer than anything.

Sighing, I apparate myself directly into our closet,. My stomach gurgles and I rub it, hanging up my duster. Pulling my hair back with the hair tie from my pocket, I ponder a shower. I'm filthy, covered in stickiness and underbrush.

Deciding I'm too tired for that, I grab a wet towel from the hamper and scrub the crud off my face and body. My clothes go flying into the hamper—write-offs unless Hex can work his own brand of magick—then I pull on one of his shirts, so exhausted I can't even contemplate buttoning it.

Once I'm clean, I pad out to where he's sitting, lowering myself to the floor at his feet with a grunt. My muscles are sore from the hunt, so I drop my head into his lap. Speaking into his mind, I sigh again. *~I heard you. ~*

His fingers rub over my jaw and I feel his heart touch mine. He begins without preamble, his tone soft. *~I love you. I'm sorry. I was wrong. ~*

He was—again—and I know it. I'm too tired to get angry right now. I want this horseshit to be over.

~ I freaked out, too. You're back; I'm back. ~

I mumble, burying my face in his tummy, sinking back into our connection.

~I didn't leave. I went into the other room to beat the hell out of the bag. We, uh, need a fresh bag. ~

I chuckle, groaning as it makes my chest muscles pull. *~Don't worry. My clothes are shot. Good thing I left the coat in a safe spot. ~*

Leaning down, he sniffs me and I feel the frown even though I don't look up. "You killed?"

One shoulder lifts and falls. "I was hungry and in a foul mood."

He doesn't question my glib response, though I know he asked because I didn't used to kill unless they left me no choice. The more connected my Beast is inside, the less concerned I am about human ethics—food is food. The line between eating a cow and, well, eating a cow has become completely blurred. I'm learning how to hunt, and since the changes in my biochemistry are ongoing, I've had to learn to save the rip and tear for emotional outlet rather than daily feeding. What I did tonight is far more significant than either of those descriptions does justice to.

Rural massacre fits. He's going to wish he'd been there.

Tilting his head, he strokes my jaw. "What's wrong? You feel uncomfortable."

"I ate too fast and made a mess. I'm sore and I have a bit of indigestion. I shouldn't have played with my food."

He arches a brow and grins. "Lucky it wasn't Thai, or you'd be a real mess. Come here, baby." Holding his hands out, he reaches for me.

"Mexican," I grumble, making a face. "It might have been worse." Scrambling onto his lap, I curl around him. His hands rub over my tummy and he rests his head on my shoulder. I comb my fingers through his hair, purring softly as we nuzzle.

Suddenly, the doors slam shut, the air thickening as the cracks seal even more than before. *~No one. No one gets in. Not here. Not even primaries tonight. ~*

His hand smooths over my stomach and his arm tightens around me, stroking my spine.

Smiling, I lean my head on his, agreeing. I close my eyes, looking inside myself to seal the doors and gateways as much as possible without severing the cords forever. They may bang on the doors, but I think with the energy I got from feeding tonight, I can keep them shut for at least a couple of hours without a slip.

I feel him calming by degrees, his lips brushing my forehead as he sinks into our connection. Letting the peace wash over me, I hold him and let the connection hum through us. The turmoil inside me wanes and my soul settles down. His thumb traces my eyebrows, down my nose and across my cheekbones, humming a soft tune in my ear.

~I love you so very much. I was so scared. ~

I blink, the scent of tears making me realize that he's crying. Taurus never cries. I mean, everyone does, but I've not seen him this unglued yet. *~Scared? Why? ~*

Brushing my knuckle under his eyes to catch them, I caress his cheekbones.

~When you left. I read the note and didn't think you were coming back. I didn't leave the house. I didn't know what to do. ~

Clucking my tongue, I shake my head. *~No, no, no. I would never leave a note to end a relationship and I would never leave for good over something that trivial. I don't know if I even can leave you now. It felt like I was being punched in the gut just to leave the house. It's gotta be something big before this reed breaks, baby. ~*

He doesn't know the level of inappropriate and painful things that people do to me, and I don't leave them. I always think I can fix the problem. It's a curse, I know, and part of why I haven't disentangled myself from Sari and Wilde yet. But why was I able to cut it off with Rhea and Alistair then?

I don't have time to ponder that oddity—though it bears much more consideration at another time—because he lets out a tremendous sigh of relief.

"Okay. Good. Because I wanted to do bad things to innocent people when you weren't here. It wasn't good. In fact, I'd like to lodge a formal request that you never leave me—ever."

"Good thing I was out doing bad things to innocent people for you, huh?" I stroke his face, smiling. "I think you've infected me."

He grins wickedly. "Christ, I hope so. I've been trying hard enough."

"Maybe I was feeling some of your rage, too." That is very possible. This is the only connection that I haven't figured out how to seal off yet.

His face drops, and he gapes, sputtering. "Oh, Christ, I didn't even think of that. Talia was unprepared and got hit with a wave. She went ape shit."

I shrug. "Guess it *could* get attributed to a random serial killer or. Or the mob, maybe, or a cartel."

"Huh?"

"A sizable group of people in the woods... Splat." I sigh. "If they hadn't run, I wouldn't have been so pissed. I might have killed them. Maybe."

Snickering, his eyes dance with wicked glee. "Have I told you that I love you, baby?"

"Yep," I grin, "but you can tell me as much as your weak heart desires." I peck his temple, my heart swelling with fondness.

~Love the killer kitty in you, baby. ~

His nose rubs against my skin as he nuzzles the mark on my neck.

Head tilted, my response is low and throaty. "I love the demon in you."

"I wish I'd been there—killing, feeding, the blood of the innocents and all."

Whispering, I correct him. "You're always with me—all the time and everywhere."

"I know, isn't it neat?" His expression is boyish for a moment, then it grows wistful. "Here, though, I meant in a more bloody and physical way."

"Yeah, but you would have leaned against a tree and watched me get pissed, running about. You'd be no help at all."

"Bloody right, I would," he growls. "More running equals more jiggle for the step."

His priorities make me giggle and my eyes dance. "I see you leaning against a tree smoking and ogling me as I run around all smeared in blood and gore. You lech."

I can tell he's imagining it as his eyes swirl and the growl that rumbles out of his chest. "Hell, yeah, love."

My arms tighten around him, grinning with mischief. "You'd get all worked up and end up doing it."

He rumbles, grinding his hips against mine. "Christ, baby."

Images fly through my head at light speed, followed by sensory impressions that rock my entire body. I groan, digging my fingers into his shoulders, barely able to hold on. Holy fuck. When did he learn to do *that*?

I feel the Beast rising, lumbering to the surface. "Fucking hell."

His grin is pure evil, and it makes me shiver as he growls. "Welcome to the life of a killer, baby."

Rubbing my cheek on his with an answering rumble, I rasp, "We should do that."

"Now?" His expression is indulgent, like he's agreeing to go to a tea party with the Queen rather than hunting people to a bloody death.

"No, but sometime soon. I'm way too comfy here right now."

He snarls at me with his fangs bared to provoke Her. My fangs drop in response and he yanks me onto his lap to straddle him. Hands scrabbling, he separates the shirt and squeezes my breasts hard. My thighs spread to hug his hips and red lines spring up on his chest as my nails rake. I hiss as his fingers and palms grope. His hips grind against mine and he lowers his voice to a rough, gravelly tone. "Yes—rough baby. Show me."

Images slip into my mind and I feel him courting the Beast, drawing Her out. Without warning, I swoop down, tearing into his shoulder as my claws rip into his hips to hold on. He roars and we join roughly. His arms band around me and hold, holding me close enough to sink his fangs deep into my breast.

~Yeah, baby. Mark me up; I'm yours—your killer kitty. ~

I whisper into his mind as I slide the sharp claw tips down his back.

His nails are blunt, but they dig in deep, gripping my waist as he meets my thrusts with his own. Ripping his fangs out of the curve, he strikes again, letting the blood flow. Stars explode behind my eyes as the pleasure rockets through me and my blood mixes with the trickles of his from the bite on his shoulder. I keep rocking on him, eyes swirling with green and gold as I moan low and dark. Leaning down, I scrape the four points across his other shoulder from neck to bicep, watching the droplets well up.

"That's it, baby, slice me, bleed me like the demon kitty you are," he mumbles, doing the same to me from the shoulder to elbow. His eyes flash as he throbs inside me, almost high on the scent of the blood. *~Fuck, you're good at this. ~*

The throaty chortle that echoes makes him growl and I bend in an impossibly fluid manner to rake my incisors over the peacock's neck, then his chest. *~Only for you, baby. ~*

His eyes roll back and he grits his teeth, shuddering hard.

I feel him steeling against the end. My tail drops in response, stroking over his slick skin as I yowl, teetering on the edge. *~Fuck baby. Going to—soon. ~*

The bottlebrush tip of his tail flicks out, wrapping around mine and tugging as he stiffens from head to toe. "Fuck! It's going to happen...*now!*" He jerks my head back, tearing into my throat as he explodes, roaring into my mind.

My screech echoes his and I bury my fangs into him, suckling, jaw working to get a better flow. Release flows over me like a crashing wave and it knocks me out. We're both drinking greedily, blood loss heady and dizzying. Connected down to our cores, the primal fades, and our tails chase, playing and stroking over the hurts.

Sighing as we whisper back and forth mentally, my hands weave into his hair, holding him in place as we feast. I feel how close to the danger zone we're getting, and I lap at the wound. He takes notice of my caution and I sense him pondering going over the line before he whispers. *~Can't we do it—once? It probably won't kill us. ~*

~What would it do? ~

I whisper, a war between curiosity, excitement, and concern starting within me.

A few seconds go by as he considers, leaving me to float in a sea of sultry sensations. *~Well, it might kill us. We'd drop out of consciousness for a bit. We'd have drunk more than anyone else I know ever has—and lived through it. Since we're mated, I'm not sure what it'd do. I've fed more from you than I ever have before. Sometimes even that's not enough.~*

His lips turn down and he stops to think. *~I don't know. The baby tosses the mix a bit. We should be on a bed if we try. ~*

He nuzzles as he suckles, still drawing on the wound.

Purrs rumble out of my chest and my tail tugs his, my voice tremulous as I respond. *~Can you get us there? I'll try to help you. ~*

He nods and my magick opens for him, letting him access it to help apparate us to the bed. In a blink, we're on the satin comforter, staining it as we suckle and bleed from various wounds. Groaning, I slide a hip on his, pressing close. *~Feel you. Taste you. Want you. ~*

~You sure? ~ he croaks. *~It's supposed to be utopian, but I'm not sure I'll stop bleeding when we pass. You will, but I'm not sure about me. ~*

~You will. My blood's in yours more than anyone else. You can do it. Since the night I healed you, you've got the power. ~

~I should have thought of that, but I'm so lightheaded. I have never hungered like this before... ~

~I know; I can't ever get enough. I crave you. ~

~It feels hot... tight... colorful. ~

The sensations flow from him to me and my head swims. I suckle more, eyes slipping closed and everything hazy inside. *~Sweet... warm... soft... ~*

Our breathing gets shallower, tasting and floating in a place with no pain, only peaceful softness. Limbs turn to water and our bodies seem to connect deeper than ever before as we whisper endearments. Passing warning level after warning level, instinct takes us further and further as spots dance in front of my eyes. My consciousness seems to shimmer like the air of the desert in the day's heat. Our hearts flutter. Like a dying waltz, they echo slowing beats until they stop.

After that, there's nothing except two bodies entwined and a glimmer of hope that our strength would save us both.

A spark of light and energy dances inside them, untouchable by their actions, and it reacts instinctively to strengthen them. The light kick-starts smaller things first, healing superficial wounds and pulling the feral faces back. The cuts seal, stopping the blood flow. A small, magickal push engulfs them in a warm glow, the baby inside guiding them gently first to life and then to reawakening.

The Cat and The Bird Are Not Zombies

❧

DELILAH

My eyelids crack open as I shift, and he rolls over, wrapping himself around me. Head swimming, I feel many things swirling around in it. A smile drifts across my face as he nuzzles my neck. Draping my arms around him, limbs feeling weightless, I cup the back of his head.

~*Well, baby,* ~ he croons, his voice vibrant in my mind. ~*How do you feel?*~

~*I'm all floaty.* ~ I chuckle, the warmth in his voice caressing me inside. ~*You?* ~

~*Ditto the floaty and toss in a sublime bliss.* ~ His grin slides down my spine and the sensations are so strong that I almost see it without even looking at his face. ~*We lived.* ~

~*I noticed. How'd that happen?* ~

~*The living? No clue. We went way past what we should have, even intending to go farther than normal. I couldn't bloody stop.* ~

~*I know. I was so hungry.* ~ I stretch my limbs before dropping back onto him.

~*I don't know why, love, but this blood craving I have for you is like nothing I've ever felt before.* ~ He strokes his hand down my back and I feel it like it's in stereo. I mean, I feel him touching me, his hand on my skin, but I also feel his hand as if it's mine feeling my skin under it. *~Well, that's new. ~*

~Whoa. ~

~It's not only me then; good to know. ~ His fingers trace up and down my spine and I know he feels the muscles relax and my heart speed up. *~Jesus, that's potent. ~*

My eyes flutter at the sensations and I reach out, tracing around his peacock. *~Good Goddess. ~* I groan.

His breath hisses as he arches his back, pressing into my hand. *~Christ. What did we do? ~*

Hands rubbing up and down his chest, I whisper. *~God, baby. I don't know. It feels amazing. ~*

Groaning darkly, he slides his hands down to span my waist, caressing. Our eyes roll back as the sensations coast over us both in shocking clarity. He gapes and blinks.

~It's like we're in the same body! ~ I rest my head on his shoulder before my palms slide over his hipbones, rubbing my thumbs on the points.

His breath comes faster and his hips sway a bit as he nods. *~That, my heart, is exactly how it feels. ~*

Leaning down, I kiss over his heart. *~This is going to take some getting used to. Can Talia feel it, you think? Or Rafe, I wonder? ~*

Eyes losing focus, he connects with his other mate. Through our bond, I see a flurry of images I assume are from Talia, and I blink. *~Whoa. ~*

He speaks into her mind and I hear it. *~Hello, love. Is everything okay? ~* She sends a questioning emotion back, along with a general sense of wellbeing.

~Did she feel us pass out? It just occurred to me they might not have known what was going on. ~

He seems to ponder this for a moment, then speaks to Talia. *~Deli and I—we drained each other completely. ~*

Talia sends a wave of shocked emotions and irritation that rolls over both of us. He tries to calm her. *~Shhh, love. It's okay, hush. ~* A flurry of images and emotions flash so quickly that neither he nor I can make them out, and he snaps. *~Damn it, woman, slow down! You know I can't... ~*

The images halt and she clamps the emotions a bit, sending a few more rapid images before the connection closes. He turns and grins sheepishly. *~Um, she's... ~*

~I'd say that's a 'no'. ~

~She's coming. Put something on. ~

~Oh, bloody hell. ~ I groan, peeling myself off the bed, staggering a little as I go to the closet. Pulling on one of his shirts, I come back over, collapsing on the bed and look over at him. *~I should see what Boneless is thinking; give me a sec. ~*

He nods, rolling off the bed and shuffling to the closet to pull on pajama bottoms. Looking shaky, he drops back onto the bed, his expression troubled, presumably by Talia's response.

I turn onto my back as the mattress dips with his weight, reaching inside and finding the right cord to tug on. *~Hello, love. ~* His response rumbles through me and it makes me smile. *~Um, so did you notice anything out of the ordinary today? ~*

His response is harsh and sarcastic, making me wince.

Wrinkling my nose, I shoot back. *~No need to get bitchy. I didn't plan it. Yeah, we did! Duh. You can kiss my... You didn't tell—okay. Calm down. She's fine. I'm fine. He's fine. Chill out. Jesus, take one of Philomena's blue pills. Yeah, Talia is on her—no. I don't think you need to—damnit, I said no. We're freaking fine. Don't bring—please listen? ~* Stopping as he cuts me off, my head flops back down and I roll over, burying my face in Taurus' chest.

He looks down at me, eyebrows raised. *~You know, when I said I wanted to meet your family, I didn't expect this. He's on his way, eh? ~*

Scratching my head, I whisper, "I'm not sure who's coming; he wasn't clear. He's usually not that worked up."

He caresses my side. "It'll be alright."
"I know," I smile and curl into his side, purring.

The Goddess is Full of Wrath

❧

TALIA

They drained each other?!

Is that flamboyant featherhead serious? What in the name of all things hot and hell bound did he think he was doing? And don't get me started on Deli. She's *supposed* to help me keep that birdbrain in check and now here she is, following him merrily down the road to *death*.

Ugh. Sometimes, I wonder if I am the only sane person in this entire universe.

I know I'm not, but humor me, okay?

My choices might not be stellar—dating Wilde — and I'm not doing so hot on listening to the people trying to protect me, but then I've never been the type to retreat from a challenge. In fact, I run at it head-on.

Before I do, I plan and consider, and I make it work. I'm the brains of the operation, which is why I work in the training and operations department at the Company. I analyze, target, and plan the things our clients need. I'm damned good at it, too.

Relationships I've never been great at—outside of Taurus. We clicked and we still do. It's been a little lonely with him so immersed in Deli. I thought a fling might be the thing to shake myself up and have a good time.

I'm not complaining about them. If I had an issue, I'd state it and fix the problem. He's different with her than I've ever seen him, and it's a good thing—when they're not conspiring to cause their own certain deaths.

I *may* have stepped a little far into the fire too quickly with Wilde. Since I spent the better part of yesterday dealing with his little 'family' breakfast from hell followed by the bird going off his rocker last night, I'm wondering if a little action with the flouncy one is even worth the trouble. Hell, a vibrator would have cost a lot less than the repairs and emotional turmoil that dating him has generated.

How could I have known that dating a mate that she didn't even care if I dated was going to cause a problem for Taurus' leading lady every time I go near the fool?

Oh, right! She bloody told us so.

At least, she tried to. I should apologize for not listening to her gentle, yet insistent decrying of the idea. I'm not sure why she was tippy toeing around the insanity when she had a definitive idea of what would happen, but I don't suppose that Taurus wanted a blow by blow of her relationship with him, either. Maybe that's why she was so vague.

Regardless, now I have to contend with the two of them diving into the shallow end and hopefully, not hitting their heads on the bottom. This car just is *not* going fast enough and I can't poof like him and his sparkly kitty, so all I can do is drive like I'm trying to break the sound barrier and stew.

Good thing they're all alive and well because I'm going to fucking kill them.

The Artist Flies to the Rescue

B*loody-fucking-hell.*

You know, I'm a laid back clone. I don't ask for a lot, don't complain, and I don't make anyone jump through hoops for me. Is it too goddamned much to ask that my primary mate and her bloody husband don't commit a Romeo and Juliet randomly at 11 pm on a Thursday?

Seriously. This is what I deal with, people.

I know she's rash and emotional and impulsive, and he's no better. I know they're in this phase of love that's so huge that it's transcending the sodding Universe, and the baby has made it that much bigger. But draining one another, knowing all three of them could die?

Christ in a fucking cartoon, I think they hit their heads in the shower or something.

My car's flying down the road like I'm in the middle of a high-speed chase and I can't get it to go fast enough. Jesus Christ, the things this woman makes me do. I'm liable to end up a smear on this windy, long-ass road up to their house.

You know, I was here when we brought the bed in and I don't

know if it's the magick of being a rich bastard, but this place is like four bloody times the size of what was here only a month ago. It's a mansion now. I park the car and sigh, trying to get myself under control. It won't help to have this turn in a screaming match, and she'll be amped up enough as it is.

Calm down. Take a breath.

Honestly, it's the most excitement I've had since the whole ex-mates affair. That, my friends, is a bleeding tragedy.

I've got to get out more.

The Goddess And The Artist Give A Lecture

DELILAH

A loud slam at the door downstairs startles us, and we jump. He groans, "Bloody hell. I forgot the lockdown." With an eye roll, he opens the wards, unlocking the doors while leaving everything else closed to the outer world. Sitting up against the pillows, he takes a deep breath and squeezes my hand. I rub my tummy and clasp his as we wait.

Talia storms in, dressed in leather from head to toe, her knife blades flashing in several places on her body. Her expression is concerned rather than angry, though she's glaring at us both. "Okay, does someone want to explain to me what the *hell* is going on? What do you mean, you drained each other completely? You're both noticeably not dead," she grits her teeth and growls, "though I can't say how long that will last for one of you."

I blink at her, feeling a wall of emotion slam into me. Taurus mentioned she was an empath; he did not mention that she was an extraordinarily strong empath who loses control of her shields when she gets upset. Sucking in a deep breath, I put a hand over my face. "Oh, fuck, dude."

Talia doesn't notice because she's too caught up in her rant.

"What was the enormous wall of woozy earlier? I was driving, and I almost wrecked my car. One minute I thought I was going to pass out; the next minute, everything was fine. I thought I had PMS."

She stares at him, then me. Her eyes widening as she realizes that I'm swaying a bit. "What's wrong? Is it the baby? Are you okay?" She turns to Taurus and hisses. "What did you do now, you nit?"

Reeling, I croak, "We're not dead; that's true."

I squeeze my eyes shut and wave my hand at the fridge, opening the panel of the wall and floating a bottle of orange juice and a few homemade nausea tablets towards the bed. Her eyes follow them until they land in my palm and I sip and chew. Once I feel my amped-up metabolism breaking them down, I sigh in relief. "He didn't do it. You're emoting huge and it's—'whoa' is the best word."

Taurus roars at his primary. "*Talia*! Block your sodding emotions, damn it. You're *hurting* her!"

"You're not hurting me. It's okay. Everyone needs to chill out." I wave my hand dismissively. It was making me a little woozy because of the size and the fact that my blood sugar hasn't evened out yet.

She looks a bit gobsmacked because I feel it and closes her eyes for a minute, ostensibly blocking her emotions. "Better?"

I nod. "You didn't have to do that. I just needed to rehydrate and replenish a little. Normally, it wouldn't bother me, but I'm on the weak side." I grin.

Talia shrugs. "No problem for me to do it, if it's easier for you."

Calming now that I'm okay, Taurus says, "Sit, love. I believe we've got company coming in the form of Deli's family and I'll explain what happened once or not at all."

She gives him another look as if she's going to kill him where he sits, but she nods. I apologize for worrying her because it feels like the polite thing to do, but it diverts my attention as I feel my mate lope into the room from the back stairs.

I look over and see him leaning against the doorjamb, eyebrow arched as he surveys the scene. "Anyone want to tell me what the bloody hell's going on?" He pushes off the doorway, slinking in, his long tresses windblown from the convertible ride over. He drops into a chair, draping over it like he's always been there. I've said it before and I'll say it again, my family knows how to enter.

I can't give him the satisfaction of knowing that, though, so I wrinkle my nose and give him a look. "Nice pose. Too bad we're not filming a sexy soft core." Rolling my eyes, I mutter, "Drama queen."

He snorts at me. "Don't get me started on what this scene looks like. It feels like I stepped into a cross between Blade," he looks at Talia, "and the Queen of the Damned. Not that any of it is unattractive, I'm a mite confused since it felt like you fucking *died*."

Taurus whips his head around to glare at him. "We didn't die, mate. We—hell, I'm really not clear on that point, but we're obviously not sodding dead.

The leather-clad woman chuckles, used to clone drama tactics. Having given up on getting a rise from Taurus, she turns to my mate, saying, "You're Rafe. I've heard interesting things about you. Jury's still out on if this is better than the first time we met, so I'll say that it's good to officially meet you. Sorry about the hair."

The long-haired clone turns his brilliant smile to Talia, ignoring Taurus' snarl for the moment. He blows her a kiss as he rolls to his feet. "I am at that, pet. It's nice to meet you when you're not throwing weaponry at my head. It makes the view a lot more pleasant." His eyes twinkle as he turns back to Taurus. "Sure, not dead *now*. Otherwise, this'd be a lot more disturbing. Good to meet you, as well." Chuckling, he moves a chair to face the crowd before settling into it like the boneless git he is.

I roll my eyes again and mutter under my breath, "Bastard. You're a complete, utter bastard."

Talia eyes him, smiling at his grace before looking back at us. "What happened?"

"I wondered that myself. Does anyone in the brain trust know?" He considers for a moment, then looks back at her. "Have a seat, pet. Let's take the tension in the room down a notch and we'll all feel a lot better, I'd wager."

I narrow my eyes at him, and then my gaze turns to my husband. "Do we know what happened? I mean, besides…" I flush a bit.

Taurus grins down at me, strumming a caress down my back with a thought, and then faces the others. Talia drops into a chair as she waits for his response, looking no less dangerous sitting than standing. "Not a clue. I mean, I heard stories, but it turns out they don't tell the tale." He shrugs. "The plan was to go past the line—a touch—nothing major. We wanted to push the envelope a bit. We'd been sharing a lot of fluids of late and spending a lot of blood. We wanted to take it to the last possible moment."

Talia crosses her arms over her chest and glares. "Remind me to renew your membership with intelligence, as it looks like your last term has lapsed."

I purr softly as he strokes me inside, soothing me, and I sip my OJ before joining in. "Yeah. We didn't intend to keep going all the way. It kind of got out of hand."

Rafe arches a brow and snorts sarcastically. "Are you trying to tell me *you*, queen of self-control that you are, never had a clue that you might push too far?"

Talia nods and points at him. "What he said."

I give him a peeved look. "Oh, yes, and you're known for your restraint. Pull on the other one, cause that one's getting uneven."

The clone wrapped around me growls a low warning. "I can't explain it. We couldn't stop. Sod that; we didn't want to."

My mate pushes his long hair back in aggravation. "Okay. Then you didn't stop, and then what? I felt empty for a few minutes, like she was gone—poof. It's why I said dead, because that's what I felt like—a minute of screaming agony and then nothing."

"Yeah," Talia pipes up. "When I felt you guys come back, it was so incredible, such a huge feeling, that I thought my emotion sensors were on the fritz. It happens sometimes when I have PM... er, when I'm not feeling well." Her eyes cut to Rafe before continuing, "Was that empathy or did you feel it, too, Rafe?"

Chuckling, he waves his hand at her. "Not a worry, pet. There are lots of women folk around our place, so feel free. Yeah, I felt it. She was gone and then *boom*—almost fell off the bloody stool."

Sighing, Taurus shakes his head. "That's the part I can't tell you. I figured we'd pass out, planned for that, but we ended up going a couple of deep darks past the level we should have. Then, near as I figure, something didn't want us croaking."

I shrug. "I don't have a clue. One minute here, and the next time I know anything, it's two hours later." Looking down at myself, I furrow my brows. "I'm feeling remarkably unblemished at that."

A rush of panic floods through our bond as he notices the scratches and bruises are missing. He's trying to remember whether we called for a healing before we went out when his hand flies to his neck, looking worried.

Not looking at him, I sip my water, adding, "Nothing is out of place or anything." I knew he'd worry about our marks—the outward signs of our mating—being erased or healed permanently. Those scars stand for much more than possession: they're a promise and a commitment. Losing them for *any* reason would be like decimating an integral part of our relationship. His freaking out is not only warranted, but a shared feeling.

I take a mental inventory, trying to find the truth of my words. He looks at me in concern, having figured out that our marks are still in place, though he waits for me to finish, ensuring that I'm okay.

The assertion of my well-being sends a flood of relief through the bond and his arm tightens around me as he murmurs to me in my mind, letting me know how relieved he is that all of our marks and scars are still in place. I smile, concurring, and snuggle into him more as we communicate mentally, not paying a bit of attention to the guests in front of us.

The lounging clone looks over at Talia with a grin as Taurus gazes at me. "Do you feel like parents who caught their kids doing the naughty in the back seat of the car yet? I'm pondering the 'I can't believe you'd do something so stupid' speech."

I glare at Rafe, then retort. "You are cruising for a bruising, buster."

Talia laughs throatily, relaxing a bit. "If you did that, your image of laid back and easy going goes poof. Maybe I should? I'm more known for my not-so-blustery."

He smirks at her. "I didn't say I had to do it. You be the bad cop, pet. I'm thinking you've got it down better than I do, anyway."

Tongue in cheek, she looks at herself. "Oh, yeah, what with the Blade look I've got going on," she grins devilishly.

"It's a sexy movie, and it's not unattractive in the least. It's right fetching, in fact. I like dangerous women." He smirks and shrugs, every inch of him moving as he does so.

Looking over at Taurus, I whisper into his mind. *~Now do you feel like we're interrupting something? ~* I chuckle.

Talia rolls her eyes at Rafe and shakes her head. "Oh yeah, you're a clone, alright. Great sexy banter."

"I didn't know my clone-ness was in question. I would have dressed nicer for sure."

Taurus smiles at me, running his fingers down my arm, sending shivers down both our spines. *~At least they stopped bellowing at us like a deranged Mum dearest. ~*

She eyes him up and down, from his toes to his long hair, and drawls, "I wouldn't worry about that, baby. You're looking fine as you are. Besides, peacocks are…" she pauses, eyes dancing, "too bloody high maintenance."

Taurus' eyes slide from me to glare at his primary. "I can *hear*, you know."

I giggle into his head. *~Distract them with each other. It's a perfect plan. We are devious. ~* Leaning into his hand, I scoot closer, feeling like I need him to touch me.

Rafe laughs, all his attention on the other woman now. "Keep that up and I might blush—or he might blow a gasket—who knows which? Though, I can think of *much* better ways to heat the skin."

Her tinkling laugh is knowing. "I bet you do, you big hedonist. As for the blush, I'll believe it when I see. No way, buddy."

My mate grins more, his hair streaming over the arm of the chair, legs dangling over the side. "It happens, but it takes the right touch, you see."

Taurus wraps his arm around my shoulder and seeps into me, calming us both as joy spreads through us. *~It wasn't my original plan, but then, I'm not one to pass up an opportunity to improvise. ~*

I reply, smiling a bit as I know it's been a while since my mate has been this playful. It's good to see him get some of his spark back. I relax into Taurus with a pleasurable sigh. *~It's almost amusing to watch, anyway. ~*

Taurus leans over and nuzzles my neck, whispering into my head. *~I'm going to boot the golden goddess in about two minutes as she's feeling much better about our almost deaths and I want to be alone with you, so enjoy it while you can. ~*

I chuckle, tilting my head into him. *~He'll take off when you do. I think once he saw we were okay, he was fine. ~*

Talia smirks boldly at Rafe, eyes flashing. "Oh, is that what it takes? What gets touched for that momentous occasion?"

He tilts his head, giving her a return smirk. "That's for me to know, pet."

She shakes her head and matches his expression. "You clones are all about your *big* secrets. You *do* remember the rest of that little ditty, don't you? If I follow you around with a teeny stick, will I find it if I poke often enough?" Pausing, the other woman seems to rethink. "Though, as you stay immobile, the following is less of an issue."

Lips pressed together, eyes dancing with mirth, Rafe replies, and "You never know. I was never one to complain about a good poking. You're welcome to find out anytime you like." She blinks at him and he blinks back, looking innocent. "Is something wrong?"

I giggle, but Taurus glowers at him. "Are you macking on my woman, you long haired Leonidas?"

Talia turns and snaps at him. "Don't *even* go there, you arrogant fowl."

Grinning mischievously, Rafe shakes his head. "Leo cooks. I'm Rafe—try to get us straight. I'm just being me. Though, nice choice of words. Macking? Wonder where that phrase comes from?"

I roll my eyes. "You are *such* a pain."

"Besides, my hair being long has nothing to do with it, Simba," he quirks a brow, looking amused.

Ignoring Talia, Taurus growls. "That's it. Out."

Talia frowns. "Taurus. Be nice."

Arching a brow at her, he says, "You, too. Out. Go flirt with Sampson over there someplace else."

My mate looks at Talia and winks. "It's okay, pet. I'm being a pain on purpose," he chuckles and offers his arm. "Shall we, my dear? It looks like we've worn out the proverbial welcome."

Giggling, I grin, "Sampson—that's a good one."

She glares at Taurus, standing and defiantly taking Rafe's arm. "Nice to know there is still a gentleman around." She sniffs over at her primary, ignoring him, though I can tell that she's glad we're okay. "I'm with you, Rafe. Let's blow this place. It's gone to the cats and birds."

"Chuckling, he gives me a wink and a mental pinch. "It's a

bloody zoo in here, alright. Off we go then, Blade, your choice. I'm game for anything you want to throw at me."

Taurus groans into my head. *~Bloody buggering hell. Doesn't he know that she's worse with the challenges than you are, Minx? He'll get no relief now.~*

I chuckle, replying to him mentally. *~He wasn't lying; he likes it dangerous. He'll take it all with a smile and a flip of the mane, love. Trust me. ~*

As he and I whisper to one another, Talia grins. "Are you now? Good. I've got a kitchen sink that I've been storing away for *just* such an occasion. Let's go."

"Then plumbing it is. Later, kids! Be good so we don't have to come back."

Taurus watches as they leave, then sinks back into the pillows. "Christ, that was bloody exhausting."

"We got spanked," I snort.

He chuckles. "Yeah, we did. I like our way better." His expression turns serious. "You know, Talia was a little concerned with Rafe's flirting. I don't know if you felt it or not."

"Concerned? No, I didn't, but I'm used to him being that way." That would be true until recently. He hasn't since Alistair. He's not shown even a whiff of interest in doing anything, even this party for him, since that happened.

Hell, I don't care if she's a ten-foot purple Martian; I'd do anything to see his gorgeous smile again. I may be ensconced with Taurus, but I love my primary and his melancholia has gone on long enough. I made it past them; he needs to now.

"It's not that. She's—she'd not want you to think she's moving in where she's not wanted. I think she enjoyed the banter, though."

"Honey, I'm not in the least worried. Rafe and I are very free with one another. Sure, I asked him about the marks, but only to let him know more than anything else. If he and Talia like each other, then good for them. It's good to see him socializing again. He needs to."

He sighs. "So you and me and this?" His hand strokes my arm, then shudders in pleasure.

I lean into his touch and my eyes close. "Feels marvelous."

"Yeah, it does. But if it doesn't wane at all or I don't get used to it, I'll be soiling pants left and right anytime I'm near you."

I laugh. "Isn't that what you do, anyway?"

He grumbles, feeling my mirth, and nips my shoulder in reproach. I groan, straining towards him, whispering, "If it makes you feel better, it affects me, too."

"Bugger."

"Yeah," I murmur, swaying a little as I feel his pleasure. "Like that."

I see him struggling to shake it off. "As I'm too drained to do you up right, we will have to persevere."

"Uh huh," I nod, laying back and stretching in a feline manner, my purr kicking up. "Perseverance is good."

Growling, he shakes his head. "I hate perseverance."

Smiling, I say, "We have plenty of time tomorrow, too, baby."

He rolls to his side. "We're..." he pinches me, and then winces. "Ow."

My nose wrinkles. "Ow is right."

Arching a brow, he shakes his head. "Near as I can figure, it connected us. I've not one clue what to do about it."

"Do we need to do anything? Maybe it'll get less, or we'll get used to it, like you said."

He looks down and mumbles, "I don't want it to get less or used to it."

I smile. "I don't either. You sounded like you wanted it to change."

He looks surprised and horrified, shaking his head. "Bloody hell, no. It's deep for me—very deep. I've never, nor can I conceive, of ever wanting anyone as I want you. Even falling asleep, I want you."

"I know, baby. It's like I feel you inside me and me inside you, all at once. Overwhelming."

Nodding, he grins ruefully. "I have this urge to slay dragons for you, too. That's new."

"You want to protect me now, love?" I wrap my length against him as he nods. "Me, too. I'd kill someone if they hurt you."

He whispers, "Never had that before. I like it."

I flush a little, scrunching. "You're that important to me."

"I'm familiar with the feeling. I'm a little awed by what we did and the effects." He shakes his head and yawns. "Sleep now. We'll suss it all out later."

Pulling me into his arms, he sets his chin on my chest and I grin. "I'm sure we'll find new stuff all the time."

"It will make sparring a blast. I can't wait to get you in the field."

I chuckle. "Oh, yeah. We'll be dangerous when we do that blood/sex/death thing." It occurs to me and I blink. "Um, unless someone has me terminated for fifteen unscheduled deaths from earlier."

"You're not an agent, so you don't have to worry. But..." He doesn't look at me for a moment, then mumbles, "Want a job with the Company? With me?"

I tilt my head, feeling shocked. I've been fighting the power with those people and the Cabal since the beginning of my time in the Rift and now, to make everything weird beyond weird, I'm mated to one and being offered a job at the other. "Would they take me? I mean, I'm not a clone. Or trained. Or docile. Or respectful. Or obedient."

Pondering for a moment, he nods. "There'd be shouts and protests and irritation that I'm a bad clone who abuses his privilege. That's a normal day for me."

"Well, you don't have to make a stink if it's trouble. I guess I could give them a blood sample if I were feeling generous, and that'd make it better."

"I'll wear them down. It might help if you go out on some kills with me. Show them what you can do. Because you're not a clone, but you're not human, either."

"You decide if you want to take that on. I'll go wherever or do whatever. You know I'm always willing to come help you, baby."

"I'd prefer you on the payroll as my partner, but we'll think about it tomorrow."

I smile and snuggle closer. "We'll talk more later. You need sleep."

"You, too," he yawns, clinging to me. "I will see you after this coma, love of my heart."

Drifting out of consciousness, I fall asleep knowing we'll deal with the ramifications when the new day comes. We have plenty more where those came from."

That is, as long as this doesn't start another fire that will consume our fragile community.

Preorder TBA Title (Book Three of Rise of the Resistance)

World & Pronunciation Guide

2

CHARACTERS, PETS, & CREATIONS

Delilah Lenore O'Hara (dee LIE luh Len ORE OH Hair-uh) numbered as x1501; human—maybe. Lived in Rift for two years, born in an Earth town called Whistler's Hollow. Thirty-five years old, lives in the Resistance Quarter in a house called The Maison with her family of clones and droids including: Rafe, Victor, Caesar, Hex, Sandrine, Siren, and Philomena. She is mated to Wilde, Sari, Rafe, Alistair, and Rhea. Rafe is her primary mate. She is one of the current Resistance leaders and mayor of the quarter with Lily. She has a pet white tiger named Aradia given to her by Preston for her birthday this past year.

Nicknames: The Cat, Nightbloom, Sandwich, Peach, Deli, Delicat, Twinkles, Darkness, Kitten, Queen D, Nancy, Juliet, Tiger Lily,

Donatella (don UH tell UH) numbered x098; human; living in Rift three and a half years. Leader of the Resistance during the Conflict, creator of droids. Lived in Down Under house with Victor and Caesar until she met James. She left the Rift with James

455

and his droid Lucinda to live on Earth, abandoning Victor and Caesar to live with their family friends at the Maison.

Nicknames: Dona

Rhea (Ree-UH) numbered x256; human—maybe? Living in the Rift for four years in Cabal Quarter. Mated to Alistair, one of the original three brothers, and close friend of Talia from life on the other side of the portal. She lives in The Firehouse with Alistair and eventually mated with Sari, Wilde, Deli, and Rafe. She has a robotic dog she used to get into the Resistance.

Nicknames: Flame, Blondie, Lady Fair,

Rafe (Ray-F) numbered 086; clone; former operative. Clone won in a contest by Dona that fell for Delilah and became her primary mate. Mated to Sari, Wilde, Alistair, and Rhea. Artistic and known for being languid. Lives in The Maison with Deli, Hex, Sandrine, Siren, Leo, Philomena, Caesar, and Victor.

Nicknames: The Artist, The Lounger, The Stoat, Royalty, Ennobled One, Tyger,

Caesar (see ZAR) numbered A001; droid. First droid created by Victor and Donatella and leaders of the Resistance in the Conflict. One of the creators of almost all droids, and a submissive. Was involved with Lucinda until she moved with Donatella and James to the other side of the portal. Likes to be on a leash. Changes his hair color frequently.

Nicknames: Puppy

Victor (Vik-tor) numbered 020; clone. Former mate of Donatella and part of the Resistance in Conflict. Lived in Down Under house with Caesar and Dona until she left for the other side with James. Lives in The Maison with Caesar along with Deli's family now. Has a deep history with Deli and Rafe. Secondary father of all droids with Caesar.

Nicknames: Vic, Fangy, Pops

Alistair (Al-is-TARE) numbered 001; clone and one of the three original brothers. Lives in Firehouse with Rhea and was a big part of the Cabal side in the Conflict. Former operative for Company. Mated to Rhea, Sari, Deli, Wilde, and Rafe. Very close to Deli at the moment because of craziness. Loves her beast.
Nicknames: Tyger, Ace,

Sari (sar-EE) numbered x260; human—maybe? Lives in Coyote Den with Wilde, Janus, Roman, and Calista. Mated to Wilde, Rhea, Deli, Rafe, and Alistair. She was a defector from the Resistance in Conflict and helped Cabal win the war. Turned to Resistance again after Cabal abandoned Rift. Convinced Deli to allow her to join their town based on her former droid turned clone, Wilde. Has a coyote mutation and is torturing people now.
Nicknames: Coyote, Gnome,

Roman (Roh-man) numbered as A201; droid. Partners with Janus and lives in Coyote Den with Sari, Wilde, Calista, and Janus. Rumored to be involved with Philomena in a threesome.
Nicknames: Hottie,

Janus (Jan-us) numbered A202; droid. Partners with Roman and lives in Coyote Den with Sari, Wilde, Calista, and Roman. Rumored to be involved with Philomena in a threesome.
Nicknames: Spicy,

Philomena (fill OH main uh) numbered A200; droid. Lives in The Maison with Deli, Hex, Rafe, Leo, Sandrine, Siren, Caesar, and Victor. Drunken pill popper but cares about her family. Rumored to be in a threesome with Roman and Janus. Fashion hound and elitist.
Nicknames: The Bitch, Duchess P

Wilde (why uhld) numbered 056; was a droid and turned into a clone by The Company after he and Sari betrayed the Resistance. Blogger and intellectual snob. Mated with Rhea, Sari, Rafe, Alistair, and Deli. Lives in Coyote Den with Sari, Calista, Janus, and Roman. Was a sweet romantic, but recent events have him allowing the suppressed demon inside free and he is using it to punish those who upset him—including Deli and Rafe.

Nicknames: the Blogger,

Sandrine (san-DREEN) numbered A124; droid. Created for Leo as a companion by Vic and Caesar. Has a panel in back that keeps Buzz, a genetically mutated spider, in it. Kicks ass and takes names. Lives at Maison with Caesar, Victor, Deli, Rafe, Leo, Hex, Siren, and Philomena. Helps care for the animals, including Aradia and Mercury's giant bugs.

Nicknames:

Leonidas (Lee-oh-nye-dis) numbered A096; droid. First droid created for Deli. Lives in Maison with Deli, Rafe, Hex, Victor, Caesar, Philomena, Siren, and Sandrine. Dates Sandrine. Chef of the household. Very easy going. Loves pulling pranks with the other earliest droids.

Nicknames: Leo, Romeo, Nuts and Bolts,

Hex (HehX) numbered A100; droid. Dates from Belle's family. Punk rocker ala Billy Idol. Lives in Maison with Deli, Rafe, Leo, Victor, Caesar, Philomena, Siren, and Sandrine. Martha Stewart of the house, runs and decorates everything. Wears frilly aprons and combat boots. Second droid Deli ordered.

Nicknames: Punk, Rocker, Sid

Theodora (thee OH door uh) numbered A050; Droid. Created by Dona to help Talia when she was ill and couldn't work. No one knew she'd been shot, but Theodora is the only droid to be modeled after a person, not a clone template. She looks exactly like Talia, but is the polar opposite in personality. Involved with Damien and they all live in the Homestead house with Talia, Taurus, and the hellhounds.

Nicknames: The Lady, T, Theo,

Damien (day ME en) numbered M001; muse. The only muse known to exist. Appeared to Talia one day and has lived with her since. He and Taurus fight constantly. He talks in riddles and visual images, making it hard to understand him. He has various forms, can hop portals of his own, and has a monstrous form he rarely shows. He is an artist and has muse magic that no one understands. He is partnered with Theodora.

Nicknames: Melted Crayon, Crayola, Monster,

Belle numbered X300; human; living in Rift for three years; Cabal Quarter home called The Shop that mostly goes unused for their home on Earth called The Ranch; joined the Resistance after Sari pressured her to be let in; she ordered Chaos first, then Veruca. Functions as Sari's bully.

Nicknames: The Bulldog,

Mayhem numbered 045; clone given to Belle during Conflict; mechanic; edgy rocker look; only mated to Belle; friendly with Sari's family; Deli thinks he's sent out to seduce people to get them to like Belle; supposedly closed to Michaela;

Nicknames:

Chaos numbered A215; droid; speaks in riddles; looney tunes; dances and sings; prophecy is supposed gift; dating Hex

Nicknames: Crazypants,

Veruca numbered A255; droid; created for Belle to shift into a wolf; edgy punk; not dating anyone friends with Calista

Nicknames: little wolf girl

Cruise numbered 004 ;clone; mated to one of the original Cabal members; left the Rift to become an A-List celeb after the Conflict

Shea numbered A116; created for Tamara after Resistance formed; lives at Tropical House; family in house Manuel, Grayson, and Derek; casual lover of Deli; also has ties to Black Rose Family

Manuel numbered 092; broken out of Company program without permission; claims to be mated with Tamara; lives in Tropical House; family in house are Derek, Tamara, Shea, and Grayson; ties to Black Rose Family

Tamara numbered X1601; human from Earth; chef; lives in Tropical House; family in house with Grayson, Shea, Derek, and Manuel; ties to Black Rose Family

Amanda numbered x1753; human; lives with Constantine; member of Widow's Peak Family; closest to Sari;
Nicknames:

Constantine numbered A120; lived here six months with Amanda in Widow's Peak Family; close with Deli; one of her non-mate lovers;
Nicknames:

Lily numbered x471; lives with Mercury; favors droids; semi-involved with Rafe; part of Captain's Ship family; co-mayor of Resistance with Deli
Nicknames:

Mercury numbered A097; droid; quirky and odd; makes genetically altered bugs; likes role play; lives with Lily in Captain's ship family; involved with Deli as non-mate lover; hurt her when beast came out; voyeur and loves to take pics/video

Nicknames: Captain

Aradia Deli's white bengal tiger; rescued from a bad circus by Preston and given to her for her birthday

Twist Deli's all black ferret produced when she dressed as a pirate for a movie opening night with Mercury

Tweedle a ghost that lives with Lily and Mercury

Grayson numbered A129; droid; considers his primary mate to be Tamara; creepy and pretends to be a Dom; ominous and unsetlling with poor social skills; made by Victor and Caesar; he is also involved with Rita

Rita numbered X1610; human recruited by Tamara; her family is called Black Rose; involved with Grayson; considers primary mate to be JJ; very submissive and self conscious.

JJ numbered A125; created by Victor and Caesar; involved with Rita as primary and Tamara; not very sharp.

Wally numbered A132; created by Victor and Caesar; part of Black Rose; droid with wolfish characteristics like Veruca; fun and loves music.

LIST OF FAMILY NAMES, HOUSES, AND MEMBERS

The Maison Family: Delilah, Rafe, Leo, Hex, Sandrine, Siren, Philomena, Victor, Caesar, Aradia, and Twist

The Homestead Family: Taurus, Talia, Theodora, and Damien, and the Hellhounds

The Den Family: Sari, Wilde, Calista, Roman, and Janus

The Firehouse Family: Rhea, Alistair, and Priscilla

The Ranch Family: Belle, Mayhem, Chaos, and Veruca

The Down Under Family: Dona, Lucinda, and James

The Captain's Ship Family: Lily, Mercury, and Tweedle

The Widow's Peak Family: Amanda and Constantine

The Tropical Family: Tamara, Shea, Manuel, Grayson, and Derek

The Black Rose Family: Rita, Wally, and JJ

The Gearhead Family: Michaela, Preston, Aramis, Kane, and Shane

The Library Family: Dahlia, Mack, and Rupert

The Tech Family: Heather and Chance

The Hallows: Dahlia, Rupert, and Mack

Jaguars: Rana and Everett

The Wilds: Amora and Strike

The Coach House: Marina and Ward

The Starship: Simone, Percy, and Wilhelmina

Maple Leaf: Penelope, Gregor, and Aramis

The Sanctum: Dove and Cherise

LOCATIONS IN AND OUT OF THE RIFT

Bytes 'N Chips- A dive bar used for one of the portals to The Rift as well as a frequent recruiting location.

Dirty Deeds- A bar created by Sari that was the location of unspeakable debauchery. How it was destroyed is unsubstantiated.

The Maison- Delilah's enormous home. It is the epicenter of Resistance activity.

The Zoo- The new karaoke bar Sari and Belle opened without permission.

The Company- A mysterious organization that created The Rift, runs the secret Project Reality, and maintains surveillance on the inhabitants of The Rift. Allegedly, they are a private mercenary organization with no ties to any government, criminals, or other governing bodies

Sacred Space- The anointed space a magick user keeps to perform rituals and spells. Only Deli has one.

Portal- The pathway to The Rift from Earth. The main one is located in Bytes 'N Chips, but there are more throughout Earth. Those who can apparate do not always use them.

The Resistance Quarter the magically protected area in the Rift where the Resistance all live

The Cabal Quarter the original spaces where families lived when the Cabal ruled and everyone first came through the portal.

Riftverse Terminlogy

*Warning, this list has potential spoilers*

Clone- created from DNA and modified through trade secrets involving quantum physics, wormholes, and the Company scientists.

Android/Droid- am artificially intelligent creation that is technologically advanced far beyond human capabilities including bodily functions, charging, and sentience. Created by Donatella, Victor, and Caesar prior to the Conflict and continually improved upon by a team of their creations.

The Rift- A pocket dimension that the Company HQ and staff, along with humans of the Cabal and Resistance live in.

Bytes 'N Chips- A dive bar used for one of the portals to The Rift as well as a frequent recruiting location.

Dirty Deeds- A bar created by Sari that was the location of unspeakable debauchery. How it was destroyed is unsubstantiated.

The Maison- Delilah's enormous home. It is the epicenter of Resistance activity.

The Cabal- A human governing body put in place by the Company to keep the human inhabitants in line.

The Resistance- Originally, the rebels and droids that fought the Cabal/Company in the Conflict. Currently, the inhabitants of Deli's hidden city.

Claiming/Marking- A ritual involving biting that is akin to engagement for clones and some droids.

Mating- A ritual like marriage that involves biting, claiming, blood exchange, and marking.

Apparate/Disapparate- A form of travel used by some clones and magicks users that is similar to teleportation.

Sacred Space- The anointed space a magick user keeps to perform rituals and spells. Only Deli has one.

The Zoo- The new karaoke bar Sari and Belle opened without permission.

The Company- A mysterious organization that created The Rift, runs the secret Project Reality, and maintains surveillance on the inhabitants of The Rift. Allegedly, they are a private mercenary organization with no ties to any government, criminals, or other governing bodies that operate as both white and black hats if you can afford them.

Familiar- An animal that facilitates magick for an extranormal, also serves as a companion and protector.

The Beast- The name for the sentient panther shifter inside of the Delilah.

Demon- All of the clones are created with one based on their template and the droids are also programmed with one if it suits their template.

Template- The base appearance and personality of the droid/clone. These were decided by the scientists of the Company and mirror a cast of individuals they cloned/passed through the wormholes.

Oversight- The individual that runs the Company. He/She is unknown to those without Alpha Level Clearance.

Clearance Level- Those involved with the Company have clearance levels for access to information and systems. It is based on the Greek alphabet with Alpha being the highest level with the least individuals.

The Conflict- The war between the droids and the clones (Resistance and Cabal) that resulted from the caste system the Cabal created.

The Battle of Blood and Steel- The final battle of the Conflict prior to peace talks.

The Creation- This refers to the process of the creating the first three clones and the subsequent process refinement.

Other Place/Side/Real World- Earth, circa now-ish

Project Reality- The name for the experiment the Company is running that contains the inhabitants of The Rift. They are unaware.

Portal- The pathway to The Rift from Earth. The main one is located in Bytes 'N Chips, but there are more throughout Earth. Those who can apparate do not always use them.

Reviews, Print, and Merchandise

If you have enjoyed this story, please review it.
It helps other readers find my work,
which helps me as an indie author.

Thank you!

Reviews for this book are appreciated on the following platforms

TikTok
Instagram
Facebook
Storygraph
YouTube
BookBub
Amazon

To purchase print copies or merchandise, go to The Worlds of Cassandra Featherstone

Secret Bonus Scenes for all the Series...

For another secret bonus scenes, *click the link below, sign up for my newsletter, and get your freebies.*
   Get your bonus scene here!

Sneak Peek: Veiled Flame

LOSER

Kat

The little blue icon on my app has been glaring at me all day, but I'm too damn nervous to open it. Everyone at Woodlawn High has been buzzing all day with their notifications and the squeals of joy and moans of despair were too much for me to take. My anxiety is through the roof—this is the moment I've been waiting for since middle school, but I can't seem to force myself to bite the billet and check.

Maybe it's because I don't have the support system most of my classmates have?

That's probably true, given I've always been a loner and I don't fit into any specific 'caste' here. It's hard to make friends when you get shuffled from foster home to foster home over the years. I've rarely stayed anywhere long enough to make a friend, much less a group of them.

I'm not delinquent or anything—the families I've been placed with just return me like a pair of pants that doesn't fit after a year or so. The caseworkers click their tongues sympathetically and hunt down a new placement, but I've never been given a reason *why* people don't want me around. One lady said I must be born under a bad sign and hell if I knew what that meant other than I'm not good enough to keep around.

It would be different, almost understandable, if I misbehaved or got bad grades. But I don't—I'm always in the top five percent of my class and I do everything I'm asked. I don't even lord my smarts over the other kids or adults. Being presentable and unassuming was something I adapted long ago to improve my probability of staying in a home long term.

Unfortunately, it never worked and though I should be a shoo-in for scholarships and acceptances galore, I can't bring myself to be rejected yet again.

So I wait for the last bell of the day, slinging my bag over my shoulder and trudging home to the latest in my temporary housing. I can't even contemplate looking at the possible heartache waiting for me in the college application system WHS insisted we use. The fear is too great and despite knowing I'll be on my own for good at the end of this year, I'm unable to risk the pain.

I hate being this way.

My court mandated therapist says it's some sort of attachment disorder that's common in foster kids, but I think that's bullshit. The problem isn't *me* not forming attachments; it's asshole adults not forming one to me. Being left at a safe haven in a fucking basket as a baby wasn't because *I* did anything wrong—again, fucking adults couldn't handle their commitments.

As usual, I arrive home to an empty house. There are two other kids who live here—Bryce and Blake—but they're at football practice. Of course, the Jamesons *love* them; they get to strut around at games because their strays are the stars of the team. I'm not mistreated, but I'm definitely an afterthought. Both of my 'parents' are still at work, so I drop my bag on the couch and head for the kitchen to get a snack:

Don't get me wrong. I *could* have been placed in far worse homes than any of the seven I've been in since elementary school. None of the ex-fosters starved, beat, molested, or abused me. They were all decent folks with jobs and houses that weren't hellholes, but they never liked me.

I have no idea why. I tried to be everything they wanted.

But when the end of each school year came, I was handed in like a textbook and off I went to some group home until the next contestant stepped up. It baffled everyone, not just me, but that's what happened every single time.

Sighing, I pull some fruit out of the fridge and grab a soda. I have homework to do and if I want to have time to work on my stories, I'll need to get it done before the house is full of people at dinner time. Bryce and Blake will have gotten messages about their applications, too, and I'd bet my pinkie toe those idiots got into some big sports school. Brett and Allison will be oozing happiness for them and I don't know if I'll be able to keep food down if I have to admit my failure when they ask.

Being eighteen sucks ass.

After I grab my books and tablet, I head down to the den. I have to give my current parents credit; they set up a very nice workspace for us to study in the converted basement. By the time they took me in, the Jamesons created a cozy room down here where the three of us could relax and do our work for school without being interrupted. It might have been more for the boys than me, but I appreciated it all the same. Desks, a couch, big chairs, and bookshelves fill the space, making it almost seem like our mini-library. They even put a small fridge for drinks and snacks in case we had to be up late to cram.

It's my favorite place in the entire house and I spend most of my time here.

I sink into the huge armchair, putting my drink and snack on the side table. It only takes a few minutes to arrange myself in the soft cushions and I pause to tug my headphones out of my pocket. Music always soothes my jagged edges and I need it to stay focused on the bullshit AP Calculus I need to keep my average up in. My course load is heavy, but I applied to tough colleges. I wouldn't have a chance to get in, especially on a scholarship, if I wasn't taking equally challenging classes in comparison to all the prep school kids.

As always, the sounds of Vivaldi carry me away as I scrawl equations on my screen and before long, thoughts of the blue notification completely fade away.

"Kat!"

The shouts barely register as I continue working on the problem set, gnawing on my lower lip in concentration.

"Jesus fuck, where is she? I could eat a hippo!"

"Kat!"

Thumping followed by what could pass for a stampede of elephants jerks me out of my math filled trance when Bryce and Blake come down the stairs. They smell as bad as the aforementioned pachyderm's cage, so they must have rushed home right after practice. The blond twins glare at me as if I'm the offending element despite being sweaty and covered in dirt and grass stains.

This doesn't bode well.

Usually, they're tired and hungry after practices so I'm used to cranky ass boys, but tonight, there's a light to their faces. That had to mean they've gotten their letters and dinner will be a gush fest in honor of their perfection. I'm going to need all of my strength to fake smile and nod as Brett and Allison fawn over them.

I don't begrudge them their success—not really. They work hard and play even harder on the field. It's not their fault they're the American dream teens and I'm the nerdy basement troll no one wants. But it's awfully hard living in the shadow of their bright light, especially when I'm no less intelligent or talented.

"I'm finishing the AP Calc, guys. What do you want?"

They roll their eyes at me before Blake scoffs. "It's not due until Monday. You're so hyper."

Duh. I take anxiety meds, douchebag; of course I'm 'hyper.'

"I can only be who I am, Blake." That earns me a snort from Bryce and I know it's because he thinks that's the problem. "Is dinner ready?"

"Almost. Get upstairs and set the table so we can shower—Brett's orders." Blake grins smugly.

The two of them seem to always arrange it so chores get passed to me for some half-assed reason and this is no exception. Sighing, I put my stuff aside, fully intending to hide down here after the dinner mess is cleaned up. Likely by me, but like I said, I could definitely live in worse foster homes so I let it go. Doing some chores isn't worth risking the group home for the last few months of my high school career.

They take off running up the stairs and I wait for them to disappear before I follow suit. My phone is tucked in my pocket and I feel like it's a stone of shame I have to bear. I know once the adults make over the twins' success, they will remember me, and I'll be forced to find out what disappointment lies in wait for me. The dread weighs on me, but I head into the sunny kitchen and pick up the pre-prepared pile of plates, silverware, and napkins on the counter.

Allison looks up from the stove and gives me a half-smile, nodding as I take the dishes into the dining room. Like I said, no one is mean or horrid, they just seem...obligated. After a while, it makes it hard to waste time trying to be bright and sunny. Being reserved makes it a hell of a lot easier not to feel rebuffed when they don't pay attention to you regardless.

"Make sure you include champagne glasses for your dad and I!" she calls from the other room.

The twins definitely got acceptance somewhere big. Brett must have gotten the bubbly on the way home.

Once I set the table, I return to help Allison bring out the roast and sides. I'm a little amazed at her efficiency when it comes to getting the housework done while working full time, but I suppose it's something people with real parents get taught as they grow up. My home life has been so fractured that I haven't learned how to cook more than very basic shit from YouTube videos. That may be a problem after graduation, but I've never felt comfortable enough to ask Allison if she'd teach me. I'm sure she would try, but it doesn't feel right.

"How was school, Kat?"

I look over my shoulder, seeing Brett in the entry to the dining room. He's already changed from work and smiling, but I see the distraction in his eyes. He's waiting for the boys to come down. "It was fine. I've got a Calc test at the end of the week. I'll be studying a lot to get ready."

"Good, good. No matter what happens with applications, keeping your grades up will ensure no one pulls any offers," he says.

Those words aren't for me. They are for the two wet haired boys who just appeared behind him.

"Kat's too much of a geek to ever let her grades slip, Dad," Blake says as he pushes past his brother and drops into his usual chair at the table. "Grab me a Powerade since you're in the kitchen, mouse!"

Both Brett and Bryce stare at me and I turn around, heading to the fridge despite the fact that I was *not* closer than the other twin. Out of habit, I take two of the drinks and a soda for myself. I've been here long enough to know Bryce will send me back to get him one as well. It would feel like typical sibling stuff, but for some reason, I just *know* they do it to fuck with me. I have no idea why I feel that way, but trusting my gut has been the one thing that helped me get through all the upheaval in my life over the years. It's a good gauge for knowing when I'll get booted or if people are being earnest in their reactions.

The therapist says that's some sort of trauma induced early trigger warning shit, by the way.

After I hand out the drinks, I sit down on my side of the table and we wait for Allison to come out. Brett is at his seat at the far end of the table and the twins are punching each other as they look at something on their phones. I know where this is all going but I drop my gaze to the table, swallowing the coppery taste of fear as it courses through my body.

I'm going to be exposed and there's nothing I can do to stop it.

Read the first three episodes free on Kindle Vella: https://www.amazon.com/kindle-vella/story/B0BSTMB1X3

Villains & Vixens
Heads will roll.
BLOODTHIRSTY
International Bestselling Author
CASSANDRA
FEATHERSTONE

QUEEN BEE

They dim the lights in the club, and the spots click on as the curtain slides open.

It's a full house tonight in the little burlesque club off the Rue Pierre Montaine.

Chez Arc En Ciel is not well known compared to the *Moulin Rouge* or *Le Lido*, but the wealthy from both sides of the Seine gather here for shows four nights a week. If you pass the various layers of security checks to even be permitted to book a reservation, you also have to be able to afford the two thousand Euro per guest cover charge. If you don't eat or drink anything, that's all it will cost; however, that would get you blacklisted.

Intro music pumps through the speakers and I stand on my mark in the opening position. My cane is resting on the wooden boards of the stage by my front foot as I pretend to lean on it. Roars of applause echo through the room as our troupe of dancers catch the lights, sequins sparkling like diamonds when the stage lights rise. We're dressed in pinstriped black pant suits and fedoras to match the big band style opening to the song. As soon as the horn-filled intro finishes, the dance begins.

I follow the routine with precision, snapping and popping my hips to the beat as we spread out across the stage. You wouldn't know by the fake smile on my face that I'm scanning the crowd. Two fan kicks later, I've rotated past the proscenium, and I think I've found my mark. Twirling, I stop in the place I need to be for the bridge, singing along as if my life depends on it. It might, to be honest, because I need to sell my cover tonight, so no one notices me.

The Guillotine moves in the shadows, but tonight, she's in the spotlight.

My ass shakes as I dance my way through the song, swinging the prop cane I'd replaced with one of my design. You wouldn't know by looking at it, but it's not the painted balsa the other dancers have for a very specific reason. I need it to complete the mission that forced me to spend two months in Paris working my way into this job at *Chez Arc En Ciel*. If I can't strike tonight, the surveillance, counterintelligence, and time spent building this cover are wasted because my mark is leaving for Asia tomorrow.

Tonight, the Cobra dies for his sins.

The break of the song slows the music and the dancers pour into the crowd to wiggle around the rich assholes. It's choreographed, but it's also to advertise each girl for private dances in the lounges upstairs. We're not strippers—not that there's a damned thing wrong with a woman using her body to support herself—but we do bare more skin in the closed rooms. The *laissez-faire* attitude of the owners means as long as we kick them thirty percent of the fees for those dances, they don't care what any of the girls do in the rooms. I'd find it sleazy, but the girls who work here are highly skilled performers who choose to make thousands of dollars a night rather than peanuts in some ballet troupe or chorus line.

By the time I've flirted my way to the VIP tables, the Cobra is staring intently at all of us. Spotlights pin each one of us on the floor at the bass hits, and I swivel my hips as my free hand slides down to the secret spot on my jacket. In unison, we tear the jackets off to reveal rhinestone studded bras with straps crisscrossing our waists like shibari ropes. A lift of the fedora and pop of my hip, along with the beat, draws the fierce-looking brawler's eyes directly to me. I pout prettily and stalk towards his table with the swagger of a tiny dicked asshole that owns a monster truck.

His thin lips pull back over the famed curving fangs he had implanted. Dark, glittering eyes follow every move I make as I approach, and I pretend to whip my hair from side to side as I check for his guards. They're here somewhere, but I need them to be far away so I can beat my escape before they notice. When I get within inches, I tap his leg with my cane and spin around to shake my ass in his face. The grunt of approval makes me want to heave, but I turn, holding onto the prop with both hands. My feet click on the floor in a soft shoe step as I make 'fuck me' eyes at the dirty bastard. He leans back, his pants tented as he gestures towards his lap.

Fucking gross.

I don't care about his weapons trade or what happens when people get the shit he moves. I have no clue why I have to take him out. The reason they have sentenced him to death isn't part of my contract, and I'm nothing if not a dispassionate observer of the darkest parts of human desires. Twelve years at *l'Academie* ensured I care very little about anything that isn't directly related to my ability to complete my jobs.

Sighing, I dance closer and drop onto his rather unimpressive erection and wiggle. There's plenty of cloth between us to prevent him from doing anything I'd make a scene over, so I focus on the task at hand. I slip the cane behind his head, resting the wood against his neck as I tug him forward. The move reads as playfully bringing his face to my breasts, but at the last second, I click the release built into the custom weapon. One end slides open to reveal the razor sharp garotte and before he can say a word, I yank it through.

Faint gurgling is the only noise besides the end of the song, and I carefully slide the sides of the cane together. Climbing off the nasty fucker, I put my hands on his cheeks so I can pretend to flirt with him while I arrange the head so it looks as if he's leaning back in the booth. It needs to look realistic to allow me to return to the stage with the others. When I have it settled, I back away from the booth, blowing fake kisses as I walk backwards through the crowd. I almost collide with a dark-haired guy with his collar pulled high as I head for the stage, and I roll my eyes. Whatever celeb that is trying to keep their face away from the paps is doing a shitty job of it.

The entire troupe takes a few bows and shuffles off of stage left to the wings. I exhale a sigh of relief when the next group enters on the opposite side. I haven't heard shouting yet, so I don't think the Cobra's men realize he's down. Now I take this emetic pill, have a vomiting episode, and I'll get sent home.

That's when Arabella Montaigne, the burlesque dancer, will cease to exist, and Remy Arsine Benoit will re-emerge.

I smile to myself as I chew on the tablet that will have me retching my guts out in a few moments. This is a more complex extermination than I usually prefer, and I can't leave my normal calling card behind. The Cobra's head had to remain in the booth rather than get delivered to his home in a basket.

Such a shame, that. I quite enjoy the reactions my little gifts engender when they're discovered.

Walking into the dressing room, I carefully strip my costume off, putting all the pieces in my bag. Every item in the locker room that belongs to gets placed in the duffel carefully as I wait for the effects to hit me. It won't do to leave loose ends, even if my prints have never touched a single surface in this place. My gut roils and I turn, facing one of the other dancers as the vomit finally comes. Gracelia screams like she's being skinned when I hurl on her and it's everything I can do *not* to smirk through the chunks.

"C'est la merde!" she shouts, running for the showers as if she's on fire.

It takes less than a minute for the owner to send me home for the night. I walk out the back door of the building with everything just as the sirens scream.

Perfect timing, as always.

I jump into the first cab I can hail, directing him to the *Hôtel de Crillon*. Their suites are the ritziest in Paris, and it's my go-to hideout when I'm here. I used to only stay in the Bernstein Suite, but some rich fuckwad purchased it six months ago. If I could track them down and beat the hell out of them, I would, but I booked my schedule until late 2025. Assassins with my skill set and accuracy are getting harder to find. They forced the old guard into retirement because they refuse to adapt to the digital age. Too many cameras, crime labs, and hackers running about to do everything Cold War style.

The future of murder for hire is millennial, people. We're old enough to be stable, but young enough to be agile with new technology. Plus, most of them are broke AF from crooked ass student loans.

It's not an issue I have, but I've been in the business since I hit double digits. You don't survive *l'Academie des Invisibles* if you haven't killed someone before the end of primary school. It's unheard of.

I was eight the first time I used the weapon that would become my signature.

Shivering, I tap on the window of the cab and bitch the driver out. He's taking a longer route than necessary to raise my fare, and I'll have his guts for garters if he doesn't knock it the fuck off. A string of curses in French erupt from him when I voice the accusation, and I slam my palm on the window with enough force to crack the plexiglass barrier. He almost drives into another car, but when he regains control, he makes the requested adjustments to our route.

We arrived at the front entrance after a few more arguments and a traffic jam around the *Champs*. I throw the euros at him in disgust, memorizing the medallion number for later. He's not worth my time, but I have quite a few contacts who might be interested in blackmailing a cabbie in town. Getaway cars are cliche in the crime world now. Most ne'er-do-wells like myself find greater comfort in anonymous taxis or ride-share accounts hacked through the deep web accessed on burner phones. If your ride doesn't know you're a villain, there's no one to flip if law enforcement comes looking.

I never look the same for any job—ever.

I will not use Arabella Montaigne as a cover in the future, and once I move to the location of my next job, I'll ensure that she meets with a terrible fate. It's a lot more work to slowly kill off my alters once I've used them, but it's also why I've never even come close to being caught. The dancer with long wavy red hair, freckles, and big green eyes will never grace the streets of Paris again after I hop a plane. She will, however, get a minor story in the paper and an obituary when I decide how she tragically dies.

The Guillotine will rise from her ashes and be reborn.

PROLOGUE

Twenty-one years ago...

A powerful wave of apprehension hits me as we approach Claridon's house. Pausing at the edge of the forest, I wait until we can see what awaits us. The silence is deafening as we take in the wreckage of what was once the home of our dear friends.

They splintered the heavy cabin door in pieces littered around their yard like an explosion sent the shards flying. When the wind shifts, the foul stench of death and rot slams into us, making my wife gag. Lights are flickering ominously in the shattered windows and another scent—burnt food—catches the breeze as we approach.

"Cast protection before we reach the porch," I murmur.

"*Ego invoco deus ab mihi. Protego mihi ab hostili et malum.*[1]"

I nod solemnly, repeating her words to invoke our Goddess' watchful eyes on me as well. The scene in front of the house does not inspire confidence about what we will find inside.

The air is thick as we step onto the porch and another smell wafts towards us—blood. Its metallic tang invades our senses almost to the point of tasting copper on my tongue. Climbing over the debris, I look at the once cozy living area. Shredded cushions, torn drapes, stuffing, and other destroyed furnishings lie scattered around the room. When I bend to examine the destruction, I find coarse animal hairs embedded in the remnants. I pick some up to sense the aura of the creature it came from, but all I feel is death.

The bloody hoof prints puzzle me—I do not recognize them as belonging to any creature I'm familiar with. Whatever came to this house was not a normal shifter, nor was it a common magic user. The level of malice and lack of emotion concerns me. Its aura is like that of a necromancer or one of their creations.

I follow a set of heavy prints to the hallway leading to the dining area and kitchen. Swallowing hard, I prepare myself for the carnage I know will appear. The rotten food and decomposition scents are so bad I have to raise my shirt to cover my nose before I vomit.

It is certain our friends are dead; no one can lose the amount of blood that coats the surfaces and walls while staying alive.

"What made those claw marks? I've never seen such deep furrows," my wife whispers.

I shake my head, holding a finger to my lips to keep her quiet. I've never seen that type of mark, either, but we don't know if there's anyone still here. We must stay silent while we explore. The food on the stovetop is burned and has flies on it—that's the rotting smell. Wood is barely burning in the oven, just a few embers remaining, but it tells me our friends were caught unaware.

It means the malevolent being that attacked the wolves did it within the past few hours.

My heart stops when I remember their baby girl. Feray had to be here when it happened; it's the New Moon and both of her parents stay home during the start of the new lunar cycle.

"Freya, forgive me. I almost forgot the baby," I hiss at my wife.

Her eyes widen and her hand flies to her mouth. I see the tears forming as she thinks about what the condition of this place means for a defenseless infant. Together, we leave the kitchen, intent on heading back through the outer room to the stairs.

Just beyond the landing, we stumble over the body of Claridon. His corpse is mutilated, but I recognize those battered hands anywhere. He clearly put up a hell of a fight to keep the intruder from making it past him. Despite that, it ripped his chest open and his intestines are hanging out. Blood spatter decorates the once lovingly decorated walls, painting them vermillion and signaling his desperation to protect his family.

Swallowing again as I look at Imogen, I tilt my head at the trail of bloody hoof prints that lead to the nursery. We were here when they found out they were expecting, when they assembled the room, and even after Feray was born. Now the beauty of that memory has been sullied by the scene before us.

We have to be strong...

Once we're both ready, we follow the prints to the door of the baby wolf's room. The sight that greets us is horrific: it splayed Lyra out as if nailed to a cross and impaled her head on a post of the baby's crib. Blood is dripping down the whitewashed wood, making its way to the pink carpet. Dead eyes stare sightlessly at us as we hold our breath and enter. The injuries to our friend are a testament to how hard she fought to protect her child, though in the end, she also failed.

I don't want to see what this monster did to the baby we considered a sister to our child. Forcing myself to approach, I stare at the empty crib in astonishment. There's no sign of Feray, nor that it harmed her in this room. I whip my head around to look at my wife in shock.

Was this a kidnapping? Why would they kill everyone so brutally instead of simply sneaking in to snatch the baby?

My eyes dart around the room until I reach the closet. I stalk over, throwing the door wide. There's a pile of dirty linens and blankets in the bottom, which is unlike Lyra. She always kept everything tidy, so much so that we all teased her about it. Tossing the clothes over my shoulder, I dig down until I reach the floor. I call for light and my magic brightens the dark space enough for me to see a tiny seam at the baseboard.

Claridon was always paranoid, and I never understood why. We both lived simple lives in a small town of magic users and shifters, well outside the dangers of the big city. He was a master craftsman and Lyra ran a bakery; there was nothing to worry about. Humans were far away from our little town and the stench of corruption from the gangs and Councils doesn't exist in Silver Falls.

But I recognize a bolt hole when I see one, so I search frantically until I find the lever that will spring the door open. It takes several tries to successfully open the door—Claridon was top-notch at his trade—but when it swings out, I gasp.

There, wrapped in her father's shirt and Lyra's clothing, is Feray. She has the warding amulet Imogen made for her on her chest, and I realize that even while scared for their lives, Lyra and Claridon ensured the beast wouldn't find their child. Between the magic of our amulet and their scent swaddling her, the baby is hungry and tired, but safe.

I lift the tiny infant out of the hole gently, my eyes filling with tears. Her baby scent makes my heart hurt for my fallen friends and I clutch her to me tightly. It's our responsibility to take care of her now; I know that. Imogen nods when I look at her with a sad expression, then walks over to the dresser, opening a drawer. When she hands me the baby sling, I know she feels the same.

Once I secure Feray to my body, we make our way back to the stairs and head out of the house. It will need to be burned to keep that creature or anyone else from following the scent trail to our home. We don't want anyone to know Feray is alive; she will be safe with us as long as we continue to have her wear the amulet that suppresses her wolf.

Raising her with our daughter, in a new town, is the only way to keep her alive.

I didn't wake up this morning knowing I'd have to abandon my entire life and our home, but I know as surely as the sun will rise tomorrow what we must do to protect this baby. Looking down at her curiously, I ponder the situation again. A magical beast used as an assassin seems like overkill if their target was the infant. Slaughtering her family was also unnecessary—that thing could have slipped into her room and killed her before anyone knew it was there.

Lifting the magic on her amulet for a moment, I wait until Feray opens her eyes. That's when I realize why my friends put it on her. My wife walks up beside me and runs a finger over her cheek. Her red hair looks very much like mine and as long as we keep the magic refreshed for the spell, she will look as though she is our natural daughter.

"We must pack up and move immediately," Imogen says as we walk out. "The capital city is vast, and no one knows us there. That will allow us to raise her as our own—a sister to Fiadh."

"Yes," I murmur. "I will send a message to the local council to inform them we are moving. The death of our friends and their daughter are too much for us to bear here. You simply need to keep her secret in our home until we leave."

She nods. "What about the monster who did this? Who would send it to kill a baby, and why?"

"Someone who scared Claridon enough to make a secret bolt hole in the nursery and forced Lyra to ask us for that amulet. I don't know what they were up to, but obviously, it was much bigger than our tiny town."

Imogen frowns. "We made three amulets, love. Why weren't Lyra and Claridon wearing theirs?"

"I don't know, Gen. Whatever the reason was, they took theirs off and someone powerful hunted down their daughter. Nothing is what it seems here, but we must protect Feray. We will keep her wolf suppressed for as long as possible—up to her Ascension if we can. She'll grow up and if she's destined for something bigger, she'll be able to assume that mantle when she's ready."

Taking this baby on and keeping her secret violates our coven laws; we both know it. Hiding her means we will always be on the run—we need completely new identities when we flee to the capital. It's a lifetime commitment, but the look on my wife's face tells me she's certain this is the right thing to do.

I know without a doubt that being was pure evil, and it came with one purpose: *assassination.*

Tomorrow, we begin our lives on the lam with two babies—there is no other option .

Get it now: **https://books2read.com/newmoonrisingCOM1**

---

1. I call on the gods. I protect myself from enemies and evil

About Cassandra Featherstone

Cassandra Featherstone has channeled her lifelong passion for writing into a flourishing career, a journey that started when she first grasped a pencil as a gifted child with ADHD.

Her debut novel, born during the solitude of COVID lockdown in March 2020, draws on a tapestry of personal encounters and insights that resonate deeply with her readers.

An international bestseller, Cassandra has topped Amazon charts in categories such as LGBT Anthologies, LGBTQ+ Mystery, and Bisexual Romance, among others. Her works navigate the complexities of bullying, PTSD, body dysmorphia, mental health struggles, personal reinvention, and the empowerment of claiming one's own space. Importantly, Cassandra offers a thoughtful and respectful portrayal of LGBTQIA+ relationships, subtly reflecting her own connection with the community through her narratives.

Her literary repertoire spans sci-fi fantasy, urban fantasy, paranormal, and comedic genres in academy whychoose settings, with a strong commitment to portraying consensual, safe, and accurately depicted BDSM and kink lifestyles. Her books are an invitation to explore transformative stories that are both inclusive and engaging.

Often affectionately called 'The Muppet' for her wacky theater kid personality, she resides in the Midwest with her tech-savvy husband, their creatively inclined college student, a literary-minded dog, and four scheming cats.

READ MORE AT CASSANDRA'S WEBSITE OR HER FACEBOOK PAGE. SIGN UP FOR EXCLUSIVE CONTENT AND UPDATES HERE.

FIND HER ON ANY OF THE SOCIAL MEDIA BELOW AS SHE *LOVES* TO CHAT AND *NEVER* SLEEPS!

Also by Cassandra Featherstone

THE MISFIT PROTECTION PROGRAM SERIES

Road to the Hollow

Return to the Hollow

Home to the Hollow

Rejected in the Hollow

Revealed in the Hollow

Healing in the Hollow

Revenge in the Hollow

AUDIO OF THE MISFIT PROTECTION PROGRAM SERIES

Road to the Hollow

APEX ACADEMY CAPERS

Come Out and Prey

Let Us Prey

In Prey We Trust

Oh Holy Spite (3.5 novella)

Eat. Prey. Love.

Prey It By Ear

AUDIO OF THE APEX ACADEMY CAPERS SERIES

Come Out & Prey

Let Us Prey

In Prey We Trust

TRANSLATIONS OF THE APEX ACADEMY CAPERS SERIES

Come Out & Prey (German)

Let Us Prey (German)

In Prey We Trust (German)

DISCORDIA UNIVERSITY

Veiled Flame (Book One)

Quiet Burn (Book Two)

SECRETS OF STATE U

Blood on the Ice (Book One)

Suspicions on the Stage (Book Two)

VILLAINS & VIXENS

Bloodthirsty (Book One)

Ruthless (Book Two)

Wicked (Book Three)

AUDIO OF THE VILLAINS & VIXENS SERIES

Bloodthirsty

Ruthless

TRIANGLES & TRIBULATIONS

Hoist the Flag (PQ)

Yo-Ho Holes (Book One)

CHILDREN OF THE MOON- WITH SERENITY RAYNE

New Moon Rising (Book One)

Waxing Crescent (Book Two)

Waxing Gibbous (Book Three)

Full Moon (Book Four)

Waning Gibbous (Book Five)

FAETAL ATTRACTION

Hell on Wheels (Book One)

TBA Title (Book Two)

RISE OF THE RESISTANCE

Ream Exclusive Prequels

Hooked on a Feline (Book One)

Peacock Me Like A Hurricane (Book Two)

TBA Title (Book Three)

REAM SERIALS

Secrets of State U

Discordia University

Denizens of the Dark

Faetal Attraction

Agents of the Ouroboros

Rise of the Resistance

F.E.A.R. Academy

ANTHOLOGIES

Unwritten

Shifters Unleashed

Jingle My Balls

Love is in the Air

Silent Night

Snowed In

All Hallows Eve

www.ingramcontent.com/pod-product-compliance
Lightning Source LLC
Chambersburg PA
CBHW070400310726
48977CB00003B/505